CU00725262

DWYERS' CROSS

DWYERS' CROSS

Pamela Edgar

Macdonald

A Macdonald Book

Copyright © 1988 by Pamela Edgar

First published in Great Britain in 1988
by Macdonald & Co (Publishers) Ltd
London & Sydney

All characters in this publication are fictitious
and any resemblance to real persons, living or dead,
is purely coincidental.

All rights reserved.
No part of this publication may be reproduced,
stored in a retrieval system, or transmitted, in
any form or by any means without the prior
permission in writing of the publisher, nor be
otherwise circulated in any form of binding or
cover other than that in which it is published and
without a similar condition including this
condition being imposed on the subsequent
purchaser.

British Library Cataloguing in Publication Data

Edgar, Pamela
    Dwyers' cross.
    I. Title
    823[F]   PR9369.3.E3

    ISBN 0-356-15420-3

Typeset by Leaper & Gard Ltd, Bristol, England
Printed and bound in Great Britain by
Mackays of Chatham Ltd

Macdonald & Co (Publishers) Ltd
Greater London House
Hampstead Road
London NW1 7QX

A Pergamon Press plc Company

*This book is dedicated to all courageous women,
especially my mother Dorothy, Dr Naomi le Roith
and the memory of Dale.*

Acknowledgements

My thanks and appreciation to my agent, Frances Bond, for her wisdom and guidance, my husband Michael, his parents, my father, my sister and all my friends whose interest inspired me.

PART ONE
1820–1824

CHAPTER
One

The Indian Ocean seethed blood-red all about the *Poseidon* and the dozen other sailing ships swaying at anchor a good mile from the shore of Algoa Bay. The dying African sun shimmered along the western horizon and sliced with scarlet smears the edges of the far-flung clouds. The sea breeze had died with the sunset and a stillness lay on the water.

Somewhere in the *Poseidon* below decks, a baby wailed faintly in the crowded steerage quarters. A hoarse drunken voice rasped out the bawdy words of an old Irish song accompanied by other raucous voices, male and female. The ship was an East-Indiaman, and ex-troop transport from the recent Napoleonic Wars, now crammed with three parties of British immigrants, two Irish and one English. They were refugees, of all types and classes, from the post-war depression and crippling taxes in Britain; refugees in search of a better life.

On the poop-deck two powerfully built men faced each other. The taller man, a leer on his savage, hook-nosed and scarred face, shouted a curse into the sunset, furious and drunk. He thrust an empty bottle, broken at the neck, before him and advanced several paces towards his opponent.

'You scurvy dog, Dwyer, like your brother and all the rest of you southerners, the worst Black Protestant traitors of the lot!' He took a pause to wipe his mouth with a sweat-soaked sleeve, breathing heavily. 'Not content are you to serve vile Saxon rogues like the rats you are, you now try to turn my own men against me in the most scurrilous fashion in order to take over the leadership of all three parties aboard this stinking ship.' He paused, then uttered the worst possible abuse from an Irishman, 'The curse of Cromwell on you!'

The bright hazel eyes of the other man gleamed, unmistakable hatred sparking in them. He spoke now, deliberately calm, and stone cold sober. 'Your papist curses are but a wisp of smoke, Septimus O'Reilly. There's not one who doesn't know that you change your spots and your religion for your own devilish purposes. You are an insult to your Catholic faith. Your men are sick to death of your rules and regulations ever since we left Cork Harbour — tis they who seek another leader and other company, even preferring the only English party aboard!' There was a terrible knowing smile on Dwyer's face as he watched O'Reilly stagger forward, noting coolly the vicious rage in his small, bloodshot eyes. 'Just wait,' he continued, 'until those vile Saxon rogues, as you call them, find out how you falsified your party records by substituting whole families for single men who cancelled their passages — and all the rest of your cunning machinations. It will give me the sweetest of all earthly pleasures to finish you off this night and have done with you so that you can no longer trouble us when we disembark on the morrow.'

'No! Uncle Cady! No!' A young woman's cry of anguish tore through the fading April light, echoing across the bay. A girl rushed forward, trying to come between the two men. Frantically she turned to Dwyer. 'By all the saints, Uncle Cady, have you finally lost all your sense?'

Her uncle wiped his mouth with a finely-turned sleeve of an Irish linen shirt, a reminder of more prosperous times. Deep laughter lines ran from the corner of his eyes which mirrored anything but good humour in that moment. He was a man of medium height, stocky and powerfully built. His stern, strong Dwyer nose was prominent in an otherwise kindly face that had the mark of class about it. His hair was thick, grizzled and coppery without a trace of grey although he was forty-seven years old.

'You stay out of this, Esther Mary,' he said, speaking with the lilting, cultured cadences of County Cork. 'Return to the cabin to your sister while I teach this varmint a lesson he'll never forget!' He stood where he was, watching his opponent like a snake about to strike.

'Oh Uncle Cady, how could you?' Ester shrieked. 'And with poor Mama hardly cold in her grave.'

But she was forced to back away as O'Reilly advanced, fingers clenched tightly around the bottle, pointing the broken edge towards Cady Dwyer, his great slab of a chin thrust forward. He had a strange almost evil quality to his face, and a light lurking deep in his slate-coloured eyes. The shoulders of his soiled blue frockcoat rose and fell with his breath. He gave a hiss of pained anger, the sabre-cut across one cheek a dirty, livid white. Thrusting the bottle downwards he lunged with one terrible cry, his breath reeking foully of potcheen.

There was a rush of feet across the wooden boards of the deck and Esther, backing to the rail, could hear panting as blows were struck and the men came together. O'Reilly roared aloud, and raised the jagged bottle, flashing in the fast fading light, above his head. As the blow still hung impending, Cady leapt to one side, a mighty oath falling from his lips. The two men suddenly locked together in deadly combat, each with a hand on the other's throat. Esther could see nothing for the moment but the two furious, encrimsoned faces swaying together, and she shut her eyes for a second. The endless singing from below came to an end just then, and all voices in the steerage broke into a dull monotonous chorus.

The ship rocked suddenly and Esther opened her eyes at once. She glanced at the men and her heart jumped against her ribs. She watched, eyes frozen as her uncle pushed O'Reilly's lumbering body backwards, instantly blinding him with a blow to his brow. With a howl of pain, O'Reilly's large hand clawed upward, losing his grip on the bottle. It crashed to the deck in an explosion of green glass as another stunning blow caused him to fall to the deck, his mind dazed by the beating and the vast amounts of potcheen that had mysteriously appeared on board during the long sea voyage.

Cady shrugged broad shoulders and dusted off his breeches with a wicked chuckle. He turned away, beckoning to three seamen who had watched the whole scene, and now ambled forward, pigtails black with tar swinging down their backs from red stocking caps. Hands burnt black with rope burns picked up the prone figure while a fourth mate cursed loudly as he swabbed away the splintered glass.

'That fire-eater of an Irish madman should have been put

away for good, even 'anging is too good for the likes of 'im. Drinking, cussin' and makin' no end o' trouble fer four bleedin' months. Let 'im waste on these God-forsaken shores of Africa and the wild beasts eat 'is bones, and good riddance too!'

Cady turned to his niece as he pulled on his dark greatcoat. 'Well, Esther, that's one party leader down and two still standing. Not bad for a night's work.' He wrinkled his nose, taking out a snuffbox from the fob pocket of his shiny black brocade waistcoat. 'The air out here does certainly not smell like roses.'

The air seethed with the rank smell of the fly-infested livestock tethered together in their boxes on the main-deck below. Cady took a large pinch of snuff as he studied Esther thoughtfully, his eyes glinting with suppressed mischief. 'And you should be using your nimble fingers on some embroidery or some such thing with your sister in the cabin.'

Esther tossed back the mane of gleaming auburn ringlets with a flick of her head. 'That was the most disgraceful exhibition of common brutality I have yet seen, Uncle Cady. What will Papa say? Besides, you could have got yourself killed, or even worse!' She glared at him, her eyes bright and scornful. 'You should be ashamed of yourself, but I can see you are not one jot embarrassed, and that is the tragedy of it! A gentleman from one of the oldest and proudest families in all of County Cork who behaves like a common criminal.'

Cady tried to control the mirth welling up inside him, her girlish scorn striking him as amusing. Then he put on that bland air he could fashion up so easily in his seamed and worldy face.

'Good heavens, my child, but it was a great relief to step down from a gentleman's exalted pedestal and breathe the air of a lusty man's world for a change. No one can tell me you're really sorry or worried about me. That wretch has never been your favourite person, mutinying against the captain, being clapped in irons and cursing the whole crew — but especially your father and me ever since we left Ireland after Christmas.'

She gave him a scornful look, dark blue eyes flashing sudden fire from under well-defined brows. 'It's no use talking any sense to you, Uncle Cady — it never was, and never will be,' she said loftily. Her mouth curved. 'I dread to think what mischief you will drag us all into on those dreary shores across the bay.'

12

Cady could not restrain a smile. 'Don't think any more about it — time and the English will do it all for you. And I might add that dreary-looking coastline and the whole colony of the Cape of Good Hope was bought by the English from the Dutch for the princely sum of fourteen million pounds, dear girl, so keep your scorn for something less valuable.'

'Glory be!' Esther cried contemptuously. 'You do go on. I do not care how much money was traded for this outlandish colony, it does not look at all promising to me, so there!'

Cady's eyes glinted. He was delighted to see how she struggled between scorn and anger. From the fob pocket of his waistcoat he drew a gold watch with its heavy chain, looked at it, then clicked it shut. His chin lifted. One hand came up to stroke his magnificent thick, copper moustache. 'It's time for evening prayers, Esther Mary, and for you to be turning back to the cabin before your papa finds you out here after sundown. To be sure, prayers are just the thing for your reckless spirit just now.'

Esther's eyes snapped with annoyance at the wicked satisfaction in her uncle's face. For one vivid moment the air between them shivered with tense friction. She was about to answer, then she drew a breath, knowing he was baiting her. She sharply turned her back on him, the soft fringes of her black shawl brushing against the folds of her simple mourning dress. It fell almost to her feet, goffered demurely high at the neck and gathered under her breasts.

But nothing was demure about Esther Mary Dwyer, second and favourite daughter of Mr Joshua Dwyer, leader of the smallest party on board, a former squire and Justice of the Peace near Cloyne, the possessor of undisputed local power. And yet for all the force and strength of her features, Esther was beautiful. Tall and shapely, she carried herself with a poise and dignity far beyond her eighteen years. She pursed her lips angrily, sweeping back her abundant hair, the colour of the flaming African sunset, coaxed into the prevailing fashion of corkscrew ringlets at her ears and framing her high, clear forehead with its striking widow's peak.

'Hm!' she heard her uncle say, as she kept a determined profile towards the shore. 'You really are the most stubborn wench. If only you would marry the first decent man who crosses your path, it will be a relief to us all — and it is not as if you've had no

13

opportunities these last four months.'

Esther stepped back, an extra flaunt to her steps. 'You have the cheek to say that to me, Uncle Cady, when you know that there is no one on board this ship who deserves to be called a real man!'

Cady looked into the brilliant, taunting face. Leaning comfortably against the rail, he snorted. 'Take the advice of one of your elders and betters and grab the first man who'll have you, for there'll be very few who'll dare, mark my words. Think of your poor father, left with two daughters to feed, clothe and marry off.'

Flushed with indignation, she leaned forward, her eyes bright and malicious. 'It will pay you to keep your nose out of my affairs, Uncle Cady. I will marry whom I choose, when, where and how I decide!' She blazed with defiance, her fingers tightening fiercely on the rails.

Cady squinted through the fast-dying sunlight, his gaze moving on to the other ships, their large pyramids of canvas sails furled to their tall, graceful masts. 'To be sure, you will only respect the first man to give you a good overdue spanking.' His musical voice was softer, more lilting than ever. 'But for now, it is time for prayers. Your father will be waiting in the cabin.'

Esther clamped her lips shut. A scowl crossed her face, but she knew she must not go too far. She turned away, dropping her uncle a sudden swift bob of respect and swept away, leaving him to stare after her, a thoughtful expression in his eyes.

Algoa Bay lay still and leaden as the last rays of light dwindled and disappeared. The oil lamps on the other ships were mere blurs in the darkness when Cady decided to follow his niece to the cabin. On shore, the glow of campfires burned warmly amongst the dunes. Lines of tents straggled along the sand against a backdrop of hills that stretched into an unknown interior and an even more unknown future for them all.

CHAPTER
Two

The oil lamps on the mast were lit, casting a faint light over the main-deck when Esther stole out from her cabin once more. She stood by the rail, alone and unchaperoned, her heart heavy with mourning. Life for her was suddenly so full of sorrow again. She shivered as cold moisture filled the air. The land breeze had begun. The water glistened darkly below and here and there were patches of white foam cresting the long rollers as they creamed out towards the shore. All around the hull the current bubbled and hissed. The hawser was so taut that it pulled and creaked the anchor. The beach had long disappeared in the darkness, the hills now shapeless and hidden. There was the creak of woodwork, of wood straining against wood and ropes twisting as the wind thrummed in the rigging.

Esther's thoughts returned once again to the recent deaths of her mother, older sister Anna and younger brother Lewis from pneumonia. It had been the most terrible experience in her short, privileged life, especially to have lost her beloved mother. She had always been there, and now Esther needed her more than ever. She doubted that she could do without her in this new alien land across the bay. The vital integrating force in her life and that of the family had gone, and she was left with her father, Uncle Cady and younger sister, Laree — lonely, bewildered individuals facing unfamiliar and frightening circumstances.

She thought of the indignity of the three burials at sea, each of her loved ones sewn up in canvas and weighted with lead. They should rightfully have been buried peacefully in the small tranquil graveyard in the grounds of Cloyne Cathedral where the Dwyers had worshipped for over two hundred years. In the pain of

15

remembering, Esther could see it all again — Longwood House where her family had lived for generations, outside Cloyne to the east of Cork City. Her memories of the past, of the home she had known all her life were as clear and bright as they had ever been. She saw it all, the thick solid wood of the front door leading into the finely-panelled rooms, the long framed windows letting in the soft golden light of the short, northern summer days. Never had the memory of her childhood home nestling in the Irish hills seemed more beautiful, or more secure in its mellowed, old dignity.

She was back again on the damp hills where time stood still, remembering the dark hedgerows, the winding leafy lanes and the rain-soaked, bright-green patchwork of fields lying about the house. She had enjoyed her life as the privileged daughter of the local squire, living in the large, graceful stone house set back among its old trees. The spreading fields had rolled out and away down to the sea in the distance where the stench of poverty had scarcely touched her.

It was all too easy to forget the grinding poverty of most of the Irish, to block out the memories of the smoke from Catholic farmsteads filling the air, burned by the English. She dismissed all that, only reliving again the picnics at the small seaside village of Ballycotton with its fingers of green land pushing out to sea. She had enjoyed the parties and dances in Cork City among the upper-class gentry whose homes were modest compared with those of their English counterparts, but fine enough for them. She could feel again the beautiful gowns, spilling yards and yards of lace and galloon ribbons, the cheeky, gay bonnets, the gloves and the dainty, square-toed shoes with assortments of silver buckles.

She remembered the piano lessons with old Count Angerstein, an impoverished Russian aristocrat who had left his native country and settled in Ireland. She thought of her first and only love, Count Angerstein's dashing, young grandson, Michael, whom she had adored, and his love letters she still kept, tied with pale pink ribbon.

And now that life was over, burnt into ashes by mounting debts caused by the post-war depression which had finally forced her father in desperation to sell the family estate. He had joined

16

the Settler Scheme to the Cape of Good Hope which did not seem to Esther to have anything good or hopeful about it at all. Her father and uncle, though, hoped to start again and build another Longwood House set in another large and lovely estate.

Uncle Cady had managed the family's sugar estates in Badajoz in the West Indies. She had been raised to the stories of his reckless ways and exciting adventures in the tropical islands until the estates had also suffered from the aftermath of the Wars and were declared insolvent. He had returnd to Cloyne after many years and agreed to join the family in its emigration to one of the remotest colonies in the Empire.

They had left Ireland in a small party of thirty-six members: blacksmiths, tenant-farmers, coopers, labourers, artisans, their women and children. The nine single men were apprenticed to her father for three years and would help build him a fitting country house and work his lands until their contracts expired. She knew that her father felt a great responsibility towards them for most of them had lived and worked on Dwyer land for years.

It had snowed when they left in the bitterest winter for forty years and they were detained in Passage West, the small village in Cork Harbour, for days at a temperature fourteen degrees below freezing. The two ships, *Poseidon* and *Rosa*, had waited in the harbour, each with an English party from London aboard. Vast quantities of plate-sized cakes and steaming whiskey-punch had kept the passengers happy at the quayside inn until the weather finally broke.

Esther's last memory of the parting was of the receding harbour wall of one of the two privately-owned quays. A group of lively, young men had run along it to the end, their shouts of farewell growing faint and distant as the ship drew further and further away. The cries of the sailors had grown louder from the rigging where they hung like spiders in their webs. And there had not been one clear eye among the passengers as Cork Harbour disappeared, never to be seen by most on board again.

The past faded with disturbing abruptness and Esther was back in the present. The sudden smell of pitch, paint and strong animal odours from the pens made her feel sick and Ireland had never seemed so far away. They had all been promised a free passage to this dismal place, the deposits for each family paid back on their arrival at their destination. A farm of a hundred acres of virgin arable land awaited them, reputed to be the finest in southern Africa for pasturage, corn and grapes. They had been given the first ten years to pay back the cost of the land, and rations were to be issued until the first harvest. It all seemed so promising, and yet . . .

She felt cold when she thought of her father, as if a sudden icy chill from the sea had crept on board. He had been under considerable strain since his wife, beloved companion for so long, had died. He had withdrawn from them all, so that not even she, his favourite, could reach him. She had come to dread the dark, brooding look so often on his face these days.

She was tired of shipboard life, of the quarrelling, the bickering, wailing babies and irritable mothers, the drunken wretches, the dreadful food, the stink and disease. All she wanted was to escape from this wooden prison.

She watched the shimmer of stars reflected in the vast blackness of the water below, then sighing, and killing all further memories, she returned to the family cabin on the upper-deck.

The following morning Esther rose early. Making her way on deck once more, she watched the first morning light catch the water so that it shone a luminous blue towards the distant horizon. A strong breeze chopped it, sending foaming spray high into the air.

On the main-deck the hoarse shouts of the crew rose; their bare feet pattered over the wooden boards, rough hands carrying buckets and holystones to scrub the decks before the passengers disembarked. Esther raised her spyglass to her eye and pursued the dark specks bobbing on the water, heading out towards the ship like great, black beetles. They were flotillas of flat-bottomed lighters.

She could see the dismal bay overlooked by a stone fort perched on a shoulder of rock on the fringe of dark, low-lying hills. Its Union Jack fluttered in the stiff breeze. It was nothing like any of the immigrants had imagined. It was far worse than anything they could have dreamed of, so remote from everywhere, so bleak and barbaric.

The bay was a large inlet where there was no harbour or jetty and the passengers and cargoes were unloaded by the lighters plying back and forth between the shore and the ships.

She lowered the spyglass and snapped it shut, now surrounded by a buzzing coil of noise as more passengers arrived on the upper-decks. The frightened animals were winched aboard the lighters bobbing on the white-capped waves fragmenting about the hull. She watched other lighters creep towards them, battling against the strong sea breeze. Between them and the shadowy green masses of the hills, the blue sea crawled to the shore.

'Good morning, Esther Mary — surprising to see you up so early after creeping out on deck again last night.' Cady Dwyer strode up to stand beside her, his greatcoat slung across his shoulders against the early autumn chill. The sun shone on his thick, coppery hair as he leaned easily against the rail. 'You thought no one saw you creep out alone on deck — but you were wrong. I was taking my last walk around the pens, luckily or unluckily for you, missy.'

Esther's dark blue eyes flashed. 'You would, Uncle Cady! Always spying on people. Why did you not tell Papa?'

He felt in his pockets and drew out a brass tobacco box and a white clay pipe. 'Your papa has enough worries on his shoulders at present,' he said conversationally. 'But I would advise you to watch yourself — it's not safe or seemly for a young woman such as yourself to be out alone, unchaperoned in the dark.'

He stuffed his pipe with tobacco with his hard, strong hands and put away the brass box. Then he lit the tobacco with a tinderbox, drew in some air and let it out, his eyes meeting hers. 'There is some sense in what I say, though you would be the last to see it, Esther Mary.'

'I am tired of being told what to do,' she retorted. 'Besides, I am old enough to look after myself.'

Cady appeared undaunted. 'In this part of the world no woman is old enough or brawny enough to look after herself in certain circumstances.'

She swung on him, her eyes glittering dangerously. 'I am old enough, and I can look after myself. There's not one weak bone in my body, d'you hear me?' Her hands, in dark, kid gloves buttoned in pearl, curled tightly around the spyglass. 'I have enough good sense in my head, which is more than I can say for Laree and that gangling, overgrown schoolboy she totes around every minute of the day!'

Cady's bright hazel eyes sharpened. He bit the stem of his pipe. 'If it's Roydon Wilson to whom you refer, then you are a hundred per cent wrong, my girl. He may look naive and innocent, but I'll wager he'll make the best husband for your sister. And mind your tongue — jealousy does not become you!' He turned away from her with more than a touch of acid, and strode off with her exasperated words, 'Jealousy indeed! I've nothing to be jealous of!' following him impotently.

A frown crossed Esther's beautiful face, then her anger fled and she knew a moment of shame. They all wanted to escape this ship. They were all weary of it, especially Uncle Cady and herself who shared the same fiery nature and restlessness. She pursed her lips and lifted a stubborn chin. Roydon Wilson was the last person she would ever desire. When her chance came she would make a brilliant match, with or without a dowry, and live for the rest of her life in fine style. And that was something Roydon Wilson would never be able to give Laree.

'Esther, Esther!' A clear, young voice with a slight Irish lilt chimed along the quarterdeck. Laree, Esther's younger sister, a girl of sixteen, ran towards her. The fresh breeze streamed through her light brown ringlets shot through with chestnut glints. It billowed through her simple black dress, sending the velvet sash of the empire waist flying back.

'You must hear our news, Esther, you have to be the very first person to know,' she piped, waving a perky black bonnet sprigged with tiny, white rosebuds.

Esther turned to face her, a ripple of impatience ruffling her expression as her eyes fell on the young man with the gleaming, wheat-white hair who followed her sister rather apprehensively. It was Roydon Wilson himself, son of Mr Arthur Wilson the leader of the only English party on board and a gentleman farmer from Newton Abbot in Devon.

Laree stood before her, her face alight with intense excitement. Her china-blue eyes never left Esther's face, the soft ringlets demurely hiding her rosy dimpled cheeks. She was tall and slender with the faintest resemblance to her older sister, but cast in a gentler, sweeter mould that Esther's nature could never imitate with success.

'Roydon wishes to ask Papa if we can marry as soon as possible.

20

Isn't that too wonderful for words?'

Esther stared at her, too surprised to speak. She looked at Roydon without warmth. He stood behind Laree, looking for all the world like one of his father's sheep, she thought uncharitably. And her Uncle Cady thought he would be a good husband for Laree, with his loose-limbed, clumsy body and hangdog expression. She was sure that if she barked at him he would die of fright.

He wore a dark blue frockcoat like a shapeless blanket; his long leggings, reaching to mid-calf, white stockings and flat black shoes with dull silver buckles, were all sea-stained. He never looked right in his best clothes, as if he wore them uncomfortably, on sufferance to please his mother. He clutched a deep beige beaver-brimmed hat in a large, bony hand, and she could see the muscles of his jaw working nervously. He was nineteen and although a year her senior she had dismissed him long ago as a person of no consequence. She wondered again what on earth Laree saw in him.

'No!' she said, her mouth snapping. 'Papa will never agree — you're far too young, Laree.' She looked directly at Roydon, his fresh, ruddy face mutely considering hers as he stood in rigid silence, waiting.

The colour rushed to Laree's face. 'But Mama was my age when she married Papa, Esther!' The bright gaiety that shone from her pretty, vulnerable face seeped away. There was a look of acute dismay in her eyes, She was in a bewildered pain of confusion — anxious for Esther's approval, worried about Roydon's embarrassment and agonisingly aware that she did not understand her sister's antagonistic behaviour.

'Papa will understand, Esther, I know he will. Roydon and I love each other — surely you of all people understand that?' She gazed at her sister with wide eyes, a shadow now in their depths. She looked so young and earnest in her pleading that Roydon looked down at her with concerned, possessive eyes.

Esther's face hardened. 'Stop being a fool, Laree. Papa will be furious when he finds out. He has been through quite enough already without your stupidity too. Besides, how can you even think of such a thing when Mama and the others were buried only a matter of weeks ago.'

Laree was stricken. She stood for a moment like a figure of stone staring at the sister she loved and admired more than anyone else,

21

whose strength and force of character were so much greater than her own. She bent her head.

Esther had seen the bleak, unhappy look and her irritation abated, leaving her ashamed of her sudden outburst. She was sharply aware that she had hurt Laree who desperately needed her support. But there was no turning back now, her pride would not let her.

As the breeze made music in the rigging and the noise from the passengers rose tumultuously, Esther and Roydon regarded each other over Laree's bent head. She was surprised at his steady look, the intenseness of his expression unusual in the easy-going boyishness of his face.

'Come, Laree,' he said gravely in his slow Devonian drawl. 'There is no more to be said now on the matter.' His pale eyebrows drew into a troubled line over his light grey eyes as he placed an awkwardly protective arm about Laree's shoulders.

When he glanced at Esther again, there was a guarded look in his eyes, not unfriendly, but wary. She recognised a new and unexpected implacability in him. In that instant a silent challenge flared between them, over Laree.

The green hills of the shore stood out boldly beyond, and between them and the ship the lighters continued to bob over the waves with the sparkle and flash of the sun in the midst of them. A crowd now thronged the rails on the main-deck, the chatter of voices almost deafening.

Roydon broke the charged atmosphere on the upper-deck by taking Laree's arm. He led her to the companionway and down towards the bustle of passengers wrestling for better places at the rails.

Esther stared after them, then she turned away, fierce resentment burning inside her.

The seaman bent to his oars, the surf-rope tightening between the bows of the lighter and the smaller surf-boat. As the boat pulled away from the *Poseidon*, its bow pointed shorewards. The passengers in the lighter looked apprehensively towards the beach as the seaman pulled the oars heavily, scraping the rowlocks as the surf-boat slowly drew ahead towing them across the dancing waters.

Esther's heart pounded with anticipation as she sat gracefully in the stern, riding the great swells of unfurling green chasing the white crests breaking like frothy necklaces on the fine, pale sands. The *Poseidon* dwindled as the two boats moved away from her, the stern wake pouring out behind them.

She had been temporarily separated from her family in the last run ashore. Her father had left the ship two days before to make arrangements for the party in the tent-town on the beach. She now fastened curious eyes on the approaching shoreline, the stretch of dark green water between them and the beach gradually narrowing. The bay opening before her was larger than had appeared from the ship, with breakers stretching out on either side of them. They passed the first line, then the second, sliding in towards the beach.

On closer inspection the shoreline was a broad, undulating shelf between the sea and the hills, covered with a writhing mass of dense jungle growth, starred here and there with the vivid flame of autumn aloes. Fort Frederick, consisting of three small buildings and a few huts, stood near the top of a shoulder of rock commanding both the landing and the ford over the Baakens River. At the river mouth a sparkling stretch of lagoon was whipped into low rippling waves by the strong sea breeze.

There were clusters of tents on the beach, smoke from cooking fires among the sand dunes, long lines of ox-wagons. Sounds from the camp came clearly over the shortening stretch of water, shouts, roars, bellows, high-pitched laughter. It all had a peculiar remoteness that, on closer sight, haunted her with a subtle hostility. Suddenly, she felt lost and lonely, and though it was a bright day, a chill ran down her spine with light, sinister fingers.

The hills and the beach closed around them and shut out the great sounding emptiness of the sea. Instead, close at hand was the wind and the whisper of the surf. The boat lifted and fell and grated on the sand in the shallows, and some of the men jumped out with the seaman and held fast to prevent the run back. Out of the bright sunshine, figures instantly came to wade into the surf to help with the unloading.

Young men tumbled out of the boat as the surf-rope unravelled, leaving the boat aground in the shallows. Throwing their legs over the side, they dropped into the ankle-deep water and splashed up the beach. A group of Seaforth Highlanders, stationed there to assist with the landing of the settlers, surrounded the lighter. Several noisy, half-naked Hottentots, a race that had lived in the Cape Colony for generations and whose lack of dress caused some consternation among the females, stood beside them.

Amid loud shouts, Esther and the women were carried by the Highlanders to the gently shelving beach. The children rode, whooping with glee, on the backs of the small nimble Hottentots.

Surrounded on the beach by an odd assortment of baggage, a dismantled carriage, and a pianoforte without legs, Esther shook her skirts free of the sand. She stared about her, one hand trying to restrain the bonnet ribbons streaming about her head. This is without doubt the windiest, most dreary place I've ever seen, she thought dismally. Her eyes raked the scene trying to find some point of optimism, of hope to stop the despair rising inside her.

The settler camp spread under a vast sky. Strings of washed clothes stretched across the evergreen bushes covering the dunes. Cooking fires still glowed, acrid wood-smoke pluming the air. Small groups of soldiers moved among the tents of the immigrants whose pale faces were lined with the weariness of the long sea-voyage. Big, rugged Colonial–Dutch Boers, the only white race beside the British to inhabit the colony, stood beside their wagons waiting to take the settlers to their farms. They were selling heaps of almonds, raisins and oranges, haggling with their customers in sign language over the stiff squares of paper-money called rixdollars, and over the silver Spanish dollars. Their Hottentot servants brandished enormous, bamboo-handled whips, reaching the flanks of all the oxen in their spans with one skilful blow. The iron-rimmed wagon-wheels jolted over the soft sand, rendered fine by the continuous wind along that part of the coast, as some of the wagons left the beach on their way to the interior with parties of settlers on board.

The sparkling ocean lay blue and wide to the horizon. Surf tumbled and tossed its foam along the edge of the shore, the great rollers runing down the coast by day and night so that the camp was never out of earshot of their thundering noise.

Esther gave up her fight against the wind and untied the black velvet ribbons of her bonnet. It was with overwhelming relief that she looked up and saw the tall, grey-haired man stride towards her, the tails of his dark frockcoat flapping behind him. It was her father.

A large flock of gulls lifted suddenly, white wings flung against the bright blue of the sky. She stared across at her father drawing closer with every determined step. She felt a rush of affection for him and

24

impulsively, bonnet in hand, ran towards him, the skirt of her pelisse swinging about her shapely, stockinged legs.

Running agilely, she closed the gap between them, fine showers of sand kicking up behind her. Clear, alert grey-green eyes glowed in a face severe above a thin wide mouth, as Joshua Dwyer drew up to her. The smile she gave him in return was so joyous, so full of relief, that his own taut face relaxed into a contented grin. Heedless of decorum, Esther flung her arms about his neck, her bright auburn ringlets streaming across her face.

'Oh Papa, this is such a lonely, barren place — I never dreamt it would be like this!' she burst out before she could stop herself.

She saw the swift, bracing movement of her father's shoulders as he drew breath, his grey-green eyes narrowing in his harsh, proud face. He stared at her, and then he shook his head.

'Esther Mary, nothing in life is quite like one imagines it will be, but we are here now, for good or ill, and we must make the best of it. There is nothing for us back in Ireland. Besides, your mama would not have liked it any other way.'

'Mama would have hated it here — I know she would. It is the most uncivilized place I have ever seen!'

Joshua said nothing at first, regaining his control. He eyed Esther enigmatically from under his thick grey brows. 'You will not talk like that again, my child,' he said with unusual vehemence. 'We are here to stay and that's the end of it. And you will refrain from speaking about your mother in such a disrespectful manner.'

Esther flared, her eyes bright, but Joshua gave her a look of such acute displeasure that she could not speak. Desperately blinking back tears of protest and frustration she looked over to the far side of the camp where the bush-covered dunes rolled upwards in green sweeps. Her own beloved father had withdrawn from her. He and she had been so close, and she had loved him through all the years that she could remember.

But as she turned her eyes once more to face his, she saw no joy there, only a bitter remembering. Mama had gone. The family was breaking apart. And Papa was becoming an unfamiliar, cold stranger.

25

CHAPTER
Three

Esther sat back on her knees in the tent which she shared with her sister, Laree. She ran her fingers over the engraving of an embossed invitation card she had pulled from the small, inlaid, rosewood trinket box she held in her lap.

Beside her, scattered on a small rug on the sand, lay a pair of ivory opera glasses and a tortoise-shell cardcase. A dull, empty feeling flooded her entire being. She replaced the card in the box lined with pale pink satin and tiny seed pearls. It had been her last invitation to a Christmas ball at the home of Count and Lady Angerstein, the grandparents of her beau, Michael. It brought back too many memories she preferred to forget of the gaiety she had once known, the gorgeous clothes, the dances, the laughter — and Michael. Her beautiful Michael who she would never forget.

Her face was sullen as she snapped shut the rosewood box. Lifting herself abruptly, she sat back on the heels of her flat, black kid slippers and watched Laree sewing. There was a choking in her throat, and she felt quite suddenly overwhelmed by rebellion, hate and despair.

'This has got to be the windiest place in the whole rotten world,' she cried in sheer exasperation. 'It has not stopped to take breath the whole morning.'

An amused giggle escaped Laree. 'Trust you to say such a thing, Esther.' She sat at a folding table set up at one end of the tent close to the two truckle beds. Her fingers worked nimbly at a pair of deep blue slippers to replace a pair badly stained by seawater.

Esther's eyes were fixed on the restless scene outside, hardly aware that Laree had spoken. Overhead shone the autumn sun, hanging in a blue sky. The crisp breeze whistled through every chink in the tent, sprinkling a fine rain of sand on the wooden brass-studded chest near the flap, and the valises stacked neatly beside it.

She looked about her with sharp revulsion. Away to the east, the air above the low green bushes and tents was smoky with cooking fires, the smoke blown into sharp spirals by the breeze. The sound of drunken voices came from the main camp, where most of the settlers were in desperate circumstances and seemed to be, to her mind, a collection of filthy, idle and insolent people.

Near her, in the privileged section with its neat marquees, the upper-class folk read and talked quietly before their immaculately arranged tents. Wagons jolted backwards and forwards, taking their parties to their farms. She could see Isaac Wilson, Roydon's uncle, standing near the shore, one hand mopping his ruddy face with a large canary-yellow handkerchief. He leant on his ivory-topped cane.

'There's that old self-righteous toad, Isaac Wilson, who talks of nothing else except his fat sheep,' she burst out with a wealth of hostile feeling. She failed to notice the quick, wounded expression in her sister's eyes, nor the stubborn look that changed her pretty face.

Laree struggled with a variety of emotions, unbearable distress conveyed by the way she stabbed her needle deep into the slipper she worked. She bit off a thread and raised her smooth, brown head, her eyes resting on Esther's back. 'That's not fair, Esther — and you know it. Isaac cannot help what he's like or your opinion of him. He's quite a mild, old gentleman really, and as harmless as they come.'

'He may not be able to help his great, empty head and sheep's eyes, but he can help his speech!' Esther swung round. 'He must be the most boring person in Africa — or England for that matter. I wonder how many he has put to sleep with his long, dreary speeches about the agricultural revolution, and if I hear the name of Jethro Tull or the rotation of crops once more, I'll scream.' She tossed her head so that the magnificent riot of red ringlets tumbled about her head, all its myriad of shades catching the sunlight streaming into the tent.

Laree suddenly rose from her work, trembling with suppressed emotion. Picking up a small musical box, she opened it and a gay, tinkling country tune filled the tent. Tears welled up in her eyes as the melody played over and over again, bringing with it bittersweet memories of the past.

'You're not still thinking of marrying Roydon, are you?' Esther's sharply discordant voice broke through the tune. 'You have been very quiet about it these last few days.'

Laree stood very still, staring at the box in her hands with its dainty harlequin figure twirling round and round to the music. The tune stopped abruptly and she did not turn it on again. In that moment she seemed almost too fragile to exist in that wild, rugged place, as out of tune with it as the tune from her musical box.

Then she lifted her head. 'I love Roydon, Esther — something which you may find hard to believe — and I know he loves me. Someday, at the right time, he will approach Papa and we will marry.' Her cheeks suddenly flushed crimson. 'But as you said on the ship, it is too soon after dear Mama's death, and I don't want to upset Papa.'

She looked at her sister with an unusually defiant expression, and Esther gazed at her, before her eyes travelled to the box. Mama had given it to Laree a long time ago. Then she looked away, embarrassed by her own untimely outburst. If Laree wanted to be a fool and marry someone with no prospects, a mere boy with no more experience in life than she had, then she was going to wash her hands of it and let Laree make her own mistake.

'This place is not so bad if you try to get used to it, Esther.' Laree spoke with unexpected spirit. 'You haven't given yourself the chance and that's why old Isaac and the others annoy you.'

Esther folded her arms across her chest resentfully. Laree would never understand how she felt. She rolled her eyes heavenward, the light of impatience glittering in them. 'It's just that you are satisfied with so little, Laree, while I — it's not only this place, it's — I'll wager anything you like that there can be no dashing gentlemen out here in this wild place.'

Laree stared at her sister; she had seen the swift film of moisture in Esther's eyes, but it had gone almost before she had realised it. She puckered her brow, her light brown ringlets outlining her head in shining softness. 'You're lonely, Esther, but you haven't given anyone a chance and heaven knows you've had plenty of opportunities. I think you are right — you ask for too much. We must be grateful for what we have. There are many unfortunates who do not have even what we have been reduced to. Besides, you do not know who could be out there waiting in the interior, near the towns. You can't judge the rest of the country by this beach. If it's anything like what we saw of Cape Town from the ship, then our lives shall be very pleasant.'

She smiled. It was impossible to remain angry with Esther for long — she was too honest, too reckless, too infectiously alive. 'When the time comes, will you believe me then?'

An almost belligerent scowl crossed Esther's face, her dark blue eyes wicked with sudden mischief. 'If and when the time comes. We shall have to see now that we're all prisoners of this barbaric land.'

'Ah, I see I have caught you girls hard at your labours.' Their father's tall figure appeared at the open flap of the tent. He stood, a faint smile creasing his wide, thin lips, his shirt sleeves unbuttoned and loose at his wrists, his black, embroidered waistcoat hanging open. He had taken his white clay pipe from his mouth and cradled the bowl between his fingers.

'A pretty sight to be sure — young ladies industriously employed.' He chuckled and clamped the pipe back in his mouth.

'Oh, Papa, it's all so — boring!' Esther hissed.

Joshua thrust out his lip, holding his pipe in one hand. 'Then I have good news for you. We finally leave for the interior early tomorrow morning with one of the Boers — a Mr Gert Venter who has loaned us his wagon for the purpose.'

He smiled as he saw Laree's face suddenly light up, eager, bright, young and alive. 'That is the best news yet, Papa. And soon we will be on our very own farm in our own home once more. Does Roydon know? Will they be travelling with us?'

Joshua nodded. 'To be sure they do, child. They will be travelling with us for most of the way. The last part we do on our own with our small party and that of Mr O'Reilly.'

'Mr O'Reilly?' Esther burst out, throwing her head back. 'That will only be trouble for us, as if we needed any more of him and his like.'

Joshua looked at her, his face grave. 'It is only to the location — there we leave the man and his men to their fate.'

Esther turned to see her father's suddenly averted head, his expression hidden from her. Joshua did not like Septimus O'Reilly any more than they all did, but she had learnt that when her father mentioned the man it was best to remain silent.

She shrugged and turned away, not noticing the pain in Laree's eyes as she regarded her father's rumpled shirt and the heavy lines in

29

his tired face. As Joshua stooped to leave the tent, Laree's heart went out to him. She knew she could not speak to him of her feelings for Roydon yet . . . But the right time would come, of that she was sure, out there on their location, in their new home.

In the pale glow of an autumnal dawn, the one English and two Irish parties from the *Poseidon* assembled about the wagons for their departure into the interior. The tent-town was just coming alive and the smoke from rekindled fires began to swirl about the dunes. The hills were lost under early morning mist, mysterious and vast, the bushes obscured, swallowed up, until the sun burst through the layers of vapour.

Little by little the Boer wagons with their spans of long-horned oxen emerged from the haze, their colours growing brighter with the slowly deepening light creeping over the sea. The loaded wagons and their rows of oxen, stamping their massive feet, stood in line, the noise of men and beasts growing to a deafening pitch.

Esther sat on the hard, wooden driver's seat of Meneer Gert Venter's wagon. Pulling her dark pelisse with the military frogging tightly about her against the damp chill, her eyes moved over the swirling mass of activity. She was pleased they were on the move at last after two weeks on the beach in the tent-town. Her youthful curiosity mingled with the uncertainty of the unknown lying ahead.

She looked out towards the sea where the east brightened to deepening gold and coral, while the north-west still slept in palest mauve and pink. Already golden patches streamed through the high formations of herringbone cloud, and outlined the irregular hem of the surf on the sand.

In a strange desolation she watched the white canvas of the last ship, so like the *Poseidon*, breaking slowly across the water until it disappeared out of sight below the horizon. One like it had carried her over a lonely sea and could never carry her back.

Feeling as if her last link with the British Isles was being taken away with the ship, she forced her eyes back to the seething mass of men and beasts around her.

A hoarse voice sounded. She looked around. A tall, angular young man of about twenty-five climbed onto the seat beside her. Samuel Pettigrew, an orphaned Englishman adopted by Gert Venter at the age of eleven, had entered the life of her family abruptly and cheerfully, as was his way. His parents had been shipwrecked on the way to India on the treacherous Cape coast. They had drowned and he had been among the very few survivors to be picked up by the Venters, almost dying of thirst. The Venters, trek-boers on their way into the interior searching for new pastures, had adopted him. He had lived with them ever since on the farm where they had eventually settled on the wild Koonap River in the Eastern Cape.

He wore a blue jacket, skin breeches and a leather belt with large pockets for powder and shot. A wide, low-brimmed hat woven from rushes was crammed on top of his unruly, straight, raven-black hair. As the wagon-drivers only spoke Colonial Dutch, it was fortunate for the Dwyers that Sam was to accompany them to their location. He had managed to keep his English alive by regular discussions with the redcoats at the few frontier posts in the vicinity and at the garrison headquarters in Grahamstown.

'We'll be leaving soon, Miss Dwyer,' he said, in a strange accent of English mixed with Dutch. She watched him soaking a piece of dried bullock's flesh, locally called biltong, with a dram of brandy from a large horn pulled from the inside of the wagon. Grimacing, she refused the piece he offered her. He sat back, his long, lean body at an awkward angle. But there was nothing ungraceful about him, and the muscles of his arms and legs were sinewy and strong, finely honed by the ruggedness of his life.

He regarded her with some amusement as he chewed on the meat. He smiled, his large teeth very white against the dark tan of his skin, but there was a disturbing glint in his black eyes.

'There's many strange ways you will have to get used to out here in the wilds, Miss Dwyer — and many rough ones you may not like, seeing as 'tis common knowledge you settlers, unlike the Boers, are forbidden to have servants.'

'I think not,' she remarked tartly, her eyes darkening somewhat stormily at the easy familiarity of his tone. 'Besides, Mr Pettigrew, that is no concern of yours!'

He looked at her keenly, his face lined prematurely so that he seemed much older than his years. 'I suppose not.' He rubbed his angular chin and pulled out a large tobacco pipe from the band of his hat and waved it in the air. 'But 'tis only fair to warn you that there be very few quality folks like yourself in these parts. I don't know what you've been expecting and I hope you won't be disappointed, Miss

Dwyer. I'm just wondering how you're going to deal with those Xhosas across the border when they get their chance to cross the Fish River into the colony.'

A rush of anger temporarily robbed Esther of coherent speech. She disliked him very much, thinking him brash, crude and far too familiar. And she was very much aware that he was trying to shock her. 'Xhosas? What Xhosas? By merciful heavens and who would they be?'

His shiny dark eyes rested on her cold face. 'Did those high-up Government nobs not tell you? All you settlers are being settled across the border from the fiercest black tribesmen in all of Africa.' She saw the shock in his face. A shock that stopped his next words for a moment, followed by such bitterness in his voice that she was appalled. 'We fought a bloody, savage war against them in this very colony only a year ago. They surrounded our biggest village, Grahamstown, in their thousands. A handful of Boer hunters and about three hundred redcoats finally succeeded in driving them away with the supremacy of their muskets and shot. The Xhosas fight with sharp-pointed sticks called assegaais — dangerous weapons, I can tell you.' There was a strange tightness about him as he paused. 'Our Colonel Lightfoot, head of the garrison, was mutilated and killed. Shocked us all. Can't understand why them government wigs never told you immigrants.'

A sense of outrage possessed her. 'No one told us about the tribesmen — or else we would never have come to this grim colony. What would be the sense in leaving Ireland with all its problems to come to this.'

Sam knitted his black brows, running a surreptitious eye over her appearance. The expression on his face seemed to say that he gave her no chance of survival here at all.

'Everything I say is the truth. You have come to a savage land, Miss Dwyer, where nature pits itself against the men who live in it. I love this land, it's in my bones, but for the likes of you and your kinsmen I have my doubts. The Boers have been talking ever since they heard you lot were coming here and it seems to them and to the redcoats that you were sent out as the first line of defence against the tribesmen.'

'What do you mean — the first line of defence?' she gasped, the light of horror appearing in her eyes.

32

Sam pursed his lips, seeking the right words. 'The authorities have placed you immigrants in the wildest parts of the colony, between the Boers and the Xhosas. There seems only one conclusion to their thinking — they want you to be the buffer for the colony against the Xhosas. There are not enough redcoats to defend our long borders, you see, so there you are smack in the midst of it all and forced to defend yourselves. And in so doing you protect the colony far more cheaply than a bigger garrison of trained men.'

Esther was numbed. She could not believe it, yet she knew that Sam, for all his outspoken manners, told the truth. She felt despair for the future. How could they remain in this dreadful place, in danger of their lives among rough farmers, uncouth redcoats and wild tribesmen — Hottentots and Xhosas?

The enormity of it overshadowed her but one thought overrode even her worst fears of the wilderness and the Xhosas. In the age of matrimony in which she lived, it was considered of utmost importance for a girl to marry well, an age in which all mothers with daughters spent much time pursuing eligible suitors. Now Esther faced the worst calamity of her life — to live and die an unmarried old maid, withered and unloved. She was being taken far into a wild interior, away from all the main centres of civilization. She saw the door closing on her to the elegant ease of her former life, surrounded by well-mannered, polished young bucks.

She looked up to see Meneer Venter doff his hat politely as he came up to the wagon to talk to Sam. He was a large-boned man, heavily lined and dewlapped, his mahogany-burnt face freckled with sunspots and framed with a magnificent thick bush of silvery-white beard. He stood back and smiled at her, then at his signal Sam struck the oxen with his long-handled whip. The wagon lurched forward. Sam settled himself on the hard seat, holding the whip easily between his long, bony fingers as the oxen were led by a Hottentot through the aromatic, evergreen bushes winding away from the coast.

The track was pot-holed and rutted deep in mud in places. The wagon jolted and heaved over the stones. All Esther wanted to do was to jump off and run away — anywhere but the place to which it was taking her. The livestock closed up behind the wagons, whips cracked and they proceeded at a slow pace to the jingling of harness of the few horses trotting alongside and the creaking of the woodwork.

Sunlight began to stream through the gaps between the bushes at the side of the animal track, throwing flickering shadows across Esther's haunted face and that of the long lean man beside her. At that moment she hated the place and him deeply; so much more because he had told her about it, and because she knew she was bound to it by seemingly unbreakable chains. I am in a prison, she thought murderously, a prison without bars, lost for ever. Why, oh why, did we come to this dreadful place?

CHAPTER
Four

The long caravan of wagons and livestock moved ponderously eastwards in a ten day journey over a stretch of country between the Sundays and Fish rivers. They travelled between ten to fifteen miles a day over rock and plain, through forests in an area veined with many small, drought-deprived streams wandering like trails of worms in soft wood. In the larger rivers hippos wallowed in the deeper pools and at night they were serenaded with the growls of leopards in the hills, and the howl of hungry hyenas and wild dogs. There were long delays when wheel-axles broke and the steep passes were difficult to climb.

A sudden storm broke out after they had made camp in a clearing. They had been travelling for two days and had wearily retired for the night with the women and children in the tents provided, the men and older boys lying under the wagons. That night it was different. As the lightning lashed the skies the men were driven into the tents by the cold rain. It pelted down on the trees, in the gorges, and in forest-choked ravines.

At about midnight there was a scream, a wild rushing of feet and the heated shouting of Boer and Hottentot. One of the oxen had broken away, swept down the raging river of water. After some time the Boers returned and sat bunched together in the covering they had made beside a wagon, the low rumble of their voices drowned by the beating of the rain.

The Dwyer girls were sound asleep in the darkness of their tent. Not even the constant drumming of the rain on its canvas disturbed them, when suddenly through the black night broke a cry of feverish urgency as a dark figure darted to their tent.

A thick Irish brogue cried out, 'Miss Esther, Miss Esther! Come quick — Hannah Byrne is near her time. Please, Miss, come quick!'

There was a sudden rustling and scuffling inside the tent. Esther sat bolt upright, her camp bed squeaking with the sudden shifting of her weight. She tried to pierce the darkness as her red braids swung abruptly down her back.

'Is that you, Amy?' she called out, searching for her flannel dressing gown. 'Do calm yourself, girl — from what little I know of it, first babes don't come all that quickly.'

Laree had risen and lit a candle. She joined her sister at the open tentflap through which the rain was pouring and where Amy Donohue stood, looking for all the world like a drowned rat. Amy had married one of the young men apprenticed to Joshua Dwyer weeks before they had left Ireland and had known the Dwyer girls for most of her life. She stood, wringing her hands together in great agitation, fear pinching her small, dark, pixie face.

'Please hurry, Miss Esther, Hannah thinks the babe is due. Your mama was the one who used to help us with birthings, on board ship and the like, and there is no midwife amongst us,' she quavered, her eyes darting from one sister to the other only to rest finally on Esther.

She and Laree stood together, the light of the candle searching their pale, tense faces. A silent, relentless struggle began in Esther, part of the legacy of pain and pride her mother had left her. It was as if all eyes, all hopes now rested on her.

On board, and during this journey inland, there was no protection from the realities of life. Esther had known about birthings although she had not given much assistance to any herself. She knew now with awful realization that she was forced to take the place of her mother, as the female head of the family and of their party. The majority of the settlers were young people under thirty years old, and she was forced to fall back on herself and her own strength. Someone had to hold the disintegrating members together and the task, it seemed, had awesomely fallen on her.

A nameless terror crept close about her heart, absorbing her in the fear that spread all over her body. She was not ready for this role, it was too much for her. If only her mother was here, everything would be all right. She would have known what to do.

There was a sudden change as she found the courage, born of desperation. 'Amy, take me to Hannah at once, and do stop shaking or you'll most surely shake yourself apart,' she snapped impatiently,

36

all at once very tall and commanding. 'Come, come Amy, at once!' The rich, dark red braids flew wildly forward in the rain blowing in through the flap. 'And let's hurry before you catch your death of cold.'

Laree came up beside her once more with a bundle of towels and a ball of twine. 'You'll need these, Esther. Mama always used them on board ship — but that's all I remember.'

Lips caught between her teeth, Esther tried to answer. She frantically tried to recall everything about the one time her mother had required her to stand near the door of the steerage quarters during a particularly difficult birth in the tropics, after the only experienced midwife had died of measles rampaging the ship.

'Please hurry, Miss,' Amy bleated in a fever of anxiety. But the words galvanised Esther into action. She took the towels and twine from Laree and propelling Amy before her, rushed from the tent and out into the rain.

She looked down at Hannah Byrne whom she had known all her life as the daughter of one of her father's tenants. Hannah lay on a truckle-bed in one corner of a tent blue with the smoke of rush candles. Esther heard her groans as mounting horror filled her eyes. She put out trembling fingers and touched Hannah's forehead. The girl screamed and looked at Esther looming over her, her face strangely altered in the candlelight. She stopped, her lips twisting, her breath short.

'Oh, Miss Esther, I am so glad you've come.' She clutched at Esther's sleeve with unexpected force. 'Amy said you'd come. Don't let me die, Miss, Michael needs me and this babe — our first.'

Esther drew a deep breath and looked down at Hannah's face so young and bewildered, and so full of tortured pain. She drew herself erect, every faculty absorbed in the process of thinking, remembering. She would not allow herself to panic.

'Now Hannah, there's nothing to get yourself stewed over — hundreds of women have babies all the time. 'Tis as natural as breathing, so they say. You just settle down and in a short while you'll be holding your own babe in your arms.' She tried to smile, while inwardly she asked forgiveness for the lack of conviction she felt.

There was an intangible pervasion of fear in the small, cramped, bell-shaped tent as the rain continued to fall, and Hannah lay back. Esther felt it all, her own instincts aroused and alert. Pushing the wet, tangled hair out of her eyes, she took charge of the situation, sending everyone out except Amy.

She heard herself tell Laree to keep water boiling and Amy to stop chewing her nails to the quick. Then she pushed the girl away and leaned over Hannah, wiping her face with a cool, wet cloth.

'The babe — it comes, Miss Esther!' Hannah whispered hoarsely through dry, cracked lips. There was a fleeting moment of terror in her eyes before the spasm of violent pain once more knotted her body, wrenching it apart.

There were shouts from outside and much bustle as the first pail of hot water, boiled over a make-shift fire was brought to the tent. More orders were issued. And through it all, Esther stood beside the bed, her heart beating rapidly each time Hannah screamed.

Esther beckoned Amy to come closer and, frowning in total concentration, she examined Hannah as gently as she could. As Hannah screamed again, Esther ordered Amy to hold the woman's arms tightly above her head and hold on no matter what happened. Then the struggle for birth began.

Esther's nightclothes were drenched with sweat as Hannah hung on to Amy's thin, wiry hands, wrenching and pulling them as the spasms of pain accelerated through her womb. There was no one to fan the burning hot face lying contorted on the bed, and Esther wished she had thought to ask Laree to stay with her.

From time to time she was dimly aware of the shadow of Amy at Hannah's head. She vaguely heard the small sounds about her, the insistent cough of someone outside. Fiercely frowning, Esther remained kneeling, careless of her own disordered nightclothes, as she struggled to help ease the baby's head out, and carefully to lift the small bloody shoulders, no longer conscious of the terrible pain of the mother in this wonderful new miracle of birth.

At last the battle was over, and she was shaking uncontrollably with relief. Esther gazed at the baby boy and touched the small, puckered brow with her finger. How tiny he was, how helpless and so perfect. She crossed over to the bed and laid him beside his mother.

Voices and sounds were now tiresomely, insistently clear. She suddenly felt so tired and drained. She had lived through a nightmare of uncertainty and now it was over. She had safely delivered her first child.

A slow smile curved her lips as she caught Amy's eye. Then she went past her, too weary and too full to say a word. She went out into the slowly growing light of the new day.

The storm had gone before the dawn. The heavy clouds had rolled away, and the sky was clear, catching all the colours of the rising sun in its depths. She stood for a moment watching Gert Venter staring silently down at the mangled lifeless body of his prize ox now wedged between two rocks in the river. A mass of sticky, dark flies already moved about it in dense, living streams. Behind them the small Hottentots scrambled crab-fashion down the rocks, with ropes to pull it out.

Esther thought of the newborn child with the large eyes swimming in the small, red, wrinkled face. And suddenly she felt ecstatic. She had taken her first real steps into a woman's world with all its mysteries, its agonising secrets of pain and joy, terror and triumph. At first, it had been only the terrible pain that had caught her in its anguish, now it was the life she thought of, the life that flowed from it.

And now the ache began, a private and lonely ache of longing and desire so swift and so strong it made her shiver. A terrible need for warm, comforting, physical love descended on her, shaking her to the core.

In that moment, she envied Hannah Byrne, the young country girl with no education and no background, for she had experienced that special satisfaction of womanly fulfilment that Esther had never known. At first her strict upbringing fought to reject the idea, for it conflicted with all the newly-awakened feelings inside her. It brought to the surface all those secrets that only a woman's husband had the privilege to teach her in the marriage bed, and of which Esther was totally ignorant. Yet she wanted to know, she wanted to experience them for herself. The ache of wasting youth and blossoming womanhood continued to spread within her, craving acceptance.

She saw Michael Byrne walking towards her, his breeches and leather jerkin still damp from the rain, his checked neckcloth askew. His attitude was guarded towards her, his landlord's daughter, but he relaxed visibly as Esther smiled at him, her wistful expression transformed. She had seen the look of unconcealed gratitude and respect in his eyes for the woman who had just delivered his first child.

* * *

Esther was jolted awake with a start, for the wagon train was toiling over a shoulder of hill alive with the shriek of cicadas. Sunlit-trailing lianas and rocks littered their path, the massive feet of the oxen lumbering over the steady, upward climb of blue-green blanketed slopes. The taste and smell of dust was everywhere, clouds of it floating in the air.

Esther straightened herself on the wooden seat beside Sam, wiping away the film of sweat on her forehead, she could feel it pouring down her face and neck and reach the top of her shoulder blades. There was no retreat from the glaring sun and she yearned for the cool dampness of the Irish hills.

She had just walked back along the caravan of wagons to see Hannah and the baby, relieved to find the new mother cheerful and coping as well as she could on such a journey, and the baby peacefully asleep.

As they jolted uncomfortably through the land where the British had reluctantly followed the Boers and annexed it in a gesture of grudging necessity, Esther longed to turn back, to return to the comforting familiarity of Cloyne or Cork City, or even London, which she had visited perhaps two or three times.

The plodding of the oxen moved her on across acres of virgin, grass-covered plains, dotted with mimosa trees, fluffed with tufts of autumn yellow, and over tangled, woodland slopes stretching endlessly as far as the eye could see. Wary quagga and zebra watched them pass and jackals and hyenas skulked in the thickets of spekboom. Large rhinoceros and elephants roamed the plains in the distance and, nearer at hand, golden-brown buck leaped and twisted through the bush, darting into the underbrush at the sound of the wagons. There were only rough animal tracks over the hills which were crowned with the crimson splash of aloes and lofty, bowl-shaped, leathery euphorbias. Green boerboom clustered along the trail where light silvered the deep recesses of undergrowth, trying to penetrate the thick liana creepers slithering among the crags and along the branches of old, gnarled trees heavy with fungus.

Then they rounded a curve, skirting thickets of evergreen, passing the remains of a leopard in a trap of large stones and timber, wild dogs having set upon it. Here and there were ominous signs of lonely, deserted Boer farmhouses, temporary huts or roofless ruins, a grim reminder of the last two frontier wars when the ground on which they

40

travelled had run with the blood of men, black and white.

Esther could feel herself diminishing against the vastness of the bush and the intense loneliness of the landscape. She felt very small and insignificant, dwarfed by the endless high sky, where the great African birds soared.

Hottentots ran along the teams of oxen shouting at the lead animals, flicking their long whips with resounding smacks. The white settler boys ran ahead of the wagons to roll the rocks and large stones away from the trail. And further ahead, she could see Laree walking beside Roydon, as close as she could without touching, in their own little world.

Laree had travelled most of the way sitting with Charity Wilson and her daughter Sophia in their wagon, while Roydon had walked beside it. Esther knew that Laree was turning more and more to Charity in place of the mother she had lost, and for a moment, she envied her this replacement. But as much as she liked Roydon's mother, she was not reconciled to the son, and she wished vainly that Laree would reconsider and find some more suitable gentleman on whom to lay her affections.

It was two o'clock in the afternoon. Esther stirred drowsily beside the camp fire in a clearing not far from the village of Grahamstown, which they planned to reach the following day. The sun was still warm, but already the first hint of winter was in the air: a faint but crisp chill, heavy with the smell of dead autumnal leaves and aromatic shrub. She felt her eyelids droop, and jolted herself awake.

Back along the track was a solid block of wagons, oxen and people. Farther back still was a short line of men, hauling a wagon with a broken wheelshaft through the shallow stream which Gert Venter's wagon had crossed only half an hour before. She felt a twinge of conscience; she was supposed to be preparing some kind of meal for the hungry.

Her Uncle Cady, Sam and some of their men had gone hunting for the pot with Septimus O'Reilly of all people, and a handful of his men. Some of the Hottentots were running to lead the oxen and stop them plunging over the unlucky wagon which had been completely unloaded. Meneer Venter, her father and some of the Boers slowly lifted it from its muddy bed in the stream. Gradually it moved, lurching for a fraction before halting again as men and oxen heaved

41

together, the white of Meneer Venter's magnificent beard shining silver in the sunshine.

There was a commotion. Everyone looked up to see the returning hunters bearing the body of one of O'Reilly's men, mutilated beyond recognition. A crowd gathered at the camp with disbelieving horror. They all stood, eyes frozen, the dense, silent ravine rising spectre-like behind them.

'What on earth possessed you to do such a fool thing as to go after a leopard, one of the most dangerous beasts in the bush?' Joshua said in a terrible voice to O'Reilly, whose eyes were fierce and wild in his bone-white face. 'And these animals, Samuel Pettigrew tells me, are nocturnal at that!'

O'Reilly licked his lips and stared at Joshua as they faced each other, their eyes only inches apart. There was bitter hatred smouldering in O'Reilly's face, and he was sweating heavily. He looked past Joshua to where the covered corpse lay cold and still on the ground. He looked like a mad man, behind his eyes his thoughts were scurrying, darting, searching for a way out.

'It's not my fault — we went out to hunt buck and came upon a flock of what Pettigrew calls hyenas, the scavengers of the land. We had to scout round them and try to scare them off, when we startled a leopard which instantly sprang on Flanagan who had got too close.' He was shouting now, his voice thick and harsh.

'But it was Cady who ran forward, I hear, to aid your man. And when the leopard attacked Cady you did nothing to help him!' Joshua said incredulously.

'It's none of your stinking business — what I did or did not do has nothing to do with you! And anyway, Pettigrew shot the beast, killing it instantly.' He turned, glaring at Cady, whose face had been torn by the animal's talons, so that his one eye was filled with blood.

Joshua persisted. 'Two men might have died, O'Reilly, if Pettigrew had not shot the leopard in time — and you were right there, with your gun in hand — why, for God's sake, did you do nothing to save them?'

'You just keep out of my way, all of you.' O'Reilly thrust his hands into the pockets of his dirty, blood-stained coat, his whole, large frame shuddering suddenly in uncontrollable spasms. 'Go away — you slobbering leeches!' he yelled, and almost in relief his men retreated, gathering further away nearer the trees.

42

Silent, Joshua looked away. Esther grimly watched her Uncle Cady leaving them all, his face haggard and drawn, every fibre of his body shrieking with the shock of it, and rage. She knew he could have killed O'Reilly then, but instead he walked away.

A black mood had fallen over the camp. They all stood stricken, men, women and children, unable to move or to think properly. But there was the stirring of a deep unease, a fear within one and all. The realization was chilling that it was easy to lose a life out here in this uncharted, uninhabited wilderness. It was too easy to die.

The next day, having fixed up Cady's face, they reached Grahamstown which was little more than a collection of some thirty small cottages on a centre ridge, one or two merchant's stores, a few modest government buildings, a shabby inn and the barracks — the headquarters of the Eastern Cape garrison — strung along a few broad dusty streets, arterial wagon roads into the interior.

It was the only village in the settlement, just six years old and a straggling outpost merging with the wilderness. Grahamstown was a last oasis on the edge of untamed bush country inhabited by a mosaic of Xhosa tribes across the Fish River, the official border between the colony and Xhosaland.

It was a relief to dine with Captain Henry Somerset, the Governor's son, who was also the Deputy Landdrost at Grahamstown, and his young wife, Frances. The Somersets lived in an elegant house at the bottom of the High Street in the part of the village inhabited by the few officers stationed there. The meeting with them was an unexpected ray of light in an otherwise disillusioning journey, and it was with great reluctance that they were forced to take their leave.

For the next seven days they penetrated the loneliest part of the colony. Grey renoster bush grew thickly on the hills, tangled with thorny mimosa, aloes, proteas and thick blombos. The landscape was bathed in a strange light, in parts curiously bleak, while lambently romantic in others.

Dawn roused the camp on the eighth day in a clearing on the banks of the Blaaukranz River, only twelve miles from their destination. A cold gloom had fallen in the lonely silence of the rolling hills. Not another living soul was to be seen. The bushes, humming with cicadas, emphasized the silence. The eye could not penetrate more than twenty feet. Anything might lie in wait, still and murderous beyond the impenetrable curtain of vegetation.

The star-filled sky was already lightening above the eastern horizon as the sound of horses' hooves broke the still. At first there were only moving smudges among the trees, and then an occasional sparkle and flash from the midst of them. A jingle of harness sounded in the chilly air and a troop of quaggas trotted quickly away.

Faint, early mist lay in the valley wreathing the surface of the river and caught in the tangled branches of thorn trees. There was the remote bark of a baboon as a pack loped rapidly up one of the hillsides. A haze of smoke hung in the tops of the tall trees whiskered with creepers, and pungent scents of burning mimosa branches and savoury roast meat rose from the early campfires, the juices already hissing and spitting into the flames.

The small body of soldiers emerged in a swirling cloud of dust, looking unreal in the early morning haze. They rode cautiously now, searching the trail before them and feeling their way along it. They drew rein, the flash of muskets glinting through the leaves. It was a welcome stop in the wearisome, back-breaking task of aiding Captain Somerset in guiding the settlers to the precise location of their farms.

Captain Garnet Fitzwilliam dismounted and tied his light roan mare to a tree as Joshua and Cady went forward to meet him. He was a tall, lean officer, strikingly elegant, in the blue velvet cloak flaring back from his shoulders to expose the tight-fitting jacket in the finest scarlet broadcloth, its gold braid and buttons flashing as he walked towards the Irishmen.

The rising sun sent shafts of light through a cleft in the rocks and softly crept through the clearing. The twisted, ancient cords of lianas hung in heavy webs as they writhed upwards in an effort to reach the light above the trees. Garnet stopped in the pool of light filtering through the trees, his shako under his arm. Introductions completed, the men exchanged bows, and began to converse.

Esther watched him, standing back among the shadows, surprised to see such a fine officer in that remote place. She heard him say he and his men had come from a vantage point in Bathurst overlooking the entire settlement to conduct the Irish parties to their locations. He spoke in the well-modulated voice of the perfect English gentleman, with that faint arrogance and authority of his class and rank. There was a nonchalance about him that she liked immediately, a debonair poise bringing a touch of culture into that most primitive region.

Unnoticed, she drew nearer and studied him at closer range. His lean, aristocratic face with its aquiline nose was clean shaven, with the exception of neat, dark sideburns. His hair, smooth and very dark, almost black, curled elegantly around his neck.

She watched, with sudden growing pleasure. So, Laree had indeed been correct, one did not know what awaited one even here, in the darkness of Africa. Here, in this untamed wilderness was, to all appearances, the answer to her dreams — provided that he was not married, of course — a dashing gentleman with the air of distinction about him. Everything around her seemed, in that moment, to lose its terror and its bleakness, brightening with unexpected promise. But first she had to find out as much about him as she could, especially if he was eligible and not spoken for.

Emerging from the shadows, she went forward towards the men, tall and graceful with her long-legged stride. The plain black mourning dress moulded her fine limbs, flowing out above the black slippers in soft, yielding folds. The empire waist gathered beneath the rounded young breasts was caught with small dark ribbons emphasising her shape. And then she raised her dark blue eyes, indifferent to all, desirous only to make the acquaintance of the gentleman wearing the culture of England about him.

Garnet turned his head as she stood beside her father. He broke off, all the breath suddenly seeming to have left him, as she stood for a moment in silence, contemplating him. She had affected him, she knew that, and it was with difficulty that she turned her own eyes away, her cheeks stained a mild pink.

She was deliberately very casual, almost cool, as her father introduced them. She warmed as he took her hand and kissed it. Then he bowed, the essence of grace and charm. The cloak thrown back from one shoulder gave a glimpse of an exquisite gold epaulette on his scarlet tunic, and immaculate blue cuffs. She liked the way he wore his uniform and carried himself as though he expected a certain deference.

'I am charmed, Miss Dwyer, to make your acquaintance, and could I apologize for the remoteness of the wild parts in which you find yourself, I would, but only God and the House of Commons can do that — the one for creating it and the other for agreeing to send you to it.'

She inclined her head towards him, looking at him through her thickly-fringed eyelashes, her eyes filled with mysterious, shifting lights, trying to find irony in his words, but there was none.

'There is no need to even think of an apology,' she said, 'for what could be more entrancing than miles and miles of green, untouched jungle and hot, blue sky.'

She smiled, expecting him to smile back. But he did not. His eyes, watching her, were unblinking, intensely dark brown. For a long moment he simply looked at her, and she felt her own smile die beneath the unexpected sadness in his face. Then a slow curve lit up the tanned skin of his jawline and he said, 'I most certainly hope that this will be a land of opportunity for you, Miss Dwyer, and that, someday, there will be the chance for you to enjoy the interests and accomplishments of a civilized country.'

She felt a stab of triumph, feeling intuitively that he liked her, but there was still a certain distance, a reserve about him, a sadness she could not define. She gave him the prettiest of smiles, filled his half-promises, boldly determined to play all the coquettish tricks she knew to full effect.

'Your wife must be very worried about you out here for weeks on end taking us all to our farms. I would be for sure.' She spoke frankly, directly, with the honesty that had always characterized her, ignoring the wicked gleam lighting her Uncle Cady's knowing face. She would show her uncle one day, when she married such a fine, respectable gentleman like the Captain. She would have the last laugh and the last word, she would make quite sure of that.

She saw a muscle flex in Garnet's jaw. Then he smiled, his even teeth very white against the tan of his skin.

'There is no Mrs Fitzwilliam, I am still heart and fancy free, as the saying goes,' he said, his voice warmed by sudden amusement.

Her father coughed. 'It is time for you to leave us, my dear, the Captain has much to tell us before we depart, and time is marching on,' he said, holding his rising impatience well in check. Esther smiled, a trifle resentfully. Bobbing a small curtsey to her father and uncle, and bidding Garnet goodbye with a graceful lift of her shoulders, she walked easily away, vanishing into the trees.

There had been no clash of cymbals, no instant pounding in her head, just the strong feeling that this man interested her. She liked everything about him from the faint smell of tobacco and pomade to his cultured, soothing voice. He fitted into her ideas of a suitable husband. She did not know about love for it now seemed to her that she had never really fallen in love with anyone, not even Michael Angerstein, though at the time it had seemed to be the case. She was now not sure that love had much to do with a good marriage, suitability seemed more sensible. And Garnet had the power to rescue her from the repulsive desolation in which she found herself.

She felt sure that Mama would have approved of him. For was he not the kind of man for whom she had trained her three daughters? Poor Anna, now she would never have a chance to put those skills to use. It was up to Laree and herself, and the way things were going Laree would end up being plain Mrs Wilson.

Her thoughts filled with images of a life beside the man she had just met — for Esther, though she would hardly admit it, was as sentimental and romantic as her ancient Celtic race, and she had that added Dwyer determination to make her dreams come true.

The air, suddenly brilliant with light, shimmered as the sun topped the nearest peak. It glistened on the exotic orange and mauve strelitzias, resembling the plumage of some tropical bird, the thorny shrubs and the rocky inclines where succulents in multitudes burst forth in pinks, reds and yellows. It heightened the greens of the never-ending hills rolling away into the distance on all sides. Over the gorge an eagle hovered and stooped, a single flash in the bright autumn sunlight, then it was gone.

Esther turned as she heard Garnet's voice, carried clearly on the still air.

'As you are well aware, Mr Dwyer, your farm is located in the land adjacent to the Neutral Territory, the no-man's land between Xhosaland and the colony. There is nothing else between them and you but thirty miles of bush. It is imperative, gentlemen, that you be armed at all times, and that you teach every woman, every child among you, to shoot, and shoot well. I shall speak with Henry Somerset to arrange a contingent of Hottentot guards to assist guarding your property for the first month at least. They are very good.'

A coldness settled around Esther's heart. It was pressing on her, making it difficult to breathe. So, they were to live in the most dangerous part of the settlement, Samuel Pettigrew was right. They would be a living wall of defence between the colonists and the tribesmen.

She looked back at her father, and saw his suffering. Now they all believed Sam and the other Boers who had tried to convince them of this fact throughout the journey. She remembered how angry her father and uncle had been when they had found out the whereabouts of their location, declaring that the Acting Governor, Sir Rufane Donkin, would hear soon enough from them. It seemed too much to bear.

Then her face cleared, a new purpose filling her mind with the ease of youth. She was more determined than ever to find out all she could about Captain Fitzwilliam now that she knew he was unmarried, and somehow escape the terrifying future facing her.

The Irish parties stood about the wagons ready to depart on the final leg of their journey. They felt chilled and strangely vulnerable in the lonely valley of silent, watchful hills. Quietly at first, and then with more chatter, the parties began to move out.

Across the dusty trail the wagons crawled to follow the soldiers riding out ahead. The trail was treacherous, and pitted with grass-fringed rocks. Here and there the tracks made by Boer wagons led through the wall of trees, deep ruts gouging the earth until even they stopped altogether. The low, undulating aloe and euphorbia-clad hills, fold on fold, curved away on all sides.

A rider loomed up beside Esther as she clung to the driver's box of the leading wagon, sitting next to Gert Venter. It was Sam. Riding beside the wagon, he said, 'I bear a gift for you, Miss Dwyer, from the wild African bees.' He presented her with a large slab of wild honeycomb, dripping golden sweetness on a dark, shiny leaf.

He threw her a teasing grin, his black eyes twinkling. Then doffing his hat, he spurred his horse forward, dust clouds flying out behind him. Esther felt irritated — he was so unbearably confident of himself.

She turned to find Gert Venter silently watching her, his calm, genial eyes set in their webs of wrinkled skin. She shrugged elegant shoulders as his mouth creased into a big smile, displaying large strong teeth.

The slow canter of another horse caught her attention. It was

48

more satisfactory this time, being Captain Fitzwilliam. He stopped briefly, expressing his hope that the journey would not prove too uncomfortable for her, the ease of his smooth voice pleasant to her ears.

She looked at the honeycomb on its leaf on her lap. A small laugh escaped her lips as her eyes met his in unspoken question and answer in the warm sunshine.

'A gift from an acquaintance.' She grinned roguishly, testing him. 'A bit rough, but sweet-smelling enough.'

He raised a finely-drawn, dark eyebrow. 'I presume you mean the gift and not the acquaintance, Miss Dwyer. I recall something in the bible about Samson finding honey in the jaws of the dead lion.'

'Sweetness coming from out of the strong, or some such thing,' she said, the soft Irish in her voice becoming more pronounced. She wanted to keep him at her side, to forget the tedious boredom of the journey ahead, saying anything which needed a reply.

He nodded his head in a careless gesture. 'I prefer it the other way around — strength coming from the sweet — but that's just personal.' A faint smile flitted across his lips. 'Now if you'll excuse me, Miss Dwyer, I am duty bound to lead this party, not to join it. I hope to see you later on.'

She inclined her head, forcibly putting aside her disappointment. She met his eyes without flinching, wondering if he was testing her. He spurred his horse and the roan mare sprang strongly forward, Garnet's blue cloak swirling.

The sky to the west was suddenly and fiercely afire as they reached the end of their journey the following day in the richly timbered, hilly country of the Coombs Valley.

The hillside around the spur, clothed with ancient cycads, renoster bush and aloes, fell away into a long, fairly shallow valley. It was studded with trees and curved away to the east. Hugging the far side, along the foothills, they could see the Kap River, a tributary of the Great Fish. Their eyes followed it until it disappeared into a narrow defile, hidden by overhanging willows festooned with the nests of weaver birds.

Meneer Venter indicated the location with an outflung hand, and climbed down heavily from the wagon. A savage and chilling silence lay all about them, lying heavy on the undulating surfaces stretching away on all sides but one, to the foot of the blue-green sea of hills. They could hardly believe that this spot was to be their home.

From their high vantage point they could see the tips of the great range of Amatole Mountains, marching across the Fish River Valley in the far distance.

There seemed a vague hostility about the hills which had crept nearer at sunset. Garnet trotted down the Xhosa trail and stopped suddenly. High above Cape vultures, brown and stark in the sky, circled and cried out, somewhere in the bush was a dead or dying carcass of a wild beast. The high shrieks of the Hadeda birds shrilled across the land, as they lifted into the air from their nests on the banks of the river.

A herd of buck ate quietly under the trees, and beside them, a party of graceful, long-legged cranes. The realization was horrifying once more — it was all too easy to die out here.

In the distance, the winding hills leading into the Neutral Territory glowed blood-red in the gathering sunset. There was a bustle of activity from the party members, and the nineteenth century took over from the timelessness of Africa's ancient past.

Garnet turned back and looked at Esther still sitting like a stone on the wagon seat, her skin taking on rosy shadows from the glowing sun.

The rest of the party gathered noisily before the wagons. Then they fell quiet, standing with eyes fixed on the dense, silent wastes rising around them. Esther stared for some moments at the valley below, her body trembling. This was to be her new home, this ghastly, desolate, wild place. Her worst nightmare had come true. She was to be buried alive in this terrible backwoods, far away from all known civilization.

She tried to block this terrible thought from her mind and made a movement to step down from the seat. Garnet was there, dismounting at once, and offering her a firm encouraging hand.

'There is little I can say to ease the shock,' he said quietly. 'There is no way of seeing into the minds of the Powers-that-be who have placed you here, my dear. But I can promise you we will get your family strong protection as soon as possible.'

Even Garnet's presence, the pressure of his hand on hers, could not take away the dreadful nightmare of the place or her anger against Sir Rufane Donkin expecting them to live out there. She stopped and stood still, noticing again the sadness about his face, speculation deep in his dark eyes. She knew he was wondering, like all the others, if they could survive here.

She lifted her face, her eyes meeting his for a second. Her face looked suddenly drawn, a mask of apprehension settling on her lively, vivid features. She opened her mouth to speak, but no sound came. She smoothed the folds of her pelisse, drawing it more tightly about her as if for some meagre comfort. I am going to die out here, she thought in total despair, I'm going to wither and die, and never shall I have lived.

Garnet bowed stiffly and walked away. She wanted to run after him, keep him with her, but decorum forbade it. She watched him stand alone, apart from the rest, and remove his shako. He placed it under one arm as he ran his fingers through his smooth, dark hair. Patting his pockets he looked about him. Thinking himself unobserved, he pulled out a small, exquisitely-carved cigar-box containing his favourite brand of cigarillos imported from Virginia. Snapping the box shut, he tapped the end of one against it. Then he slowly placed it in his mouth, lighting it from a tinderbox.

Esther saw him interrupted by her father and one of the redcoats. He crushed the cigarillo beneath his heel and turned away, disappearing with them out of sight. She shivered. The stillness of the rugged, uncultivated land was all about her. She seemed to be on an island in a wild, tangled, green sea rising towards the rolling hills like wave upon wave. The bloody glory of the African sunset splashed the patches of poor, yellowish-grey earth gouged between the old, gnarled trees covered with snarls of liana ropes. The evening was suddenly so still and quiet she could hear the insects in the grass. The sharp sound of a twig snapping electrified the air.

Everyone was moving away towards the wagons once more. There was nothing unusual about the scene but her heart began to beat fast. The silence about her became frightening in those short, intense moments. She sensed some ancient primeval presence all around her, her mind conjuring up all the stories she had ever heard about the place and the tribesmen since she arrived.

She turned her head towards the dense bushes and trees, her eyes fastening on the deep green drifts of dusty leaves. It seemed to her then that because of her fears, every leaf, every dark space between the foliage had eyes, watching and waiting, alien eyes in the depths of the palisade of undergrowth. Her heart thundering, she glanced apprehensively about, but nothing moved. She was overpowered then by a nameless and terrible fear. She felt vulnerable because she felt so helpless. It was as if the ancient forces of Africa were gathering against her — against them all.

Oh, come on Esther, she told herself, you are not one of those simple-minded superstitious countryfolk who sees things in every shadow — full of gremlins and leprechauns and such. Your mind is playing tricks on you, so full it is of the wild stories you have heard. This is a land like any other. But the feeling of uneasiness grew. This land was like no other she had ever known, and never would it be.

Suddenly, she thought of her mother's sweet, comforting face. Her eyes filled with tears. We are alone out here, my darling Mama, and there is no one to help us. There is no one who really cares if we live or die.

The sun slid down through the western clouds, changing the hills from red-gold to grey with southern rapidity, and she saw only the menace, the veiled hostility of it.

CHAPTER
Five

Winter had come with a vengeance, full of cold rains and high winds, leaking tents and soggy living conditions. The girls' tent was blown over and they were forced to move into a make-shift hut, clad in flannel petticoats, pantalettes borrowed impudently from their menfolk, stuff dresses and pelisses or redingotes.

As Joshua could not make progress with the authorities on the matter of having his party moved nearer to Grahamstown, he was forced to start a temporary dwelling for his family. A place was selected, set far back from the river for protection. It faced a field of wheat and Indian corn, the ground now broken and cleared with a simple homemade plough, the seeds planted.

The settlers were forbidden to own cattle because of their proximity to the border and the cattle-hungry Xhosas, so they were encouraged to cultivate crops in the poor, sour soil on a hundred acres of land, which by South African standards was far too small. Another discouraging factor was that, unlike the Boers, they were not allowed to have servants, so they were forced to do all the work themselves. The indentured men, heartily sick of leaking tents, built booths from leafy branches and each day set off into the hills to range the wooded kloofs for door posts and rafters for the new cottages.

The women and girls were given the unenviable task of cutting wattles and collecting six-foot-long reeds from the river for the walls and thatching for the roof. Backs ached continually, and much to the growing disgust of the Dwyer girls, their once fine, soft white hands became progressively rough, sore and calloused.

The air rang with activity and the cottage grew, made from mortar of the well-watered earth, layer upon layer, drying rapidly in the days when there was strong sun and wind. Soon it resembled a simple wooden cabin, plastered with clay. The front door consisted of packing-cases hung in two halves, and a bolt of Irish cotton was stretched over the glassless windows for curtains.

The cottage contained only three rooms: two bedrooms and a very large kitchen that soon became the nerve-centre of the family and the men who shared the evening meal with them every day. On the one side of the cottage, adjoining it, stood the long, narrow wattle building housing the men and the few families among them.

As they had not brought much household furniture, everyone had to make their own beds, tables, stools and cupboards for immediate use. The barks of several watchdogs were now heard in the clearing and the lower field was populated with a small collection of peaceful draught oxen, broadtailed sheep providing five pounds of fat in each tail for soap, candles and cooking fat, and some horses brought back from Bathurst. And being Irish, some goats were always kept with the horses for good luck.

The winter sun glittered on the crude stone-coloured cottage with its strong, simple lines standing out in contrast to the surrounding greens and the puffed, scarlet tubes of feathery ericas. The cultivated fields ran away before it, glistening with the recent rains.

It was called Dwyers' Cross, symbolic of the suffering and anguish they were enduring, trying to make a home out of the harsh wilderness about them. It also came to be associated with the loss of Emma and her two children, Anna and Lewis, on board the *Poseidon.*

Now ready, it waited through the remaining winter weeks for the coming of the new southern spring. The wheat and Indian corn began to grow in the warm womb of the earth with the promise of a rich harvest. The rain continued, fine as mist, wrapping about the homestead like a damp, clinging, vaporous curtain.

In those waiting weeks, Joshua campaigned hard with the authorities for the removal of his party to a more suitable place nearer to Grahamstown. Donkin was sympathetic, but hard pressed to fulfil his request, and those of many others. In the end, after weeks of delay, Joshua and Cady decided that as they and their men had put so much hard work into the Coombs Valley, they would remain there and make it into a permanent home. From then on the determination grew that it was their land, and no one, black or white, would ever take it from them.

There was the unmistakable smell of spring in the air. A deep cobalt-blue sky smiled over the green crests of the hills, golden sunlight pouring down the slopes, flooding the valley with light. It was early September and the uncultivated parts of the fields were strewn with a carpet of tiny, white flowers. Succulents glowed over the jagged rock faces, blazing bronze and scarlets, contrasting with the gentle whites and pinks and the vibrant tomato-red climbing aloes aflame over the banks of the river. Tiny, brown sugar birds fluttered like insects in and out of the blossoms, and insistent bright-green grasshoppers chirred in the long grass. High overhead, a kite hawked for fledglings, while a brilliant Paradise flycatcher perched in a milkwood tree, its small nest wedged in the fork of a branch.

There was an emptiness inside Esther. She flung herself into the kitchen with suppressed rage, banging the pots on to the rough yellowwood table and reaching for a pitcher of water from the dresser. Tipping some of it into the bowl of flour before her, she pummelled it with furious energy, her arms covered with dough up to her elbows.

She threw a vicious glance at the heavy sack of flour, newly brought from Bathurst, propped up against the wall, and cursed its existence. Fiercely she tipped the soft dough on to the table, scrubbed clean with woodash, and reached for the heavy wooden rolling-pin. She held it in her hand, testing it like a weapon, then rolled it defiantly over the ever-growing sheet of pale cream-coloured dough.

Her face tightened angrily as she looked down at her hands with their broken nails and grained skin that had once been her pride and joy. Since coming to this dreadful place all she did was to cook enormous meals, sew rough garments, clean and clean until she could scream, and have shooting lessons every day with her Uncle Cady. She could think of a hundred more interesting things she could do given the chance, and the beautiful clothes she could make, given the cloth.

In an agony of mounting frustration she thought of all the years tutored by her mother in the upbringing of a genteel lady, for the purpose of marriage to some gentleman of means and breeding. She had been taught how to supervise a large household, to play hostess and entertain well-connected and interesting guests. All that now seemed like some hopeless dream as day after day she plodded on like some rough farm-girl with no hopes higher in her life than to become an efficient and practical farmer's wife.

55

There would be no balls, no soirées, no fine house with servants, no gorgeous gowns. The only charming, eligible gentleman she had met was Captain Garnet Fitzwilliam, but she had not seen him for weeks. He had sent a fine horse as a gift to her father and there was word that he was still arranging a Hottentot guard for the farm.

She had heard along the colonial grapevine that he was the second of three sons of one of the oldest and wealthiest families in England. Even though his father was only a baronet, it was rumoured that they had so much wealth and influence that they had friendships with the Prince Regent, Prince Prinny himself. Garnet was thirty years old and single with no sign of a betrothal in sight. She knew also that all the snobbish settler elite had set their caps at him for their daughters, that every mother in that circle was determined to pursue him as a golden prize in the matrimonial stakes.

Esther despaired. She had no mother to compete with those over-eager, unscrupulous matrons. Her father was so busy fighting the cause of the settlers with Donkin and trying to overcome his own awesome problems that he gave no thought to her plight. She would have to do it all herself without the most enviable and necessary asset of a dowry. But now, Garnet would not even look at her showing all the signs of hard work. It was all so dreadfully unfair.

The morning filled with the sound of hoarse, male voices, and now and then, rough laughter. There was the faint shriek of some bird in the trees and the gentle cooing of turtle doves. Joshua had departed to Grahamstown on urgent business matters and Cady was in charge. Samuel Pettigrew had returned to help them and had stayed ever since. He was now regaling the men outside with amusing stories about bush life.

A light trail of flour trickled from a burst seam in the canvas flour-bag near the door and a small fieldmouse scampered away from it and into the dark recesses of a corner while a harmless, brown house-snake slithered through the rafters in the roof. Esther's eyes followed it without feeling, for she was too upset about her own affairs to bother any longer about the creatures inhabiting the cottage with her.

She was possessed of such exuberant health, such unflagging energy, and was so full of life that the thought of spending the rest of her days holed up here, wasting her youth, caused a sudden stream of unfamiliar and endless tears. She brushed them away as the sound of a horse's hooves thudded on the turf outside. A rider came round the

56

curve towards the kitchen at a brisk canter and drew rein hard outside. He dismounted and stalked up, punching viciously at the door.

Hastily drying her eyes, Esther reached for the woollen shawl she kept hung behind the door. Flinging the latter open, she stood facing Septimus O'Reilly. She still loathed him, and he had done nothing to change her opinion of him. He had never been a kind man, and she had heard from the men who had run away from his farm recently to live at Dwyer's Cross — men like James Coffee and Murtagh Dougherty from Baltinglas — that he was still bad-tempered and difficult, with the same foul mouth and quick fists. During the past months on the frontier, he and the Dwyer brothers had never come to any understanding; he preferred to view them as rivals, and the feud between them grew with every passing day. He was a cold and dangerous man who would never give an inch.

His slate-coloured eyes sharpened in a hard, malignant stare as he faced Esther and now Laree, who had been weeding the vegetable garden.

'Where is that father of yours, wench?' he snarled at Esther, his Wicklow brogue stronger than usual.

Esther loosened the shawl she had thrown over her shoulders and tucked it into the belt of her full, white pinafore. She tossed her head, the auburn curls spilling from under the frilled housecap. 'And what can you be wanting with him Mr O'Reilly?' she asked in a tart, accusing voice before she could stop herself. Her dark blue eyes snapped with unfriendly fire.

'Esther, do be careful!' Laree warned, looking at her from a suddenly pale, drawn face.

Esther ignored her, and continued, stiff-lipped. 'For your information, my father is not here.'

'No matter. I will see Mr O'Reilly.' Cudy's soft, musical voice sang out from around the corner of the cottage. He stepped forward in a frockcoat of black cloth buttoned almost up to the chin, his breeches and much-worn Hessian boots laden with dust. A neckcloth of white silk with many folds spilled from the top of his coat.

O'Reilly's eyes narrowed dangerously. His savage vulture-like face with its hook-nose suffused with instant animosity. 'You have stolen six of my best men, Dwyer, I have come to take them back to my farm, or Captain Somerset will hear about it.' He stood taller than

Cady, but carried more weight, and this time he was cold sober.

'Those men have come of their own free will, O'Reilly, because of your ill-treatment of them. They claim that you have not paid them since they arrived on African soil and you have put them on half rations. And you continue to flog them and force them to build you a mansion without enough food and no money.' Cady's hazel eyes gleamed sardonically. 'The sooner we settle this matter before the court and Captain Somerset, the better for us all.'

O'Reilly spat derisively on the ground, his hard unblinking eyes fixed on Cady. 'I am going to teach you a lesson you will never forget, Dwyer — knocking me down on board ship, goading me and blaming me for Flanagan's death and now sneaking away my best men!' He flung up his fists.

Laree screamed, backing away with Esther through the doorway. Cady slapped his thigh, his powerful fists itching and bunching at his sides. 'It will be a cold day in hell before you defeat me, O'Reilly! And if this is the way you want it, I'll be only too pleased to oblige.' He lowered his body and prepared to lunge, pulling the neckcloth from his neck and flinging it aside, then taking off his coat and waistcoat.

A small crowd began to gather about them. O'Reilly spat on his hands and rubbed them before he drew them up, his whole stance and expression rigid with hostility.

'This time, Dwyer, you have taken on too much, and I'm stone-cold sober.' The two men watched each other, bristling and tight-muscled.

There was a shriek from one of the women as he lunged at Cady with his arm raised. Cady saw it coming, for he jerked his head back and the arm cracked his shoulder. Pain creased across his face and he fell against the wall behind him.

Esther's hand flew to her face as Cady pulled himself up, breathing hard, and the two men grappled, reeling against the wall. Hypnotized, as if caught in a terrible dream, she called to them but they did not hear. They were fighting to kill, and there was nothing she could do to stop it. She had never seen her uncle in such a raging mood before.

O'Reilly grasped the collar of Cady's shirt and again they stumbled back against the wall. The men broke apart and silver flashed in the short space between them.

'Holy Mother! That devil has a knife! E's going to kill Mr Cady, 'e is!' one of the women cried, and Esther lifted terrified hands to cover her face.

Her heart hammered in her chest. This could not be happening. She could hardly bear to look as her uncle sank to his knees. The knife thrown by O'Reilly grazed his shoulder and fell to the ground some feet away. The thought struck her with full force that her uncle was about to be murdered and she ran from the doorway, out of Laree's resisting arms and towards the men.

She heard her sister sobbing, and the loud cries of encouragement for her uncle from the crowd. O'Reilly looked about him savagely, from face to face, and saw that they were all glittering with hatred for him, like vultures waiting for his demise.

Esther stopped as she saw Cady stagger to his feet, catching O'Reilly's ankle and pulling him flat. Again, Cady lunged, throwing his body forward, as O'Reilly crawled in the direction of the knife.

He hit O'Reilly so hard, with the full force of his body behind his fist, that the man cried out in pain and stumbled back, clutching his face, the pistol he had taken from his coat falling to the ground. There was a loud gasp from the onlookers as his shoulders sagged. Blood poured through his cupped hands and spattered in red streams down his pale, lined shirt and mustard coat.

Cady pulled himself shakily to his feet. There was blood on his face and his shirt was torn. 'Get up, you miserable wretch!' he ordered, standing over O'Reilly, breathing heavily. 'That will teach you to come over to Dwyers' Cross causing trouble. You will rot in hell before I'm through with you and your underhand mean tricks. All prepared with a knife and a pistol, were you — well, now you'll learn just what I am made of!' He leant forward and pulled O'Reilly up.

'No more, Uncle Cady, please!' Esther cried. 'There's been enough harm done already.' Without thinking twice, she flew towards the pistol on the ground and picked it up before O'Reilly saw it.

'You will pay for this, Dwyer!' O'Reilly screamed through broken lips, hitting out at Cady. But Cady had sidestepped and the punch hit the air.

Amidst the rousing, frenzied cheers of the men Cady struck out with his fist again. It took O'Reilly on the cheek, then he slammed him against the wall of the cottage and scooped up the knife that had fallen half-buried in the earth. He held it against O'Reilly's throat.

'Enough, Uncle Cady! Enough — you'll get yourself in prison for this!' Esther shrieked, running blindly forward, careless of her own safety. Her face was drained of all colour. She saw a blur of faces, then her gaze fixed, and she saw shapes — a small party of horsemen coming up the rise — redcoats!

She stared, round-eyed. They were coming closer, the jingling of harness becoming insistent and clear as the crowd quietened. The air was hazed with dust as she stood there, numb and immobile, the pistol still in her hands. Suddenly she came alive.

She turned towards her uncle still holding the knife menacingly to O'Reilly's throat. 'Uncle Cady — there's a party of redcoats coming this way — they're almost upon us — please take that knife away and let Mr O'Reilly go!'

'You stay out of this, Esther Mary!' Cady hissed, his face seething with such loathing for O'Reilly that she hardly recognized him. 'This is a matter between him and me.' Esther whirled around at the sound of horses' hooves. The small body of soldiers rode swiftly towards them, the light of the sun gleaming on muskets and swords. Then without warning, a husky voice with a rounded, Sussex burr and a ring of authority, called out: 'What in devil's name goes on here?'

The tall, well-built figure of a tanned sergeant in his late twenties, rode up to them, followed by nine or ten armed Hottentot guardsmen.

Cady looked up, never leaving his hold of O'Reilly. A look of unusual defeat settled on his face. He waited as a hush fell on the spectators, their faces becoming wary and guarded.

Esther watched the guards dismount, the blue cloak of the sergeant flaring from his broad shoulders. The glint of muskets soon flecked the crowd as the soldiers strode towards them.

The crowd melted a pathway before the sergeant as he marched through them, spurs clinking at his heels. From her place in his path, Esther had a clear, uninterrupted view of him. His face under the black leather shako, its red plume fluttering, was not handsome, but strong, striking, disciplined and exceptionally attractive: the expression cool. The tight-fitting, scarlet jacket was now exposed, its cross-belt a white strip across the sergeant's powerful chest. The long, tapering, dusty-white trousers he wore seemed to emphasize the muscular length of his legs. She hardly noticed anyone else, her attention was entirely focused on him.

As her thoughts raced, he looked at her and the pistol in her hands. In that moment she noticed the startling, intense blue of his eyes, and again she thought how extraordinarily attractive he was. Her heart seemed suddenly to leap into her throat in a ridiculous, choking way and she chided herself for being so foolish. He was, after all, a stranger to her, and a non-commissioned officer from the rank and file, a common soldier far beneath her own social level.

He bowed. 'Sergeant Buckmaster Jones at your service, Miss. I've brought the armed guard for Mr Joshua Dwyer as requested by Captain Fitzwilliam.' He straightened to his full height. She knew instinctively that he was just as aware of her as she was of him, and she bent her head so that he should not see her confusion.

'Kindly explain what has been going on here, Miss — it looked like a minor riot to me. And why is it that you should be holding a pistol in such a way as it could do much harm?'

She lifted her eyes. He was studying her closely and she was aware of the tension and nervousness in herself. Her heart thudded and she was afraid he would hear.

'I am Esther Dwyer, daughter of Mr Joshua Dwyer. That is my Uncle Cady over there with the knife — he — he was fighting with Mr Septimus O'Reilly who came to this farm to cause trouble, as he has done for all the time we've known him! My uncle has had enough of him, and so have we all,' she burst out, for it was suddenly important that this man understand the truth. 'O'Reilly's men left him because of his ill-treatment and he came to take them back. They do not want to go.'

'And the pistol, Miss Dwyer?' He indicated the gun in her hands. 'I suppose that was part of the — remedy against this Mr O'Reilly?' He removed his shako, his curly brown hair springing thickly, vibrantly, from his head, and curling about his tanned neck.

The amazing eyes still focused on her as he waited for an answer. She drew a deep breath. 'It fell to the ground during the fight — it belonged to Mr O'Reilly. He was going to kill my uncle. I picked it up before Mr O'Reilly could get it again.'

'And were you going to use it to help your uncle?'

She lifted her chin as her eyes caught his flickering appreciatively over her from the large white collar of her dress to the black slippers peeping from the hem of her skirts.

'No, I was not, Sergeant Jones! I was taking it out of harm's way.' There was a deep blush on her cheekbones, as much to her gathering annoyance she found herself actually enjoying his calm, unhurried appraisal of her.

'Harm being Mr O'Reilly, I take it?' His gaze returned to her face. He gave her a long slow look, a twist of humour around his beautifully moulded lips. The smile building about his mouth creased the clear hardness of his jaw and made him appear in that moment as the most handsome man in the world.

Then, suddenly, his direct, masculine assurance disconcerted her. She was vividly conscious of his proximity to her. She felt the mad, unfamiliar rush of blood singing through her veins which she had never experienced before, not even with Michael Angerstein, back in Ireland.

Instantly she felt resentful towards him. He had made too much of an impact on her, and she was afraid that if he looked at her much longer he would read her thoughts with those brilliant eyes of his.

He replaced his shako and moved away, striding past her towards her uncle and O'Reilly. Those around him looked oddly dowdy in comparison. She saw her uncle hand him the knife, resignation in his eyes.

'You, sir, and Mr O'Reilly, will have to return to Grahamstown with me.' Sergeant Jones' voice was firm. 'Attempted murder is a criminal offence even in these backwaters.'

'You'll pay dearly for this, Dwyer!' O'Reilly bellowed, choking with rage. 'That is the one thing you can be sure of.'

Cady turned, his voice like steel. 'If I was you, O'Reilly, I'd be content to get on with breathing for now, and save that hot air for the judge. You'll need it.' He put the waistcoat and coat on again over his torn and blood-stained shirt, stuffing the neckcloth into a pocket.

O'Reilly was so angry that for some moments he was speechless. 'We leave without delay, gentlemen,' Buck Jones said, his tone carrying more hidden steel than a rapier. 'Collect sufficient for your needs, your horses and come with me.' He turned to Cady. 'You party will be safe here, sir, under the guards I have brought, while you are away.'

Cady acknowledged the delivery of the guards, whereupon Buck Jones chose the oldest and shrewdest of the men as sergeant to be responsible for their good conduct.

He turned away, his gaze again falling on Esther still standing in the same spot. His eyes narrowed, half-shaded by his lids as he coolly stared at her.

She was immediately furious with him. The glow in her face now faded. She straightened her back, her chin moving slightly upwards in an effort to break the spell he wove about her with his eyes.

He threw her a salute, bowing ever so slightly, then he was gone, striding rapidly to his horse. Dazed, Esther walked back towards the cottage to help Laree fill her uncle's saddle-bags.

She had not taken more than a few steps when she heard a cry from John Tobias, one of the young men standing at the edge of the disappearing crowd.

'Sweet mercy!' he cried. 'There's a huge snake on my greatcoat under the trees!'

Esther turned back. Then she froze with shock and revulsion. An enormous puff-adder rested on his greatcoat where he had left it earlier, folded beneath a large acacia tree. He had stooped to pick it up, his right arm still outstretched.

She watched in horror as he recoiled. The thick body of the snake with its distinctive black and yellow markings lay across the front of the coat where it had gone for warmth. The squat head with its malicious eyes fixed its enraged stare on the figure above it as it advanced slowly and puffed itself aggressively.

In Esther there was room for nothing now except crippling fear. Her blood pounded, her face growing hot and all she could do was to stare, transfixed with dread. A scream arose from her throat, and died as the snake, irritated in being disturbed, began to hiss and inflate its terrible jaws. All the while its malignant eyes gleamed.

For once Esther's courage and decisiveness left her, her eyes frozen on the swaying form.

'Don't move, lad, keep perfectly still.' It was Sergeant Buck Jones somewhere behind John. 'And don't you move either, Miss Dwyer, you may startle the snake.'

Esther remained motionless. She had forgotten him in her fright. Out of the corner of her eye she saw the tall redcoat's powerful frame work its way to John, feeling for his sword with one hand, the sharp blade ready to bite. Everyone had backed away in fright, except Sam, who crept up behind the Sergeant, to back him up if necessary.

Buck Jones continued to speak softly while moving closer all the time. 'Puff-adders won't move out of your way like most other snakes, lad, but will lunge forward suddenly to strike.'

John involuntarily moved his raised right arm to his side and in that instant the snake struck. He cried out sharply in pain. Buck leapt then and quick as a flash, seized the snake by its tail. He pulled it with a sudden, dreadful jerk and threw it violently some paces away. Esther saw him clearly now; his head was bare, his sword raised.

He struck down hard, where the body and the head joined, severing the great reptile behind the skull. It convulsively reared into the air with one last, mighty heave, and then fell.

Buck stepped away as the group of chattering Hottentot guards ran up and grabbed hold of the severed snake's head. They carried it off to bury it in their belief that anyone treading accidentally on the head could injure himself from the fangs which they believed remained venomous for months afterwards.

John cried out again from the fierce pain of the bite. Sheathing his sword and whipping out a penknife from a pocket, Buck turned to John. He took the young man's arm and cut away the sleeve. A small crowd gathered in horrified silence. It was deathly quiet as Buck scarified the livid, violently inflamed wound and allowed it to bleed freely.

'Hold still now, lad, and clench your teeth,' he ordered as John, sitting before him, willed the pain to go away. Buck leaned forward and bent his head, sucking out the venom until his jaw muscles ached. He spat out the venom, and still holding his arm, lifted his head as Sam hurried up and knelt beside him with a bottle and a bowl.

'Here, Sergeant Jones, I've brought you as much brandy and milk as I could scrounge.'

Buck nodded and poured great quantities of the brandy over the wound, as Sam wadded up a brandy-soaked bandage from the torn sleeve. It was patted onto the dreadful gash, which was losing some of its livid hue, as Sam ordered John to drink as much of the sweetened milk as he could manage.

Buck rose from his knees and looked down at John. Sam stood beside him in his goatskin trousers, his broad-rimmed hat pulled far back on his head, his pipe stuck, as always, in its brim.

'The best remedy for snake-bite, as far as I know, is the one that the Hottentots use,' he said conversationally to Buck whom he seemed to know fairly well. 'They take a live fowl, cut open the fleshy part of the breast and press it on the open wound. The venom is then drawn out. If it's deadly, the fowl dies from the poison drawn into its own body. A good remedy to remember, John Tobias, in this harsh and merciless land.'

An excited babbling broke out from the crowd, and suddenly Esther found it all too much. She swayed back, faintness sweeping over her, her stays feeling far too tight and constricting. Her ears began to ring alarmingly. Putting her hands out she tried desperately not to fall. All around her figures seemed to be moving and heaving. The air crackled with humming and hoarse shouts, and she felt ice-cold.

Vaguely she was aware of the seething mass of humanity after the shock of the fight, and then the snake, but only the tall redcoat coming towards her was real. The only flash of brightness recognizable to her was his scarlet jacket, exposed as his bright blue cloak fell back, caught at the shoulder with its black, leather strap. He put out his hand, as she fell, unable to save herself.

He went down on one knee and raised her face, lifting her in his arms. She leaned against him in a dizzy, helpless silence, feeling the warmth of his touch, the muscular chest beneath the red jacket as he balanced her against him.

Even in her dazed state she was shaken to the core by the bewildering sensations racing through her body. She tried to turn her head away but his extraordinary eyes drew her back. She choked back a sudden, hysterical laugh, her teeth suddenly chattering from shock.

A shadow fell across them. Looking up she saw Laree's pale, tense face. She was bending over her, a bottle of sal volatile in her hands. Then Buck Jones released her as Laree helped to raise her to her feet.

Esther looked away. Her hands were trembling and she found herself wildly hoping he would not notice. She started to move away unsteadily. His figure became a shadow, surrounded by a kaleidoscope of other shadows, indistinct, gone.

She put a hand to her head, feeling strangely lightheaded. Leaning heavily against Laree, she suddenly needed her support very much. She had never met anyone quite like Sergeant Buckmaster Jones. She felt naked, sick and weary, conscious of nothing except the lingering riot in her own body and mind. She tried to think of

Garnet Fitzwilliam, and finally succeeded with a sense of wild and sweet relief.

Garnet was right for her. He was a gentleman from the right background with the wealth, the connections, everything.

CHAPTER
Six

The case of Cady Dwyer and Septimus O'Reilly took several days and drew the attention of the entire settlement. It was the first case of its kind to stir up so much interest and sides were taken as speculation grew about its outcome.

Cady gave a spirited defence of his action, aided by strong evidence presented by Joshua and O'Reilly's men who went to great lengths to describe the constant brawls, the half rations and the fact that no wages had been paid since their arrival in the Cape. The men had built him an impressive farmhouse where he could live in style, but had received nothing for it.

Joshua's evidence in particular was articulate, well-informed and eloquent. It finally demolished the case led by O'Reilly with facts and figures and impressive details, even down to the falsification O'Reilly had made on the records of those in his party. At the end of the proceedings, Captain Henry Somerset summed up strongly in favour of Cady, on the grounds that, under direct provocation, his action had been understandable, if not justifiable.

The two *heemraden*, the assessors, agreed to the verdict and Somerset, having the final say, ordered O'Reilly to pay all the wages owing his men, backdated to the time of arrival on his farm, under the penalty of a fifty-pounds fine. The men had to return to work for him, still being under contract.

O'Reilly thundered at the injustice of the verdict and returned to his farm accompanied by the reluctant and resentful men. It all caused a fine uproar in the gossip-hungry, isolated frontier districts. Not long afterwards he left the settlement for Cape Town and returned to Ireland, much to the relief of everyone. Several of his best men joined Dwyers' Cross and became staunch supporters of the

Dwyer brothers throughout the troubled period that lay ahead.

Joshua and Cady, with Sam, Michael Byrne, James Coffee and Murtagh Dougherty, worked together to form the men into a cohesive group to forge out of the wilderness a habitable, productive environment. Soon there were horses, cows, poultry, pigs and draughts animals in the wattle enclosures surrounded by grey renoster bush. Beyond the developing orchard, which was fast becoming Joshua's pride, the gentle, rippling wheat and the green, feathery tufts of Indian corn stretched across the fields, reaching out towards the hills.

As spring enveloped the land, the weaver birds made their nests in the branches of the trees at the water's edge. Stretching back from the homestead, there rose the smoke from the new men's huts. Summer came with long days of dappled sunlight on the veld and in the woods, lying along the hills and in the kloofs.

The fields of ripening grain spread lushly out before the homestead, the air filled with the wild sweetness of summer blooms. On the wooded hills above the river, evergreen succulents lay glistening and fat. A battle began against the armies of caterpillars, lice, grubs and other pests enticed by the lushness of the season, as they attacked the wheat, corn and vegetables.

One early morning in mid November, the day promising to be warm, Esther filled a pitcher of foaming goat's milk in the kitchen, for breakfast. She looked up sharply as her father galloped towards the cottage and drew rein angrily. She was alarmed as he dismounted in haste, tethering his horse to the hitching-post across the yard. He strode inside, his boots caked with red dust that fell in clouds on to the floor. 'Where is your uncle and Pettigrew?' he demanded, taking a step forward, his dark frockcoat tails flapping against his leather breeches.

'Why, whatever is the matter, Papa?' Esther looked at him, noting the burning fire in his grey-green eyes, his fierce face, with its stern, grey eyebrows, drawn with bitterness. The stubborn line of his wide, thin lips, was tight, angry, the jutting chin taut.

'There's goddamned mildew on the wheat,' he thundered, blocking out the light spilling through the doorway. 'The whole field is covered with the muck — not one plant has escaped.'

Esther's face stiffened with mounting consternation. The wheat was their biggest source of livelihood. Everything depended on it.

The government rations were to stop after the wheat harvest.

She followed him out of the door. 'Surely there is some hope, Papa? There must be some plants that have escaped the worst of the blight.'

'Child, we are ruined. Come,' he said abruptly, 'I need to talk with your uncle and Samuel — they must be at the sheepfold.'

She followed his tall, erect figure rapidly eating up the distance towards the enclosure, hoping that it was all some huge mistake, but knowing in the ruthlessness of her natural honesty, that it could not be so.

They stood before the kraal, encircled by its fence of renoster bush. Sam was erecting a double barricade around the poultry pens after a large, spotted genet had stolen two chickens in the night. Joshua's expression was stony as he watched Cady tense himself, circling a single-barrelled, smooth-bore flintlock, with his initials engraved on its silver plate above the pistol grip. Following a bustard, big as a turkey, on the edge of a covey in heavy flight above his head, he bent swiftly taking aim, the shot humming through the air. It took the bird with a fierce blow, while the others screeched overhead in alarm and made off in clumsy haste. Lowering the flintlock, he smiled until he saw Joshua's face. He put away the gun and came forward.

'And what may be the trouble, Joshua? I can see it sticking out a mile on your face this beautiful morning,' he asked, wiping his brow with a handkerchief.

'The whole wheat crop is ruined, Cady — riddled with some mildew, my boots are full of it.'

Cady smote his fists together with a resounding smack. 'You cannot be serious, that is our livelihood.'

Joshua regarded him with steel eyes. 'You can believe it, Cady, it is true, every word. Our entire wheat crop is ruined before its first harvest, and our hopes with it. Samuel, I want you to examine the plants and tell me what it is.' His eyes took on a sudden harsh gleam. 'We have nothing left except the Indian corn and the vegetables left by the pests.'

Sam's black eyes clouded. 'There is no need for me to examine them, sir, I can see by the dust on your boots. Your plants have been attacked by rust. That dust on your boots kills the plant by attacking the stalk, spreading like wildfire until the whole plant is infected.

69

There's nothing anyone can do once it has started. It's rather like an incurable disease.'

A protest had risen to Esther's lips but she knew from the look on Sam's face that all he said was true. There was no way out of this ugly dream. Their livelihood had been vanishing before their eyes, all the while they had looked at it, watched it, dreamt about it, unsuspected until it was too late. The tops of the plants looked so healthy still, waving in the breeze like a rich green sea.

She turned, feeling the acrid and unfamiliar taste of defeat. Joshua drew out a snuffbox from one of his pockets, and took a good, hard pinch of snuff. There was a dangerous gleam in his eyes. 'We will examine the entire field once more, Samuel — and then I will have something to throw at Donkin that will stick in his craw and quite possibly choke him.'

Esther's heart sank as the three men moved off to investigate the field. The rough, home-made wooden cart rattled away over the turf, clods of earth flying up in its wake.

Without waiting for another second, Esther ran towards the stable and jumped on the back of the first horse she saw, astride like a boy. Driving her heels into the animal's side, she buried her hands in its mane. Across the yard the horse galloped, its hoofs ringing loudly on the stones, down towards the fields along the glade path, plunging towards the men and the disastrous field of wheat.

Samuel was right, it was rust, cruelly infesting the wheat like a terminal disease. The entire wheatfield was ruined and the whole season had been wasted.

A row of men stood before Joshua and Cady, highly-inflamed and impatient for a decision, the silence of the lands around them. Joshua looked down the line, from the lean defiance of James Coffee at one end, to the broad, weather-beaten face of Murtagh Dougherty at the other. He and Cady knew their men, their heated passions, their fears, the swerving loyalties of those whose livelihood is threatened.

It only needed this to cause an ugly situation. Joshua could feel the mutinous rebellion flaring among them, and knew he must douse the first flicker of the flames before it became a raging fire. The men had been through so much already, how much more could they take?

The silence was now shattered as they gesticulated and cursed, raising their voices roughly in anger and bitter disillusionment.

'And what in hell's name do we do now?' Michael Byrne

demanded above the rest. 'We have many mouths to feed. I tell you, we are ruined good and proper and I with a wife and son.'

Cady stood, his stocky legs astride, the muzzle of his musket glinting from his shoulder strap. There was a sound of footsteps behind them as Esther ran up, the breeze lifting her ringlets from under her housecap.

Cady's eyes were fierce and uncompromising. 'And that is no kind of talk I wish to hear on Dwyers' Cross, do you hear me? That kind of talk gets you defeated before you've begun. One more word of defeat and you'll be thrown off this land, is that clear?' The blood seemed to drain from his face as he stood rooted to the spot.

'One crop failure and you're all bleating like gutless sheep. Do *we* win, or does this stubborn, unresisting land?' While he spoke he grinned mirthlessly, but his eyes held theirs and most shrank back from him a little. They knew he meant every word he said, and had proved it often, as had his brother. They knew that beneath the controlled, good-natured manner, there was a fiery temper that brooked no opposition when tested — different, but as potent as his brother's.

Esther looked at each man in turn, knowing that much depended on what her uncle had said to them, on the strength and the hope he could still give them.

Joshua regarded the men with outward composure but an unmistakable gleam of anger kindled his grey-green eyes. With a single gesture he brushed his hand in the direction of the fields.

'We find ourselves, men, in a manner of speaking, a human island in the middle of desolation. But I don't want weak resignation to fate. I want a fight, plain and simple, and fighters to the end — or we will die starving. And I cannot think of a worse fate.'

The men ranged themselves in a ragged line, all of them sullen-faced and angry. Joshua cast his eye over the group, silently waiting. For a moment it seemed that the men would rush them in blind despair and frustration.

At last Joshua spoke again. 'Remember Ireland, men — have you come all this way to give up at the first setback. Stick with us, united against the forces of nature here. And we will surely succeed. We must plant ourselves firmly in this soil and slowly, as we take root, we will prosper like the sturdy evergreens and hardy succulents around us. But that thirst for success must first come from within us all, or we are lost forever.'

Esther hoped that her father's words would freeze their thoughts and hold them, knowing that one word from Coffee and Dougherty could erupt into violence.

Joshua could find no further reasons to lecture them. And there was work to be done — the ruined crops waited to be cleared and anything saved could be used for shooks, hayricks and bran.

'My brother is right,' Cady said finally, the growing bitterness in his eyes clearly visible. 'We cannot give in. The only way is to fight the land and subdue it, harness it for our own good. We must fight the government for our rights — better conditions, more say in our own affairs — and never give up until it is done.'

The air crackled with tension as Joshua turned on his heel and strode off. Slowly the men walked away. Esther followed them, knowing that each was trying to find the courage to hide the terrible depths of disillusionment in their hearts, as she was in hers. She looked back across the ruined wheatfields; the thin wisps of smoke from the homestead behind her seemed miles away.

The rust had attacked the wheatfields of the entire settlement, and later it was found that blight had killed the potato crops. Many of the settlers were destitute, with no other resources left for the next year. Certain ruin and starvation stared them bleakly in the face. Joshua was appointed *Heemraden,* assistant to the magistrate, at Bathurst in addition to his post as leader of the two Irish parties. These were now breaking up, as were most of the other parties, as a direct result of the harvest failure.

Joshua and Cady had managed to avert a serious situation at Dwyers' Cross. They set about working for a change at once and called a meeting of all the leading farmers in the area, only to bring the wrath of the law down on them and to be told that no public meetings were allowed.

The Acting Governor, Donkin, did however agree to the extension of the time for rations, and he gave permission for a number of redundant men, particularly non-farmers, to leave the land, causing the further break-up of the larger parties. He had the colonial boundary moved from the Fish River further east to the Keiskamma and the entire settlement, including the Neutral Territory, became the new district of Albany. Bathurst was to be the new capital as Grahamstown was too far north and many miles from the furthest locations.

More land was granted to leading settlers, including Joshua and Cady, who set about extending their farmlands.

December approached and the heat intensified, shimmering far out where the sky and land met. There was no wheat to bake bread; Indian corn was used until the rations were distributed once more. Tea and coffee had run out, so they made coffee from aromatic leaves growing in the hills and dried out potato-tops for tobacco. The vegetables served in a variety of different ways.

December died in a welter of heat and New Year passed uneventfully, the past drowned in a glaze of sentiment and longing. As the pinpricks of light from the pungent-smelling, thick tallow candles spread warmly about the kitchen one summer evening in January, Laree took up her embroidery silks. The threads ran like glowing rivers, her fingers working deftly without a break.

Esther picked up a leather-bound book by Jane Austen and tried to read. Not being much of a reader, she was soon bored and threw the book down on a table. After pacing up and down several times without in the least disturbing Laree, she flopped down on a stool, her arms crossed defiantly under her breasts.

If only Mama was here, she thought crossly, she would have given parties and balls, and set about securing fine husbands for Laree and me. Esther knew that Laree still silently pined for Roydon Wilson. Now, seeing the wistful, unhappy look on her sister's face at times, she was no longer sure whether she was right about Roydon, and if she should have been so emphatic in her rejection of him.

She rose and picked up a sampler from the table. She glanced at Laree, her slender fingers flying as they formed the perfect tiny stitches. Sam Pettigrew was in love with Laree, even she could see that, though Laree hardly seemed to notice. Perhaps even Sam might be better than Roydon, because he was a man of experience. He was interesting, though hardly the right match for a Dwyer. But even on that matter she was now quite unsure of her feelings.

Esther, like the rest of the family, had come to feel comforted by the presence of Sam. He knew so much about the country and the rugged, hospitable Boers who had helped the settlers through their first, hard year. It seemed to her that before Sam's arrival, she and Laree had been unaware of the nature around them: the movements of the animals, the birds and their calls, the constant changes in the wind — all of which he had taught them over the months. It seemed that she had been too preoccupied about the society she had been born into and known all her life. She had taken that enjoyable life and its comforts so for granted, it was as if she had not been fully awake until now. Perhaps that was what she was hungering for — new experiences. This country was slowly but surely changing her.

She gazed down helplessly at the tangle of jewel-tinted silks on the table and wondered which colour to choose. She sighed in exasperation. How boring it was! She loathed embroidery of any kind! Sewing was a challenge, especially making lovely clothes to wear for special occasions, but embroidering samplers was so . . . so . . . pointless. She pursed her lips resentfully as she threaded her needle.

She thought about Garnet Fitzwilliam. Sir Rufane Donkin, in accordance with ruling procedures for meritorious military officers, had granted Garnet two hundred and ninety-six morgen of land, a mile from Grahamstown, last August. It had been surveyed the previous spring and the title granted. He had begun to build a two-storey house and set about commissioning one of the settlers, a former architect, and some of his men, to build on the estate, which he had called Glendower Park after a property belonging to his family in England. And when it was finally completed Garnet was planning to hold a dinner-dance to which they were already invited. Esther's eyes gleamed as she tried to concentrate on her sewing.

Speculation was rife among the leading matrons, and the only possible conclusion they could arrive at was that he desired to marry.

Esther made a mistake and pricked her finger. She threw down the sampler contemptuously on the table and walked over to the window, peering into the blackness of the country quiet that lay about the cottage. She thought of Sergeant Buck Jones. Although he was her social inferior in every way there was something about him that evoked in her a wicked but exciting feeling. She had not seen him since their first meeting, but she had learned that he was the illegitimate son of an actress, who had died in his youth, and some unknown regency buck, one of her highborn and influential lovers.

Buck Jones, it was rumoured, was having an illicit and passionate affair with the widow of the late Commander of the Grahamstown garrison, Lady Amanda Lightfoot. She was reputed to be gay, witty and attractive, at least seven or eight years older than her lover. It was also common knowledge that she had chased him outrageously ever since her husband's death during the Fifth Frontier War, and had even cast surreptitious eyes at him when they both arrived in the colony five years before.

Esther heard of their escapades along the grapevine and of how they flouted the conformity of the tight, insular society around them, by daring to act as they pleased. Lady Lightfoot's past was lurid and steamy, filled with a string of lovers, one reputedly the Prince Regent himself. But never had she so extravagantly thrown herself at any one of them as she had at Buck Jones.

And it was he who had captured Esther's reluctant imagination and fired her bored, restless spirit, though she tried to fight against his effect on her through the succeeding days and nights.

Now, as she peered out into the night with the savage land lying silently about her, she recalled the day she had first met him. She could feel again the closeness of him as he had held her in his arms after the snake scare. He had not held her like an inept, clumsy boy, but as a man, experienced, bold, dashing. Yet he was so totally unsuitable for her in every way.

Shocked by her thoughts, she fought those memories by trying to turn her attention once more to Garnet Fitzwilliam and his forthcoming party.

CHAPTER
Seven

On a midsummer's evening in February, 1821, a select company of leading settlers and officers of the garrison gathered at Glendower Park, Garnet Fitzwilliam's newly-completed residence.

In the short space of time since the settlers had arrived, the small outpost known as Grahamstown had begun to leap to life. It was still the only village in the settlement, as Bathurst, the proposed new capital, was still under construction. Grahamstown had started to sprawl, forming the nucleus of the new commercial and farming centre.

Along the ridge more cottages had been built after the crop failure. Now patchworks of fields embroidered the land, thrusting out bravely towards the peaceful hills over which thousands of Xhosa feet had swept in the two recent, bloody wars.

A network of streams wound slowly from the Kowie, looping and fading into the distance in the pale, smokey haze of the last evening light. Renoster bush surrendered to the sudden, sweet fields of Glendower Park and beyond the low wall of a long driveway, set among its gardens, stood the house, large and grey. The dying light veneered the stone facings and the tall, narrow entrance with gold and ruby gleams. The rows of long, sash windows glimmered faintly, hiding the elegance inside. Behind and high up, rose a backdrop of rocks, gazing out on to the rolling, woodclad hills.

A few refurbished carriages, some Cape carts, a wagon or two, were outspanned near the entrance in the large sweep of driveway.

The buzz of conversation rose from the spacious lawns as the guests gathered about Garnet and his officers dotting the grass with their smart, freshly-pressed mess uniforms. The newly-promoted Major Somerset and his wife were absent as Henry had taken the post of Commander of Simonstown.

As congenial company in Albany was strictly limited, friends were compelled to make long and difficult journeys for social gatherings. This was one of those occasions when the cream of settler society had been brought together by Garnet.

The smoke from the spits, where the meats roasted, curled upwards in lazy spirals, to be held and caught for the briefest of seconds in the branches of the trees. Long trestle-tables were laid out on the lawns, covered with the finest white linen and laden with crystal glasses and polished silver. Wine pails were placed at convenient places on the grass near the tables. Many candles, in unusual wood and tin chandeliers, were strung about the trees, glimmering in the fast-fading light. Laughter ran out across the lawns, heavy with gathering shadows and the sparks of glowing fireflies.

Esther walked gracefully from the front entrance of the house where she had changed into party clothes with the other young ladies after the long, dusty journey from Dwyers' Cross. She re-arranged the soft folds of the deep blue, sarsenet gown, a few seasons old, but still flattering with its short ballooned sleeves and rows of tiny, silver galloon ribbons below the firm swell of her breasts. The matching, ruched neckband, holding a clasp of small flowers to one side, was a stroke of genius, enhancing the sparkle and colour of her eyes. She was positively breathtaking. Her beauty, added to her boldness, instantly fascinated the young men, exciting them and thrusting from their thoughts all the other young women decorating the lawns.

She was aware of the stir she created. She had gone to great lengths over her appearance, and none could guess the irritated moments spent with the hot tongs, coaxing and forcing the riot of deep wine-red curls into the profusion of glorious ringlets about her neck, held tightly together at her ears by knots of silver galloon ribbons.

And it was all on account of Captain Garnet Fitzwilliam. She had not seen him for months, but she was determined to capture him that night.

She stopped, tapping a white silk fan framed in ivory with an impatient hand. She looked towards Garnet conversing with a group of guests, the young women in the knot eyeing him with encouraging, flirtatious glances over their fans, tittering and giggling. Never had Esther seen such a figure of masculine elegance, resplendent in his red mess jacket with gold braid and shining epaulettes, the spotless white trousers and high, polished hessian boots, worn only on special occasions. He looked so poised, so debonair with the coal-black hair feathering his cheeks and the nape of his neck. A slow, half smile curved his lips, and she saw him give a careless shrug. He raised his fine, dark eyebrows at some remark, and finally looked in her direction.

He stood watching her in silent fascination, then he smiled as their eyes met, excused himself and came forward to meet her. There was a stir of interest among the crowd. The frosty eyes of the older matrons pierced his back with a thousand darts as they fanned themselves with growing annoyance, their overloaded bonnets and turbans turning to follow him. At the sight of Esther Dwyer, their eyes became frostier still.

Taking her hand, he gallantly bowed over it. As she lightly rested her fingers in his, he brushed a kiss on her hand with a disarming smile. 'You look very beautiful tonight, Miss Dwyer, a real jewel adorning my garden.'

How dashing he is, Esther thought, smiling triumphantly at him and ignoring the other young women struggling to maintain their composure as they tried to hide their hostility towards her.

'So,' she said, taking a deep breath, 'What it is to be so popular, Captain Fitzwilliam.' She gave him the full benefit of her most provocative smile.

He looked at her searchingly, his deep, dark gaze missing nothing. Her body gleamed in the last glow of the sunset, rounded and disturbing in its femininity. The swell of her hips was outlined softly beneath her gown, her breasts just exposed enough above the low neckline to hint at their firm shapeliness. Esther, delighted with the effect produced, was watching the expression on his face.

'Playing host has its rewards, my dear.' There was something about the amused tilt of his eyebrows, the sudden mischievousness in his eyes that made her laugh.

'And I have seen many of them surround you like moths around a candle.'

The dark liquid of his eyes deepened as he became caught up in the excitement of her presence. 'Many moths but only one rare butterfly. Besides, I have never been partial to moths,' he answered with a smile, and she read in his face such evident desire that heat flamed for a moment in her cheeks.

He was silent for a moment as if he wanted to say something else, and she noticed that for an instant the look went from his eyes. Then it was over, and she allowed him to lead her to one of the tables as the musicians bent over their instruments and started to play. The last trailing patterns of daylight moved quietly out of the sky and the darkness of the veld and trees was lit only by the many candle chandeliers and the fireflies.

Her eyes sparkling like dark sapphires, bright with triumph, Esther's senses drank in the intoxication of it all. She suddenly felt like a gilded bird freed from its cage for a few, precious hours. And all the while she was conscious of being the focus of curious eyes.

The smoking-hot food was brought to the tables in covered dishes by Hottentot servants: gleaming platters piled with venison, roasted lamb in a delicious sauce, pork covered with russet crackling, and golden partridge, the flesh crumbling from the knife. Wooden boards carried grapes, apples, nuts and cheeses and a selection of delicate puddings: pastries oozing with juicy plums, iced cakes and syllabub with assorted sweetmeats. It had been a very long time, if at all, since the settlers present had enjoyed such a feast, now spread so opulently before them.

As a pendant of bright stars was framed against the sky, and from the hills came the long churring of a nightjar, Amanda, Lady Lightfoot, made her late and daring entrance. A small, confident woman of about thirty-five, glided on to the lawn, her arm possessively looped through Garnet's. All eyes automatically turned in their direction.

A gown of the sheerest, silver-grey tissue enveloped her small, rounded, mature figure, flowing about her and revealing more than a hint of the voluptuousness of her full, soft body. She sailed forward, very much aware of the stir she had created, and obviously enjoying it. Her ash-blonde curls, obviously dyed, were banded with silver ribbons in a most unmatronly manner, and her gemmed bracelets flashed on her full, rounded arms like dazzling points of fire.

She was not beautiful, or even pretty, but alarmingly lively and arresting, and very, very interesting. Her amber eyes sparkled with excitement, their tracery of laughter lines cleverly concealed by cosmetics. If Garnet was at all embarrassed by her attire, he gave no

79

sign of it, escorting her before them with easy courtesy. It was a daring entrance carried out as only Amanda could, with enormous panache, and Esther was grudgingly forced to admire it.

She had never seen Amanda before, and she was not disappointed. The older woman was warmly welcomed by the officers and talked easily with Garnet, whom she appeared to know very well, in a deep, husky voice that was curiously fascinating. A coterie of gentlemen soon gathered about her, and Esther and the rest of the women, young and old were instantly ignored. Amanda hardly seemed to notice the icy antagonism she drew from most of the members of her own sex, in whom she had not the slightest interest, her eyes and her charms reserved only for the men.

Esther, watching her, was resentful and fascinated. She, who had drawn all eyes, and especially Garnet's, on herself moments ago, was forgotten. It was not often that she had to surrender the centre of the stage to another woman, and she was definitely not used to it. Whatever she had expected of Amanda Lightfoot, nothing had prepared her for the remarkable presence of the tiny woman. She enchanted those about her with sophisticated charm and wit, possessing a bubbling and infectious laugh, which she used with effortless ease, infusing the company with its gaiety.

Esther remembered everything she had ever heard about her, and now she could believe it all. She had the magnetism and the power to have seduced Sheridan, enchanted Prinny, the Prince Regent, inflamed the poet Lord Byron, and many more. She had held Regency society in the palm of her small hands as the young child-bride of Colonel Lightfoot, many years her senior, and had brought money to his titled, but impoverished family. And she intoxicated Buck Jones.

Esther felt strangely inadequate, knowing she could never compete with the worldly experience and fascination of the older woman. She felt vulnerable and gauche — and, worst of all, so very young.

The meal ended with the singing of glees and catches by the guests to a musical accompaniment. These were followed by dancing, as soft radiance emanated from the wood chandeliers. The small band of musicians struck up a waltz and Amanda was the first to be claimed to dance.

Esther watched her, as more and more dancers filled the lawn.

80

She herself was claimed by a young officer for the quadrille. The dancers pirouetted, bowing and stepping, turning on heels, holding hands, pointing toes — forming and reforming. The lawns and trees were dark against a vast sky stippled with stars, the air full of fireflies.

Esther tried to forget Lady Lightfoot as the band began a minuet and she was claimed at last by Garnet. Relief flooded ridiculously through her. All was not lost. He had not forgotten her — she could still work her own magic on him even though Amanda seemed to treat him as if he was her special possession.

She summoned up the old familiar spirit to bewitch him, her eyes glowing with brilliance and fire, as with a sweep of his arm he brought her to the centre of the shimmering sea of silk, satins and muslins. She felt the pressure of his strong fingers through the thin material of her gown.

Suddenly there was a commotion from the driveway. Two horses galloped through the gates, their riders urging them on. Those nearest to the driveway recognized the head and shoulders of two redcoats coming out of the darkness in clouds of dust! The leading one waved a flaming mimosa branch in his hand. He slowed to a trot as clods of earth thudded on to the grass. Garnet, a frown on his face, excused himself and went forward to meet them.

In the pulsating light of the torches, Esther saw the tall, muscular figure of Buck Jones stride towards Garnet, the folds of the long blue cloak flaring from his broad shoulders. They all heard his husky voice in the sudden silence that had fallen, announcing that Chieftain Mazwi's son, Lungelo, who had been refused permission to occupy some of the former Neutral Territory, had attacked one of the Missions under Reverend Allen, and carried off two hundred and seventy-four head of cattle.

A loud gasp ran through the guests as they gathered about the soldiers. There was the slightest movement of acknowledgement from Garnet as Buck Jones said, 'I bring urgent orders from the Commandant of the Frontier, Colonel Scott, Sir — I have 'em here.' He pulled a letter from a pouch slung over his shoulder and handed it to Garnet in the deep hush that followed.

Garnet excused himself to read it. He looked up and faced his guests. 'I am forced to apologize to all you good people present, but I have to leave you in the middle of the entertainment. His Excellency has ordered Colonel Scott to send men at once to seize the Xhosa

81

chieftain, Mazwi, and to hold him until all the cattle are restored. It is only fair to tell you that I am to proceed to the former Neutral Territory with Sergeant Jones, Corporal Pickering and one hundred men immediately. I am deeply sorry, but the matter is urgent.'

He smiled thinly, waving the letter in his hands. 'But I would like you all to stay and enjoy yourselves even if I cannot be here with you.' He paused, pursing his lips. Then he turned to one of the officers at his side. 'Lieutenant Jackson, I want you to take over as host, nothing must interfere with the pleasure and comfort of my guests.'

He looked at Buck. 'Sergeant Jones, wait for me here with Pickering. I will change into field dress and be down directly.'

He made his way to the house as the murmur and buzz of apprehension grew loud among the guests. By now they had all heard of Mazwi and Lungelo, most having suffered cattle thefts and the killing of herdboys.

Lieutenant Jackson took over immediately, requesting the musicians to continue and the dancing to proceed as if nothing had happened. Esther remained behind while the others trailed back towards the lawn and music throbbed through the air again. She felt sudden resentment towards the tall soldier who had come to call Garnet away. He was under orders, but that did not make it better in her eyes. Closing her eyes for an instant, she fought down the mounting, angry frustration. She had been getting along with Garnet so well until then.

A sound made her look up and Buck stood before her. The flowing cloak and tapering white trousers accentuated the long lines of his body, and she noticed again how incredibly blue his eyes were in the flare of the torch. It was impossible not to respond to this man as his masculine magnetism dominated the scene. A curious sharp thrill ran through her as the force between them seemed to explode wordlessly. He watched her, his eyes alert above the faintly smiling mouth, and she promptly forgot Garnet Fitzwilliam.

They faced one another now, the English sergeant and the young, Irish gentlewoman, and although neither abated one ounce of their dignity, or their unspoken opposition, the attraction between them was almost palpable.

He cocked an eye at her, the flame of the torch wavering and setting strange shadows dancing around them. Its light flickered over

82

his thick brown hair outlining his face. Then a full smile touched his lips.

'You are cross with me, Miss Dwyer — for calling away the Captain — but duty calls and soldiers must obey.'

There was a moment of silence, and her annoyance faded. A surge of irrepressible excitement rose in her. She had not seen him since that first time at Dwyers' Cross, but she had heard so much about him that she felt she knew him.

Looking up now into that strong face, she believed all she had heard — of how he had taken command of Grahamstown barracks at the height of the most savage fighting during the last war, when Garnet had been badly wounded and thousands of Xhosa had surrounded it. He had led one of the finest and most daring defences of the entire war, succeeding in holding out the enemy. It was well-known that he had strode up and down the barrack walls for hours, urging his men on, seemingly unafraid for his own safety.

It had been recounted often how Amanda's husband, Colonel Lightfoot, had held the thin, red line of defence at Kowie Ditch for hours waiting for reinforcements, preventing the rest of the Xhosas advancing on the village. He had been mutilated and killed and Amanda had thrown herself at Buck Jones.

'I would think, Sergeant Jones, that it is much more comforting to stay here than to travel through the darkness after a black savage,' she said with sudden impudent defiance as she tried to fight the power of his charm. He seemed amused as he studied her.

She saw the twinkle in his eye, the twist of humour about his beautiful mouth. 'Each to his own, Miss Dwyer. There are more discomforting experiences than chasing black savages, as you choose to call them — I prefer the word "tribesmen". Here, for instance, in this very smart gathering of civilized beings, there run many dangerous and treacherous undercurrents, like dark, bottomless pools. The women, with their little jealousies and intrigues, have much war-mongering amongst them, weaving webs of deceit. And the men are just as bad with their love of competition, of bettering the next man, their pious, self-righteous condemnations.' He continued to look at her, his eyes narrowing with mockery.

She was surprised at the length of his speech, at the cynicism of its content, then seeing the teasing expression in his startling blue eyes, allowed the rich peals of laughter to escape from her throat.

83

'I do believe you jest with me, Sergeant — quite an unexpected pleasure from one of such rank as yourself. And why, seeing you are so learned and clever, are you still a non-commissioned officer taking orders when you should be making them?'

For a fleeting second the intensity of his blue eyes seemed to explode. An expression she did not understand flashed through them, then was gone.

He smiled sardonically, the dimples deep in his cheeks. 'We are not all as fortunate as you and your kin, Miss Dwyer. It is not for want of trying on my part, I can assure you.' His husky voice with its rounded burr was softly, thickly edged with irony. 'But without money and influence one has no chance. I have neither the means nor the influence to buy a commission in an army where most are still bought and sold — and my lack of background I think, speaks for itself.' His cool eyes rested on her face without a trace of self-pity.

She regarded him with new respect, realizing that he had been promoted to the rank of sergeant not only because of his ability, but because he could read in a time when very few of the rank and file could. He had been promoted above many older men who were stuck on the tediously slow ladder of regimental promotions because of their inabilities, while he had mastered them and gone ahead.

She had always felt that all soldiers below commissioned officers were uncouth ruffians, not the kind of men she had ever given much thought to. But, somehow, Buck Jones was different.

'But surely there are ways to right a wrong?' she said without thinking. She wished she could bite her tongue. He made a mockingly deprecating gesture that did not fit the expression in his eyes, a movement that flashed a dark blue cuff and a glint of brass buttons.

'My dear, Miss Dwyer, it is not for small fish like me to argue with the select clique of powers-that-be! That is not a right expected by underlings such as myself.'

She took a deep breath, not knowing what to say, but she felt the bite of cruel truth in his words.

'Surely there are ways to help you — someone with influence and means?'

'Are you suggesting that in your generosity you would care to redress the wrongs of our misguided society, Miss Dwyer? If so, your concern touches me deeply.' His voice was casual, softer than before, and his face was serious, but she distrusted the gleam of mocking humour lurking in his gaze. He did not believe for one minute that she or anyone of her class cared one jot what happened to those in his position.

'I see that good manners forbid you to be honest with me, Miss Dwyer. Lud! How tiresome good manners can be.' As she struggled for the vestiges of thin control which had never been one of her strong points, he lifted his brows quizzically.

Two spots of dark colour appeared high on her cheeks. Never had any man looked so attractive or so distant, and never had her heart called out so strongly to anyone. As she continued to look up into his eyes, they were unfathomable. All at once she knew she must fight her attraction for him. It would be madness to consider him anything but out of her class, a social inferior. And his standards were not hers. She tried to pull her wits together, all too aware that the other girls were whispering behind their fans, that they studied her with furtive curiosity and hostility, exchanging sly glances full of dark significance. There was something repulsive in their lusting for the meat of a scandal, especially as she was conversing with the one man who had the smell of scandal so strongly about him. And his possessive mistress was present. Esther had forgotten all about Amanda Lightfoot.

She shrugged it all off, considering the other girls to be petty and spiteful, and, lacking her admirers, plainly jealous. Abruptly she inclined her head towards him.

'You are indeed the most unmannerly of men!' she hissed under her breath, a storm brewing in her fine eyes.

Quite undaunted, a dazzling smile broke the determined line of his mouth. 'I never pretended to be otherwise, but you, Miss Dwyer, are indeed the most attractive.'

Vividly conscious of her proximity to him, she sharply turned away before he could realize just how much he had affected her. Without a word, laughter in his eyes, he moved towards Corporal Pickering, quietly observing the whole scene.

Esther walked away, her eyes darting across the gay sea of soft, filmy gowns, bobbing ringlets and waving fans, as each girl vied for the eligible men, their smug mothers sitting apart and gossiping about the passing parade.

Suddenly, her eyes encountered Amanda Lightfoot, standing not

85

far away and regarding her with all the chill of an Arctic winter. All too clearly she was made conscious of the older woman, an almost tangible hostility emanating from her, as naked rivalry stood between them.

Esther was stunned. Amanda continued to stare at her, rigid with hatred, her amber eyes glittering and sparkling as if she longed to destroy her. So fierce was the feeling from her that Esther was momentarily intimidated.

But then a puzzling change came over her. A strange sense of power filled her as she took in the painted face, past its prime, the too bright ash-coloured hair, the over-ripe lips, the too eager eyes. Too much plumage on too little a bird, she thought with the callousness of youth. She was interrupted by a movement at her side.

Garnet stood looking down at her, his dark eyes sparks in the shadows thrown by the candles.

'I apologize, my dear,' he said softly, 'but when duty calls a soldier must unfortunately obey. This is not an enviable task, but a necessary one. I hope you understand?'

She lowered her gaze, for his eyes seemed to penetrate her very soul, searching out her feelings, all those thoughts she would rather keep hidden. When she dared to look at him again, he was watching her, his dark eyes filled with some indefinable emotion.

'Is there anything wrong, Esther? You don't look quite as lively as usual.' His voice, which had been evenly-paced, now took on an edge of concern. 'I hope I haven't inconvenienced you as much as all that?'

Before her encounter with Buck Jones she would have been delighted at his concern, his obvious feeling for her, now all she could feel was a strange flatness. Then she recovered her composure, falsely smiling. 'It was — is — the heat and the dancing. Goodbye, Captain Fitzwilliam — God be with you.'

'Thank you, my dear,' he said, bowing to her before he turned and left.

Esther did not know when she became aware of Buck Jones and Amanda Lightfoot together. They were standing near his horse under the light of his torch.

She managed to retain a cool and unruffled expression as she watched Amanda's diamond earrings flash against her cheeks. The hum of voices and laughter rose and mingled with the music throbbing and swelling as the musicians once more bent over their instruments.

She saw Buck smile and shrug broad, red-jacketed shoulders. For one terrible moment she was seized with passionate hatred for the other woman, so terrible and so unexpected that the triumphant glow of her earlier scorn faded.

Then she saw Amanda draw herself up stiffly, her eyes smouldering in a face suddenly distorted with rage, uncaring of those around her.

Buck's face changed in the hissing light, a strange forbidding look on it. He bowed slightly and mounted his horse, calling Corporal Pickering. Garnet had joined them and the three horses thundered away, their hooves lost in the darkness.

Esther saw Amanda look fleetingly about her, then called for her carriage. So, thought Esther, it is true that Lady Lightfoot jumps more to the tune of the Sergeant than he does to hers. She was madly in love with him, and the fact that she was jealous of any rival was thrown into sharp focus by what Esther had witnessed.

She could now understand why it was that someone of Amanda's sophistication stayed on in this uncivilized frontier. It was only to be near Sergeant Jones, he was the reason for her remaining here. Esther sighed inwardly, wondering in that moment what it would be like to be kissed by a man such as he. Suddenly embarrassed by her thoughts, she flushed and turned away.

The only way to stop the grey desolation spreading over her was to devote all her talents to capturing Garnet, who represented to her everything she really valued in life. The desperation to escape the danger and wildness of Dwyers' Cross lent energy to her thoughts. She looked back towards Garnet's house, its tall, graceful chimneys rising like dark shadows high above the wood chandeliers at the entrance. She wanted to be the mistress of this lovely, elegant house. She wanted that with all her heart.

CHAPTER
Eight

After the party at Glendower Park the Dwyers remained for some days in Grahamstown with friends. The following morning Lady Amanda Lightfoot's maid arrived with an invitation for Esther to take tea with her that afternoon.

Esther knew that she should refuse, and at first her feelings for the woman were so strong that she almost threw the invitation right back in the maid's face. But her upbringing and breeding forbade such a gesture, and the more she thought about it, the more her curiosity got the better of her. All her instincts urged her not to become involved with Amanda in any way — that she should distance herself from the woman, and her association with Buck Jones. But she was intrigued by Amanda, and that intrigue reached out to her affair with the extraordinary sergeant. She accepted the invitation, much against her own good sense, feeling a curious excitement. Dressed with elaborate care, she entered Amanda's smart phaeton outside the front door at three o'clock.

As it drew off down the dusty High Street Esther straightened the soft, sprigged green muslin and adjusted her small-brimmed straw hat, festooned with green and white galloon ribbons. Glancing out of the window, she pondered again why Amanda wanted to see her. Curiosity once more quickened her. She and the older woman had very little in common, except a certain roguish, reckless lust for life. But it was certainly never displayed in the same way. She could never wantonly throw caution to the wind and flout every convention in the way Amanda had done all her life. They swerved to avoid an ox-cart laden with goods, the cries of the farmers and Hottentots loud on the streets. A new community was growing around the few original dwellings. The carriage swept past recently-erected, rough-stone cottages, with their newly-dug gardens and fruit trees. Along the street several new buildings were being constructed, marking off the distance to Amanda's house. It was an attractive two-storied residence at the bottom of the High Street, built by her late husband. It stood on a slope in an acre of garden running down to the river at the bottom, and boasted a fine stable of five horses.

At last the carriage came to a complete stop and the door opened. Esther's gloved hand reached out as the footman assisted her down. Clutching her green reticule, gathered at the opening with a drawstring, she nervously walked to the front door, hoping that her sudden uncertainty did not show.

Inside, she was shown into an elegant drawing-room at the back of the house. All the draperies, in varying shades of blue with contrasting white and gold, were fine and expensive. The exquisite furniture was upholstered in flowered white and blue brocade, the afternoon sunlight reflecting the gilt-framed mirrors on to the silver and the polished wood surfaces.

Amanda was seated at her tapestry frame, dressed in a gown of palest powder-blue. Her silver-blonde hair was piled on top of her head, cascades of ringlets at the nape of her neck. Esther's eyes took in all the details, from the thin-fringed, Chinese-silk shawl of the most magnificent peacock blue, thrown carelessly about her small, rounded shoulders, to the pale blue, embroidered satin slippers.

Her heart set up a sudden, unreasoning fast beat. She swiftly glanced at herself critically in the Chippendale mirror near the door, nervously patting a bright red curl in place. She felt instantly too tall, gauche and vivid in colouring, beside this small, dainty, porcelain woman.

Amanda raised her head in feigned surprise, a dazzle of diamond frost in fine, old silver swinging from her ears. Her deep, husky voice rolled between them, mellifluous and soft. 'Ah, Miss Dwyer, how very nice of you to accept my invitation, at first I thought you may well refuse.'

'And why should I refuse, Lady Lightfoot?' Esther asked before she could stop herself.

Amanda looked across at her, an enigmatic expression in the cool, light-amber eyes. She rose, adjusting the low cut, rounded neckline of her bodice, exposing a glimpse of full, creamy breasts. Everything about her was precise and impeccable, her dyed hair groomed, the fingernails of her pale, small, lively hands immaculate.

'No reason in particular,' she mused.

Esther remained staring at the face, motionless in a shaft of sunlight, so skilfully painted as to hide the faint wrinkles about the eyes and mouth. She was a woman desperately fighting age, and trying to combat it in every way she could. Esther did not know what to reply, intuitively feeling that there was some special reason for the invitation.

She tried to still her racing thoughts as Amanda beckoned her to a chair. She patted a fat, blue and gold tasselled, velvet cushion. 'Do sit down, Miss Dwyer, there is no need to be so ill at ease, I can assure you. I bark, but never have I been known to bite.'

The heavy, gold mourning band flashed on her finger as she moved her hands. She studied Esther, eyeing her clothes in a manner suggesting she was well aware of the hard times on which the Dwyers had fallen.

In that intense moment, surrounded by the opulence of the room, Esther felt some emotion from the woman, pressing in on her, squeezing her with icy, inflexible fingers. She ignored Amanda's offer of a seat and remained standing, feeling more at an advantage from there. Amanda shrugged eloquent shoulders. She spread her arms and eased her body against the chaise-longue, one exquisitely embroidered, slippered foot peeping from the beaded hem of her gown, unconsciously showing the slightest hint of showers and flounces of pale Brussels lace.

'As you wish, Miss Dwyer — but I always think it far more comfortable and companionable to sit.' Esther was once more surprised at the unusual beauty of the older woman's voice, its deep pitch edged with laughter that never grated on the nerves. She could understand how many men had been mesmerised by it, trapped by its silvery charm.

She resented suddenly the full rounded curves, the silver hair piled up on the small, fascinating head. Her own eyes narrowed. 'Why do you wish to see me, Lady Lightfoot?' she asked, the resentment heavy in her voice. 'I am sure it was not to discuss the fashions or the weather.' Her voice, beneath the gentility, was Irish, touched with a certain lilt, and full of innocent sensuousness that was not lost on Amanda.

For one vivid instant the air between them shivered with tense friction. But if Amanda was disconcerted by Esther's abrupt manner, she hid it quickly under a mask of light gaiety. She gave the younger woman a sidelong glance. 'I do wish you would sit down, Miss Dwyer, you are like a cat walking gingerly on hot coals.'

She smiled and stood up, reaching for the bellrope. 'Perhaps a dish of tea will calm your nerves.'

'I am quite calm, thank you,' Esther said, aware that Amanda was playing with her like a cat with a mouse. 'I do wish you would get to the heart of what you wish to discuss.'

Amanda stood before a chessboard of inlaid ivory, set out on a low rosewood table, the delicate red and white carved pieces abandoned. The aroma from an orange pomander swinging on its ribbon, clove-struck and fresh, pervaded the air as she picked up one of the white pieces, idly caressing it with her fingers.

'Sergeant Jones plays a good game of chess, did you know that, Miss Dwyer? Rather like a general deploying his troops in some war zone. Clever man, shrewd tactician, for all his rather lowly rank — but perhaps you have already found this out. Ever had a game with him, my dear?' The words uttered stood out in startling relief against the hypnotically musical voice, still warm, dark and velvety.

Esther could feel a gathering of concentration, like shadows entering the bright, elegant room, a dark force of will being directly focused on her. Her heart skipped a beat as she met Amanda's eyes steadily, seeing the amber flames within their depths. So this was it — she wanted to find out how well Esther knew the Sergeant. That surely meant she was not as sure of him as she pretended.

'So,' Esther said sharply, with a quick intake of breath. 'The pretence of a tea invitation was all in aid of the Sergeant.' She gave Amanda a look of acute displeasure, watching her as she replaced the chess piece on the board.

Amanda turned away, picking up a goblet from the table. She was disconcerted, beginning to wonder if she had underestimated the Irish girl. She said nothing, holding the glass between her pale, well-manicured fingers so that the light reflected from the crystal cuttings. She looked up, the light, translucent lustre of her eyes brilliant with suppressed emotion.

'You are still so very young, my dear, such a child really. I had no idea,' she murmured, declaring war.

Esther stared at her, her eyes on fire as the blandest of smiles broke about Amanda's taunting lips. She watched mercilessly as Esther struggled for self-control.

'You have got me here under false pretences, Lady Lightfoot,' she burst out hotly, 'and I resent that deeply.'

She could feel the heat of her temper spreading inside her as the oppressive warmth of the room seemed suddenly heavy and all-enveloping. She felt as if she was suffocating, caught in the subtle threads of some unseen and sinister spider's web. She should never have come, she should have listened to her reason and not her heart.

Amanda smiled, her eyes cooling perceptibly. She put down the goblet. 'You have fire and spirit and that is what interests Sergeant Jones — it is a challenge to his strength, his masculinity, that daring recklessness in him that attracts so many women, and, as I have seen, attracts you. You remind me a lot of myself as a younger woman, my dear — so you see, I understand what you want, and what attracts you as it does me. But I must warn you, Miss Dwyer, you are still far too young and inexperienced for him. I see that now — in fact it has been a great relief for me to see it all so openly displayed. You are so innocent deep down, and innocence has a way of palling even the most reckless heart.' She emphasised 'innocence' as if it was some kind of despicable disease.

'Buck Jones likes his women mature, more sophisticated. I have spoilt him for ingenues such as yourself — for you see, I taught him much of what he knows, and what could you possibly know of such matters?' She laughed, deliberately weighing her up with contempt and scorn.

She leaned forward, her clear, amber eyes never leaving Esther's face. 'He was a young corporal when I first rescued him, straight from the battlefields of Europe. What did he know of women then? The only kind he had any experience with were those following the army from camp to camp — poor, street women who could teach him only to a point. It was I who uplifted him, taught him the finesse of a fine lover, and he was eager to learn. We know each other very well, he and I.'

Esther's face was still, as if she was considering the advisability of telling Amanda just what she thought of her. Then, unexpectedly, she flared, 'Why are you telling me all this? I hardly know the man.'

An ominous glitter appeared in Amanda's eyes. 'But would like to know him a lot better. I am no greenhorn, Miss Dwyer. I have lived long enough, have gone through enough, to know an infatuated, moon-eyed calf when I see one. If you play with Buck Jones, you play with fire, and you will burn those innocent, unstained young fingers. You may burn yourself so badly that you will never recover.'

Esther could hardly believe her ears. The amber eyes never wavered, locking on to hers with a bitter coldness she did not dare to understand.

'How dare you say those things to me, Lady Lightfoot! What gives you the right to sit there and throw such talk at me? It is absolutely none of your business how I feel or do not feel about anyone,' she said heatedly, her eyes snapping.

'You are an impertinent young woman! It has everything to do with me!' Amanda clipped the words without raising her voice. She hastily reached for the goblet and took a deep gulp of the tawny liquid.

She turned away as a maid brought in the tea on a silver tray. Esther looked at Amanda for one wild, crazed moment. The fury in her eyes made everything indistinct. She thought she was going mad in that expensive, suffocating room.

Looking away through one of the long sash windows, she could see a landscape of green, falling away to the river, the trees standing out like a water-colour painting. Distressed, she forced her eyes back into the room where Amanda was pouring the tea.

Inexplicable hostility from some elemental instinct of rivalry welled inside her. It was in this room that Buck Jones visited this woman, upstairs in the bedroom that they had been together. She tried to shut out the unwelcome, disturbing vision, knowing that they had nothing to do with her — it was all part of a life that was not for her, never would be. And she did not want it to be.

The room was filled with mid-afternoon quiet. Everything in it swam in sunlight that hurt her eyes — shooting rays of fire from the prisms hanging from a pair of gold-edged crystal candlesticks on the mantelpiece, pools of light thrown across a swirling Turner painting, on to a fine, jasper Wedgewood vase. Everything was bathed in warmth, except Esther's heart which felt heavy with despair.

She took an involuntary step forward. 'Is there anything else you have to say to me, Lady Lightfoot? If not, I will not stay for tea, thank you.'

Amanda raised her hand and shot her a venomous glance. 'I want you to stay away from Buck Jones — completely. He is mine. It's hands off, Miss Dwyer, if you know what's good for you. If you choose to disregard my warning. I will do all I can to make it very unpleasant for you in this colony. I will do all in my power to undermine your so-called respectability, which I know matters to you very much. There are ways and means, and your reputation will be ruined. I know Captain Garnet Fitzwilliam very well, and he won't like to hear certain things about you. You see, my dear Garnet values decorum and respectability even higher than you do.'

Esther looked at her incredulously. 'What are you saying? I hardly know the Sergeant. Besides, there are many who would never believe you.'

Amanda took another sip of wine from the goblet. The girl was too bold, too fearless to be either threatened or cowed. Her poise wavered before those merciless, bright, young eyes.

'You are an arrogant, poverty-stricken minx!' she said, breathing heavily as the wine began to take hold of her. She drew a deep breath. 'If you take Buck Jones away from me, I will see to it that you never become mistress of Glendower Park. Do I make myself quite clear? Buck Jones belongs to me. I worship him — for the first time in my miserable life I really love someone other than myself. I would do anything for him — I've offered to buy him a commission in the army, to give him money, take away the hardships, the struggles he's always known. And he's refused it all with his stupid, pig-headed pride! Now he and I are all but finished and all because you threw yourself at him, titillated his senses, his masculinity!'

Esther felt the cruelty of it all. She understood then just how madly possessive Amanda was over Buck Jones, that he did not love her in return, that she was being blamed for Amanda's unrequited love — although she had only seen the man twice in her life.

Before she had time to assimilate completely the full significance of what was happening, Amanda rushed at her and slapped Esther across the face with the palm of her ringed hand.

She was oblivious of the goblet falling and smashing against the table in a shower of tiny crystals. Her amber eyes blazed as Esther's hand flew to her cheek.

'How dare you, Lady Lightfoot!' Esther breathed, trying to control the murder in her heart, which was soaring by the minute, threatening to overwhelm them both.

94

Amanda leaned against the table for support, cutting her hand on a small shard of glass. 'You have ruined me, you stupid, shallow, Irish strumpet!' Her words hissed ruthlessly through the awful silence that followed, falling like a whiplash on Esther, who knew, by age and breeding, she could never hit this woman back. 'He never would have left me if it hadn't been for you!'

Esther was stunned. It was not the words themselves that appalled her, it was the hatred behind them that was so horrifying. Such a transformation had come over Amanda's features that she recoiled before the change. All that had ever been pleasant and beguiling had given way to a wild and frightening malevolence.

Esther's eyes widened in horror as she stood rooted to the spot. The woman was mad, utterly mad.

Esther backed away to the door. 'I have not done this to you, Lady Lightfoot!' she cried, 'You have done it to yourself!' She opened the door wanting only to escape the dreadful woman and her rich, terrible room.

'I hate you!' Amanda screamed, hysterical. 'I hate you more than I have ever hated anyone in my entire life!'

'You can hate me all you like, Lady Lightfoot, it will not change a thing!' Esther slammed the door angrily behind her. She had to get away from this horrible house.

Momentarily, the feel of the sun and the sound of movement, the crowding of colour and life along the street, eased the sickness in her, warming the numbness which was confusing her. But she felt inside the real disturbance of something she did not fully understand.

CHAPTER
Nine

Throughout the months on the frontier, Esther had come to realize that the feeling between Laree and Roydon was far deeper and far stronger than she had ever imagined. She had never thought it would last, but it had survived against great obstacles. Now, when Laree told her that Roydon wanted to approach Joshua on the matter of a marriage between them, Esther felt she could no longer stand in her sister's way. And after all the months of trial and tribulation she no longer wanted to keep Laree from a happiness she herself longed to experience. She offered to broach the subject to her father, thus paving the way for Roydon. Joshua agreed as he was in dire financial straits and he knew that Laree would be well looked after by the Wilsons, his staunchest friends and allies in frontier affairs.

The young couple's happiness was obvious to all as arrangements were made for a spring wedding. A marriage licence was obtained in Grahamstown, through the help of Garnet, now a more frequent visitor to Dwyers' Cross. If Esther expected him to address her about his own serious intentions she was to be disappointed. Although he was attentive to her, he was astute and careful enough not to compromise himself. So she languished on the farm, going about her daily routine, trying to devise ways and means of forcing his hand without appearing to do so. Even though he tried to spread his attentions to other unmarried women, she knew that it was she who held his interest. But she had learned that he was a cautious man who had enjoyed the freedom of his bachelorhood for a long time, and he would not want to give it up to just anyone. When he did, it would have to be to a woman he loved and respected, and who loved and respected him. She could not therefore push him too far or too fast, or she would risk breaking their friendship, and so she was forced, against her nature, to bide her time.

It was autumn. The wily Mazwi had escaped Garnet and his men, but the cattle were reclaimed. A fort was constructed on the Keiskamma River commanding the narrowest neck of the neutral territory. It was called after Colonel Willshire, former commandant of the forces on the frontier. This fort now stood on the lands close to those of the Mazwis.

At Dwyers' Cross the wheat and Indian corn had been planted in the renewed hope of a good harvest. The Acting-Governor, Sir Rufane Donkin, visited the frontier, staying overnight with the Dwyers in their recently completed, double-storied, stone house — one of the few settlers' homes boasting a pan-tiled roof made on their own land.

Autumn fled and winter advanced, with the warmth of summer a forgotten memory. Bitterly cold days and nights followed, but still there was no sign of the expected rain. The time allotted for the help of the Hottentot guards ended, and they left to work for their own masters, various Boers near Grahamstown, who had lent them out.

As the unsuitability of the soil for crops became clearer, the settlers, including the Dwyers, had acquired more and more cattle. Sir Rufane Donkin, on his visit to the location, discussed this matter with Joshua and Cady and agreed to suggest to Lord Charles Somerset, the absent Governor, on his return to the colony, that the lands be extended considerably to make pastoral farming a feasible proposition.

It was not long however before some cattle were stolen by a party of Xhosas on their way to the clay pits, not more than half a mile from the farmhouse. Consternation raged among those still living on the farm, and immediately Cady and Sam rode out to confront the marauders, only to find that they had mysteriously melted away into the seemingly impenetrable bush. From then on the men had shifts of guard duty near the pits.

Spring burst forth in Albany with the vivid, scarlet fowers of the kaffirbooms spotting the kloofs, and here and there, the tufted gold of the mimosa and the delicate pink frothing of peach blossoms. As the sweet, elusive fragrance of wild jasmine and honeysuckle scented the air, Laree was married to Roydon at Dwyers' Cross by the visiting preacher, the festivities continuing long after the bridal couple had left for their honeymoon in Port Elizabeth. Arthur and

Charity Wilson had rallied to help Joshua with the preparations, as had several of the neighbouring farmers' wives. The Wilsons had a small cottage prepared for the couple in the grounds of their farm, Sunfield Park, in the Blaaukranz Valley.

As soon as the wedding was over, the shattering news that the wheat crop had failed a second time flashed from one end of the frontier to the other. More men left the land to seek work in the growing towns of Grahamstown, Port Elizabeth and even as far as Uitenhage and Graff-Reinet. The mass of defections grew daily, proving that the strict pass-system forbidding the settlers to move from one place to another without permission had failed.

Joshua and Cady managed to keep their party together and to prevent the total disintegration by forceful authority and the giving of helpful advice to those who remained. And still Somerset Farm, belonging to the government, at the foot of the Boschberg, continued to hold the monopoly of produce for the colonists and the military.

It was in December that the good news of Laree's pregnancy was made known, and Esther set about making and stitching hundreds and hundreds of tiny tucks into a growing mound of baby garments — yards and yards of binders, matinee jackets, veils, shawls, socks, gloves and nightgowns of flannel embroidered in silk, from all the scraps and cast-offs she could find.

Esther was well aware that although two years older than Laree, it was she who was still single and unattached. Partly because she was so beautiful and therefore a dangerous rival for the other women of Albany in their search for suitable husbands, and partly because she was so arrogantly scornful of the looks and remarks that came her way, Esther was singled out for ostracism. Carefully and unobtrusively she was left out of certain entertainments and parties, slyly ignored by those who resented her most and feared her competition.

But they would never know the loneliness, the frustrations and the despair she kept hidden from them. In her own private misery she weathered the storm until other more pressing matters came to the fore.

The new year of 1822 sped by and it was early autumn once more, and still hot. The sky was a hard brilliant blue against the hills. Little hamlets had sprung up, and criss-crossing the countryside were new tracks winding through the bush.

The labour shortage had become acute, and the menace of the tribesmen encroaching on the colonial borders was growing. Lord Charles Somerset, the Cape governor, had returned some months previously from England, furious at the drastic changes made by Sir Rufane Donkin in his absence. Promptly Lord Somerset changed back most of the departing Governor's policies, causing more conflict and confusion among the settlers. And pervading the whole atmosphere was the continuing lack of rain.

It was at this time that Joshua and Cady faced a large crowd of Xhosas, men and women, fetching ochre clay at the pits near the farmhouse. They were on the point of firing into the hostile crowd when a redcoat charged up and stopped them. He explained that the Xhosas had been given permission to collect the clay by Colonel Willshire at the fort on the Keiskamma River.

The Dwyers returned to the farm, angry at having been kept in ignorance of the permission granted to the Xhosas. It was becoming obvious that their irascible attitude towards the Xhosas was causing growing hostility among the tribesmen, who did not understand their behaviour, having always collected their clay at the pits.

The Dwyers, in turn, did not understand the importance of the clay to the Xhosas and regarded its collection as a violation of their land. Feelings of antagonism mounted on both sides.

A week later, on a hot afternoon, Esther and Joshua waited for Cady, Sam, James Coffee and a young farmhand to return from getting supplies in Bathurst.

Another day, Esther thought hopelessly, hoeing the vegetable garden listlessly, another day of endless drudgery with very little fun in sight. And now there was the added problem of the Xhosas waiting their chance to come over the hills to steal their cattle. She wondered dully if perhaps Lord Charles Somerset had been right in dictating that they should not have cattle, for surely he had known the price they would pay for it? But that was a matter she could never discuss with her father or Uncle Cady who were hotly against the Governor on that issue.

She felt so tired of it all, the struggles, the disappointments, the dreadful bordeom. This place frightened her, she who had seldom been frightened easily by anything in her life.

She lifted her head, her eyes stopping abruptly at some point on the far side of the fields. Shading her eyes with one hand, she made out the figure of a man weaving towards the farmstead across the fields, as if he was drunk . . .

There was something familiar about the man, but he was still too far away to recognize. Then she knew — it was Sam. She would know that tall, lanky frame anywhere, the coal-black hair without a hat.

Something was wrong. Terribly, terribly wrong. She looked about for the cart and the other men who had gone with him to Bathurst. But of them, there was nothing.

Without further hesitation, she threw down the hoe and started to run towards Sam, her cotton skirts flying out behind her.

'By all the saints, Sam!' she cried aghast as he staggered towards her, his face haggard. 'Whatever has happened? Where is my uncle and James Coffee, and Andrew Harding, the new boy?'

'Miss Esther,' he gasped, trying to regain his breath, 'the cart was ambushed — and attacked by — by a band of Xhosa warriors, a few miles from Dwyers' Cross. They jumped at us — from the overhanging rocks — and fell on the cart with assegaais!' He watched her closely as he spoke. There was a kindling in his black eyes, and his mouth took on a harder, more bitter line.

Esther could hardly breathe and when she spoke her voice was hardly recognizable. 'Mercy be! And what has happened to my uncle and the others?'

'Mr Cady was wounded in the leg but he managed to crawl to safety, dragging James Coffee with him — Coffee was badly hit, I don't think he has a chance — and young Harding — he was killed outright. I managed to escape to get help — with the Xhosas after me. I didn't think I'd make it!'

'Oh Sam — come back to the farmhouse — we must tell my father at once!'

Sam's voice rose to harsh coldness. 'That we must, Miss Esther, those tribesmen are not going to get away with this — and we need to find your uncle as quickly as possible.'

'I'll go then, Sam. I'll run back to tell my father and you follow as best as you can.' Before he could say any more, Esther, with red curls streaming from underneath her housecap, was running back to the house at full speed. She left Sam staring after her in surprised silence, then slowly he forced himself on after her with tired urgency.

From far away, he saw Joshua emerge from the cottage, and before he reached it, the older man was mounted on his horse. Pulling

100

Sam up behind him, they were soon speeding away in the direction of the ambush.

Joshua came back with Sam some hours later with the news that neither Cady nor James Coffee could be found. They had brought back the body of Andrew Harding which was lying in the dust beside the upturned cart. Then, taking the rest of the men with them, they scoured the bush and on the following day, after an exhausting search, they found Cady stumbling home. He had left Coffee's body in the shelter of bushes where he had died during the night. Cady was taken to the Kaffir Drift military post, thirteen miles away, for medical attention, and later brought back, barely alive.

That August Cady gradually recovered, spurred on by the birth of Laree's daughter, and named after her late grandmother Emma, which delighted them all.

The general economic position became alarmingly critical through roaring days of wind and no rain. In early spring the new type of beardless Bengal wheat, supposed to be free of rust, started to poke through the thirsty earth, as anxious eyes searched the sky for rain. Then before them all, the dreaded rust appeared, dashing their hopes for a third season.

It was at that time, under a sky pocked with a few feathery clouds moving before a light wind, that a scream wailed, high and terrified, its echoes rolling down the Coombs Valley. Everyone stopped in their tracks at the farm, then grabbed muskets and pistols. It was learned soon afterwards that Patrick O'Leary, the fourteen-year-old herdboy had disappeared while tending the sheep near the river.

A full week later his body was discovered in a kloof, mutilated by hundreds of assegaai wounds. He was buried on a vacant piece of land beside James Coffee. Joshua performed the short burial service amid the silence of the small group of men and women around him. There was an awful stillness when he finished, broken only by the chirping of the weaver-birds flying backwards and forwards to their nests hanging from the willows beside the river.

They stood, a handful of people, in the vast silence, small and insignificant. As they returned their brother to the earth, their hearts filled with terrible bitterness and hatred that only man can have for man — a dreadful blackness that would grow as day followed day. The hope of revenge would become the sweetest thing on earth, a

101

terrifying point when respect and love of life becomes distorted, vanishing in the primitive laws of the jungle, where there is no justice, only the law of survival.

Frustration, fear and outrage reduced the concepts of good and evil in the minds of those standing under the sun's warming rays, where nothing was considered sacred anymore, and all the Xhosas without exception became to them, dangerous and savage enemies. As the days passed and the warmth of the sun strengthened, so did the blackness in their hearts.

In October a scheme was drawn up for the formation of a local militia to patrol the border against cattle raids. It was only to last three years, as regular patrolling could not take place owing to the militia-men's need to attend to their farming. But in the short time it lasted, it was to have a certain restraining influence on the tribesmen across the border.

The pleasant hamlet of Longwood had grown up some miles from the farm, and a store, a blacksmith's shop and a brandy tavern had been opened. It was to be the latter from which either Joshua or Cady had to regularly rescue their remaining men. Both of them still rode from farm to farm in the area in an effort to keep the location going.

Before the local militia had been formed and could operate, the removing of all military protection from the Coombs Valley locations had allowed the cattle thefts to grow alarmingly, much to the mounting fury of the farmers. There was more trouble between the Dwyers and the Xhosas near the pits, and some more cattle were stolen towards the end of February.

It was an oppressively hot day. There had been a mild storm of scattered showers the day before, but nothing else. The curtains of the house had scarcely stirred in the early morning and Esther had known as she woke that it would be another scorching day.

A bright light lay everywhere. The trees were chocked with dust and where streams had once run there were now straggles of dry soil over the stricken earth. The drought from the far northern wastelands had arrived with a vengeance, days of burning glare and hot, berg winds.

She stood in the heat of the kitchen, the room buzzing with sticky flies. The iron pot swung gently on its corner over the fire, the air full of the odour of thick soup. Damp tendrils of hair stuck to her forehead about her ears, giving her an almost raffish look, accentuating the grace of her neck.

She rolled up her sleeves and placed a bacon dish and black pudding on the table in preparation for the midday meal. The house steamed with the brassy glare of sunshine pouring in through the door, thrown open on to the kitchen garden. The bright light took all colour from outside as the loud clang of hammer and anvil echoed from Murtagh Dougherty's forge across the yard. The sound was broken only by the low, steady whirr of a flight of plump quails disappearing among the thickets of spekboom. A hoepoe took off from under a mimosa tree and armies of ants trailed across the dust.

Esther ran a tongue over dry lips. The flies buzzed continuously, onc lighting on her hair. With growing irritation she brushed it away and looked out of the open door. Her dark blue eyes followed a hawk as it rose from a thorny acacia, beating upwards in a slow majestic spiral and then drifting eastwards on a cushion of air.

How she longed to be that bird just then, to soar from the imprisoning cage in which she found herself, break the bars and fly away, free. How she longed to wear lovely clothes again, eat delicious, exotic foods, and feel the texture of soft, fine sheets around her body.

There were very few vegetables left, and very little flour. A sack of American flour stood against one wall, brought all the way from Cape Town during the continual drought.

She was restless, her temper simmering with the increasing heat. It did not matter to her in that moment that the hated pass-system was finally abolished. She cared little for the fact that her father and uncle had helped Mr Thomas Pringle try to establish a free press in the colony, or that they struggled against the Governor's opposition to their setting up a monthly magazine. She spared no thought for the continual smuggling between border farmers and the Xhosas, or for the settler scheme that was being eroded by the severe economic disasters.

What she did care about was the fact that, because more men were moving away into the towns, she was now required to milk the cows. She could hear the endless swish of the milk into the pail, and the heartbeat of the cows. She could feel their warmth in the cold barn in the early morning. She had to stick to it, because the cows had got used to her, and liked to be milked by one person only.

103

The anthill oven was heated twice a week and she baked all the bread required, there being only a few women left to help her. She made teacakes and johnny cakes as only the Indian corn had survived.

Now she clenched her fists crossly. She had become a farm girl. Her fine breeding meant nothing, nothing at all. Her worst fears still haunted her. She did not want to become a lonely spinster untouched by feelings for any man, she could not bear the thought. But as the days passed it seemed to become more of an ugly reality.

She had seen Garnet a few times, and although he still seemed to be attracted to her, he was suspiciously non-committal about his feelings for her. Now that she was no longer invited to many of the parties where she could meet him, she had to rely on those times when he chose to visit the farm.

Her growing desire to escape Dwyers' Cross with all its dangers and fears, grew. So she waited day after day, week after week, for Garnet's decision, in the dwindling hope that he had not found someone else.

The barking of a watchdog suddenly disturbed the quiet. In the distance she could hear the pounding of horses' hooves over the turf. Her curiosity was instantly aroused. Peeling off her soiled apron, she walked to the door and out into the bright sunshine.

At first she thought that it was possibly one of the new smouses who loaded their wagons with trinkets and household goods, travelling about the settlement selling and bartering their wares. Then she realized there were horses but no wagon.

Searching the brassy sky for signs of rain clouds, she was pleased with a diversion in her long day. She was all smiles until the leading rider came into sight, his tall figure outlined against the sky. Then she felt suddenly cold. It was Sergeant Buck Jones and two Hottentot Cape Corps cavalrymen, leading two familiar Dwyers' Cross black cows. They were obviously the ones stolen from the farm.

She stood still as the horses' hooves threw clods of sand high across the wild fields. Buck Jones moved forward, ahead of the others on a large chestnut horse. He leapt a sprawling, dry ditch, the galloping hooves tearing up the turf, his jacket a scarlet flash. The dust he raised hid the men and the cows behind him.

Esther watched him, conscious of the sudden tension and nervousness in her. She had not seen him since the party at

Glendower Park, and she did not know how to behave towards him. She was uncomfortably aware of all that she now knew of him and the scene with Amanda Lightfoot flashed into her mind with all its searing pain and bitterness. Her only salvation was to think of Garnet and her plan to marry him. It gave her the courage to face the sergeant.

She drew herself up proudly as he dismounted, tethering his horse to a stake under a large mimosa tree across the yard, and strode towards her, spur rowels clinking behind him. The glare of his red jacket and the white crossbelt hurt her eyes. For one wild, unreasoning moment her life flared into vivid, lively colour, all the drab routine, the isolation about her, faded away.

'Well, this is a pleasant surprise, Miss Dwyer,' he said, and there was a touch of irony in his mocking tone. He bowed, smiling at her from familiar blue eyes. The dimples in his cheeks were deeply and wickedly cleft as he stood before her. The spectre of Amanda Lightfoot rose between them, intangible but strong, and an unexpected sense of pain filled Esther's heart. She knew what she must do.

With an effort she said, in the coldest and most condescending manner, 'Good day, Sergeant Jones, and what brings you in such haste to this remote spot?'

He raised one thick, well-defined eyebrow, watching her. A faint half-smile now played on his lips as if he knew exactly what was going on in her mind. 'While we were out hunting tigers in the jungle we happened upon two stolen black cows, Your Highness, branded with the mark of Dwyers' Cross.'

'There are no tigers in Africa, Sergeant Jones, as you well know,' she retorted, resenting his effect on her, the masculine assurance of his bearing. But she was conscious of an unwilling excitement, seeing him arrogantly mocking, and recklessly attractive. Here they were, just the two of them, together in a wild place where only the elements really ruled, in an atmosphere bristling with tension.

His husky voice broke into her thoughts. 'Bravo, Miss Dwyer — you are learning faster than some. If I recall correctly, there were some settlers who mistook the glow of fireflies for tiger's eyes.'

Her eyes lost their excitement at seeing him, and she blushed scarlet. There was still so much of the girl in her at war with the young woman, and this man had the knack of bringing it quickly to

105

the surface. Yet, for all her annoyance with him, she was very much aware of everything about him — of the long, strong lines of his body, of the skin above the jacket, tanned and healthy. She was surprised to see, at close quarters, faint lines of weariness about his face as silently, reluctantly, she felt drawn once more towards him. She understood very well what such feelings had done to Amanda Lightfoot, and she did not want them to do the same to her.

She tried to change her thoughts, finding her emotions distasteful. The dog bounded up with the two other horsemen, and whimpered and sniffed about Buck's legs.

'You have a good animal here,' he said, bending down. There was a note of affection in his voice as he patted the dog's head, fondling its ears.

Carelessly his hand brushed hers. She felt a sudden stillness envelop them. Vividly aware of the heat of the sun and the spicy scent of the shrubs, she was still overwhelmingly conscious of the man facing her. Confused, she looked away. She was irritated by the way in which he had skilfully cut through her superior attitude, the artificial postering she had assumed to save herself from him. She knew she had asked for it. But the magnetic attraction still remained beneath all the irritation.

However, she would not give him his victory. 'Mind your manners, Sergeant Jones,' she said with tart insolence, referring to his former statement about tiger's eyes. 'Please remember who you are addressing.'

She saw his cheeks crease again with a maddeningly slow and mischievous smile. 'As if you would ever let me forget, Miss Dwyer.' He folded his arms, still clasping his riding whip.

The temper that had simmered all morning now flared.

'You must really be the vilest of toads that I have ever had the misfortune to meet, Sergeant Jones!' she snapped, with more than a touch of spirit.

He did not seem surprised or insulted. Undaunted, he lifted his brows quizzically, a twist of humour about his beautifully moulded lips. But never had he looked more challenging. 'This is indeed a crushing moment, Miss! I have been called some names in my life, but I must confess never to have been called "a toad".'

She saw him struggling to hold back his deep amusement. Then, to her rising dismay, he threw back his head, letting out rich, infectious laughter. 'This has really made my day — the vilest of toads!'

'Oh, but you are insufferable!' Esther cried angrily, her rage pouring out. She stamped her foot. 'You just get off this land, do you hear me — this instant!'

'And take your father's cows with me?' The laughter suddenly died away. He was smiling no longer. She saw before her the firm, tanned face, strong nose and hard eyes, which the sunlight had turned to steel. A frown darkened his attractive face and his eyes locked on to hers with a cool cynicism she did not understand. 'My dear young woman, if it were not for these two men and myself, those cows would have ended up as karosses for some dusky maidens in Xhosaland by now — black karosses being much favoured in those parts, I'll have you know.'

A hot flush sprang to her cheeks. With confused, angry thoughts, she tried to make up for her rude behaviour without apologizing. 'It is all the fault of the Governor — by allowing clay fairs at the pits he has encouraged the Xhosa on to our land. They steal our cattle and as we have been successfully cut off from trade with them completely, we are forbidden any legal contact with them which might help matters between us.'

Behind the pattern of her beautiful face, she was outraged. The red blushes on her cheeks had settled into a dark glow, the flush of sudden battle in her face.

He was surprised; it showed in his voice. 'Let me remind you, sweetheart, that your kinsmen have done nothing to endear themselves to the Xhosas. There is a disturbing sign of revenge and bloodlust among 'em. Most of your men want a fight because fighting will unleash that suppressed savagery in 'em.' His jaw tightened, and there was a grim expression on his face. 'I've seen that same lust often on the battlefield. You would do well to remember it.'

'It is the policy of Lord Charles Somerset and no one else, that has led to this dreadful state of affairs. This is our land, Sergeant Jones. My kinsmen have suffered to break this soil and make homes here. They have endured too much at the hands of those black savages across the border.' Her hands trembled slightly. His eyes held hers. There was a fire in their startling depths, and she felt the colour deepen in her cheeks.

'It is not as simple as that.' His tone underlined the inadequacy of

107

her statement. 'The Xhosas have also in their turn suffered at the hands of the white men — especially old Chieftain Mazwi and his tribe, living closest to the border. He remembers, while a boy, the first friendly meetings between white and black near the Fish River — each looking for new lands, new pastures for their cattle,' he said curtly, looking down at her. 'He fought as a young warrior against the white man later, lusting for blood with the rest, but now he is old and wants only peace for his people.'

His eyes were still on her, gauging her, watching for every shade of thought and emotion in her. She flushed with indignation. 'If he wants peace then he should keep his warriors off our land. They take what is not theirs.'

'Who is to say what land is rightfully ours or theirs, Miss Dwyer? You — or they? Mazwi and his people claim that the land between the Fish River and Sundays River is theirs by right of conquest and occupation before 1812 when the Fourth Frontier War drove them out forever.' He paused, a frown creasing his brow once more.

Esther looked at him, wondering suddenly what memories lived behind those vivid eyes.

'That old man is one of our few allies in a territory combed by hostile clans. Your kinsmen are making all the enemies they can among his people.'

The effect of his words was disconcerting. The red head lifted proudly as she stared at him, keeping her hands folded tightly before her. 'If the old chieftain is right then all our lands here belong to him, and that I do not believe for one minute. We have been given these lands by a rightful government. What Mazwi says is backed by nothing but words.' She was now full of stiff indignation.

She saw something flash in his eyes but it was gone before she could be sure of what it was. 'The white man has set himself up through force of conquest and accumulated wealth, sweetheart, as prince of it all. He has his own privileges and forces them on those he considers weaker and more primitive than himself. He has the stronger weapons, the more experience, so who is right? The conqueror or the conquered when force has made it so?'

The statement provoked Esther like a slap in the face. She bridled angrily. 'You make a mockery and a farce of it all, Sergeant! My kinsmen own this land for whatever reason, and they shall keep it in the way they see fit!'

108

Buck seemed about to say something, then stopped. He shrugged his broad shoulders, his face enigmatic. 'If they have the right, then they have the greatest responsibility for peace here on the border, and that must not be lightly taken.'

'By what right have you to say this?' she retorted. 'And how is it you claim to know so much about the thoughts of the Xhosas? So much more than most?'

'I happen to speak the Xhosa language — an accomplishment I share with Captain Somerset among very few others.' He drew a breath, studying her with cool appraisal. 'I would say I am a good ten years older than yourself, Miss Dwyer, and that in spite of my so-called lowly station, I am a fairly knowledgeable fellow. But don't hold that against me, just call it experience,' he said, the mockery once more disturbing the blueness of his gaze.

She knew he spoke the truth without boasting, but meeting it so directly, she resented it. She saw that she was fighting too many feelings for him and about him. She wanted him to like her, but she was afraid. Then, recovering, she burst out, 'You are arrogant, Sergeant Jones — please leave now. I never want to see you again.'

'Never is a very long time, Miss Dwyer.' The blue eyes were suddenly nonchalant, and yet, watchful. 'I had best get the cows to your father without further delay.' There was the slightest hint of impatience, as if he no longer wanted to stay, and she felt a rush of disappointment.

Angry and confused, she turned away and flew back to the kitchen, her face aflame once more. There she became a whirlwind of activity, taking her anger out on the dishes lying on the table.

Now the blustery, hot wind had arisen and she could hear it in the trees, a constant low whistle, and dervishes of pale dust spun across the open spaces. But no matter how hard she worked, there was no way to blot out her need to love and be loved.

She looked down at her strong-fingered hands. She usually found cooking satisfying, and in housework she could force herself to forget, but nothing in her life could ever be a substitute for loving, caring flesh and blood.

CHAPTER
Ten

March of 1823 found the settlers again frustrated as they still were not allowed to hold public meetings. A memorandum was signed and sent to England, setting out their grievances. Sir Rufane Donkin defended his recent administration before the government in England, and the British press took up the matter. Debates began in the House of Commons, bringing the state of affairs to the British public.

But many thousands of miles away, on the frontier, the land was dying. The scattered showers ceased and the relentless sun called attention to the overwhelming thirst of men, beast and earth.

At Dwyers' Cross the river began slowly to dry up and there was only enough water in the pools for drinking purposes. There was not enough to drive the flour mills on the river or to grind the Indian corn into flour. For several weeks they ground a small daily supply with the coffee mill, but as the handle kept breaking they were reduced to bruising the corn by crushing a few grains at a time with a round stone on a flat one. In this way they managed to get a few small cakes of very sweet, coarse meal daily.

Soap was made from pumpkins which they were told by the Boers would last at least a year. In Joshua's vineyard the terraces of leaves browned in the autumn, the first season of wizened grapes still clutching the tendrils.

The winter that year turned especially bitter and cold, the winds high, whipping through the fields like some wild creature bent on destruction. The piling clouds were rent in shreds and blown away by its force. It shrieked through the choked ravines and forests of close-packed trees, up the kranzes and down from the snowcapped

Amatole Mountains, spreading like a gigantic chain across the Fish River Valley.

The ploughlands at Dwyers' Cross lay quiet and full under the restless sky, the cycle of creation slowly begining in the weeks ahead, carrying in their earthly womb the hopes of the men for the following spring.

By the end of September the rains had still not broken. Small clouds gathered in the afternoon, but by evening they disappeared. At Dwyers' Cross they had made barley bread, ground Indian corn for johnny cakes and porridge, and preparations were now well under way for the evening meal. Esther stood at the kitchen door, checks flushed, her dark blue eyes alive with laughter. Cocked saucily over her red-gold curls, was her muslin cap, daintily frilled.

Her mouth wrinkled, suppressing mirth as she watched Sam giving the men gathered around a skilful display of handling his twenty-foot long oxhide whip, by flicking off the necks of a dozen bottles in a row, standing some distance away. There were hoots of laughter as John Tobias tried, and only managed to get the whip tangled in a knot.

The glowing colour of the sun spread over the western hills, fringing the high milkwoods in the early evening. And beyond, the forest of lichen-covered trees rose, covering the hillside. The loud squawk of Hadeda birds rose into the sunset and swifts sped across the sky after insects.

Through the open kitchen door the smell of earth, foliage and manure invaded the room glimmering with the light from newly-lit candles. In the thick undergrowth, bullfrogs croaked and Esther was no longer startled when a bat ghosted silently by her, across the yard. A small barn owl shrieked suddenly nearby, as the dying sun cast a deeper red-golden wash over the landscape.

The watchdogs lay down outside, waiting for the scraps from the table, guarding the farmstead. A deep peace settled with the cooing of turtledoves in the tall milkwood trees rising up to the sky, on the edge of the clearing.

Suddenly a spasm of barking from a pack of wild dogs in the hills broke out, echoing eerily across the valley. Many pairs of eyes looked in the direction of the sound, the whip and bottles abruptly forgotten, as the laughter died away. Then they fell silent, listening.

After some seconds they all turned back as nothing more was

111

heard. Beyond the yard the dogs were alert, watching the milkwoods and the thickets of spekboom and wag-'n-bietjie bushes around the clearing on which the house and its lands stood. They barked, their hackles rising as they padded up and down the turf.

Through the stillness of the evening, another sound of barking rose, this time much nearer. Sam grabbed his musket and rushed across the yard. 'I think those brutes are after the sheep! And they sound ravenous to me!' he cried, calling the men who were moving back towards their huts.

The next moment, the noise split the surroundings with searing, dreadful howls coming from the direction of the sheep kraal. Joshua reached the door, followed by Cady, in time to hear that there was a pack of about thirty of the ferocious beasts after the sheep.

'Esther — you stay here!' Joshua ordered, immediately reaching for his musket leaning near the door. 'Go inside, girl, there may be trouble — and close the door.'

For a brief second Esther was alarmed. She felt the quick prick of fear tingle her scalp, then she slammed the door shut and ran to the window where she pulled back the curtains.

Most of the watchdogs had bounded off, rushing wildly across the rectangle of cleared ground. The sound of rushing feet in all directions blotted out all other sounds for a while, and raised voices yelled to one another as the men mustered for the attack. All around, the wild dogs set up a howling, savaging fifteen sheep before the retort of a gun hit the air. Not even fierce watchdogs could stand against the vicious, hungry packs of some of the worst killers in Africa.

Soon, in frenzied pain, six of the watchdogs were killed, savaged beyond recognition. The wild dogs were chased from the kraal; John Tobias, tragically, was in their way, and one of the wild dogs leapt at him, and felled him to the ground in an instant, in a furious ball of ferocity. John's high-pitched screams of terror and pain rent the air, lacerating it with agony. Another wild dog ran up, biting and snapping at his legs. He screamed again in mad terror, and this time the men were running up in blinding mad rage. One of the surviving watchdogs hurtled forward and jumped towards the throat of one of the wild dogs. The animal was thrown off as the fangs of the wild dog sank into its neck.

Esther froze with fright. She saw her uncle raise his musket coming in fairly close to the wild beast, and aim. For one sharp instant he and the dog stared at each other with burning hatred. Cady let the shot free and the dog fell, its jaws flecked with white foam. The other dog left John and bounded away in wild crazy flight. Sam managed to shoot it as it leapt away, and it dropped to the ground, howling.

Murtagh Dougherty gave a stricken cry and ran forward. He bent over the broken body of John, and wept openly. The rest of the men stood aghast, staring down at him.

Esther knew the young man was dead. Her eyes filled with tears as she remembered how John had arrived in Passage West with O'Reilly's party to see his aunt who lived in Cork City. He was seventeen years old. While waiting for the others to sail, he had asked to join the ships going to the Cape. After some time he had been accepted, but only on the condition that he worked as a member of the crew. She remembered how he had been tied to the masts of the *Poseidon* during one of the worst storms of the voyage around Cape Point, to prevent him from falling overboard. He had been the one bitten by the puff-adder, had recovered, and now, after all those hardships, he had gone, never to smile and laugh again.

She watched her father and uncle walk over to Murtagh who had become friendly with the young man, treating him like a younger brother. They stood over him for some agonising moments. Murtagh looked up empty-eyed, his brown jerkin soaked in blood. The laughter of only minutes before had turned into sorrow and bloodshed.

Esther turned away in that lonely, silent kitchen and wept as if her heart would break. She leaned against the wall, her shoulders heaving with painful, wracking sobs as she had not done in years.

She had learned in her months on the frontier, that Nature was full of death and cruelty, and even though it was a savagery without real evil, as man did to man, this was the final straw which broke her down. It let out all the repressed feelings of months, years — all the grief, the sorrow, the frustrations, the fears flowed out in a full, never-ending stream, until she thought she would never have any tears left to cry again.

The wind rose that night, drumming loudly against the windows and doors and among the trees. Esther tossed and turned in her bed, listening to the rattle of the branches carried by the increased howl of the wind. The cold moon, blanketed by thin cloud, slipped behind one of the far crests of the hills and left the valley in darkness, the terror of the bush lost in it.

It was a long, restless night, a churning of thoughts and images, terrifying and fierce. Esther fell into a doze and woke again, her heart galloping with fear. Her mind was distorted by a nightmare from which she had rudely awakened. She was cold with sweat, the morbid atmosphere of the dream still clinging around her.

It was still pitch dark, the blackness closing in on her as the old ghosts of the past nudged their way into her mind, carefree days speeding by on wings of forgotten gaiety, laughter and security. They faded and she was surrounded by a horror she had never known existed. The shock of what had happened had violated her mind far more deeply than she had realized up until then.

She lay in the darkness, clenching her fists as the shadow of fear once more placed a cold hand on her heart. Unbidden the terrible images of the wild dogs and the dead Irish boy forced themselves on her. They swarmed about her, pressing down into her fevered, tortured mind. She thrashed backwards and forwards, trying to free herself of their dreadful clutches. A wild impulse to beat on the door, to scream in futile terror overtook her, and she needed all her powers of control to calm herself.

Hours later, the clouds had been blown away and the wind dropped. It was still outside, the fields and hills, stretching away into the velvet night, under its canopy of bright stars, so low that they seemed to be falling down the distant horizon. So quiet and peaceful, yet holding so many dangers. Finally she slipped into an exhausted, dreamless sleep as the first rays of dawn crept over the hills to the east.

Esther surfaced slowly from a deep sleep. For some moments she had no idea where she was or what she had dreamt. She opened her eyes and it all came flooding back — the nightmare, the death of John Tobias. She felt swamped suddenly by the prospect of facing the simple funeral ahead, but she refused to show it. She heard her uncle calling her from downstairs, heard her father saddle his horse for his early routine inspection of the lands with Cady and Sam. And she recalled with a start that she was late cooking the breakfast.

Rising quickly, her fingers fumbled with buttons and arranging her hair. She looked pale and there were dark hollows under her eyes.

I hate this harsh place, she thought, with the impulse of deep resentment. It was as if the land was living, being capable of wreaking a vengeance all its own, a sleeping dragon, breathing fire and brimstone at whim, bringing terror and hardship to all who dared to carve out a living on it.

Outside the air was once more full of the high shriek of the Hadeda birds. She picked up the brush again, pulling it fiercely through the tangle of curls. If she had any sense at all she would fight tooth and nail to get away from this place before it was too late and she became an old maid, prematurely worn and faded.

Then she thought of Garnet Fitzwilliam. She had almost given up all dreams of him. The hope now came to her that one day he would come and take her away from Dwyers' Cross — to his home at Glendower Park, as his wife. She threw the brush on to the dressing table in a fit of pique. How she wanted to be the mistress of Glendower Park! All the doors to high society would be open to her then, to enter and ignore as she wished. She would have servants, wonderful clothes, jewels, fine horses, entertainments — everything. And she would never have to think about farm work again.

Her firm jaw tightened. Then she smiled to herself, her resilient spirits stretching themselves once more. If he does not get around to thinking of me anymore, I will just have to remind him to do so.

She straightened her back, loosening the shawl she had thrown about her shoulders, and tucking it into the wide, white pinafore. She nodded her head, setting the wine-red curls dancing, as she reached for her housecap, a new gleam in her eye. That was what she would do. She would find a way of reaching Captain Fitzwilliam.

It seemed an impossible task as she now saw him so seldom, but she was determined she would succeed in spite of the obstacles, in spite of all those sour, self-satisfied, old matrons who wanted him for their own washed-out, simpering daughters, and in spite of Miss Beatrice Cummings, the most pretty and intelligent of them all, who seemed to be the main contender for Garnet's hand.

Suddenly an idea began to form in her mind. She remembered that Garnet was intending to stay for a few weeks with friends of his near Port Frances. She knew that her father's friends, Major and Mrs Powell, the Resident of Kowie and Harbour Master, lived there and that her father regularly saw them when he was at the Port.

Somehow she would tell her father about the dreadful nightmares and ask if she could stay for a few weeks with the Powells to get away for a rest, and she would see to it that the time coincided with the dates of Garnet's stay near the Port. She would find out through her father when Garnet would be there and she would make sure that he knew she would be staying with the Powells.

Hugging her new idea to herself, she started to run downstairs, humming out of tune under her breath. The world had suddenly and unexpectedly taken a new turn, and a quite different and brighter light.

Major Powell and his wife, Lydia, were a childless couple who adored young people. They were only too eager to have Esther to stay, and so it was that Sam took her in the wagon to their cottage set on a hill overlooking the sea and the river mouth.

Esther enjoyed the delightful company of the couple who took her to their hearts with such warmth and kindness that the horrifying memories at Dwyers' Cross and the nightmares slowly receded from her mind. The days were filled with sun, sea and walks along the beach, with its few boats and as yet only fragments of river activity. The nights were spent singing duets at the pianoforte, which Lydia played almost as well as Esther's late mother, and playing chess and backgammon, at which Esther soon became as adept as the Major.

It was spring as Esther stole outside one morning with shoes and stockings in hand, the early sun thin behind a pearly-grey wash of clouds. The strong smell of salt drifted up to her as she walked down the tangled, grassy path to the deserted beach. She could hear the dull pounding of the surf on the fine, ivory-coloured sand, the waves twinkling in the watery light as they broke in steady rhythm on the hard-packed sand. The dew, still lying on the grass in dark patches, brushed her bare ankles. The fat leaves of an old, gnarled fig tree made a skirt of deep shadow on the ground where the small, over-ripe fruits had fallen, sparkling wet with moisture.

She felt a curious sense of detachment as she stopped and gazed out across the shining water, tiny points of whirling light dancing on its surface as it rose towards the pale, ghostly grey of the sky. The air was filled with the shriek of the lazy, circling gulls, flying further out, and their marauding swoops as they chased their prey and dived into the water.

She looked about her, the delicious feel of the fine sand between her toes. High dunes covered with coarse water-grass and thorny bushes, housing colonies of grey mousebirds with tufted crest and long sweeping tails, rose to her right, the bush filled with the chuck and chirr of wings and busy flutterings. The tide was out and stretches of beach lay uncovered. A boat twisted gently on its moorings near the river mouth and further back the river was a sombre, inky darkness from the cliff shadows still lying across it where it narrowed between them. She climbed a dune and threw herself in the lee of a large mound of sand. She wondered when Garnet would arrive for so far she had heard nothing.

She looked towards the half-dozen, small, thatched rough stone cottages built where the ground rose from the river and formed a shelf. The custom house at the shore end of the east bank stood in barren loneliness, a reminder of the work her father and Major Powell were setting in motion. They were attempting to develop Port Frances into a viable port for trading along the coast between there and Cape Town. Still there remained the problem of the landing of vessels over the treacherous sandbar at the entrance to the river mouth.

A voice startled her, coming some way above her from the path leading down from the Powell's cottage. She jumped up, not expecting anyone at this early hour.

She stood very still, staring with open amazement at the tall, powerful figure of Buck Jones striding towards her over the stones. He was the very last person she ever expected to see.

She watched him come towards her, carrying his black, leather shako under one arm, his brown curls attractively ruffled. The strengthening light caught the buttons of his scarlet jacket flashing bronze fire as he stopped before her.

His hand rose in salute. 'Miss Esther Dwyer.'

At the sound of his husky voice she experienced a rush of feeling, a bittersweet joy in view of what stood between them. She had felt loneliness deep inside, but his just being there sent a message of warmth — despite the fact that she had tried to forget him. Her cheeks flushed crimson; she was aware that she was in no proper state to receive visitors, especially such a notorious and dangerous one. And now, confronted by him, she was only too conscious of her own inadequacy — of her old faded, blue-striped gingham that no elegant lady would ever wear, of her tangled undressed hair, her bare legs and feet.

She took a deep breath, trying to stifle her rising embarrassment. Buck Jones somehow always caught her at her most vulnerable. She saw how at one he was with the environment, as if he had been born to it, the rugged wildness matching his own. In this background of Africa, with its untamed savagery, all her own breeding, her innocent youth seemed, beside his experience and worldliness, unaccountably ineffectual, making her an insubstantial shadow with only her beauty and quick wits on which to fall back. He was ten years older than her and she was out of her depth.

'And what brings you to Port Frances, Sergeant Jones?'

'To see you — with a message from Captain Fitzwilliam. As I did not want to disturb Major Powell at such an hour, his valet told me where I would find you.' His tone of voice made her look more closely at him. She detected some indefinable, underlying emotion in it as his brilliant blue eyes gleamed beneath the well-defined brows. 'As I was travelling in this area the Captain asked me to deliver his letter — personally.'

'I suppose I should be deeply honoured,' she said, his manner setting her on edge. 'But you see I am not in any proper state to receive you.'

'You could be wearing sack-cloth and ashes for all I care,' he said. 'I assure you, Miss Dwyer, that gingham is most provocative at this time of the morning.'

She was unaware that the dark red hair, tumbling unfashionably about her shoulders, was a hundred different shades and dazzling lights, as her eyes flared to life. He gazed down into her face, a smile beginning to curve his lips. His expression was as yet unreadable, smiling, watchful, a knowing look in his eyes.

What kind of man *are* you, Buck Jones, she wondered, and realized she had no idea at all.

A light blazed briefly in his eyes, then was extinguished. She gave him a speculative look, deeply conscious that his easy, mocking exterior hid the inner man. There was a withheld power to command in him that was as impressive as it was irritating. She was determined he would not get the better of her, and although she was not properly dressed, she could meet him with dignity. She lowered her eyes and could see the fine brown hairs where his wrists left the dark blue cuffs

118

of his jacket. For some reason she found herself trembling as he pulled out a letter from the inner pocket of his jacket.

'The letter, Miss Dwyer, is to tell you no doubt that the Captain is leaving for England — on compassionate leave for one year.'

She looked at him aghast, stung into attention. This was the last thing she expected. Just when she needed time to work on Garnet. It could not be true.

'Leaving? I don't believe you — you're mocking me, Sergeant, and I think in very poor taste.'

'It's true, sweetheart — the Captain is returning to England on account of his father who is desperately ill. I haven't read your letter, but methink it will be all there.' He held it out to her and she took it with shaking hands.

'I cannot believe you. A year is such a long time, especially in this God-forsaken country.'

He stared at her in a new way, the blue eyes behind the thick lashes crinkled at the corners. 'Time has a habit of passing, Miss Dwyer, even though sometimes we would hold it back.'

'You do not understand — you will never understand,' she burst out before she could stop herself. The lights in her wonderful hair changed colour rapidly, from deepest wine to earth-brown to gold, as she abruptly moved her head.

'Ah, I can understand only too well, but don't you worry your lovely head — he'll come back to you well-oiled with a slice of his father's fortune.' He grinned at her, his cheeks deeply dimpled.

Her hands clenched the letter he had given her so that the knuckles showed white, her mouth tense with astonished rage. Then she drew herself even more upright. The letter flickered to the sand.

'How dare you?' she hissed, all fired-up in an instant. 'How dare you speak to me like that! You — who are you anyway, to come here insulting a superior in birth and manners — you, who are not even good enough to lick my father's boots.'

His eyes met hers in fearless, half-challenging amusement, saying things she dared not think about. 'Now that is going too far — licking boots is not my stock in trade.'

She struggled impotently for the last vestiges of thin control, feeling it crack under the strain as he studied her, unabashed.

He moved closer. Electric blue eyes stared into dark indigo ones for a long moment, and Esther had a strange sensation of falling. He was so close. She put up her hands to push him away, and at the same moment a gust of chill air broke into their solitary world, bringing cold reality with it. She both hated and wanted this detestable man!

She watched him, noting the authority, the strength held in check as he handled the shako in his hands. So many conflicting emotions swirled inside her, fighting for ascendancy. Week after week she had not seen him and she told herself to forget him. She had told herself that when she met him again he would seem less attractive, and that the image she held of him that last time she had seen him at Dwyers' Cross would vanish. Her thoughts had not gone beyond holding and caressing; not knowing much beyond that, she had felt the delight of secrecy and a dizzying madness at her forbidden thoughts. But now, as he stood so close to her, he was more attractive than ever, more desirable, and the urgency to be even closer to him, was more vivid than before.

She watched him, entranced, hardly breathing, as the sun came up, triumphantly gold in an apricot sky streaked with the last remnant of cloud. And behind him rose the hilly bush, the Powell's whitewashed cottage perched above, its walls gleaming in the growing light.

He eyed her curiously, and she saw the welling and deepening light in his eyes and the long, silken lashes. She saw the thick, defined, brown brows and wanted to touch him as one touches a bird's feathers.

She turned and fled, the motion abrupt but not ungraceful; the long flow of bare calf and ankles above her well-shaped feet, gleaming and pale beneath the rapid whirl of frilled petticoats and drawers. She heard him call after her, but she ran on, not looking until she was well within the safety and refuge of a larger sand dune. She stopped to catch her breath, her heart hammering in her chest. She suddenly felt, standing there alone against the dune, that without Buck, there was an emptiness in her life that she did not want to admit, like a clock that had stopped ticking. It was as though she had wittingly slammed a door in her own face.

Then there he was, his tall figure dark against the shadows of the dune. He caught up with her, riotous red curls in his face as he turned her roughly around, linking them. She lifted her head and stared into his eyes. Her face seemed to swell and become hot with mingled embarrassment, anger and desire.

120

He reached for her arm, his touch running up it like a bolt of lightning.

'Leave me alone — you — you brute! Let me go!'

'It's time you had a lesson you'll never forget, sweetheart, one that will make nonsense of all your false airs and graces.'

'I'll scream if you don't let me go!' She struggled futilely against the strength of his arms around her.

'Then there's only one way to stop you, Miss Wildcat,' he growled under his breath, and his lips moved against hers, his breath on her mouth.

She fought as if her life depended on it, until there was no more fight left and her senses staggered with ecstasy. Her whole being seemed to burst into flame, sensations she had never imagined overwhelming her. The feel of him, the smell of him, all combined to transfix her. She had no real intimate experience with men, especially one as powerful as Buck Jones, and she was lost.

He slid his fingers along her body, pushing the rim of her faded dress from her shoulders, revealing the cleft of her hard-nippled breasts. Her breath caught in her throat as her whole body contracted painfully. Her chemise fell and she caught a flash of her own rounded thighs, as pale and lustrous as her arm. She then became aware that she was holding her breath, that her face and breasts were as hot as if the sun had struck them. She was conscious of a fine trembling through her body and desired, above all things, to touch the iron-hard muscles of his shoulders and arms, now exposed by his ripped-open jacket and shirt. She wanted to feel the broad expanse of chest covered with brown curls, to kiss again those beautifully moulded lips that must be the most wonderful lips in the world, and run her fingers through his hair.

Then she was naked, the light of the dawn stippling her body, hiding as it revealed. He held one breast in the cup of his hand. She had never been touched there by a man before, and the feel of his hand drove her almost out of her mind. She felt a moment of terror for an instant as he moved and ripped off the rest of his clothes, enchanting her body, arousing it until thought and feeling, heart and head became one liquid flame. He drew out her suppressed longings, freeing her passion and she could deny him nothing.

Together, still clinging, they fell on to the cool, fine sand and the world became one deep drum of passion and incoherent sound and heat and delicious struggle.

Above them, the sky brightened as gulls screeched, wheeling. Esther obeyed the passions of her body, caught up in an agonisingly sweet, yet terrible, urgent intensity. Buck lay on her and took her, and she held him to her, moaning with pleasure and pain. Entwined, she was conscious after the first initial pain of nothing but a wild ecstasy, as like a flame they merged together. The firm voluptuous body beneath his was like a yielding, living substance as she gave all her desire, passion, love, responding to his inner heat. Deeply penetrating and infusing her, they became one, each fulfilling the other in a most sublime act of love. His lips were sweet and moist against her, murmuring, she knew not what. When it was over, she had no immediate thoughts. She had only the memory of something immense, of incredible joy, beyond which nothing was comparable.

Strands of auburn hair drifting over her eyes and ears, she saw his face bent over her, and it was more beautiful than she had ever known. Slowly he moved away. Then, like a cold hand squeezing her heart, she heard the husky savagery of his voice that shocked her to intense awareness.

'I have ruined and ravaged an innocent child — and I am cursed.'

'No, Buck, don't say that.' Esther was alarmed. 'I am not a child, I am a woman.'

The metallic blue of his eyes was dim as he buttoned up his shirt. 'You have the body of a woman, Esther Dwyer, but in worldly experience you are still a child. I should have known better.' He let out a long sigh. 'I have wronged you and taken advantage of your lonely state. It will be wise for us to see each other only when necessary.'

Abruptly, Esther sat upright. Stunned, stricken and dumb, she listened to that low, deep voice and thought she understood.

She had thought that she meant as much to him as he had to her. She had given herself to him because of deeper feelings she hardly fully understood. But he — he had been born and reared in an atmosphere alien to her and her understanding. He had taken his pleasure where he found it — for instant gratification, to be forgotten and discarded soon afterwards. Now he no longer wanted to see her. He was a fitting son for that disreputable actress mother of his. Now she could believe all she had ever heard of him.

She thought of Amanda Lightfoot to her shame, and knew she

122

could never match that other woman's sexual experience. She had fallen for his charm, his attractive body and she was lost, dirtied and corrupted beyond forgiveness. She had given herself to an adventurer who would scorn her, laugh about her with his rough, soldier friends. She was now a fallen woman.

Her face was suddenly pinched and all colour seemed to have faded from her cheeks. Then, without speaking, she hurriedly dressed and fled from him, soon lost up the path to the cottage, and leaving him to wonder at the peculiar behaviour of one who had loved him so passionately only moments before.

The sun was warm now. Above the path the morning breeze shivered the bushes. There was a good view of the flaring red geraniums, and through them, a glimpse of the cottage to which she ran as to a refuge where she could hide and lick her wounds.

CHAPTER
Eleven

It was the first week of October. Laree had given birth to her second child, a son Joseph, and her daughter Emma was a bouncy, flaxen-haired little girl, just over a year old.

At Dwyers' Cross the men looked up at the threatening sky. The sound of distant thunder rolled from the heavy, low-lying clouds on the horizon, echoing eerily faraway across the valley. Lightning flickered briefly as it steadily grew darker and rain spat in the wind that had sprung up in cold gusts, howling and roaring with continuing strength across the hills. Suddenly, there came a great, stabbing, downward thrust of lightning that turned the whole world into a blue and yellow dazzle of light. All doors and windows were boarded up and made fast as the great mass of clouds grew heavier and more menacing by the minute.

It was not a gale, but a mighty storm, as if the forces of a gathering anger had been stifled for two years and finally must be spent. Lightning cut the sky with jagged ferocity, brightening it for a brief second. Then day was turned to night and the rain teemed down, drowning out all colour. Thunder continued to roll overhead and the rain became a torrential downpour that washed away all tracks and paths in a mighty rushing avalanche. The river rose, surging and swirling, until the pressure of the rising water built up at its narrowest point, swelling dangerously. It thundered over its banks to join other streams and rivulets cutting across necks of land to swell the mainstream.

All the rivers in Albany became high, swift, cutting all contact with other parts. Great tracts of land were isolated from the rest of the colony, standing in five to six feet of water in parts.

The roof of the farmhouse at Dwyers' Cross began to leak

ominously. Large, icy drops of water plopped on to the floor, seeping in until the kitchen stood a few feet deep in water. It took hours to soak up the mess and to board up the gaps in the tiles.

The garden was washed away. The fields became a vast sea of running water, not only the crops, but the soil itself being carried away. All but destroyed were the orchards and vineyard, and the sheep and cattle kraals gave way, the few animals left drowned in terror under the merciless, lashing rain. Sam struggled to save them with the help of the men. Joshua and Cady were in Grahamstown at the time, and nothing had been heard of them since. Michael Byrne sank into the river of chocolate-coloured water rushing down the yard in an angry boiling mass as he and Hannah managed to save their children as their cottage was swept away. They were able to swim to the main house with Sam's help. The handful of men, the few women and the children were brought in from the storm and soon the main house was crowded with fugitives from the flood.

Esther judged the stock food available to feed them and soon had a stew bubbling over the fire, its savoury smells filling the house. She turned and sighed with impatience as she looked around the room. Even the strongest person would swoon in the presence of such noise and stink. She approached Hannah and Amy and asked them to help her supervise the children and organize some routine. As her forthright manner would not accept refusal or disrespect, they readily obeyed and some kind of order was created.

Esther, already tired and eager to have done with the crowd, and the flood, was quick and decisive, and impatient with any slowness or tediousness from the others, most of whom stood in awe of her. When all was done and, in near exhaustion, she leaned her forehead against the damp wall of the sitting room, she prayed for there to be an end to it all. She was sticky and grimy, her hair limp and dirty. All thoughts and images of Garnet that before had sustained her at depressing times, making her feel her life would be better, seemed so long ago and faraway. And she forced herself to suffocate all thoughts and feelings for Buck Jones, after the experience in the dunes. It was something she preferred to forget, as she thought no doubt, he had already.

What had happened between them had been a sudden overwhelming passion, irresistible, heightened in intensity by the knowledge that it shouldn't be happening, that it couldn't last. She

125

found that her attitude to him had completely changed. His gentleness and passion towards her had shown her something of the man beneath the worldly, rugged surface, and melted her self-engendered resistance. It was not so much what happened between them that horrified her, but his reaction afterwards — that had shocked her more deeply than she knew. He had rejected her, diminished her in some irreparable way.

She still wanted to love him, but it was impossible. Love and companionship would never be theirs to share, although he had taken her heart, and for that she would never forgive him. She must not even think of him as having any intimate connection with her. She would have to force herself to believe that nothing had happened, that everything was as before, if she could — and she must never compare other men with him.

The calamity came to be called 'The Great Flood', and there was not a house in Grahamstown that escaped damage. The entire settlement was in ruins. Abject poverty and dreadful suffering were everywhere. There were so many who had lost everything, including the Dwyers.

The land outside the farmhouse was a seething swamp. Great trees lay uprooted in the dark, muddy wasteland. The river flowed sluggish, brown, floating debris and carcasses fouling its waters. The air was fetid with the sickly stench of mud and decay as the dreadful week ended. The Dwyers had lost everything. The so-called Albany elite, the party leaders and independent settlers who had sunk most, if not all, of their capital, into their allotments, were the most unfortunate of all. It would take many months to relieve the suffering caused by one of nature's worst disasters.

A watery sun struggled to shine through the few clouds still gathered over the land. The wind had died and a deep, eerie stillness lay everywhere. The sodden bushes still standing dripped with water, the grass in the higher places steamed. Then the grey bank of low clouds lifted and a glorious rainbow arched itself across the heavens. As the sun's rays brightened, each layer of distinct colour shimmered triumphantly above the earth. The flood itself became a thing of the past, but its ravaging effects were to last much longer.

Esther stood on the knoll of oozing mud, and looked across the stricken lands. There was nothing left and the future had never looked bleaker than it did then. Only that morning Sam had told her that any crops remaining after the flood had been attacked again by rust. Her father and Cady had returned from Grahamstown as soon as the storm was over and they could travel over the impassable tracks of land to face their ruination.

She was about to turn away when Sam caught her by the arm. He pointed to the hills. 'Miss Esther, get inside quick, coming our way are swarms and swarms of locusts to complete the destruction of the land.'

It was all too true. As she looked it seemed as if enormous clouds of snow had formed over the hills. The thrum of the destructive insects filled her head as she allowed herself to be hustled inside. The air all about was suddenly darkened by a thick cloud of whirring creatures for about half a mile, obscuring the sky as the locusts approached the land. The rushing sound of millions of wings filled the valley. The ground was strewn with wounded insects, their wings broken by those with which they collided. After that, great armies of caterpillars ravaged what was left of the land.

'Of all the plagues of Egypt,' Sam said afterwards, 'the locusts must have been the worst.' He looked up at the sky with a face both grim and taut.

Esther stood beside him, the destroyed land all about them. In her mind's eye she saw it as it should have been — a field of healthy, waving wheat. She saw herds of cattle grazing peacefully on the lands, and a gracious house, much like Longwood House, rising on its gentle knoll. She lifted her head as the vision vanished, her profile suddenly flooded with sunlight.

Sam's words interrupted her thoughts. 'Despite everything,' he said, 'I love this land — the wildness of it, pulsing with life and power, and the beautiful strength of its countryside. There's a voice here, ancient and wild, that speaks to me.' The hard features of his lean, brown face softened as he looked out towards the hills and the deepening brilliance of the sun. He watched as the sombre landscape came alive under the gold of the light.

The skin between Esther's brows puckered, giving her face a sullen look. 'I could leave it, and the sooner the better. I could go back to Ireland or England tomorrow.'

'Pah!' Sam looked at her, grinning. 'You forget the suffering back in the old country, Miss Esther — only the upper-class quality have the vote in parliament, the rest struggle in overcrowded, filthy towns,

127

eking out a living. My father was a lawyer, an educated man, yet he had no say in the ruling of the country, of his life — no power to change injustices against him and his kind.'

He looked out across the sodden fields, his black brows furrowed. 'Here there is room, space for a man to move, for his soul — if there is such a thing — to breathe. There's a kind of freedom for men like me, space, rawness, newness in the ancient soil. I wouldn't change this for anything in the old country, with its decadent king and his scandalous wife living off the fat of the land, while the rest starve, forgotten and outnumbered.

He turned for a moment to look at her. 'I tell you, Miss Esther, once we have replanted this land, it will grow again and spread under God's own sky. It will all come right in the end. I've seen it happen time and time again, droughts, floods, insects. This land was made for strong men like your papa and Mr Cady. Only such as them can harness it. Africa is not to be forced or trapped, it is to be harnessed, coaxed and tamed, according to its own ancient laws. There is a way of working with Africa, and a man must listen to its mysterious voice.'

He grinned again suddenly. 'Believe me, Miss Esther, you'll make a good frontierwoman yet, though I would never have said that at the start. You will love this place as I do and never want to leave it, mark my words. There's something in the wind tells me so.'

'Pox on your words, Samuel Pettigrow! That I will never do,' she scoffed as she stared into his hard, but compassionate face. 'So believe it, for I will never change.'

She turned away, vowing silently that she would not stop trying to escape from this place, and once away, she would never return.

In the gloom that followed the flood, Esther was as unprepared as the rest for the scandal that tore through the settlement, ripping it open from end to end.

Amanda Lightfoot had been brutally murdered and it was believed that Buck Jones was the murderer. Everything seemed to point to him. According to reports from her servants and the people nearby, violent screams came from her bedroom in the early hours of the morning. The maid and other servants had tried the door but found it bolted. When they eventually managed to break it open, the room was in a shambles: the bed was disordered, the rich hangings

128

spattered with blood, chairs and tables were overturned and costly ornaments were scattered on the carpet where pools of blood dried in dark patches. Nothing appeared to have been stolen, and Amanda lay dead from many vicious wounds and a brutal beating, the red prints from her fingers groping desperately to find the bell rope.

The news was so shattering, but still Esther found it unbelievable that Amanda, that small, lively, silver-haired woman, whose storm of jealousy she had known, had gone in such a dreadful way.

Amanda, it seemed, had put up a fierce struggle against her attacker, who, it was believed, escaped through the window and out into the garden towards the river. It was known that she had quarrelled with her lover, Buck, only weeks before the flood, and he had left the house never to return. Now he had been taken to gaol as the prime suspect in a murder so terrible in its implications that it had the entire settlement in an uproar.

In vain Esther tried to work out an explanation for the ghastly crime, but she could not get beyond the fact that for all that happened between them, Buck was not a murderer. She had tried to forget him but again he was thrown back dramatically into her life. She thought of Buck, now in gaol in Graaff-Reinet, awaiting trial before the next session of the Circuit Court — his life, his destiny, now entirely out of his hands. It was this idea that had obsessed her ever since she had first heard the news. For a while she lost the power to think, much less to feel. It surprised her that she could still move her limbs without trembling and go about her daily tasks as she had always done.

In the pretty country town of Graaff-Reinet at the southern base of the Sneeuwberge, the two judges of the Circuit Court arrived earlier than usual. Owing to the seriousness of the case and the social prominence of the murdered woman, Lord Charles Somerset intervened and ordered the judges to open a special session for the trial without delay.

Garnet, whose leave to England had been delayed by the flood, postponed it further to help Buck, whom he believed was innocent.

During the next few weeks all Albany reeled with horrified fascination at the further revelations in the Lightfoot murder case. Not only in Grahamstown, but in Graaff-Reinet, Uitenhage and as far afield as Cape Town, men and women discussed it in shocked voices, eager for details. It would be another few months before the news reached London, and Amanda's brother, Andrew Lotharton, a

129

prominent member of parliament.

The servants testified, including Sims the butler who had recently left Amanda's employ over some domestic dispute. Their testimony was united, though at times given reluctantly, in their accounts of discord between their mistress and the Sergeant and their insistence that the chief cause of their mistress' distress had been the end of her affair with him, and it appeared that Sims, who had been a loyal servant in the employ of the late Colonel Lightfoot for years, had advised the court not to search for the murderer anywhere but in the Sergeant's quarters.

All the time, Buck stubbornly stuck to his statement that he and some of his men had been cut off from the rest at the height of the flood by the raging Kowie River. He swore that he had been nowhere near the scene of the murder, but trying to save his men by swimming across the raging waters and bringing them all to safety. There was admiration for the heroic manner in which he had helped his men, but the opinion was unanimous that he was the only one with a motive strong enough to have, at some time, slipped away from the men in the driving rain and, in a last quarrel, murdered her. As he was an excellent horseman, he could have ridden there and back without any of the men missing him. Public opinion was also strongly against him because of his background. His illegitimacy was not so much spoken about as implied, as was the opinion that he carried himself with far too superior an air for one of his dubious beginnings. And the fact that he disagreed with the colonists on the frontier policy towards the Xhosas in no way endeared him to them.

Evidence was heard that one of Amanda's servants, a stable boy, had actually ridden out to find Buck and, failing to locate him, had given a message to a worthy source that his mistress was calling for him in her delirium. Buck denied having received any such message, but there was growing doubt about the honesty of his evidence. He was regarded as the inhuman murderer of a woman less than half his size and weight — hanging was too good for such a fiend. Public opinion weighed heavily against Buck.

They looked for another woman in the case, and Esther quailed lest the argument between her and Amanda after the Glendower dance was discovered. But as the days passed, nothing was said.

Most agreed that no man hacked his ex-lover to death unless some other woman had driven him to madness. They could not prove it, because he had not been seen in any other woman's company after becoming Amanda's lover, but they seemed determined to find one, somewhere.

In the midst of all the intrigue surrounding the trial, the next few weeks passed in deep gloom and depression as the effects of the flood were fully realized. Many of the older settlers took to drink. All available financial help, rations and clothing were distributed by the Society for Distressed Settlers. Even as far as Britain and India, assistance was mobilised for the enormous task of the recovery of the Eastern Cape.

For many hundreds of acres, the land still lay under dank, oozing mud. The tracks and paths that had been washed away remained impassable. The clearing of the land was slow and arduous; the river flats were covered with silt brought down from the hills, and the swamplands yielded grudgingly. Everywhere people felt the weight of hardship, shortages and toil, but there was a grim handful of men like Joshua and Cady who had the dogged spirit to keep going, and who did not turn to the bottle to escape the grimness of reality.

The Dwyers were part of that band of men and women determined to survive at all costs. A long hard struggle lay ahead against the environment, the government and the Xhosa. This band was embittered, but never broken. In them confidence in their ultimate victory never died. But for Esther, this struggle was pushed to the background of her life for a while as another, far more urgent, personal problem reared its ominous head.

It was near the beginning of November and the deepness of the country quiet settled on the land before the evening meal. The low clatter of pots and pans filled the kitchen, then stopped as Esther, her abundant curls hidden by a frilled housecap, set a rush taper to the cooking fire laid in the fireplace to light a tallow candle.

The plastered walls about her shimmered with reflections from the firelight, and outside the purple and crimson of the sunset glimmered over the lonely fields and beyond, where the broad rectangles of cultivated wheat and corn patches on the hills were ablaze with colour.

Esther sighed, thinking of the empty nights stretching ahead of her like a long, lonely road. She could see no more hope for herself without a dowry. Garnet had all the unmarried girls pursuing him relentlessly, and their mothers hatching plans to trap him into matrimony.

The sudden feeling of nausea flooding over her, threatening to make her retch, alarmed her. She rose, a lighted candle in her hand. Quickly she placed it on the table and sat down again with her head on her arms, feeling thoroughly wretched. This was not the first time she had felt nauseous. It had been happening a whole week. At first she had thought she was sickening in some dreaded way, then as the tenderness of her breasts became apparent, the idea that she was with child filtered through her brain like some unwelcome shockwave.

She had not seen Buck Jones since the day in the sand-dunes, but she knew, no matter how hard she tried to think otherwise, that since then nothing had been the same. The pleasure and the intensity she had experienced then were now too painful to contemplate. Ever since the murder of Amanda, she had not been able to put him out of her thoughts. Her mind was suddenly filled with images of him as he had been that morning, and she swallowed hard, trembling and sweating, all at once.

Choking back a sob of great agitation, she knew she was carrying Buck's child. Slowly the silent tears began to flow. Pressing her hands lightly together in her lap, she looked up. What was she to do? What would everyone say? They would say that she was a wanton woman, a strumpet, carrying the child of one of the most notorious bastards on the frontier, and a suspected murderer.

What would her father say? Uncle Cady? She could not bear to think of that. Her father would throw her out, it was his right, or he would send her away to a retreat somewhere where she would be buried alive for the rest of her life. All those years of family pride and respectability, their standing in society, had suddenly vanished.

She wrung her hands together. She had tried to forget about that day in Port Frances, to forget that Buck had ever existed, but everything about it was still so vividly etched and clear. And now it was done.

She turned her thoughts back to her present predicament, and cringed inside at the thought of the outcome. It's this dreadful place, she thought bitterly, it's the loneliness, the savagery, the fears and the insecurity. It would never have happened back in Ireland, in that comforting world when Mama was still alive. She would never had let it happen.

She had been lonely, afraid and restless, and she had allowed Buck Jones to take advantage of her, and to her eternal shame, she had enjoyed it all, revelled in it before she had known he did not feel anything for her. Now, more than ever, she needed the strength of her forceful personality to keep her sane in the days, weeks to come.

A conflict raged in her mind, between shock and anger. Shock that it should have happened to her — and anger against Buck that he had done the most terrible thing that could happen to an unmarried girl of her class and station. Worst of all, she had been deflowered by a lowly sergeant: a man of the rank and file, and that, in the eyes of her class, was unpardonable. She sat very still, her face ashen in the candlelight, as the situation and its seriousness crystallized in her mind.

It seemed to her suddenly as if all her innocence had vanished, that she had gone far beyond the safe bounds of carnal knowledge that had so carefully sheltered her. It seemed that there was a terrifying new depth to life that she had not noticed before. She was filled with such despair that she even thought of suicide. But somehow, even in the extremity of her despair, life was sweet.

Then the sinister foreboding took shape in her mind, that if it ever became known that Buck Jones was the father of her child, the conclusion would be readily reached that they were having an affair to rival that of the one with Amanda Lightfoot, that Amanda had found out, and Buck had killed her, either to silence her, or in a mad rage. She would then be completely doomed, and he would most certainly lose his life in the most horrible manner of being slowly strangled to death.

It was very quiet, nothing seemed to stir except her restless, agitated thoughts. It's done and no one can take it away. Or can they? She sought desperately for a remedy. She thought back to all those unmarried girls labouring on her father's estate back in Ireland. There were women who took away unwanted babies, but their methods were vile, or so she had heard, and rumours always got out.

She was forced to keep absolutely silent on the matter, and suffer it alone. She looked about her with haunted eyes. No man would have her now!

Rough boots sounded outside in the yard. Startled, she looked in the direction of the door. No one must see her like this, no one must guess her condition, for not only her reputation, but a man's life was at stake.

She rose to stir the thick, meaty soup, which made her feel even more sick, in its iron pot over the fire. The bright flames rose higher, the smoke snaking upwards. It crackled loudly, the large pot swinging slightly on its hook. Her brows drew together in a deep, frantic frown. She had to find some solution and it had to be something that would stop the scandal that was threatening to break about her head.

CHAPTER
Twelve

'And what news of your uncle and father, Esther?' Garnet Fitzwilliam asked, standing at the side of the heavy, oak desk in his administrative office in Grahamstown.

It was a morning in late November and there was a fresh south-easterly wind blowing. It drove the summer clouds across the sky and rattled door and window frames, moaning outside the government offices in the Dundas Buildings, at the corner of High and Hill Streets.

He studied the bright young woman sitting in a chair opposite him. He fashioned up a quizzical smile as he followed her eyes to the unfinished game of chess standing on an oak table under the long, sash window overlooking the blustery street.

'A game Henry Somerset and I play to take our minds off more pressing matters,' he said in explanation, his voice quiet and low, as usual, and pleasing to the ear.

Esther drew a breath, rather like a sigh. 'I believe that Sergeant Buckmaster Jones plays a good game — rather like some war strategy,' she said, her voice lilting and invitingly sensuous. Hiding the pain she felt at the mention of Buck's name, she smiled at him with all the arts she had learned. Esther was playing one of the most desperate games of her young life, and if she lost, she lost everything as a woman in respectable, upper-class society. She had persuaded her father to allow her to accompany Sam to market, and he had agreed, knowing nothing of her plan. She had left Sam at the market on the excuse of extra shopping, and had made her way to Garnet's office, dressed in all the finery she possessed.

'He does,' Garnet said, a sudden shadow falling across his face. 'He learned the noble skill from me, here in this very town. We've had

135

some fine games at this very table until that wretched murder.'

Esther was surprised that an officer of his rank should fraternise in any way with a non-commissioned officer, even one as distinct and extraordinary as Buck Jones.

Garnet lifted the lid of an inlaid box of sweetmeats, and offered them to her. As she ate slowly, he watched her.

'I've known the sergeant a long time,' he ventured. 'We served in the same regiment against Bonaparte, cut our teeth on the Frenchies together. He was one of the best boxers at the time — I won many a bet on his winning a bout. Very quick on his feet for such a big man. But he let me down once as I recall — in Spain, he was a very young private then, up against a real tiger of a man, Ironside Griffith, by name — that was the only time I've really seen him knocked out, completely out. But you can't be interested in this army talk, my dear, it must be detestably boring to a charming and beautiful, young lady.'

Dark blue eyes, wide with surprise, gazed at him beneath the brim of the small, frilled, vanilla bonnet with moss-green trimmings, decorated with a jaunty, emerald feather. She tossed back her head with a movement that emphasized the proud swell of her breasts in the new vanilla mull gown she had made from the last bolt of cloth brought out from Ireland.

To his own amused vexation, Garnet's gaze wandered over her slim figure, her fitted gown revealing the outline of her firm breasts and shapely hips, the folds of material billowing to her dainty, slippered feet. There was colour in her cheeks as she leaned forward, the curls warm against them when she moved her head.

'The talk certainly doesn't bore me, Captain. After all, the Sergeant's trial is the talk of the colony. It is a dreadful affair, and I cannot bring myself to believe that he is guilty, though, of course, my father and uncle think differently.'

'I can no more think he is guilty than you,' Garnet said suddenly, and she found him returning her regard with calm approval. 'Although none of us officers approved of his affair with Lady Lightfoot, he is one of our best men — with the courage of a lion and a closed mouth, discreet, a rare quality in the army out here where many rogues and wastrels have been attracted to our rank and file.' He bit his lip. There was silence. The noise of the wind outside seemed to heighten in the quiet room. He picked up a new-style, steel-nibbed pen, unconsciously toying with it. 'We need men of Jones' calibre — a born leader with an intimate knowledge of the bush. I intend to fight for his acquittal.'

Esther lifted her chin. 'There are many who disagree, my kinsmen among them. They think he had the motive and the strength to have done such a dastardly thing.' She noted his reaction as a glint of something close to annoyance sparked in his narrowed eyes.

'Then I am sorry to say they are all wrong, including your kinsmen, which is a pity because they have so much influence on the rest. I would lay my head on a block that Jones is not a sadistic murderer. I think I know him better than most, and many times in the heat of a battle it was he who saved the lives of his own men, and never lost his sense of control.'

Abruptly Esther rose and he watched her stroll over towards the chess set on the table, swaying on her long, shapely legs, the perfection of her body emphasized by her gown. She heard him say, a little hoarsely, 'He saved my life during the seige of this town in '19, and I owe him his life now.' He knitted his black brows, then a ghost of a smile lit his face, his eyes crinkling ever so slightly. 'But come, we are far too serious.'

She turned slowly, thinking bitterly of another chess set in another room on a hot, bright afternoon — a room of gold and blue. Hiding her thoughts, she turned sideways so that he could see the bold curve of her breasts and, below them, the exquisite moulding of her stomach and softly rounded hips. She stole a look at him from under her eyelashes, wondering what he would say if he knew she was carrying Buck Jones' child. His dark eyes never left her, glimmering and shining and changing with his thoughts. He had long, black and silken lashes and his eyebrows were arched, giving him a faintly sardonic air. She thought, here is a man who reveals nothing of his thoughts and passions, and he rules himself like steel. Garnet Fitzwilliam, she knew, would never allow vulgar displays in himself. And yet, she must win him over, she must make him succumb to her charms, her power. She must force him to marry her and give her child a name, a background of respectability.

'Would you like some refreshments, Esther? A dish of tea, a glass of wine, perhaps?'

She was frowning deeply as she turned the top of the ivory parasol handle in her fingers. Suddenly everything she was doing, the parade she was making of herself before him, seemed so shabby, so tawdry — especially after what she had done, had allowed to happen with Buck at Port Frances.

She gazed at Garnet suddenly blankly, unable to answer his question. She saw again the image of Buck on the beach, her mind etched sharply with the love and pain of the outcome of that brief, intense, encounter. She did not love Garnet, she never had, and perhaps she never would. A strange, bitter smile on her lips, she remained deep in thought, the whole reason for her visit forgotten.

Raising her eyes to the mantelshelf, somewhere to Garnet's right, her gaze met the vacant stare of the bronze bust of the Duke of Wellington, and slid to the brass bullet-mould beside it. Garnet's life was filled with weighty matters. She must look ridiculous, parading before him, trying to entice him with her silly, flirtatious ways. A side table held an inlaid mahogany-on-oak decanter box containing six decanters with gilded shoulders and on one wall, suspended in brackets, hung his Brown Bess musket and a brace of expensive pistols, symbols of the nature and danger of his work out here, where women were a light diversion, the frivolous moments between matters of state.

Her face proud and pale, she looked at him and saw his face through a sudden, embarrassing haze of uncontrollable tears. She who never cried in front of others, was now hopelessly undone before such a controlled and elegant gentleman.

'What is it, Esther? Have I said something to upset you, my dear?'

She heard the scrape of his chair, the instant concern in his voice. She saw the appalled look on his face and knew that she was embarrassing him. She felt the pressure of his hand on hers, and the world came back. Her flesh was warm but his hand was icy cold. Slowly she shook her head, ashamed she had exposed her feelings, and allowed him to lead her back to her chair where she took the fine cambric handkerchief he offered.

Silently she dried her tears. It had all turned out so differently from what she had planned. She had failed and she had made a fool of herself. She had wanted him to propose, and could not raise the subject herself. Sitting there, she heard her voice telling him about the struggles at the farm, of the loneliness and the boredom, when she should have been coquettish. Normally any obstacle became a challenge that stirred her spirit, but not now. Perhaps it was because she was pregnant, but she was so weepy these days, a thing she had never been in her life.

All she was conscious of was a sense of complication, and confusion. Everything had suddenly changed. She closed her eyes. Out at Dwyers' Cross it had all been so different in her mind. But here, facing him, her plan had dropped away. Garnet was not like that — he was not easy to impress. She wondered briefly if Amanda Lightfoot had said anything to him about her.

Mulling over this, she raised only embarrassment in herself, making conversation with him harder and more artificial. His face was unreadable. His whole posture was contained, and yet alert, like a cheetah lying in the shade.

'Is there something I can do, Esther?' he said, very slowly, as if considering his words.

'No one can help me, Captain — it is just a female weakness.' Her tone was self-mocking, but it did not match the expression in her eyes. A flash of pain crossed her face as she realized all was lost. Then her pride came to her rescue. She was a woman of the Irish gentry, with a proud and vigorous heritage behind her. She had been educated and trained to be the wife of such a man as he.

The light from the window revealed the faint lines about his lips and the tiny grooves across his forehead as his brows gathered in the beginnings of another frown. 'It's been all this talk of Sergeant Jones — it has upset you. You are very caring to be troubled by what happens to him, my dear. You have my word that I will collect enough evidence from his records to acquit him.'

She looked into his lean face, knowing that he would do as he promised. She found herself wishing he would take her into his arms and kiss her passionately as Buck had done. She sighed inwardly, striving to control her feelings, suddenly stirred once more with terrible unrest. She knew that his house had been destroyed in the flood and that it was in the process of being rebuilt; a new mansion, it was rumoured, of eighteen rooms, double-storied, with three interlinking reception rooms, and tall serrated chimneys. It would have been such a fitting place to raise her child. Garnet must be planning to marry, as some said. In fact, it was such talk that had prompted her to visit him in the desperate hope that it might be she who was the fortunate one. But now she had suspicions that Beatrice Cummings or some other young woman had already got there before her, and that he was designing the house for his new wife-to-be. She felt strangely deflated, but not resigned.

She told him about the stealing of cattle by the Xhosas, the barbarity of the frontier and the struggle of her kinsmen to wrest a living from the soil. Fluttering her hands in an uncharacteristic gesture of defeat, she ended with, 'And we are so inadequately defended that it hardly seems as if we will survive at all against the odds.'

There was a long pause. Garnet still studied her, his dark eyes unfathomable but giving an almost lazy expression to his aquiline face that was grossly misleading.

He spoke at last. 'I cannot deny what you say is true, Esther, but do not forget that we have just recovered from one bloody war on this very ground with the Xhosas, and it would seem that the larger herds your kinsmen have accumulated are attracting the tribesmen's attention, and aggravating an already pressing frontier problem beyond all proportion.'

He paused, giving a little shrug of his shoulders, the well-chiselled lips curling slightly. He was speaking the truth as he knew it, and it seemed to Esther that he had nothing to hide from her.

'The wars against the Xhosas have been the most expensive item in the colony's budget, my dear — and that is not taking into account that we are only one small, but strategic part of an already over-extended Empire where these problems form only a slice of other conflicts worldwide.'

Esther's feelings surged immediately against what he was saying, yet she could not help being swayed grudgingly by his complete lack of pretence. She rested her eyes on him, in all candour. 'While the politicians haggle over budgets in faraway England, we starve. While they plunder the colonies, growing rich on arguments, we die — or so I have heard it said.'

Garnet raised a finely-drawn eyebrow, giving her a penetrating look. 'There are no solutions for this frontier, Esther, there are just next steps, new frameworks. His Excellency, the Governor Lord Charles's original plan was to have ex-soldiers out here who could defend themselves. It was the Colonial Office who saw fit to send civilians without telllng them what they faced.'

She said, with a sad smile, 'I am sorry to have taken up your valuable time, Captain, and I have bored you with my problems.'

140

He touched her shoulder lightly, bending down to do so and she regarded him in silence. She saw his face and something mysterious in his subtle eyes. I want to marry him, Esther thought in wonder, I would go with him even though I do not love him for I feel he is kind and a man of honour. But he seems to have other plans.

He stood up, and raised her up beside him. He took her hand, the barrier disappearing between them. 'On the contrary, my dear, it has been most enlightening. I am most concerned about your kinsmen. I know how much you have suffered, but up until now, I had not realized how much it affected you personally. I will do all in my power to help you.' He smiled and touched the red curls at her cheeks, the feel of his hand reassuring her. For a long moment Esther thought that he was going to kiss her. Then he took her hand, looking directly into her eyes.

'If I can ever be of assistance in any way, please do not hesitate to ask me.' His eyes smiling at her with a certain promise, he released her hand and let her go. She felt a rush of disappointment as he retreated once more into his urbane, controlled self.

For a moment she had thought he had felt some desire for her, then she realized his interest in that direction had only been momentary. He had no intention of being anything else to her than what he was at present, a comforting family friend on whom she could rely. Lightening her tone, she smiled in mock gaiety as she made to leave. 'Thank you for your concern, Captain. I appreciate it.'

He glanced at her, and he no longer smiled as he reached for her pelisse, casually draped over the back of her chair. He was so elegant, so commanding in his scarlet broadcloth jacket, white trousers and highly-polished, black leather boots. He closed his eyes and she saw that he was suddenly weary as she bade him goodbye, puzzled. Imperceptibly he nodded his head and offered to see her to the wagon, but she politely refused, only wanting to be alone before she had to face Sam again. She had failed in her plan, and she would be the outcast of the entire community — and the laughing stock, if anyone found out about the reason for her visit to Garnet. Just then, she wanted to get away from him as quickly as possible.

She stood in the street, trying to calm her anguish as she battled against the shrieking wind, the air full of choking, yellow-brown dust. The enormous hooves of oxen churned up pale clouds as their

141

masters shouted above the wind. A troop of soldiers rode by, their blue cloaks wrapped about them in an effort to keep out the dust, and passers-by hurried around her, doubled up against the gale.

It had all gone so wrong. Neither he nor she had reacted as she had expected, and she obviously did not exert her feminine power over him as strongly as she had thought she did. Esther battled on, trying to push the terrible predicament she was in, from her mind. She would have to find someone else to marry as soon as possible. There was no other man she wanted to spend the rest of her life with. There was no one else she respected, except of course the child's natural father — and that was impossible. But in her condition she would have to find someone, someone who would agree to marry her at short notice. But who?

She thought of the remoteness of the lonely frontier farms so near the border. She would never be allowed to remain there once her condition became known. Or would she? Would she be forced to remain there, an unmarried mother, shunned by society all her life? She tried to dash the thought from her mind.

Only the robust strength and boldness of her kinsmen for survival, the kindness and assistance of their neighbours, the stalwart Boers, and the soldiers of Grahamstown garrison stood between them and the mounting misfortune and disasters facing them out there. And she was one of them.

She could see Sam in the distance, among the wagons around the square. She was beginning to realize that something beyond her control was pulling her into a net, enmeshing her and those at Dwyers' Cross, and from which it seemed she would never be allowed to escape.

CHAPTER
Thirteen

As the days passed, the Lightfoot murder case proceeded slowly, guided by English Law, struggling with the evidence presented. It was held in the Drostdy, and every word was hungrily devoured, spewed across the desert sands to other centres eagerly awaiting further developments. And every day the outcome for Buck looked more ominous.

November withered into a hot December. Garnet walked purposefully towards the farmstead at Dwyers' Cross and stopped within easy distance of the main house. Standing with military straightness, he watched Esther beating a threadbare blanket that was stretched between an upright frame of stout poles hammered into the ground, her movements rhythmic with the stiff broom in her hands.

The air was brilliant with light. Limp, dead weeds were the only sign of vegetation, apart from the thickets of bedraggled willows and spekboom. The birds had returned, flashing down the water, while long-legged cranes timidly stalked the swamp. And in the distance, Hannah Byrne kneeled and swayed up and down rinsing wet clothes in the river and smacking them on the rocks. The laughter of her young son and her tiny daughter floated all the way over the wastelands.

Garnet had started towards Esther when a watchdog ran from the house, barking. It rushed up to him, raising its head, hackles rising. He bent down encouraging the dog to approach him. It sniffed around, excited, then came to him, sitting down on its haunches as he patted the thick fur of its large head.

Esther looked up and turned as she heard the dog bark and then was silenced. She stared across at him, his polished, steel scabbard, spurs and gold epaulettes sparking fire in the sunlight. The morning breeze tugged at her flaming red curls, freed from their restricting housecap. Her plain, blue calico dress, much washed and mended, and the white pinafore over it showed old, faded stains. Clearly visible from beneath the hem were the leather home-made shoes, of which she was all too aware. She regretted him seeing her in such attire, little realizing that she made the simple, cheap clothes seem stylish, almost elegant.

He had been there for a few seconds, but she had the distinct feeling that he had been watching her for much longer, and she felt at a disadvantage. Nevertheless she placed a hand on the rounded swell of her hip as she looked at him, surprised.

'I didn't expect to see you here, Captain Fitzwilliam, I thought you were in Graaff-Reinet attending the murder trial.' She went forward with easy grace that had grown more pronounced throughout the months on the frontier.

'I returned two days ago, Esther, and I have come to see you on a matter of some urgency,' he said, bowing.

She saw a smile lurking in his dark eyes and for a moment she wondered if he had come to propose to her, though she hardly dared expect it after that ill-fated visit to his office. In fact, she had not expected to see him again, and she tried hard to forget it.

For a moment she could not speak, she could only hold her breath in anticipation, hoping desperately not to be disappointed once more. Then she broke the silence. 'Indeed, Captain,' she said, striving to sound normal, 'I am honoured.'

He was obliged to smile as he looked at her candid gaze, her face suddenly alight with expectation, yet trying so hard to keep the formality of such occasions.

He banished her suspense by coming straight to the point. 'I have spoken to your father, my dear, and he has graciously given me his permission to ask you to become my wife — after a short argument, I might add. I have been thinking along these lines for months now — that is the reason I rebuilt Glendower Park — but, as you no doubt realize, I am a cautious man and there were many aspects to consider.'

After she fully understood what he was saying, Esther's eyes began to sparkle, the blood coursing excitedly through her veins. After all the months of trying to impress him she could hardly believe that what she was hearing was true. After all the heartaches, the pain, the rejection and failure she had felt, here he was doing just what she had wanted him to do. About her, the broken fences, the ruined huts, the destroyed fields and the damp walls of the house ceased to exist. She was saved, and so was her child.

She lifted her chin, colouring under his concerted gaze. Although he was tall, she found herself almost on a level with his penetrating, dark eyes. 'I want to marry you, Captain Fitzwilliam, more than anything in the whole world.' She was breathless, a wide, spontaneous smile sweeping across her face. 'I will make you the finest wife an officer ever had,' she added with involuntary honesty. 'But why would Papa argue with you, pray?'

'You have made me very happy, Esther — and please call me Garnet, Captain Fitzwilliam is far too formal in the circumstances. Your father had a few reservations, my dear, concerning the fact that you are Irish and I am English. He has a certain mistrust of the English, which is natural enough — but that was the lesser worry — the other more serious one was the fact that he has very little money, and you have no dowry. Your father is a very proud man.'

Esther stiffened. 'He is that — as proud as I am, to our cost most probably. But he gave in, he agreed. How ever did you get him to do that? And don't his objections worry you?'

He was silent and she wondered what he was thinking. She saw the expression on his face change, and an odd, almost haunted look pass over it. Then it disappeared, but not before she had felt a swift pang of apprehension.

'Do yourself a favour, my dear, and don't let it trouble you. I have come to terms with both aspects; your Irishness only enhances you in my eyes, and the fact that you have no dowry is amply compensated by my own fortune. When my father dies one day, I will inherit a princely sum plus a property in Dorset, which will more than make up for the inadequacies of my army pay. At the moment I have a handsome allowance until the death of my father, and I have applied to buy a major's commission only this morning. The letter will be sent to London post-haste.'

Esther frowned, and said, to reassure herself, 'I can hardly believe what you are saying — that you have chosen me above all the other young women of means. Why, you've had your choice of the entire settlement and no one can say that they or their mamas haven't tried hard enough.'

145

At last, he stepped forward and, smiling at her, gently cupped her chin. 'Believe it because it is true, Esther. Ever since I first saw you at the Blaaukranz River, I knew that no other woman could come near you for beauty, intelligence and spirit. I should have approached you sooner, but I was not sure of how you would feel about me. You see, you also have had your fair share of admirers. No wonder all the other young maids have been so jealous!'

'And I thought you hadn't noticed,' she murmured, a gleam of mischief in the dark blue, uptilted eyes. 'I thought that Beatrice Cummings had won the day, especially after my silly behaviour in your office the last time we met.'

His arms went around her, and her heart thudded with increasing delight. 'A pox on boring Miss Cummings,' he breathed, his fingers following the line of her chin. 'She pales into insignificance beside you — so very lovely, proud, defiant, and so very courageous, as I found out in my office, and when you broke down and showed that inner vulnerability to me, I finally made up my mind. It was not very fair of you, my dear, to have shot down all my defences in one go!'

She stood unmoving, afraid to break the moment lest by her impulsiveness she would cause it to shatter and crumble, all the enchantment lost. Closing her eyes she tilted her face for his kiss, when they heard the high-spirited shouts from the Byrne children at the river and Garnet quickly disengaged himself, his hands gripping her shoulders.

'I forgot how public we were for a moment — a pity, but there it is. I shall take you away from these ruins, Esther, to Glendower Park where you have always belonged, and which was built with you in mind — and you shall reign supreme.'

She felt let down and lost without his kiss to seal their relationship, but his words filled her with growing pleasure.

Seeing her crushed face, he smiled, 'We will have plenty of time to get to know each other, my sweeting, and it will be my pleasure. Come, I have a gift for you.' Leading her to his horse tethered to a large tree, he untied a parcel from the crupper, his saddlebag crammed with gifts for the family.

'I apologize for the state of my offering, but this was the only way I could bring it in haste.' He handed it to her, and as she pulled out a dress of exquisite, pale lilac silk, embroidered with silver stitching and gathered with dark violet galloon ribbons, warmth spread

146

through her. It had been so long since she had held in her hands the texture of such fine cloth.

She laughed, utterly charmed with the gown and with him, and clapped her hands. 'Glory be! What a wonderful surprise. Oh Garnet, I do love you so!' Impulsively she held the gown against her. The absolute transformation in her face and appearance was complete. Garnet looked astounded. She drew a deep breath. 'How does it look?' she asked, all excited animation, the words bursting from her.

His lips curved into a smile that drew out all the uncertainty in her soul and sent it soaring into happiness. 'You look so ravishing, it is positively affronting, my dear,' he said.

She blushed. 'You can't mean that.' Then she stopped, realizing he was teasing her, and that his eyes now also danced with pleasure.

'You shall be the most cossetted, the most beloved wife any man has ever been fortunate enough to marry.' He smiled broadly with a flash of white teeth.

She suddenly thought of the child she was carrying. She could never tell him, it would spoil everything if she did and he would refuse to marry her, but time was passing and before long her condition would be apparent. 'Can we marry as soon as possible, Garnet?' she asked, taking the dress down and folding it under one arm. 'Very, very soon — I see no need to wait.'

He put his hands on her shoulders and she took one of his fingers in the way of a small child. 'If that is what you want, Esther, I'm sure it can be arranged. Your father has agreed reluctantly for me to take care of all the wedding arrangements. Buck Jones' case has been referred to the High Court in Cape Town because the Circuit court cannot pass the death sentence. I will go to town to present evidence on his behalf and we could proceed there together on our honeymoon. The case could go on for months, so perhaps it is better for a marriage without delay. Glendower Park will be restored by the end of the month.'

Esther met his look with a frown. 'Papa must have hated not being able to finance the wedding arrangements himself.'

Garnet smiled and dropped his hands. 'He did, but necessity must be faced. He can't and I can, and I am very pleased to be able to do so. I can promise you it will be one of the largest social occasions of the year.'

147

She lowered her eyes, hesitating. 'And your family — will they not mind missing it? Has your father recovered?'

Garnet bit his lip, then said, 'My father's health has declined even more, unfortunately, but there is no way I can leave for England now, as you know. The rest of my family will agree to whatever I decide but in due time I shall take you to meet them, never fear.'

Esther stared straight ahead, watching the dragonflies dart into the air, hearing the gentle cooing of the turtledoves. She thought of Buck Jones on his way to languish in Cape Town gaol waiting for his trial to begin anew.

Garnet put his hand gently on her arm and said, 'All will be well, and now regrettably I must take my leave of you, for there is much to be done now that we are to be married sooner than anticipated.'

'Will you not stay for a dish of tea?' she enquired hopefully. He shook his head. 'There is no time, my sweeting, but I thank you all the same.'

He mounted his horse at once, leaving her to stare after him, the dress and the other gifts pressed close to her heart.

She was saved. Her child would have a father and she would leave Dwyers' Cross. In a whirl of petticoats and skirts she ran back to the house to spread the news.

The weeks passed swiftly for Esther, who was in such a dreamlike state that the events forming around her making history on the frontier, and the wretched state of her family's affairs, no longer reached her as the day of her wedding approached.

It was set for the end of December, to be held in the small church of St George's in Grahamstown, and celebrated afterwards with a luncheon in the restored gardens of Glendower Park. The day of the wedding dawned sunny and bright, with the lick of the wind in it. All the garrison, leading settler families and influential dignatories were invited. Among the latter were Mr Biggs and Major Colebrooke of the Committee of Enquiry, sent out from England to investigate the settlers' complaints. Lord Charles Somerset, being indisposed, regretfully sent his apologies, but hoped to see Garnet and his young bride on their honeymoon in Cape Town. He had not visited the frontier once since his return from England, and did not seem likely to do so.

Garnet had a banquet sent up from Cape Town, accompanied by

the very best Constantia and imported wines. He had purchased a splendid trousseau for his bride, and his mansion was cleaned from top to bottom until it gleamed, graced with the most exquisite silver and gold for her pleasure. He had chosen her wedding gown with infinite care, and had it sent around to the cottage of the friends with whom she was staying in Hill Street, Grahamstown.

Esther woke early. She sat up, stretching, and gazed across at the white silk wedding gown, striped in pale gold, draped carefully over the back of her chair. She was entranced by it and could not wait to put it on. Her pregnancy had not yet begun to show, and it fitted her figure to perfection, bringing out the new woman in her.

She left the bed and picked it up, whirling around the room, a faint, exultant flush under her skin. She was intoxicated by the events shaping themselves around her. Soon Garnet would be her husband and she the mistress of Glendower Park. She threw the gown carelessly across the bed and examined her hands. For weeks she had rubbed them with goose-grease to make them soft and white. Her nose wrinkled distastefully; they would have to do. She sat on the bed, fingering with delight the pile of gowns lying on the new wooden chest, waiting to be packed. The almost-forgotten feel of expensive silks, velvets, the festoons of gloriously coloured laces and ribbons running through her restless fingers.

Sitting back sighing, she watched the moving reflections of the early morning light shimmer in mother-of-pearl patterns on the ceiling, feeling her hair falling free in shining, tremulous waves about her shoulders and down her back. From now on she would be a wife in every sense of the word, she thought, puckering her brows with anticipation and a certain amount of uncertainty. She wished her mother were here to guide her first steps in the biggest adventure of her life.

She rose and stared out of the window at the silent hills, their growths of shrub and trees of green running down the gullies like stubble, and dominating it all, the square grey bulk of Fort England. She wondered what the future would bring in this new world of hers.

The babble of conversation stopped abruptly in the new, small church, already named the Cathedral, as Esther appeared at the threshold on the arm of her father. There was a subdued murmur of admiration and envy as she walked forward, tall, proud and very

149

beautiful. The folds of the white silk gown billowed softly almost to her exquisitely-slippered feet. A necklace of pale peridotstones sparkled around her slim neck, a gift from Garnet, the symbol of everlasting faithfulness. She carried a finely-embroidered, cream satin bag, silk tassells at the corners, in one long, white silk gloved hand.

Every head turned towards her, but she gazed straight ahead to where Garnet waited for her at the altar. There was a certain tension in his body, his eyes transfixed by her beauty, as he turned to watch her slowly walk down the aisle towards him.

Without warning, Esther knew a moment of blind panic. Somewhere in her mind a voice cried out that she was making a terrible mistake, committing herself to a man whom, deep in her heart, she did not love. From this point there would be no turning back. She wondered if he shared this sense of being caught up in an implacable destiny, that whatever the future held, they had to endure it together all their lives. And what would happen if he ever found out about the child?

But the chill in her heart was momentary. She found it was not too hard to dismiss it. After all, she had thought about it for a long time and it was the only sensible course of action to follow.

As every neck in the church craned towards them, her mind cleared, and her head went up. She had made her decision and she would not be afraid to see it through to the end.

Laree followed in rose bombaset and a Dunstable hat, as Matron of Honour, standing behind the bride as Esther knelt beside Garnet on the red velvet cushions made and embroidered by the women of the congregation.

How handsome he looks, Esther thought, as she stole a glance at Garnet's disciplined, classical profile. Her ringlets trembled beneath her cream bonnet as she surreptitiously studied his bright red tunic with its gold epaulettes and revers of black silk striped in gold. He wore his ceremonial sword in its decorated scabbard at his side, the pommel wrought in purest gold, embellished with small sapphires and rubies, glowing like rainbow prisms, entwined with seed pearls.

The carriage stood outside the church in the dusty street as the bridal pair emerged later and climbed in. Sand was sprinkled in its path to ensure a fruitful marriage, the outriders started and the carriage set off at a spanking speed to Glendower Park for the wedding luncheon. The late morning light suffused evenly with gold splashes of colour the trees and bushes that had escaped the flood damage.

They entered the massive, imported gates, passing a mantle of red geraniums escaping over the low wall of the long driveway. And there was the new house, large, impressive and grey, long sash windows thrown open to the sunshine and air.

Esther could hardly breathe with admiration. This was to be her new home. She beamed at Garnet as he led her into the house filled with cream and gold, regency-striped furniture. They went through the large, stone-flagged entrance hall, from where a graceful flight of stairs led up to the bed-chambers. She clapped her hands with delight as she glided after him into one of the reception rooms leading off the entrance hall, where the important guests were assembled with crystal goblets of red Constantia wine, a choice of clarets, madeiras and champagne. Large doors opened out on to the spacious garden where the tables for the men of Garnet's company had been set out under the trees.

The luncheon passed in a euphoric dream for Esther. The buzz of talk, toasts and music rose and fell as she laughed and smiled, totally untouched by the envious, sour looks directed at her from the unmarried young women and their mothers.

Later she stood for a brief, sweet moment gazing out of the window, savouring the pleasure of it all. Her eyes travelled over the garden where the faint wind plumed the tips of the milkwood trees, and the guests performed the minuet. She was now mistress of it all, with a husband who loved and wanted her.

Her hands twirling the goblet of sweet wine, so favoured by the late Napoleon, her attention wandered past the dancers to the men's table where drink and laughter flowed richly on the warm, summer air. There was one person missing: Buck Jones with his amused, mocking assurance. She felt a strange plummeting of her spirits when she thought of him now, fighting for his life, so far away.

She turned away so violently from her memories that she spilled a drop of red wine down the front of her wedding gown. It lay like a splash of blood on the pale silk. She shivered superstitiously at the sight of it.

Looking up, she saw Garnet weaving his way through the throng of guests towards her. He seemed not to want to let her out of his sight, almost as if he feared she would vanish, disappear from his life

151

like a wisp of Irish smoke. Against the background of talk and music, his face lit up in an eager smile as he saw her still standing at the window.

Esther took a deep, steadying breath, and ignoring those around her, she went forward to meet her husband, her face miraculously wreathed in smiles.

CHAPTER
Fourteen

The bedchamber seemed gay in its green and gold drapes. Esther stood before the rosewood dressing table looking at the new set of silver-backed brushes, at the oval mirror framed with delicate, silver scroll-work. The long, crimson candles flickered and dripped wax down their silver sconces on the small table beside the great, canopied, four-poster bed, with its deep green, velvet curtains, edged with gold tassels.

Now that the excitement of the celebration was over and she was alone in her new bedchamber waiting for Garnet, she wondered if it would be like the time with Buck. Everything had been so different from her dreams and fantasies, that she hardly knew what to think anymore. Now that the moment of her surrender had come, she wanted it to be as intense, as complete, as that first time in the dunes at Port Frances. She felt that then everything would be right again, that all her fears and her feelings for Buck would vanish, and Garnet would safely take his place in her mind, in her life.

'You are so beautiful,' Garnet said deeply, as he emerged from his dressing-room, his nightshirt elegantly frilled and crested and open at the neck to reveal a lean and muscular chest. His shadow fell on the thick carpet lying like soft, green moss beneath his feet.

She felt the excitement rise within her. Everything was so right — the atmosphere, the man, the setting in the lovely home. For once, it was just as she had ever dreamed.

His glance flickered over the shadow of her breasts through the diaphanous folds of the pale lemon nightgown, provocative and arresting. Yet the gown was so simply cut that her nakedness beneath seemed innocent, almost vulnerable. He stood looking at her, as if not wanting to spoil the lovely picture she made, not wanting to disturb that beguiling innocence that hid the burning fire within. She inclined her head towards him, with that familiar mischievous look, her eyes clear and eager. This was the night she would believe her child had been conceived, with this dashing man in this most elegant of homes. Never would it know the truth about its origins.

In the flames of the flickering candles, the room swayed in to life as she walked towards him, her nightgown swinging about her shapely legs, the golden light moulding her figure exotically against the gloom. She saw Garnet in a new light, noticing the swift and unfamiliar excitement deep in his eyes. She had never noticed it before.

'You are in truth the most handsome, the most desirable man in all the world,' she smiled, her voice having the edge of triumph in it.

He was faintly disconcerted. She noticed it, but decided to ignore it. Now was the time to charm him, beguile him, capture him for ever.

He took a step towards her, his long, supple fingers under her chin, lifting her face so that her eyes were full on him. 'I am indeed the most fortunate man in the world,' he said huskily. 'I won't hurt you, I promise you. The first pain won't last, my sweeting, it will soon be over.'

For the first time that evening she suddenly felt lost and hesitant. The sudden, cold truth was that he was talking to her as a virgin maid, someone to be led into the secrets of the marriage bed gently and slowly, when she, who had already enjoyed the bittersweet joys of union with a man, was impatient to experience them all over again. She was conscious for a sharp second of nothing except the strange, desolate void of deception that enclosed her, separating her from everything she had known.

Taking her face in his hands with infinite gentleness, he kissed her on the lips. Without shame, in her desperation to calm her own fears, she threw her arms up to his neck, pressing her body against his. She felt him tighten as she pulled his face down to hers again, her long strong legs moulded against him. Her lips were moist and slightly parted as she deliberately flaunted her striking, sensual beauty in the flimsy nightgown. She felt him respond as he bent his head and put his lips to hers, brushing them gently at first, but with increasing pressure, hard and deliberate. Then his hands came up to cover hers. He removed them from his neck and held them in a strong clasp.

154

Her lips felt bruised, her face flamed, it was as though he was putting a brand on her. Garnet Fitzwilliam had kissed her, something she had wanted for years, but the rhythm of her pulse remained unchanged. The room around her dissolved in a mist of acute disappointment, and reshaped itself as he led her to the bed, smelling faintly and pleasantly of sandalwood, and on to the satin sheets. Then he drew her to himself, kissing her as he gathered up the fierce offering she wanted him to take.

Later, she lay in the great bed feeling bitterly disappointed. She sighed to herself, her hand reaching up and pulling the lace-edged pillow closer to her. Sleep would not come. Garnet had been caring and pleasant, but something gnawed at her, that core of unsatisfied longing, that deep passion within her still untapped, unspent. It had been a disappointment after all her expectations. Nothing about it had been like the time with Buck. She wondered now, if she had imagined it, heightened it too much in her mind. But she knew that Garnet was not a passionate man, he preferred the caresses to the actual passion of love. She felt that, deep down, he had been shocked at her abandonment, at her wild eagerness, and now she felt ashamed of her wanton display. He had expected a hesitant maid, and instead found a full-blooded woman ready and eager to enjoy their marriage night together.

Slowly, against her will, her thoughts became a sharp disturbance. Without warning she saw the image of Buck Jones. The darkness was full of him. She knew every detail of his powerful presence — the unforgettable moulding of his face, his body, the eyes so full of light, the beautiful mouth curling at the corners, the dimples deeply cleft even as he moved his mouth. By day she could put him out of her mind, but tonight the thoughts would not go. They were in the room, haunting her like a restless, bitter memory she did not want and hated herself for having.

Turning over, she pressed her face into the pillow. Closing her eyes in shame, the tears of mortification rolled down her cheeks, as suddenly she was seized by a nameless, crushing black fear, and a sense of her own weakness. Nothing must go wrong with her marriage, nothing must spoil it, she would see to that — she had to. After a while she turned back, staring into the darkness, and slowly as the minutes ticked away on the small ormolu clock on the mantelpiece, the storm inside her passed.

It was then that she became aware that Garnet's place beside her was empty . . .

She found him in the oak-lined library, with its low-beamed ceiling, the red damask curtains drawn full over the long sash windows. He sat in a brocaded armchair near the fireplace, his long, lean legs stretched out before him, the graceful body looking unusually crumpled and dishevelled. An empty bottle of cognac stood beside him on the desk, a glass and an unlit cigarillo dangling from one hand, the gold signet ring with the Fitzwilliam crest glinting on his little finger in the light of one guttering, wax candle. The few portraits of the Fitzwilliam clan appeared to frown down upon him from their frames on the panelled walls.

She saw him watching her as she stood in the doorway, a lighted candle in her hand, his features a shadowy mask of planes and angles. Just then, she wanted to kiss him with passionate urgency, and was about to hold out her arms to him, when his expression stopped her as he lifted his face to the light of the candle.

Her eyes, straying to the desk, became aware of the heap of used cigarillo-butts incongruously lying in a dainty Wedgwood dish, the stale smell very strong in the musty room. For a moderate man such as Garnet, that in itself was very unusual.

'Is anything wrong, Garnet?' she asked, approaching him, very much aware that she was almost naked and very vulnerable.

He remained still, looking at her, and with a sense of deep dismay, she saw that he had been drinking most uncharacteristically. He was not drunk, but just enough to have become hostile.

Quickly she placed the candle on the desk and went to him. 'What is it, my dear, has something happened to upset you?'

His usually well-groomed, smooth dark hair was tousled, his face unshaven and haggard. He looked like a very old man. Raising his glass slowly, tauntingly at her, a contemptuous curl to his lips, he said, 'A toast, madam — to your hideous deceit.' There was nothing wrong with his speech, and he was still very much in command of his senses, or appeared to be. 'Your beguiling beauty and vulnerability have quite undone me — had me completely fooled — forsooth, but you must be the cleverest whore this side of the Keiskamma River.'

'Garnet — have you taken leave of your senses? Whatever are you talking about? In your condition you should be in bed.'

He put down his goblet with a shuddering clatter, knocking over the Limoges vase used for spills beside it. 'I will go to bed when and with whom I choose, woman — but never again with you. You have made a fool of me on my wedding night, pretending to be as pure as the driven snow, when all the time you are used goods! To your credit, I would never have found out if you had been clever enough to simulate a virgin's first night. But you are too innocent for that, too inexperienced, madam — and that makes me even more angry. You did not know enough to deceive me and yet you have dallied with another behind my back. I demand to know, as your husband, why you did not see fit to tell me that last night was not your first with a man? How could you, after all I have done for you, your family? I have taken you in without a dowry, I have laid the world at your feet, and you deceive me in the vilest manner possible! Your father is the biggest blackguard I know — sending you to my office to bid for my favours to hide what you were, to keep his own name, *his* reputation clean, whilst mine must become defiled, dishonoured.'

His mouth sat in a bitter line, his black brows drawn in a straight bar across his brooding, dark eyes. It was then that fear struck her, a fear so profound that she became cold as death. He knew, and there was no way she could fool him. He was too experienced, as she was not. It was useless to try.

'My father is ignorant of any such matters concerning me. He is not to blame for anything I have done,' she turned on him, snapping.

He threw down the cigarillo, and rose, standing before her, glowering. 'So! You admit it. How dare you shame me like this.'

'I do not admit anything!' She stamped her foot, shaking her hair off her neck and shoulders. It was a cloud of red-gold in the candlelight.

'You will admit it, my dear — I am your husband, and I have a right to know about the most important matter between a man and his wife!' He threw her into a chair with cruel strength. His hands bunched into two tight fists, and she knew that if she had been a man, he would have knocked her senseless, and that it was her female vulnerability at that moment that saved her.

She pulled herself up with as much composure as her shaking limbs would allow, but the dark eyes meeting hers gave her no reassurance. She could have faced the blows from his hands better than the furious intensity of his gaze. Her usually robust self-confidence began to ebb.

'Well, madam, and what have you to say for yourself? Marrying me under false pretences. What are you, Esther, some kind of strumpet?' The admiration she was used to seeing in his face was gone, his expression now set and hard, his breath smelling strongly of brandy.

Her pride stopped her for a moment, but the words burst out. 'You treat me like some sinner — some wicked, unrepentant, scarlet woman of the streets. It's so — so humiliating!'

Her voice was vibrant with emotion. The ever present temper threatened to erupt in an embarrassing display. He frowned heavily to silence her. 'That is what you can expect when your behaviour is nothing less than scandalous. You disgust me, you know that?'

He looked at her hard, and paused. The expression on his face was difficult to read, but some new darkness seemed to move at the back of his eyes.

'You may not love me, you may not care a damn about my feelings, but do you realize what would happen if ever this got out? It will cause the biggest scandal not only here, but in England. It will bring disrepute on my family, ruin my careeer — and your reputation. I will be disinherited and forced to live on the meagre offerings I can get. Not that I suppose you care too much about that!' he said, ominously, his face white and strained.

Her dark blue eyes were wide with an effort to hold back the tears of angry despair. All that had been beautiful, exciting, now lay in a heap of ashes at her feet, and all because of a brief moment of intense madness with Buck Jones. If Garnet ever found out about Buck, she knew he would not lift a finger to help him in the trial. He must never find out — for it would not only cost Buck his job, but also his life.

The utter helplessness of being a woman totally at the mercy of her husband struck her with full force. Then her dominant self-respect flared into life. His manner riled her. 'What do you want me to do with all this talk of your self-righteous and holy background? Grovel at your feet?'

He glared at the empty glass on the desk, seeming to gather words to answer her. When he spoke, his voice was unrecognizably rough, harsh, unforgiving. 'Throwing you out on the street will be too good for you — and it will ruin me. No, you will be forced to live under the same roof as the man whom you have shamed — and to the world we will assume a happy, united front. No one — no one at all, will ever know what you have done. And before I close this — distasteful subject — you owe me an explanation. I want to know who it was you dallied with, and how many times?'

There was a silence. She looked away from him, now afraid, so terribly afraid that she had reached that point at which everything between them would be finished, that there would be no reunion between them. She pushed a loose curl from her forehead. She felt bereft, lonely, confused and painfully aware that what she said in the next few minutes would scar her life.

'I don't care,' she said angrily, rising from the chair to draw herself up to her imperious height, 'I don't care what you think of me. There's nothing I can do about that now, but don't you dare treat me like some despicable baggage.'

He stared at her with a look of contempt. 'That is exactly what you are — a baggage, giving yourself away freely before your marriage. So that is how I will treat you.'

He looked at her with sudden desire mingled with bitterness. 'You are mine, and mine you will stay,' he rasped, his voice thick, the sight of her almost naked body sending him into a mad, unfamiliar frenzy. 'No one in this earth shall take you away from me, d'you hear? If you act like a whore I shall treat you like one.'

With an oath he seized her hair with one hand and with the other he ripped and tore the nightgown from her shoulders and forced her to her knees. She cried out, striving to push him away, but he held her in a steel-like grasp and she was helpless against his strength. He tore at the nightgown until it was in shreds and she was exposed before him in the wavering candlelight. She tried to cover herself but it was too late. His lips were all over her, pressing her to him. There was no gentleness, no love, only the angry desire to teach her a lesson she would never forget.

She fell backwards with him on top of her, her eyes open wide as her heart contracted in terror. Pain almost overwhelmed her, her pale flesh quivered, then her whole body was in flames, tortured almost beyond what she could endure. It was as if she was spinning down some awful, suffocating tunnel with this unrecognizable figure bent over her, furiously administering a terrible punishment so that her heart and flesh burned as if in hell.

Once she thought she would faint, but not once did she beg for mercy. Then she screamed thickly as her raw nerves overcame the shock, and pain once more flashed through her. She reached up with claw-like fingers, and rent his back until she could feel the blood run and she was spent with exhaustion and agony.

At last he rolled from her with a sound of detestation, as if awakening from some kind of nightmare. She looked up at the grey, deflated face. How she cried out silently against the way he had used and punished her, and his final anger that had caused this most dreadful outrage. Sick and dizzy and only half-conscious, she closed her eyes. Her face was now quiet, the vitality gone out of her. His fierce, wild reaction had seemingly killed her completely. All she felt was the deep weariness of shock and disillusionment after some hope has been shattered and crushed in the dust. The light from the ornate candle on the desk fell revealingly on her pale, lifeless body, but still she could not move.

Garnet was uttering gasping words, incoherent, almost moaning. 'I have ravaged a woman for the first time in my life,' he groaned heavily, dropping into the chair near the fireplace. His hands distractedly ran through the tousled dark hair, his voice like a shell, transparent and empty within. 'How could I have done it? What possessed me to do such a terrible thing?' The pain was back inside him, writhing and living and ugly. 'God help me, for I have shamed myself.'

He looked at her, her crumpled form still lying with her legs drawn up into a foetal position on the carpet. Unsteadily he rose and weaved his way to the door, disappearing into the shadows beyond as if trying to hide himself from her, from himself.

It seemed long afterwards that she pushed herself on to her haunches, her whole body in bruised torment. She pulled the torn pieces of the nightgown around her, her head buried in her hands. A small line of blood dripped from her lip as she rocked back and forth and wept bitter, agonising tears, drenched in utter despair and self-loathing.

Then, quite suddenly, there was a lurch of pain in her womb, and she felt a trickle of blood down her legs. Clutching the remnants of her nightgown in agitation, she pulled herself up from the floor and, half crawling, she groped her way to the staircase, leaving small, tell-tale spots of bright red blood along the floor.

It was there, struggling towards the first stair, that the pain overtook her. She cried out, trying to throw out her arms to protect

160

herself and had the sensation of falling forward into complete blackness.

A face swam into view, seeming to descend from the curtains above her head. The bedchamber was warm, the steady light given out by the candles about the room throwing their full glow on the large, canopied bed. Esther came back to consciousness to see Karmela, a wizened, bent little woman, the oldest of the Hottentot servants, bending over her. Esther saw her eyes, dark and bright as apple pips and thought that in that moment she had never seen an angel of mercy so beautiful and comforting.

Karmela put down the candle-holder she had been carrying and bent to examine Esther. She shook her head, her forehead puckered with hundreds of small wrinkles, as Garnet appeared in the doorway.

Karmela left the room and he approached the bed. 'Karmela has tried to stop the bleeding with dressings, but now she says that she has an old tribal remedy — a potion of certain leaves which will stop it altogether and not harm the child you carry.'

Esther stiffened. Looking at his pale, tortured face, she knew that Karmela had told him. She felt anguish and pain that he should have learned of her condition in such a fashion from a servant. He turned away from the bed, fingering the gold signet ring on the little finger of his left hand, with obvious, deep embarrassment. She gazed at him silently, strangely ill at ease.

They were interrupted by Karmela's return, bearing a dish of ground leaves. Esther swallowed the bitter herbal concoction and Karmela said nothing until she had finished and was satisfied that it had all gone. Then she smiled down at Esther with a sudden puckish warmth.

'Please thank her for her kindness,' Esther managed to say, surprising herself with her own self-consciousness. Karmela remained tactfully impassive from then on because she knew they were both uneasy. She watched them for a moment longer and then disappeared from the room.

Garnet turned back, frowning, and adjusted the frilled cuff of his dressing-gown. He looked across at her, a film of quick emotion over his eyes. His tousled dark hair gleamed in the soft light as he moved his head.

'You need not be concerned that knowledge of your — condition

161

— will get out. Karmela is the only one who knows, and she can be trusted.' He took a gold snuffbox from his pocket and took a strong pinch of snuff, trying to control the violent trembling in his fingers. 'You know as well as I that we will have to play a charade during our stay in Cape Town. I have to go and I cannot leave you here for your own good. It would only cause talk which we can do without. Karmela says you must rest for some days, and then we will leave.' He paused as though collecting his thoughts. 'I will tell the servants that not being used to the house, you lost your way in the darkness and fell down the stairs. You will be escorted carefully in the curricle as soon as you are well enough.' He did not look at her as he spoke. 'You will understand that your condition will have to be concealed for the time being. It wouldn't do to have it revealed so soon after our wedding, as you will appreciate. That will only give rise to more rumours. There will be functions to attend. Our presence will be required — any absence will be suspect.'

Esther lay still and pale in the vast green and gold bed, surrounded by a sea of palest silk and lace-edged pillows. Only the gentle ticking sound of the ormolu clock was heard. A candle flickered in its bulbous, pale-gold glass shade, the prisms of crystal winking and twinkling with the rising heat on the bedside table, throwing shadows across the bed.

She remained very still in shocked silence. Her hand was limp and hot, the gold wedding ring flashing incongruously in the light. Her face, usually reflecting her impulsive warmth and gaiety, was now deathly pale. She could not believe that she would ever be reduced to this joyless, lifeless shadow. All the laughter, the dizzy excitement had gone. It was the lonely, bleak morning after the fun of the ball was long past, and only the dusty memories and the waste was left behind.

Her eyes misting with agonised tears, she cleared her throat. 'I suppose you want to know the identity of the father?'

Through the tears she saw his face, marked with such pain it horrified her. She was strangely moved.

'I would rather not know — it would do no good — not after what I did to you.' His face tightened with the futility of it all. 'It doesn't matter now — for all intents and purposes, the child is mine.'

She stared at the unfathomable depths in his eyes, his face now set in hard, bitter lines. She closed her eyes with a heart full of heavy

162

foreboding. The physical pain remained intensively alive. It was too late to save her marriage, her relationship with Garnet — and what was there to save? It would be a marriage in name only, there would be no life in it, no love, only a dead, respectable shell.

Something deep inside her had turned to ice. She suddenly felt utterly exhausted and very sleepy. She had lost everything she had ever wanted. She would never be a real wife to Garnet — there was nothing left except his anger, her disillusionment, and the unwanted child inside her, clinging to the grudging life that awaited it.

CHAPTER
Fifteen

While Joshua, Cady and the other settlers were deep in discussion with the Commissioners of Enquiry, and busy with the clearing of the lands and the re-building of homes, Garnet took his newly-wed wife to Cape Town. Although he had withdrawn from her since the wedding night, he maintained a reserved composure before the servants and the world.

Garnet was better than Esther at putting a fine cutting edge on his civility, but desperation taught her to become more adept at it. She had found the days long, and the nights longer. The only bright spot was the approaching journey to Cape Town.

Nothing more was said about the wedding night, but it hovered like a dark spectre on the horizon of their marriage, and the growing child inside her distanced them even more. Garnet was concerned that she travel with ease and saw to it that they did, by curricle, a fine vehicle made of polished wood. In every way outwardly, he was the perfect, solicitous husband. In this manner they settled into an uneasy state of polite neutrality which carried them through the times that were shared with company.

They arrived in Cape Town on one of those days of dazzling clearness and an intensely blue sky. The air was warm and balmy as their carriage gambolled down the sunlit streets drowsing in the shade of old oaks in the town, climbing the edge of Table Bay. There was a soft, golden light, which gave an aura of enchantment to the scene, and Esther felt her spirits rising. She loved the wide streets, at the end of which she could see the bay, ready to admit that she had never dreamt it could be like this. She was charmed with the magnificent blue mountains towering above the town with its tree-lined squares.

Light-skinned Hottentots and ebony Malays with their glossy hair, wooden clogs and conical straw hats, stood in conclaves or carried trays of fruit and vegetables slung from bamboo poles. Tall, dignified Muslim priests walked past, their long robes flowing out behind them. There were even one or two Americans with close-cropped hair. The town was smaller than Cork City, but it was quaint and interesting, the wide beautiful thoroughfares cheek by jowl with narrow, ill-paved ones.

They were in a different world, far removed from the turbulence and conflicts of the frontier. The carriage swung into the Heerengracht, where the river from Platteklip Gorge ran down the centre of the street in long water-furrows. They passed the Parade, the oldest public square in the colony, not far from the harbour and stretching before the castle gates. A large ornate fountain splashed in the centre of it, the majestic backdrop of Table Mountain and Devil's Peak rising behind it. Elegantly dressed women on the arms of soldiers strolled across it, and children ran, rolling hoops.

Beyond the castle walls, the bay danced with silver chips of light, with tall troopships, brigs, cargo schooners and coasting sloops, bobbing on the tide.

Esther adjusted the skirts of her new gown of sprigged muslin, frilled and trimmed with yards and yards of green and white galloon ribbons and flounces of Brussels lace, a new straw hat plumed with white ostrich feathers perched over her bright red ringlets. She had requested Garnet to stop at a coaching house outside the town so that she could change from her travelling habit and arrive in the town in style.

The noonday gun from the castle boomed out over the town as the curricle stopped at a well-known lodging house where they were to stay.

Although the law now forbid the importation of slaves, there were still many living in the town, in the straggling clusters of square, whitewashed houses with their large, untidy gardens and verandahs, and on the farms stretching through the beautiful Constantia Valley and the Boland.

There was unpleasant conflict between Lord Charles, the writer Thomas Pringle, and the publisher Fairbairn over the freedom of the press. There was also ugly gossip, growing in alarming proportions, alleging an unnatural relationship between Lord Charles and his

165

physician, the enigmatic Dr James Barry. But the Cape Town Garnet showed Esther was the gayest place she had seen since arriving in Africa, and she saw no sign of any undercurrents.

He introduced her to the snobbish clique of officers' wives, with soft hands and pretty clothes, who never talked of weighty, colonial matters and hard times, and who warily accepted her because she was Garnet's wife. She did not care a hoot what they really thought of her, delighting in the regimental balls, soirees, the whist parties, the wagers and the visits to dramatic performances at the Garrison Theatre. Due to the estrangement from her husband, she enjoyed the coterie of young officers who gathered about her.

Esther and Garnet visited the Fish Market near the beach. At the harbour they watched great casks filled with brandy and muscadel rolled down the wharves by sailors, and loaded on board ships. They lingered to see the fishing boats return with their catches of shining fish. From the boats came the high-pitched, tinny wailing of the fish horns that echoed back from the mountains and the sea-lapped, castle walls, setting the gulls screeching into the air, and drawing crowds, laughing and shouting, to the water's edge. One by one the boats came crowding to the shore beaching their craft stern first to lessen the risk of broaching-to in the surf, the bright bloom of the fish catching the sun's rays.

Malay women, turbaned priests and armies of fezzed small boys waited at the landing. Afterwards the fish-hawkers, in their wide pagoda hats, carried away their twin baskets strung on bamboo yokes across their shoulders, to sell from door to door, and the fish carts rumbled off with much hooting and whistling from their occupants.

Esther was appalled, however, at a sale of slaves in one of the squares, by the way such things were still taken as a matter of fact; a young pregnant female fetched the highest price, to be used as a wet-nurse.

The town was rough and ready in parts, picturesque and exciting in others. It was filled with lodging and Eating Houses and dining with Garnet was an adventure for Esther, for he knew what to order and how it should be cooked. The best Cape and imported wines, the liquers, especially the mysteriously blended old Cape liquer, Van Der Hum, were exciting to her, and best of all was the traditional Cape cookery. After so many months of deprivation and simple farm cooking on the frontier, Esther thought she had never tasted such delicious food. She took the greatest pleasure in eating dishes she had not herself cooked, from tables sparkling with silver and polished glass. Steaming periwinkle soup, piquantly flavoured bredies, especially tomato bredie, boosted by a drop of sherry, spiced curried fish, sosasties, rice sprinkled with dark, plump raisins. Then there was the Malay relish, Blatjang, with its apricots in vinegar, red chillies and coriander seeds, the chutneys and mebos.

She never tired of tasting the light, fluffy, golden brown pancakes, dusted with cinnamon, the green melon preserve frosted with sugar, and the freshly ground coffee. And not once in all that time did Garnet show the world that he was anything other than the devoted, thoughtful husband.

Lord Charles invited Esther and Garnet, who was one of his favourites, to the lavish dinner parties he still held and for which he was justly famous. He invited them to his greatest love, the racing at the Turf Club at Green Point. Here Esther sat in her carriage surrounded by the other ladies, watching the men on horseback riding in the then fashionable system of wagering one horse against another. She watched Garnet race one of the Governor's own thoroughbreds, sitting back on the concourse of open ground where the recently-built, square lighthouse, carrying its own two fixed lights formed a distinctive focal point for the scheme.

Lord Charles was present in his English coach, his officers from the castle on horseback, while farmers camped beside their wagons and Hottentots sold pickled fish and watermelon konfyt. Liveried Malay coachmen in buckled footwear and wide-brimmed straw hats, sat on the drivers' boxes of carriages and Cape carts, while their masters' wives and children were jammed inside between hampers of food.

The coloureds sang and played their home-made guitars, the plaintive notes of their songs drifting on the air, carrying years of the colony's history, the sufferings of their slavery and their hopes for freedom.

The carriages decanted their frothy cargoes, then it was hampers out, gloves off and into the delicacies, the ladies elegantly toying with their fishy hors d'oeuvres.

Esther had been curious to meet Lord Charles, the arch enemy of the settlers on the frontier, of whom she had heard: 'His power is absolute and his resentment ruin'. She was pleasantly surprised to find him a conscientious man with brilliant, dark eyes and a stern, Beaufort nose, trying to work through the maze of strange and conflicting currents in this former Dutch colony. He invited her and Garnet to dine often with him and his second wife, Lady Mary, at Newlands House, a single-storeyed residence standing in the shelter of Devil's Peak, set back from the road amid spacious lawns and gardens and surrounded by sprawling Cape Dutch verandahs.

There he spent many hours cloistered with Garnet discussing the problems and the clashes on the frontier, six hundred miles away, concerned with finding a way of curbing the Xhosa cattle raids and the latest murders from a centre of government so far away. There they also discussed the coming murder trial and its implications.

Esther was torn. She felt increasingly sorry for the Governor and his growing need of help and comfort as his enemies hurled into the attack against him, but she also felt sorry for her father and uncle and the rest in their predicament. It was only then that she began to wonder vaguely at the toll the whole settler scheme had taken. She remembered her father's long, brooding silences, the deep bitterness etched into his face.

Lord Charles was furious with Sir Rufane Donkin's changes to his house and gardens during his leave of absence, the petty interference in his household affairs that he thought had been a deliberate attempt to make him appear an extravagant autocrat. He was also convinced that the continued cattle raiding and the murders of several settlers were the inevitable result of Sir Rufane altering Lord Charles' policy of forbidding settlers to own cattle. He had heard the most alarming and critical reports, calling the settlers idle troublemakers, from his landdrost Henry Rivers, who was much hated by the settlers. He said he was unable, at such a far distance, to distinguish the many troublemakers from those who had real grievances.

And so the days passed as Garnet tried to encourage him to visit the frontier as soon as possible, to see for himself what was going on, and to meet the settlers personally. While Garnet was called more and more often to discussions with Lord Charles, to spend time with the military at the castle, or to live for days in suburban camps such as Wynberg, Esther explored the town, dragging her maid Phoebe along everywhere with her.

168

They visited the market square where wagons were drawn up under the trees, the Boer families bringing their produce to sell. They explored the Malay tailors, the saddlers and the merchants' shops, delighting in the English gingerbread, bakers, Dutch brewers, German gold, silver and coppersmiths, the comfit shops run by Chinamen with pigtails. It was as if she had been starved for so long in every way through the forced austerity of her life in Albany, that now, given the opportunity, all her suppressed feelings were unleashing themselves in a great, overwhelming desire for beautiful things, for newer and greater excitements, and a deep, never-ending craving for love.

She found increasingly that Garnet's sense of duty and purpose, second only to Lord Charles himself, was becoming more and more of an annoyance and disturbance to her. He had, she had learned, a strongly embedded sense of right and wrong, honour and hard work, which he used to deliberately shut her out from a large part of his life.

Her marriage was so different from what she had imagined. There were strict rules and regulations to which she had to conform. Garnet and everyone else expected that of her. She hated being a demure, submissive wife, treated with polite reserve and icy courtesy — so different from the picture she had formed of him up until their wedding night when the other side of him had been brutally exposed.

It all came to a head at the Artillery Ball, which they were forced to attend for the sake of protocol, in the large central room of the white, colonnaded Commercial Exchange on the Grand Parade, at the side of the Heerengracht.

The noise and chatter grew less as the eyes of three hundred guests in the ballroom swung in the direction of Garnet's entrance with Esther. There had been much talk of his marriage and speculation about his new wife. Now curiosity was matched by envy from the women, open admiration from the men, as Esther stood beside her husband, swathed in a shimmer of cream satin, ruched and flounced with lavender ribbons, which successfully hid any signs of her pregnancy. Her glowing hair was upswept into a matching crepe turban, close fitting around the elaboration of ringlets and the twist of corkscrew curls at the nape of her neck.

Garnet allowed himself a look of approval at her, his eyes

lingering on the burnished ringlets at either cheek, and the glitter of gold at her ears.

The large room, peopled with men and women dressed in silks and satins with gold and silver trimmings, filled Esther with an admiration which her pride forbade her to show. Alongside all this, Grahamstown was no better than a drab village, and Bathurst a molehill.

All chatter stopped. The stylishly-dressed single girls eyed her behind their gay, fluttering fans. They had all heard about Garnet's wife and her beauty, fearing and admiring her at once. The chaperones and married women sat on benches running around the ballroom, watching her with the greatest disapproval. They considered her far too flamboyant for a married woman, having heard of her exploits around the town with her maid, and the extravagant manner of her dress. A wife was expected to be more sedate than an unmarried girl, expected to wear forever a matron's cap at home. She was regarded as a romp who tossed custom aside, letting all her magnificent hair tumble exposed at home, or so they were told by those who had called upon her. They had heard about that impossibly-coloured hair.

Esther was surrounded immediately by an admiring coterie of young officers, and she danced as much as her condition allowed, to the rousing, military brass band. As she whirled by she was subjected to searching scrutiny by the older women, their cold eyes set hard and uncompromising behind their fans. They distorted her behaviour into something sordid and disgusting, her every look into the ugly proportions of a dangerous and wanton woman. She was wicked, tantalising and gay, claiming the attention of all the men, who had completely lost interest in the wilting, single girls propping up the walls. She chatted, she laughed and danced among the ornately-designed skirts swinging around the floor, lavish ostrich plumes adorning heads.

Esther was only too aware of herself and the enormous power of her attraction over the men. After all those dangerous months in the Coombs Valley, coupled with the dreadful experience on her wedding night and Garnet's continuing coldness, she emerged like some exotically-beautiful butterfly out of a despised chrysalis to flutter from one admirer to the next with dizzy delight. She had never felt more physically fit in months, and stood up more than well to the rigours of that night, determined that no one would ever guess at her condition.

The officers were mesmerised by her. She was quite different from anyone they had known. All the other women paled into insipidness beside her vivid beauty and vitality.

Garnet watched her across the crowded room. She smiled and laughed with a group of interested officers, all vying for her attention. He was standing beside a colonel, his polite expression becoming colder with every passing second. Much to her annoyance, Esther became aware of him.

'I do think it would be seemly and wise if we left now, my dear,' he said, casually advancing upon her through the sea of glimmering, fluttering colour. She drew a furious breath, feeling irrationally irritated with him after all his coldness towards her.

'Glory be — it is early yet. I am not tired,' she replied, with growing annoyance at what she had come to consider as his high-handed manner. With a rustle of satin and a clink of bracelets, she gave him a sarcastic look which provoked him. She saw his lips tighten and a moment of anger pass over his face.

'We are leaving now, my dear, I shall collect your wrap. Excuse me.' He forced a smile, inclining his head towards the younger men, who quickly snapped to attention.

Resentment and disappointment surged through Esther. With a sharp inner exclamation of exasperation she faced him. As though some stranger inside her spoke, she heard herself say witheringly, 'I shall not leave. Need I make myself plainer?'

He looked at her, his eyes narrowing as his face moved from surprise to grimness. 'I say it is time to leave, Esther. You will do as I say.'

The younger officers were embarrassed. They had no desire to infuriate the Captain in any way. The one nearest to her, a placating smile on his pleasant, if bland, face, turned to her: 'Do as your husband asks, madam, you will only cause a scene.'

Esther's temper soared. She threw her eyes heavenward, then gave him a quelling smile. 'Keep out of this, Lieutenant Patterson, this is a private matter between the Captain and myself.'

Submissively he gave her a faint smile and headed for the door, slowly followed by the others as the band struck up a waltz.

Garnet held out a white-gloved hand. 'You are being most

indiscreet and immature, my dear. You need to take every care of your health in your condition — let us leave before any scandal blows up, for I see a volcano simmering. You have over-tired yourself again.'

She held her arm stiffly to her side. Her face had the petulant sullenness of a child denied a Christmas present. 'I have done no such thing. If anything did happen to me or the chlld, I am sure it would please you tremendously. I am totally disgusted by your odious behaviour. I shall stay,' she said, refusing to allow him any victory.

He bowed suddenly with cool hauteur, his hand on her arm. 'Well then, I shall claim this waltz.'

Startled, Esther's eyes flew to his, and took new meaning from the steely quality of his dark expression. She had once known him as a kind and considerate suitor: she had come to know him as an angry and humiliated lover, and now he was a cool, proper and aloof military man, doing the right things at the right time without any feeling. She tried to forget it, but it was there at the back of her mind as he brought her into the centre of the dancers before she could protest.

He looked at her, an ironic twist to his finely-chiselled lips in an otherwise cold face. 'Am I so repulsive to dance with, my dear? It is not so bad after all, is it now?'

His voice was so cool that she lifted her chin in hot indignation. 'It is the privilege of a woman to speak with and act as she chooses in public.'

He faced her with a challenging eye. 'I might remind you, Mrs Fitzwilliam, that it is the privilege and prerogative of a man, and especially a husband, to command. You shall do as you are told.'

She glanced at him from two stormy eyes. 'You do not command me any more, not now, not ever.'

The dance ended and he swept her a bow, a determined glint in his aristocratic features. He held out his arm. 'Now I shall escort you back to our rooms.'

The musicians stopped for a short respite, and in the crush of guests, Garnet led her determinedly away, not stopping for any further argument.

She faced him, the pale cashmere shawl looped across her back, coming through her arms to fall almost to the ground. Then, because it was all so ridiculous, she began to laugh which

172

only caused him to be more angry.

'But you look so absurd, Garnet, like some dark, cold bear waiting to pounce on a poor, innocent butterfly.' She threw back her head, loosing a bubbling, infectious laugh before everyone present. He did not speak to her throughout the short journey back to the lodging house. She was left clenching her hands hard on the lavender, beaded reticule in her lap. Her flashing eyes stared out of the carriage window where she could just see the soft sprinkle of light from the carriage lamp out in front.

Lights from the small paned windows of the houses glowed like hot coals in a fire and lit up the uneven cobbles. The trees lining the street flickered with the shadows of watchmen in dark greatcoats patrolling the town from nightfall till morning gunfire, with their lighted lanterns, arms and rattles. Sedan bearers were drawn up at the door of an evening party waiting to carry the visitors home. Then they were past, into a quieter street where the only sound to be heard in the sudden, sombre silence was the clip-clop of the horses pulling the carriage.

Garnet faced her across the thick carpet of the room in the lodging house that they shared for the sake of decorum, his face a mask of familiar rage. 'And what do you hope to achieve by making a show of yourself, openly courting every officer in sight — and you carrying a child? By right, you should not be seen in public in your condition. You are now a married woman, a mother-to-be — but you seem to need constant reminding of the fact.'

'And you get a perverted sense of pleasure in reminding me! Mercy on us all! Nothing I did could harm the child, or your impossible reputation.' She felt weary of it all, and bored. She stifled a yawn, tossing her gleaming hair as she swept past him to the dressing table where she threw down the turban, reticule and shawl.

He folded his arms tightly across his chest, his dark brows drawing together menacingly. 'In case it has slipped your mind, I have a position to uphold. The way in which you shamelessly flaunt yourself before the society of this town is disgracing us both.'

She undid all the buttons of her cream gown with impatient hands, and it fell in a shining heap at her ankles. Then it was the turn of the stays and chemise. Finally she took up her nightgown, a froth of ice-blue silk and lace, carefully laid out across the turned-down covers of the bed. Her eyes flashing, she pulled it on, taunting him with her beauty.

'I do not intend to spend the rest of my life living like a nun in some recluse just because I happen to be Mrs Garnet Fitzwilliam and with child. Perhaps it would be as well if I did lose the child after all the trouble it has caused.'

There was a tight edge to his voice as he said, 'That you do not care about anything but yourself is clear to us all. If something happened to the child now it would be all over the town in no time. And I might remind you that you would be shunned by all decent society, never able to hold up your head again in public.'

She stood very still beside the bed, the candlelight slanting across her strong cheekbones and firm jaw, emphasising the graceful line of her neck and shoulders, smooth as satin. The firm breasts, the slightly rounded belly and the shapely hips were outlined through the softness of the pale nightgown.

What he said was true, she could not deny it, but she was far too cross to agree with anything he said. She turned and sat down at the dressing table, brushing her hair as the moths flew around the candle, with now and then a beetle smacking into the flame.

Without thinking, Garnet threw himself across the room. He snatched the brush from her fingers and swung her around to face him, one hand mercilessly pulling back her head. The bright hair entangled itself in his fingers.

'Don't you dare taunt me, do you hear? Even if you are a strumpet at heart, you are my wife — and if you care about nothing else, you can start thinking about my position,' he roared, his face close to hers.

She struggled at first in the vicelike grip of his arms and then, with visions of her wedding night flooding back, she forced herself to be still. She did not flinch. For a second she stood there, stunned, trying to dismiss the unpleasant scene. She had only seen him so angry once before. Her heart thumped in her breast but there was no visible fear in her eyes as she faced him.

'And just what do you intend to do about me if I refuse — rape me again?' She spoke with immense dignity, a challenge flaring in her eyes.

His eyes filled with sudden pain, but his anger died and she knew she had won. She felt suddenly boldly audacious in her new power

174

over men, and her growing maturity. It was as though an intoxication of spirit was working through her. Warm with confidence in herself, she felt the strength and pleasure that came from the acknowledgement of her power.

'You really deserve a spanking, but I won't be the one to administer it — life will do that for you, eventually. I will sleep in the dressing room tonight.' Slowly Garnet turned away and picked up the fine, white linen nightrobe and abruptly left the room

Esther stole a quick look at his departing figure, feeling an unexpected disappointment. Her anger had subsided, the fire was burnt out. Suddenly she felt the hollowness of her victory over him, and very much alone. She was ashamed of the things she had said to him, of the way she had flaunted herself at the ball. She had seen the pain in his eyes at the mention of the rape, and at the end of the day, he had given her so much, except himself! If it had not been for him, she would still be at Dwyers' Cross and an unmarried mother, despised as an outcast from those she loved. And he had saved her father from knowing and suffering the outcome of her condition.

She wanted someone like Buck Jones to claim her, to love her with all the masculine authority at his command, to fill the empty void in her marriage, to make it warm and real. She lowered her brush, flushing scarlet, instantly ashamed of her thoughts. But she could not deny them. She did want someone.

Later she tiptoed to the dressing-room door and peeped into the room. Garnet had fallen asleep in a chair, a handsome, first edition, red leather volume of Lord Byron's 'Childe Harold' in his hands. He looked so handsome with the candlelight casting a warm halo about his bent, dark head. She wanted to tell him how sorry she was for all that had happened between them, but her pride came forward, forbidding her that comfort.

Furious at her own betrayal by her feelings, she walked back to the dressing table, picked up the brush and brushed her hair until her arms ached.

CHAPTER
Sixteen

The incident at the ball soon became the latest talking point of the regimental clique. Garnet was deeply embarrassed and avoided Esther even more in private, taking her only to those public functions he could not avoid.

Soon afterwards, it was mercifully eclipsed by the start of Buck's trial before the High Court. Every day placards announced the latest developments which were hungrily devoured. The entire affair between him and Amanda was exposed, piece by sordid piece, and it became the only topic of conversation at the fashionable dinner table.

Amanda had been both admired and disliked, and divisions were created among the entire Cape Town community. Buck Jones was a lesser-known quantity which caused much speculation about him. Amanda's biggest weaknesses had been her indiscretions. She had flaunted herself, embarrassing her late husband who had been indulgent and soft with his much younger and reckless wife.

Reliable witnesses recounted how, from the moment Amanda had set eyes on the then Corporal Buck Jones at the Cape garrison in 1816, she had set out to bewitch him. She had arrived from the gaiety of the regimental life in Brussels and he from the horrors of the European battlefields, both posted to the Cape at the same time. She had been bored and set about catching his attention at every possible moment. It was known in certain quarters how he avoided her, and had requested other duties at times when he knew she would be present. It was disclosed that she had indiscreetly told another lady that, one day, Buck Jones would grace her bed. If Jones had been an officer there would have been more merit in the shocking suggestion, but as he was only a man of the rank and file the idea was tantamount to degeneracy. They were all forced to admit that the man was unique among his fellows, but his background was nothing less than deplorable.

Scattered information was gathered as to how he had been sent with his regiment to the Eastern frontier at the end of that year, followed soon afterwards by the new garrison commander, Colonel Lightfoot and his wife. And it was there, some months after the Colonel's grisly death during the Fifth Frontier War, that Amanda finally achieved her objective and Buck Jones became her lover, setting the few Grahamstown inhabitants buzzing.

Garnet gave evidence of the incredible bravery and courage of the man during the siege of Grahamstown, saving his life and taking command of the men inside the barrack walls. He described how the siege became the most notable event and victory of the war, due to the efforts of Jones, who was promoted to sergeant in recognition of his services. He told the court of the man's calm and dynamic leadership under fire, of how the men rallied at the sight of his figure striding up and down the lines, and his voice bellowing at them not to give up. How could such a man, he argued, become a raving lunatic and murder a woman, a helpless woman, even if he had not loved her? A crime of passion was not in the nature of such a man.

It was revealed that Amanda had offered to buy him a commission but he had refused. Since he was therefore in no way indebted to her, Buck would have had no fear of losing anything should he wish to end their affair. This, said Garnet, proved that Buck had no need to murder Lady Lightfoot in order to be rid of her.

Every passing ship carried back to England more news of the case and it was only a matter of time before it became known to the British public.

It seemed during this stage that everything was going Buck's way, and Esther felt an unexpected rush of relief, but the situation was thwart with unpredictability as the evidence mounted on both sides.

A few days later, when she was feeling that the outcome would be positive, and she was safe and unprepared, the blow fell.

The evidence from the servants' previous statements in Graaff-Reinet had been read and dissected, when Sims, the butler, appeared in the town with additional evidence against Buck. He disclosed the visit of Esther to Amanda after the Glendower Dance and Esther was called to testify.

Esther prepared herself for the most terrible ordeal of her life as the town hummed with new evidence, and the gossip about her heightened among the regimental wives. Garnet was shocked at the disclosure, and once more highly embarrassed to have the focus of attention back on his marriage. If his manner towards her privately had been reserved and cool, it now became as cold as Arctic ice.

Esther entered the courtroom, a square-fronted white building beside the Public Offices at the top of the Heerengrecht, on the day of her evidence, her face calm but rigid. It was held in open court and she had dressed with great care. Everyone looking at her was conscious of her striking beauty, youth and grace as she walked alone through the crowd.

She wore a simple yet exquisitely-cut dress of sapphire blue, touched here and there with lace and navy blue ribbon, flattering to her breasts, but falling free and hiding her slightly-expanded waist and belly in gathers and flares. The people filling the courtroom and the guards stared after her with undisguised curiosity and muffled whisperings, but she was unaware of the morbid interest she had created. The faces around her were so many blank discs to her as she took her place in their midst and waited for the questioning to begin.

The shock had left her numb with the same incredulous despair she had felt when she had discovered she was pregnant. It surprised her that she could seat herself calmly on the chair that was placed for her near the judge's desk.

The man who was to interrogate her barely looked up when she entered. He was talking in low tones with another man, surrounded by numerous papers, while everyone in the hot, ill-ventilated room regarded her, still making whispered comments among themselves.

It was then she saw Buck Jones for the first time. She had been so nervous up until then that she had hardly noticed anyone. She stiffened suddenly, wildly confused, his presence at once a provocation and a deep disturbance. The last time she had seen him was that fateful day in Port Frances, and she was shocked at the change in him. He was standing in the prisoner's dock, his scarlet jacket crumpled and worn, the crossbelt over his broad chest showing a dingy white in the light of the room. The brown curls about his head, curling into the nape of his neck, feathered cheeks drawn and pale under his tan. There was the same strong jaw, the same clear-cut features, but the square-cut face was thinner, the

178

strong nose more prominent. There were sinister shadows under his eyes — from where the amusement, the laughter was lacking.

After she got over the shock of his appearance, she was only aware of his height and vital strength, that subtle power of his masculinity still so much a part of him, even now in his depressing condition. Her legs turned to jelly as his incredible eyes gave her a keen, quick glance which went through her like a sword. A hot flush sprang to her cheeks which she tried to still as she felt dizzy in the heat of the room and her condition. She held her breath as she watched him. He was not indifferent to her, any more than she was to him, she knew that then with startling revelation. Deep down she must always have known it, and she had misread it and turned her back on him.

She was so absorbed in her thoughts that she hardly realized the hearing had begun until she was addressed. They were speaking her name, yet it seemed to belong to someone else.

The first questions were simple ones as to how long she had been on the frontier, the length of her present marriage, how long she had known her husband and Amanda Lightfoot.

Then the next question was asked in a different tone. 'We have already learned that you visited Lady Lightfoot in her house in February 1821, that you and the lady had a violent quarrel. Is this true?'

Everyone in the room leaned forward in their places. Esther felt a tremor of fear and she knew the time had come to answer the questions more carefully. All eyes fastened on her as they waited for her answer. She was revolted by the reminder of the visit, but the will to survive was too strong. She had to think, and to think carefully how to speak.

'I visited Lady Lightfoot, yes.' She spoke clearly and without hesitation. 'It was at her request, and we did not have a violent quarrel.'

'But there is overwhelming evidence from the butler and the other servants that they heard shouting from Lady Lightfoot's drawing room, that you and she were having an altercation, and that as you left the house in great agitation the lady fainted and had to be revived with sal-volatile.'

There was a sudden buzz throughout the room which soon died down, as Esther opened her mouth to answer. 'We had a disagreement.'

179

'A disagreement, Mrs Fitzwilliam? That is hard to believe when Sims, the butler, heard his mistress distinctly scream that she hated you — that you had taken the accused, Sergeant Jones, from her.' The questioning, accusing voice, filled the room where another excited hum had started.

'Lady Lightfoot was distraught,' she said shortly, aware that anything more might be too much, confused and strung up as she was, unsure of her own instincts, all of which screamed at her that her very reputation was in danger, and a man's life at stake ...

'And what was the cause of Lady Lightfoot's agitated state of mind?'

Bewildered, her mind chaotic, Esther felt disorientated. She cleared her throat, not daring to look at Buck. 'She — Lady Lightfoot was distraught because she — she thought Sergeant Jones was interested in me.'

'And was he?'

There was an expectant hush. 'No — Sergeant Jones and I hardly knew each other.' She made the denial swiftly, then she spoke more slowly, weighing her words with care, realizing as she did the significance of the question. 'I had only seen the Sergeant once or twice before that day.'

A long pause followed while the man made notes on the paper beside him. Then he looked up for his next salvo. The tense quiet of the room was ominous.

'Is it not true,' he asked, 'that Lady Lightfoot believed that a relationship existed between yourself and the Sergeant?'

Esther had known this would come, and she was prepared to face it. 'No — never that! She never thought that. She knew such a relationship could not have existed without common knowledge. She never accused me of it. She may have said it to others, but never to me. She only suspected that Sergeant Jones had a superficial and passing interest in me, which was not true.'

'A superficial, passing interest, Mrs Fitzwilliam? But how could a superficial and passing interest bring about such a heated argument between the two of you — an argument in which she screamed that she hated you, that you had taken the Sergeant from her?'

'She was a jealous woman — she imagined things that never existed.'

There was a surge of excited muttering among those in court, and she heard it but did not look at them. Her eyes were fixed on her questioner, the colour gone from her lips and cheeks. Inside the crowded room the air grew heavy, and a merciless glare filled the unshaded windows. People's faces gleamed with heat. Esther felt dizzy again as she accepted a sip of water from a glass offered by an attendant. She had to keep alert.

It was the next question that alarmed her, her eyes wide and distraught as they turned on her questioner once more.

'Did the Sergeant ever show that he was interested in you, Mrs Fitzwilliam. Did he by any look, any token, betray his feelings?'

'No, no — he did not. He never treated me in any way other than a person he knew by sight. He knew my kinsmen better through the frontier defence system. There was nothing between us, I tell you.'

She found herself searching faces one by one in frantic appeal. She saw Garnet glance at her sharply. Somehow she must make them believe her. But no one reassured her; the eyes continued to watch the effect of the question on her. She felt as if she was dying of shame.

'You have heard the grave charges against Sergeant Jones. You know that he is believed to have murdered Lady Lightfoot in a rage, driven to it by the woman's insane jealousy after he ended their affair. It is thought that the Sergeant wanted to end it because of his interest in you, Mrs Fitzwilliam — that Lady Lightfoot knew of it, and that is why she asked you to visit her, to persuade you to give him up.'

Her knees were shaking, her hands clasping and unclasping. She heard herself deny this, babbling in broken, incoherent phrases. 'Please believe me — he could never have done this terrible thing. If he did do it, then it was not on account of me. There was nothing between us. If there had been, I would never have married my husband.'

Her interrogator's voice cut into her words, cool and precise and edged with irony. 'That proves nothing, Mrs Fitzwilliam. Ladies of your status don't usually marry below their station, and that the Sergeant is below yours you will agree. You may never have felt anything for him. There may not have been anything between you. But he may have felt altogether different towards you — so differently that it was his feelings for you that drove him to commit this most heinous of crimes against the demented woman he spurned. He knew he could never cement a real relationship with you, madam, yet he has proved his liking for women of higher birth and breeding, has he not? This unattainability could have driven him to madness.'

He seemed to believe her denials that there had been nothing between them, but determined to prove her guilty of a far less obvious crime. His questions now centred on Buck's interest in her, of her unwitting influence on him. It was a clever move to shift the emphasis in order to prove her guilty of estranging Buck from Amanda without doing much else.

There was an outburst from the crowd, and Esther, looking at Garnet's unsmiling profile, wondered with a deep foreboding if he was suspicious, but his dark, intelligent face had become expressionless. He was deep in thoughts of his own.

She looked at Buck quickly, then looked away. Was he a man sadistic enough to have killed Amanda? People did not go around murdering others unless they were mad — or obsessed like Amanda herself. And Buck was not; he was sane, calmly, coolly sane. 'I would trust him with my life,' she suddenly thought soberly, before her attention was brought back to her questioner once more.

Question followed question, but she answered without hesitation now that she had rallied from the first shock. Her wits returned and she was able to deal with the cold implications. She met the challenge from then on with squared shoulders and swift, sure words that kept all eyes on her, drawing the grudging admiration of even the questioner and Garnet.

She did not look at Buck again, as she knew much depended on her answers. And all the time she knew that the interrogator waited to twist anything that could be turned as evidence against her. None but Buck saw her paleness, nor the fear in her eyes. She no longer remembered her ecstasy in his arms. She was only determined that he would not suffer any more from her evidence. In spite of the extremity of her own fear, she was no longer aware of Garnet, or the others. She only knew that Buck must be saved.

Then it was over. There were no more questions and she was free to leave. Holding up her head proudly, she walked out through the crowded room unaware of all eyes on her.

The noon sun stood high over the roofs and oaks of the town as she stared down the shade-dappled Heerengracht to the metallic glitter

182

of the bay. For a moment she could not believe it was over, then dully she realized that even though her evidence was over, it had seemingly brought Buck closer to hanging. She found her eyes full of tears. Her heart was breaking. She felt the knowledge so keenly that it cut her like a heated knife; she and he could never be one. And he could lose his life.

The pain grew worse in Esther from then, filling the days ahead with an inner despair which she strove to hide, burying it deep inside her. Her father wrote saying he would be arriving to help her, but, terrified that he should discover too much, she sent an urgent message back telling him not to come, that all was well, his presence was not needed as it would only complicate matters.

Speculation was rife after her evidence. She was gossiped about and revealed as a woman with a past. Tongues wagged as the rumours grew, giving the gossipmongers something more to colour their lives. The placards were full of it. No one knew what new turn the case might take from hour to hour, and people even left their work to crowd the benches at the public hearings. Amanda's brother, Andrew Lotharton, arrived at the end of April, and the trial aroused the interest of the Commissioners of Enquiry still on the frontier investigating the problems there.

And all through the quagmire of detail and revelation, Garnet strove to help Buck. As Buck had saved his life during the Xhosa war, he felt himself honour bound to free him, no matter what the cost. As Esther observed him at work, growing respect came out of her frustration and unhappiness. She became, on the surface, the perfect wife.

No one could fault the skills learned long ago at her mother's knee that she now brought to the entertaining for her husband in the manner to which he was entitled. Talk spread around at the miraculous change in Mrs Fitzwilliam. No more were there scandals surrounding her. She was the epitome of proper and correct behaviour, and her hospitality was carried out with great flair and distinction for one still so young.

Esther found herself in great demand as a guest and a hostess if only for the reason of the curiosity about her, her past and her present unaccountable change of attitude. It was believed by some that she was atoning for her bad past behaviour, and to dispel any rumour of trouble in their marriage, Garnet made every show of kind, thoughtful behaviour towards her before the world.

Yet, underneath it all, the pain remained, that frustrated longing for something that was not there. She could suppress it, but she could not obliterate it altogether. She may have become sought after in regimental society, but privately it was a very uncomfortable time for her.

Garnet took a house for Esther and himself in Strand Street, running alongside the gleaming curve of the bay, not far from the flat-roofed, gabled houses where the merchants and citizens congregated on the high stoeps at noon, smoking pipes and cigars while they discussed the business of the day and the progress of the trial.

The news was to reach Britain four months later, and heated debates would begin over whether Buck was guilty or not, causing divisions among rich and poor alike. It would also begin to cause a rumble in the House of Commons, among the government and opposition parties. Cartoons and lampoons were to appear in several publications, depicting Buck either as a villain with a hairy face and forked tail, stealing Esther, as a wicked Irish witch, from a virtuous, upright Garnet with a poor cowering Amanda in the background, or as a knight in shining armour, slaying Amanda who appeared as the dragon at his feet, with a beautiful and frightened Esther hiding behind his back — all depending on which side of the political fence the publications represented. Even the Irish were to have a go — anonymous cartoonists depicting Esther as a goddess of all virtues, maligned by a haughty and cruel Buck in redcoat uniform thrusting a sword into Amanda's chest. Amanda was depicted by the Irish cartoonists as a corrupt, rich Englishwoman.

Esther continued with her duties as mistress of an elegant home and a small army of servants. All the lessons her mother had taught her concerning the supervision of a large and important household now came into action, balanced with the down-to-earth practicality of the day-to-day tasks she had been forced to learn at Dwyers' Cross. The servants found her a generous, but hard taskmaster, and hastened at the slightest frown on her face to do her bidding, knowing that she had done everything they did and more during the long four years in the Coombs Valley.

It was on the day before Garnet decided to discreetly let Esther's rapidly-growing condition be known, that he took her to the coachmaker's not far from Greenmarket Square, and showed her a smart phaeton, similar to those used by the other officers' wives, together with an attractive, mischievous little bay. Esther loved the horse at once, but she did not want the phaeton, thinking it too impractical for the roads of the Eastern Cape. She preferred a Cape cart, a conveyance found only in the colony and nowhere else. Garnet agreed, seeing her point, and allowed her to choose one.

The one she picked was covered with a painted canvas hood, with reversible seats and sunblinds at back and front with side curtains. It was light and strong and built to resist the rain, dust and glaring sun of the climate. She chattered away to the coachmaker, using her magnetic charm on the large, thickset German. Once the purchase was finished she entered their carriage, her enthusiasm spent. It seemed to her then, inexplicably, that she was throwing all her enthusiasm into everything around her to quieten her own inner restlessness. There seemed no outlet for the vital passion that possessed her; she fervently hoped that it would not break loose.

She watched Garnet walk towards her. He belonged to a world where men were highly disciplined, self-controlled to perhaps too stern a degree — a world of tradition, reputation and sober manners. As he climbed up into the carriage and sat down beside her, she prayed desperately that she would be able to really change herself inside and adapt completely to the life chosen for her, by what — Fate, or her own stubborn wilfulness?

The violent south-easters of summer and the hot bergwinds gave way to the winter north-westers as May passed into June. Still there were pressing matters that forced them to remain in the town. As Esther was now well advanced in her pregnancy she retired to her home in Strand Street.

Through the winter Lord Charles was in residence at his official quarters in Government House. There Garnet visited him regularly, attempting to pacify him when the gossip about him and his physician, Dr James Barry, grew to hideous proportions after a placard concerning the matter was posted in the town in a prominent place.

There was trouble brewing too with Thomas Pringle who had left the frontier and was running the only worthwhile school for English gentry in Cape Town. He had published in his newspaper, *The South*

African Commercial Advertiser, an article about the trial criticizing the corrupt and unjust proceedings, without waiting for official sanction. Apart from small presses in far distant mission stations, the only active press in the colony was that of the Government Gazette from the castle, and Pringle's newspaper containing the article caused an uproar in government circles. There was a stormy meeting between him and Lord Charles and he had been forced to retract it. Now he was getting his own back by unofficially speaking out about the situation, in which he reckoned the evidence was biased against an innocent man.

It was on a Wednesday that placards announced that Sergeant Buckmaster Jones had been condemned to death by the High Court. He was to be placed in the condemned cell of the prison at the lower end of the Heerengracht until his execution a week from the day of the verdict. Despite the fact that there had not been conclusive and final proof of his guilt, the pressure of public opinion and the influence of Amanda's brother had succeeded in pushing the judges of the Court to their decision. There were many who were amazed that the Sergeant still reiterated his denials of guilt when there was no one else who could have done it. How, they declared, could he cling so stubbornly to his story in the face of such overwhelming proof of his guilt? The opinion everywhere was strong in branding him a most inhuman criminal who deserved the hanging he was to receive.

Esther was not prepared for the shocking outcome. Though she had known it could happen, her mind had always pushed away the reality. Now all hope was gone. The sleeplessness from which she suffered and the strain of the waiting had taken its toll. She felt limp and exhausted, as shaken and spent as an old woman. The store of energy she had always called upon was gone. She could not swallow her meals, and refused all attentions. So everyone left her and she sat in her room, staring out to sea, alone with her memories.

Could she have saved him? Was there anything she could still do? They all believed him guilty, and that, in some way, she was involved. Though she had denied it, and they never said it to her face, they all believed she had a part in the horror.

She remembered the strained, weary expression on Buck's face as she had seen it last in the courtroom. She thought of his strong, broad hands that had once caressed her. And now, they seemed stained

186

with blood. Yet she could not believe he was guilty; would not ever believe it, even when he was no more ...

Sobs shook her as they had not shaken her through any of the long, dark hours of her life. There was nothing she could do for him. He was going to die, and that knowledge crushed her completely.

Just two days before the hanging was due to take place, Lord Charles intervened after an urgent request from Garnet, backed by Thomas Pringle, to delay the execution through a final lack of evidence against Buck. Garnet was allowed to proceed to the frontier to try to obtain fresh evidence. Once published, the news spread rapidly. Everywhere people grew intense with indignation against a governor who had agreed to such a delay. One fact they all agreed upon: the prisoner should meet the fate of the murderer he was. Andrew Lotharton, Amanda's brother, was incensed by the stay of execution, demanding that he see justice done.

Garnet was sent to the frontier after new evidence and in the time that he was absent Esther remained in her room, wondering what Buck was thinking, holed up in the condemned cell in the prison near the beach. Again and again she could only admire his courage as he faced imminent death. If Garnet failed in his mission, then Buck would surely die, there would be no more second chances.

Esther was sitting in a high-backed chair facing the window, watching the fiery sunset in deep depression, when there was a knock on the door of her room. She had no wishes to see anyone, and did not answer.

It was moments later that she became aware of Phoebe, her maid, standing beside the chair, with trembling hands and a tremulous smile on her face.

'What is it, Phoebe?' Esther asked irritably. 'You know I don't want to be disturbed.'

'I know ma'am, I know, but I have such good news, ma'am — news that will give you life again.'

Esther turned her head suspiciously. 'Whatever do you mean, Phoebe? If this is some kind of joke ...'

'Oh no, ma'am, it be no joke. It's the Sergeant — the one in gaol —'

'The Sergeant — good news?' Esther hardly dared to breathe. She did not want to think, dared not hope ... and yet ...

187

'Yes, ma'am — there's a big stir in the town, ma'am — I been there meself — the Captain, he's tracked down Sims, Lady Lightfoot's ex-butler, and a real bag o' worms he is, to be sure. He was in a seedy inn in Port Elizabeth, ma'am — when the Captain found him.'

'Yes, Phoebe — go on!' Esther could now hardly contain her growing hope as her eyes never left Phoebe's face.

'Well, ma'am, a frightened witness was pressurised by them Commissioners of Enquiry, so to speak, to come forward in Grahamstown — and he saw this Sims leave the scene of the murder.'

'He did?' Esther was incredulous.

Phoebe nodded vigorously. 'That he did, ma'am — and the knife he used to kill the poor Lady has been found on the banks of the river near her house, true as bob.'

Esther turned away, her heart racing, overcome with relief. Then a thought struck her. 'But the Sergeant — will he be freed? I mean — this man Sims, will he confess his guilt?'

Pheobe smiled, her eyes gleaming like two large saucers. 'He has done, ma'am — just in the last hour or so. I heard him with me own ears. He murdered the Lady because she dismissed him for misconduct and refused to have him back in her employ and no one would have blamed her none. He said he had served her late husband for years and then the Lady, who was the worst she-devil he had ever met, got rid of him just like a piece of dirt — his very words. He had gone to the brandy tavern at Assegaai Bush and got roaring drunk, then in the early hours he had returned to the Lady's house and done her in good and proper.'

Esther felt limp as she sagged back into her chair. 'I can't believe it, Phoebe — justice has been done at last and now the Sergeant will be free — I can't believe it.'

And for all the great flood of joy that swept over her in that moment, in her heart she knew that she would never be able to see him again . . .

The Court of Appeal overturned the High Court's decision and reprieved Buck, sentencing Sims instead, and Andrew Lotharton returned to England, furious at what he called a miscarriage of justice. He was outspoken in the House of Commons, getting the newspapers to condemn the Governor at the Cape and the entire judicial system.

In the colony, public opinion was now united in condemning the High Court whose decisions were often overruled by the Court of Appeal on lack of evidence. Public pressure played a large part in the decisions of the Court and now all officials, including the Governor himself, suffered severe censure.

An innocent man had been saved from the gallows in the nick of time, and indignation against a corrupt judicial system was rife. The Commissioners of Enquiry investigated the legal system and the Lightfoot murder case became a key issue as far as the law of the colony was concerned. It illustrated the inadequacy of the system and in the months to follow the Commissioners were to use it to condemn it. It was swept away by new laws in 1827. But spectres shadowing governments are not easily dismissed as Lord Charles was to discover to his cost. Meanwhile the case had been reviewed and found to have no tangible evidence against either Buck or Esther.

Esther had made a remarkable impression on her examiners during the hours of questioning. She had become, alone with Buck Jones, the most talked-of person in the colony. There were those who still believed her guilty and would have gloated had it been proved. But, there were also those, including Thomas Pringle, who saw her in a more heroic light, as the much maligned innocent in a horror which had bewildered her as much as they — but they were very few, and one, the much condemned Governor himself.

It was essential now that the whole matter be forgotten, and as her pregnancy progressed, that she remain out of the public view, so she kept to the house seeing no one, and the subject of future plans was carefully avoided.

She was able to feel human again with the courage to live and feel, once the knowledge that Buck was to live became a reality. He was freed and sent back to the frontier, and she longed to see him again. It seemed strange to know that her body, her mind, her heart would never be warmed by him again, that he and she would remain miles apart, and so it must be forever.

CHAPTER
Seventeen

In the last week of June Esther awoke one night to the sharp, full pains of labour. Contractions gripped her body and after a moment's panic, she was struck by the enormity of the situation. She was about to birth her child and there was no one around close enough to trust with her life.

Waves of pain assaulted her and took control as she managed to take hold of the bell-rope beside the bed and pull it.

Outside it was raining, the sound drumming against the windows. Through the haze of pain as the contractions mounted, she was aware of Garnet, leaning over her. He was already dressed and in a greatcoat, and she could see the anxiety written on his face, the dark shadows beneath his eyes.

'I will go for Dr Barry immediately,' he said, studying her pale, drawn face. 'Phoebe is awake, please ask her for anything you need.'

Esther nodded. She knew it was useless asking hin to stay, to be with her, to comfort her. She would have to see this through alone.

'Please hurry,' she gasped, clutching her belly as her womb heaved in another spasm of excrutiating pain, now coming in regular waves and threatening to make her faint.

His shadow fell across the walls and marched across the room to the door which he flung open on his way to call Phoebe. Then the maid was with her, and he was gone, the sound of his horse clattering over the cobbles, soon to be lost in the muted sound of the rain.

Phoebe wasted no time in waking up the Javanese slave and ordering her to light the fire and put the kettle on to boil. She was quiet and efficient with no fuss, and very anxious that her mistress get over the ordeal quickly.

'Phoebe help me — please.' Esther flung her arms across her face, bathed in sweat as the tempo of the pains quickened and the creature inside her took complete control.

'Twill be fine, ma'am, you'll see — the first 'un is always the worst,' Phoebe said, wiping her practical hands on the wide skirt of her apron. 'And Captain will be ever so proud.'

Everything was blotted from Esther's mind then, the centre of her being focussing only on getting the struggling baby out as soon as possible. It seemed much later that she became aware of small, cool hands soothing the damp tendrils of hair back from her wet face. 'Just be brave, Mrs Fitzwilliam,' Dr Barry's unusually light voice said, 'and it will be over sooner than you think.'

The voice merged into the slim, boyish figure at her side. 'Hang on to the bedposts as hard as you can — it helps at times like this.'

Esther wanted to scream as her hands felt for the rungs of the wooden posts and tightened about them with almost superhuman strength. She wanted to die, but she also wanted to live, and she wanted the bruising, crushing pain to go.

'Take deep breaths, my dear, it eases the pain.'

From a long way off she heard the doctor's voice and felt his cool, confident hands on her forehead, wiping away the sweat with a damp cloth. He picked up Esther's writhing hand and felt her pulse. 'It should not be long now,' he nodded with calm satisfaction.

Oh, if only Buck was here, Esther thought wildly, not knowing why she thought of him. If only everything was as it should be . . . If only Garnet loved me, loved the child . . .

Opening her eyes, through mists of pain she saw Dr Barry frowning and felt him examining her belly. The knitted points of his brows quickly smoothed as he became aware of Esther's eyes on him, to be replaced by an expression of deep compassion.

'It will take longer than I thought, Mrs Fitzwilliam, but try to keep calm, the baby is well on its way.'

Esther's breathing rasped as she writhed now in savage agony, clutching at the hand on her forehead with surprising force. She was crushed by the dreadful feeling of helplessness. There was nothing in her power she could do to take away the pain.

The doctor looked down at Esther's face, her eyes full of tormented pain. 'Try to relax, my dear, I know it is hard, but it is the only way.'

Esther lay on her back on the sweat-soaked pillow, her disordered hair streaming about her and darkening with perspiration. Spasms of pain again rocked her body, knotting it and wrenching it apart as she vaguely heard Dr Barry's voice from a long way off, at the door where he thought she could not hear him. The words 'complications' and 'prolonged labour' flashed dully through the air and there was a fleeting moment of terror searing Esther's brain until she thought she could stand it no longer. She, in her innocence, had imagined that it would soon be over like the birth of Hannah Byrne's son so long ago. But she had been mistaken; she was, because of her guilt, not to be let off lightly. She was to be tortured on the rack of her wrongs — never, never would she be allowed to forget it.

She screamed in agony, biting her lips raw like a helpless animal caught in some cruel trap. Dr Barry pulled aside the blanket and turned back Esther's nightdress. He gently pushed his slender fingers into her body and as Esther screamed again, Phoebe took both her hands from the bedposts and held them tightly in her own.

'Poor, dear young thing — 'tis a frightening experience — but one we women have to suffer for 'em tiny bairns, all said an' done.'

Esther's nightdress was drenched with sweat as she hung onto Phoebe's strong, capable hands, wrenching and pulling them as the continuing pain knifed through her womb.

She swam in and out of consciousness for two days, and at times lost all care about her life or the child's. The pain was so bad that she was given laudanum and slept fitfully for some hours.

There was talk of performing a Caesarean section which had never been done before in the colony, but as the hours progressed Dr Barry thought better of it.

Esther's painful breathing filled the room but she uttered no more complaint. Then at dawn on the third day, when the clouds trailed skirts of mist, the child was finally born. She looked down at the small figure lying between her thighs and a sudden pang of pain stabbed her heart, and with a harsh breath she turned her head away. Then it was separated from her and Dr Barry spent several anxious moments trying to get the baby to breathe. There was a breathless hush, then a sharp, angry wail throbbing through the air and he appeared at the bedside. 'You have a fine little daughter, Mrs Fitzwilliam.'

Lying limp and drawn and shivering uncontrollably with shock, Esther felt the child laid beside her and she turned to look at the small, red, wrinkled face, the body tightly wrapped in many

192

blankets, Buck's daughter.

Esther's legs felt weak, and her body very tired, but her mind felt strangely liberated as if her duty was done, and only great relief was left. In that moment, only her beautiful blue eyes with their thick lashes had a look of youth.

A hot brick, wrapped in a flannel was brought and placed in the bed. A dog barked and a voice called somewhere faraway. A heavy silence fell on the room as Dr Barry walked away with the light, springing step of one used to much exercise, a delighted Phoebe at his heels. And outside the world began to glow softly with the growing radiance of light and colour.

Esther symbolically named her daughter, Aurora, but for several days after the birth she was in a deep depression, her dreams of the future destroyed by the child. Garnet refused to see the baby and she would have no visitors, ignoring all the messages sent up to her room by a perplexed Phoebe.

Her shame was overwhelming and her soul burned with it. At first her conflicting emotions for her daughter were so powerful that she shuddered at their strength. Garnet's attitude did nothing to make it any easier. He only visited her to go through the motions of a proud father. Otherwise he remained withdrawn, aloof and unbearably distant.

After some weeks she was aware of a strange, fierce possessive feeling towards the infant, so small and so helpless. She began to understand that her violent feelings were not for the child, but for herself and what she had done. A terrible despair engulfed her, and with it rose the shame. She felt trapped by her guilt, knowing her impulsive action had endangered not only her future, but that of the child. Through it all, Esther was determined that Aurora would never learn that Garnet was not her father. When she thought back on it all, she saw so clearly that the baby's true father was unlike all the other men she had known or would meet again in the future. Buck was a very special man and the memory of the incident in the dunes pierced her thoughts with such clarity whenever she was in the presence of his child.

She had thought she could never forgive him, and then on seeing him in court, fighting for his life with such dignity and courage, knew it was herself she could never forgive.

Although Esther never knew it, throughout all this Garnet had not stopped loving her. She filled his thoughts and he knew that, to him, no other woman could outshine her. Separated from her, he recalled how he had been blindly devastated at the discovery of her condition on their wedding night and all his illusions, all his dreams of her, had died. He had seen her revulsion and her disgust after the rape, and he was deeply humiliated. She had been married to him now for six months, and she still remained blind and without understanding. She had never discussed her deception, not even after he had agreed to remain married to her and give her child his name.

He had found it hard to find a woman who came up to his high standards, and she had seemed to have such great promise, not only being beautiful and refined, but also possessing such spirit and intelligence.

Everything had come to nothing. He was still proud of her, and never more than during her appearance in the courtroom during Buck Jones' trial — but she had disappointed him. He wanted to tell her, and to hold her in his arms, but she would not understand. She did not love him, and she would take it as a sign of his weakness.

He, too, was filled with pain as well as anger. She would never understand that he loved her, and he dared not try to convince her.

CHAPTER
Eighteen

Spring had reached the settlement in full bloom, buds swelling wherever a tree or shrub grew on high ground, when Esther, Garnet and a little Aurora returned to Glendower Park with hampers filled with wines, oranges, cakes and dried apples. Wild jasmine lay like mist on the overhanging rocks and along the branches of trees. Bushpigs, hares and mongooses kept to the purple shade thrown by the thickets of light green spekboom dusted with sprays of lilac blossoms, wag-'n-bietjie bushes and boerbooms.

The air was fresh, the harvest looked good and slowly, through the recurring seasons, the settlers came to know their new country and their neighbours, the Boers, as they shared common experiences and grievances and together looked with confidence to the Commissioners of Enquiry for the solution of their problems.

Esther and Garnet found a turning point had been reached in the developing community and very few now talked of wanting to go back to the old country.

However there were continuous quarrels among the settlers still leaving the land in ever-growing numbers for the towns and villages to use their non-farming skills. These quarrels only added to the great difficulties and dangers still facing the settlement, aggravated by the fact that they were still forbidden to hold public meetings to discuss their problems, or to have a free press.

Garnet found a still uncertain life, where his position and that of Lieutenant Colonel Henry Somerset (a rank purchased that July) as Commandant of the Frontier were in danger of being abolished by the British government in a policy of strict economy. The strength of the Cape Corps had been severely cut back, so that it was at that point almost non-existent. Their services were kept only by three petitions set out in Settler Memorials pleading for their retention and sent to the two Commissioners of Enquiry. The fate of the Corps still hung precariously in the balance.

Esther was left once more in the gracious and elegant house at Glendower Park as Garnet went to the aid of Henry Somerset and visited the tribesmen in Xhosaland, where there had been a shifting of forces among the tribes. The majority were now looking to Chief Hintza in the north as the most powerful chief among them. Garnet and Henry were constantly in the saddle, riding for hours with the small force under their command to the kraals of chieftains.

While Esther threw herself into the organization of the house, rode her favourite chestnut horse from the stable of twelve thoroughbreds, and ordered beautiful gowns, bonnets, stockings and slippers, the small detatchment of Cape Corps watched the plots and counterplots taking place in Xhosaland, pouncing on them as swiftly as they were able. Garnet and Henry were still convinced that the best answer to peace was to control the tribes without force, and Henry now joined voice with Garnet in persuading his father, the Governor, to interview both the colonists and the Xhosa chiefs.

As the spring slipped into summer heat and bergwinds once more, the duties of the soldiers continued to be made very difficult by the changing policy of constantly-new officials who seldom accepted the advice of those on the spot.

November brought a letter from England for Garnet, and Esther knew it was from his family. With a certain curiosity she waited for him to mention it, but all he did was to stride into the library and close the door. There he remained for over an hour.

Having prepared herself for her morning ride, decked smartly in an emerald riding habit and a small, bright green hat with a long, black plume, she descended the stairs, carrying her riding crop in one hand. Her steps slowed as she saw Garnet emerge from the library, look up and wait for her at the foot of the stairs, one hand on the newel post.

Today he was not in uniform. She noticed the first few premature silver hairs at his temple, giving an added air of distinction to his thirty-three years. Again she wished that things were good between them, that he was a real husband to her and that he would allow her to be a real wife, that he would accept her as she was with all her

196

strengths and weaknesses.

Reaching the bottom step, she stopped, her eyes level with him. Dust motes danced in a shaft of light from the half-open library door as he looked at her, an ironic twist to his lips. He maintained a cool poise, the rest of his face impassive, but there was a pain behind his eyes.

'My father died in July, soon after news of your evidence in court reached them. My mother thinks that the scandal — that your part in the Lightfoot murder case — finally killed him. As you know he had been ill for a long time. I must go to her. I will apply for compassionate leave and will be away for about a year.'

His voice was so cool, the news so unexpected, that her chin came up in consternation. 'I am sorry to hear it. Will Aurora and I be joining you?'

He faced her with a challenging eye. 'It will not be wise for you to accompany me at this time — you have caused enough misery already. And I trust that in my absence you will not try to get into too much mischief.'

'You do, do you?' She drew herself up, white-lipped. 'For all that I have caused, I am still, for better or worse, your wife. You would do well to remember it. What will the family think if I do not accompany you?'

A glint of something close to admiration sparked unexpectedly in his eyes as he searched her face. Then recovering himself, he leaned forward. 'You are, after all is said and done, only my wife in name, and it is for me to decide what is to happen regarding the visit to my family, is that understood? I have made my decision. You and your daughter will remain here on the estate in my absence.'

They had not moved. The light in his eyes intensified as he watched her set, furious gaze, her cheeks ablaze. 'And what about Aurora? They must have heard about your daughter by now. Don't you think they will think it strange for you not to take her to see them — their grandchild?' She stamped her foot. 'While you return to those civilized surroundings you leave me in this barbaric country!'

He frowned tightly, keeping himself under iron control. 'You will manage very nicely in this barbaric country, as you always have done, my dear. As to Aurora — my family know nothing about her. It won't take them long to work out certain facts and discover that either you or I or both have been deceiving them — and that I won't lay at their door. As far as I am concerned they will never know about her.'

She winced at the sharpness of his tone. 'Damn you to hell's flames! It's not the fault of the child. Is she to be condemned for something she had nothing to do with?'

For a brief second the aristocratic features seemed to soften. It was almost as if he was struggling with himself for one brief moment. When she looked into his eyes and saw the suffering in them, she was unusually and strangely moved, for she was not a woman easily sympathetic or tolerant towards those who had spurned her. Then it was gone, and a slow smile curved his lips. But there was no echoing smile in his eyes.

'That child has unfortunately to suffer for the crime of her parents. She has too much the look of a certain sergeant about her for me to claim any part of her as my own. You would do well to remember that — for she will be your constant reminder as she grows older. Would that she has his character but not his deception, a quality I never knew existed in him until the child was born. And it was for this that I helped save his life.' The sarcasm was heavy in his voice, biting into her like a finely-honed blade.

Esther stood staring at him, the colour drained from her face, her ears searing with pain as if he had struck her physically.

He stood looking at her for a moment, then he said, the ice back in his voice, 'I see by your expression that at last I have hit home. Live with your guilt, my dear, and his.'

He strode away without another glance at her, closing the library door behind him. She was left to stare in its direction, empty and destroyed. What would Garnet do, now that he had discovered the truth? What would happen to Aurora, Buck and herself?

A deep weariness took the place of the pleasure she had felt only moments before, all anticipation of the morning ride completely extinguished.

It had been decided that before Garnet left for England he, Esther and the baby would join Laree at Sunfield Park for Christmas and Esther was looking forward to seeing her new little nephew, Morris.

She lay dreamily in the great, canopied bed, the sweetness of ripe grass filling the room through the open window with pre-dawn fragrance. Garnet lay sleeping in the room next door.

198

She snuggled down further into the silk, monogrammed sheets, wrapped in the warmth and excitement of the coming visit. It was wonderful to lie in the depths of a soft bed with fine linen, the scent of lavender bags between the pillows. She snuggled further into the bed. She could summon a maid to draw the curtains, light a fire, fetch hot water, just by reaching for the bell-rope beside her. She smiled to herself, her eyes falling on the dark shapes of the clothes draped over trunks and valises in careless disorder for the trip to Sunfield Park. She loved this room, still heavy with intimate smells, mingled odours of perfume, real candlewax and the scent of a clove-struck pomander. She loved the elegant chairs, the Louis XV *chaise-longue* beneath the windows. A bowl of fruit stood on the exquisite marquetry dressing table with its delicately painted panels, the crystal prisms of a pair of candlesticks falling like silver showers in the gloom.

She was aroused by the sound of horses' hooves beating up the long driveway, the echo muted on the soft, pre-dawn air. Minutes later the front-door bell clanged ponderously with impatient urgency. She started up as the rustle of starched skirts sounded on the landing and Phoebe knocked on Garnet's bedroom door.

Garnet pulled his door open and all Esther could hear were muted voices on the landing. Whatever it was, she did not want it to intrude into her day, or dampen her excitement. But for some unknown reason she was uneasy.

She opened her eyes almost immediately at the sound of his footsteps outside the door. He opened it and walked into the room, a lighted candle in his hand. Something about him filled her with misgivings. She sat up straighter.

'What the devil was that all about?' she asked, anxiety sharpening her tone. Weak, grey light filled the room, making Garnet's face seem unnaturally pale and strained, washed-out. He spoke with controlled directness as he placed the candlestick on the dressing table.

'I have orders to leave immediately to lead a patrol into Xhosaland. A great number of cattle have been stolen from several farms near the border, by the Mazwis again. That poor, old chieftain Mazwi's wily son Lungelo is once more suspected of being the ringleader. Henry has ordered us to hold him and get all the cattle back.

'I will not be able to accompany you to Sunfield Park,' he said darkly. 'It is my hope, however, that it will all be over by Christmas and I will join you then. By the way, Aurora's father will accompany me.' There were a few brief seconds of shocked silence as her mind caught at his words, and his mention of Buck. Rage built up inside her and unleashed itself.

'Oh, I'm sick of it!' she cried. 'Always — always there is something more important than Aurora and me — there is always some urgent mission you have to carry out for dear Henry! Why can't he go himself if it's that important to him! I've had enough of it all. You have been visiting the tribes for weeks, and now that savage Lungelo has spoilt my Christmas!' She bristled with fury, her voice raised and defiant. 'Go to them then if that's what you want — go to them and stay there for all I care, and forget about Buck Jones!'

She picked up a long, exquisite candlestick from the bedside table. 'I'm sick to death of taking your taunting, of being treated like some stupid, wicked child. You know how much I wanted us to go to Laree on our first Christmas together. How I hate you, Garnet Fitzwilliam!'

Garnet strode across the room towards her. 'Do not throw that piece of excellent workmanship, my dear. Can you not be more selective in your choice of throwing objects? If you insist on hurling something, do choose something more expendable — like that hideous, green vase from that relation of yours, Sophia Wilson.'

He was frowning blackly as he took it from her taut, angry fingers after a short struggle, replacing it carefully in its original position. 'Really, Esther, you have no sense at all about the intrinsic value of anything.'

'I like that,' Esther shouted in a demented rage. 'I am even less important than a — a — a piece of cursed glass!'

He raised his arms in sheer exasperation. 'Esther, do please calm yourself. You are distraught. And do keep your voice down. One of my men waits in the hallway and I'll wager he has heard every word you have shouted at me. It is most unseemly for a person in your position.'

He brought his head up sharply, his eyes suddenly distant and cool. 'It is not right that one of my subordinate officers should hear me abused by my wife — it leads to talk, scandal, and it's bad for discipline among the rank and file. We have had enough scandal in our marriage to last a lifetime. Besides,' he added coldly, 'you can go ahead to Sunfield Park. I hardly think you will miss me.

'I have a job to do in a difficult and dangerous area — a complex task. As a soldier I am not required to question orders. One last thing — Sergeant Buck Jones will always stand between us, whether you like it or not. He was the one man I trusted, respected above all men, and now I despise him, revile him — and his daughter with him.'

He stared at her, tensions simmering beneath his controlled exterior, shown in the odd flash of his dark eyes. Then his face tightened and became a mask as he strode across the carpet to the dressing room. 'I will see you at Sunfield Park on my return. It wouldn't do not to keep up appearances after this scene, now would it?'

He closed the bedroom door quietly behind him, as if to shut out her wild, uncontrolled anger. She glared at the door, her eyes glimmering with bitter, impotent rage. But she knew the real reason for her outburst. She could no longer deceive herself; she was not the satisfied, triumphant or powerful lady she had wanted to be, but a woman unfulfilled in her deepest passions, restless and searching, and not all the riches or the luxury or the outward position in the world could put that right. And she knew, for the first time, what Amanda must have suffered when she thought she had lost Buck, what boredom and searching must have led her to him in the first place, after years of extravagance, wealth and a surfeit of pleasures in high society. She, too, had been looking for herself, but she had never found the true Amanda. And Esther was not going to allow that to happen to her.

Making up her mind, she pulled on a deep-blue, lawn peignoir over her nightgown, fastening the pale gold ribbons at the neck, and swept back her two bright braids. Throwing open the door, she sailed from the room. She would deal with Garnet once and for all. No longer would she be at the receiving end of his scorn and cool contempt. He would feel the full impact of her wrath.

She met him as he walked across the carpet of his room, resplendent in his uniform, black boots highly polished, the blue cloak, revealing a thick slice of rich red lining, swirling over one arm. She stood watching him, still heaving with anger inside her.

He patted his pockets to make sure he had all he needed. Then he turned and saw her, his fingers gripping the handle of the broad, curved sword that hung in its steel scabbard against his left leg.

'Do not pine too heavily for me, my dear, I will be back sooner than you think,' he said mockingly, watching her reaction. 'It is just as well I take your former lover with me, at least that reduces the chance of another bastard in my house.'

With a mighty effort she kept her anger controlled, and lifting her chin, she stared at him as if he was a stranger. 'I do not care if I never see you again — you can stay on that cursed border for all I care,' she snapped back, and then before she could stop herself, 'And for your information, Buck Jones was a far better lover than you ever were!'

A moment's outrage sprang into the dark eyes facing her, at the final insult, then he almost instantly controlled himself. He hesitated a minute as his eyes swept over her, taking in every detail, the peignoir falling to her feet, cool and crisp with its high neck and long frilled cuffs, its deep blue reflected in her eyes. Though she did not know it, her face was suffused with warm colour, and only for that moment did she feel the force of emotions he kept so tightly in check. Then, holding his cloak by the black leather strap, he swung it about his shoulders, and moved to the dressing table where he picked up his shako, pulling it on his head.

Reaching the door, he turned, 'One day, Esther Fitzwilliam, you will be very sorry for what you have just said. Then even the fires of hell will be too good for the both of you.'

He hurried down the stairs to join his man waiting in the entrance hall. With his departure, the angry trembling inside Esther died down. A sudden feeling of remorse rushed through her, and she rushed down the stairs and threw open the front door. She had to apologize to him for the first time in their marriage. She had not been fair to him from the beginning — agreeing to marry him under false pretences, expecting him to take in her child, the fruit of a forbidden liaison. She had taken so much from him, and now she had taken away his masculine pride as well.

Her blue eyes enormous in the paleness of her face, she saw only clouds of dust left in the wake of the galloping horses. As the sun mounted the farthest ridge of hills, silvering the sky for a dazzling day, she felt scalding tears spring under her eyelids so that everything grew indistinct and misty.

When he comes back, I will make it all up to him, she thought, I will tell him I'm sorry, that I did not mean what I said. I shall beg him for forgiveness. I will try to love him, I really will.

Resolutely she fought back the tears, hearing for the first time the screeching and whistling of the colony of birds in the giant yellowwoods, the high screech of the hadedas above the rest.

Please let me make it up to him when he returns, she prayed, with sick bitterness, her eyes staring down at the empty driveway. To her the day had become suddenly heavy and grey, for all its brightness, as she tried to pierce the numbness that was enveloping her.

I will never treat him like that again, I promise. I will never do that to him again.

CHAPTER
Nineteen

A week later Garnet's troop of just under fifty men, consisting of one lieutenant, Sergeant Buck Jones, a small party of Hottentot cavalry and eleven men following with the supply wagon, entered the narrow defile of the Bama Pass high up in the Amatole Mountains in the heart of Xhosaland.

They had chased Lungelo and his warriors for miles across the bush and Garnet sent Buck and the Hottentots through the pass to scout out if it was safe for the main troop to cross. The devious Lungelo had waited for them, and allowed the reconnoitering party to pass through unscathed. Garnet, hearing no sound of an ambush, ordered the main troop through the pass, and there in the centre, where there was no means of escape, they were attacked and massacred to the last man.

A razor-sharp assegaai, thrown hard through the air from the overhanging rocks, hit Garnet in the chest and plunged into his heart. And it was there, soon afterwards, that Buck and the Hottentots found the bodies in a silence and stench of death.

He ordered the Hottentots on a crazed, wild pursuit of the attackers and finally, deep in the mountains they found them, eating the remains of the cattle they had stolen. For the second time in his life, Buck Jones allowed his emotions to rule his actions, and he and his men set upon their enemies with murderous intensity and killed each one, except for Lungelo, who after a long chase, escaped unharmed.

Buck returned to Grahamstown with no sense of triumph, only a leaden sickness of mounting disillusion. He asked permission to take the terrible news to Esther, and Henry Somerset, knowing the high regard in which Garnet had held him, and knowing that Buck wanted to do something for the way Garnet had helped to save him from the gallows, agreed.

It was four days after Christmas and Esther stood before the narrow yellowwood staircase in the entrance of the lovely farmhouse at Sunfield Park. The doors stood open, the spill of afternoon sunlight streaming through adding a rich hue to the golden wood of the staircase.

There had been a thunderstorm, but now the land was bathed in the mellow, gold light of a lazy summer afternoon, the fields fragrant after the recent rain. The clink of an anvil from the forge was heard outside, and the whining of a dog. From the kitchen at the back a kettle sang over the fire, and nearer at hand a clock ticked a gentle comforting sound. A bubble of laughter came from the sitting room.

The hall suddenly seemed too small for the great height of Buck Jones, who stood facing Esther. Her heart set up its familiar, wild beating as she looked up into his face, then she knew something was wrong. The lines were heavy about his mouth and cheeks, there were pouches of fatigue and strain under the blue eyes. He gave her a long, thoughtful stare. She felt fear as the silence between them seemed to stretch into infinity. She knew that look on his face, that almost hesitant dread. She had seen it on other faces when there was news of disaster, on her father's face when he had brought the news of her mother's death. Her mother's death. A chill ran through her, and she knew it was something to do with Garnet.

Suddenly she cried out, 'Sergeant Jones — it's about my husband, I know it is!'

Unable to hide the sudden pain, Buck drew a deep breath and nodded slowly. The weariness in him was accentuated as he spoke. 'Your husband, Captain Fitzwilliam, is dead, ma'am. I am deeply sorry, more sorry than I can ever say. All I can tell you is that he did not suffer much, if at all.'

Whatever she had expected him to say, nothing could have prepared her for that. Her eyes remained frozen on his face, as she gripped her hands together to stop the violent trembling. She looked away, then turned to him feverishly.

She could not believe it. 'My husband, Garnet Fitzwilliam — is dead? It cannot be true.'

Buck inhaled deeply, and took his time in replying, the expression of anguish on his face deepening. 'It is true, ma'am. He was killed by Xhosas in an ambush in the Bama Pass along with most of the men.'

She stared at him, her face suddenly so stark and still, like a graven image. Her shock complete, she could not answer him, she could only watch him. Numbness crept over her, her throat ached, holding back the scream she must not utter. She had the awful, blinding feeling that in some indefinable way she had sent Garnet to his death.

When Buck broke the silence, his voice was more husky than ever. 'In all truth, ma'am, we have lost a very brave man and one of the finest builders of peace on this frontier. He knew, he understood it all.' He paused, white-lipped. 'While he lived there was some hope for both sides of the border. We all, black and white, have destroyed much by his going.'

Her eyes widened in horror as his fierce exclamation rang around the hallway. He cleared his throat, mastering his anger. 'If there is any way I can be of help, you only have need to ask, ma'am.'

Esther stared beyond him, seeing things he could not see, desperately wishing that Garnet would walk through the door, his dark head shining in sunshine, that familiar, lazy smile she had known before their marriage curving his lips. She became aware that Buck had spoken to her. Bewildered by his offer, she did not know how to reply. All she saw was that the strong-boned face before her was white; aware in the haze of mounting pain that the scarlet jacket and white crossbelt were very dusty. She saw sympathy in his eyes and she remembered the Buck Jones she had known, cool, mocking, self-confident. Now he stood before her, dignified in the face of death.

When she spoke, her voice sounded distant, thick with unshed tears. 'Thank you, Sergeant Jones. I do not think there is anything you — anyone — can do.'

She put a hand to her temple. It was so hard for her to talk. She tried to swallow, to ask him how it all happened, and precisely where was the Bama Pass. How was it that he had come back alive to tell her? But she could not say a word. Through the rapidly-forming mist of anguished tears, she saw him hold out a brown leather pouch to her, half-apologetically.

'These are the Captain's personal effects, ma'am, all he had on him at the time. And this — he kept in his inner pocket, closest to his heart.' It was the miniature painting of herself that she had given him before their marriage — the glass now shattered. Slowly she took the pouch from him, struck by a sense of dreadful desolation, by a feeling

206

of utter remorse as grief encircled her heart and shadowed her mind. Now she knew it was true, Garnet had gone forever, he was never coming back. She would never see him again, never be able to tell him how sorry she was about their last quarrel, of his inability to come to terms with what she had done, of what she'd done to his pride, to the inner man who had wanted to love her as a pure, untarnished girl. Her disbelief shattered, she felt the slow, terrible breaking of her heart. She stared at Buck as if he was not there.

He lifted his hands, then wearily let them fall. She heard him bid her farewell and impulsively she turned to him, looking at his face as if seeing him for the first time. She felt the familiar, warm strength of his tall frame so close to her and wanted, for a brief, insane moment, to lean against it, be comforted by it.

He hesitated, then inclined his head and picked up his shako from the chair beside the door. She watched him go, repressing a strong urge to run after him and fling herself into his arms and cling to his strength in the weakness of her grief. Then he was gone.

She felt so very alone. In her ears rang the thud of his horse's hooves on the turf outside. Then she gave a loud, terrified scream as if she was in pain. She was unaware of Laree rushing out from the sitting room with Charity Wilson behind her, flushed and anxious, a bottle of sal-volatile in her hands. Her eyes did not focus on Arthur Wilson limping up with the aid of a stick, moving with the rheumatic actions of a weary, old man. She was not conscious of Roydon's arms lifting her up and carrying her upstairs as she screamed and screamed, beating him with her fists. And, unseen, the miniature lay face upwards at the bottom of the stairs, its dark blue eyes staring mischievously into space.

CHAPTER
Twenty

Long afterwards she continued lying on her bed, her eyes gazing
lifelessly at the window. She had never known such suffering, such
deep anguish.

Turning her head, her eyes fell on the document on the table
beside the bed. It was Garnet's commission as a major that had
finally arrived on the day before Christmas. Major Garnet
Fitzwilliam — with the extra pay and privileges that went with it.

It was impossible to believe that his elegant, debonair presence
was no longer there, impossible that the life in him had been
extinguished by some savages in a lonely remote pass somewhere
high up in the Amotole Mountains. She wanted to strike back in rage,
to lash out at those who had done it, who had changed her life to a
living hell. In the few days since she had heard the news, she had been
wracked with considerable guilt and remorse such as she had never
known before. It was she who had made his life a purgatory, a
nightmare of disappointment, and it was she who had wounded him
as surely as if she had seared him with his own sword. She could only
think of those terrible, brutal words she had hurled at him the last
time she had seen him alive. She had told him she had not cared if he
never returned, and she had shocked him with the revelation of
Buck's prowess as a lover. How could she have done it? How could
she have been so insensitive to his pain?

How he must have hated her, especially at the last, even though he
had carried her picture into danger and death. She began to weep so
hard that it was difficult to breathe. She had never meant half of
what she had said, never meant this to happen. Surely it was because
of her that he had made a fatal error, and underestimated the
cunning of Lungelo? It was almost as if he had courted death at the

208

last, wanted it to happen.

If only she could make it up to him, bring him back. It was impossible at twenty-three, with warm blood in her veins, and a child to rear, with new adventures waiting to be explored, to believe in such bleak emptiness and death. Even Buck had cheated death on the gallows, so why not Garnet?

Her eyes slid back to the document on the table, then to Garnet's bible which Charity had placed there for her comfort. Dear Charity, always thinking of those around her. How fortunate Laree was to have such a mother-in-law, so like their own mother whose memory had become blurred through the weeks, the months since her death on the *Poseidon*. Now even the ship and the journey from Ireland seemed like some half-remembered dream.

Her attention turned to the window. It was the time of day when the sun was just sinking below the dark line of the horizon, the time when the herdboys were bringing the sheep and cattle back to the kraals for the night, when the busy clatter of pots and pans would be heard in the kitchen downstairs.

The sky deepened to mauve and her listless fingers groped for the bible beside the bed. It had been in the brown leather pouch Buck had brought back from the Bama Pass, the last book Garnet had read in this life ... There was still just enough light to read. It was always a sweet and precious hour, but tonight there was something infinitely sad, even bitter about it which she could not define. It might have been the document beside the bed, reminding her, or her own thoughts of Garnet, or the clouds that came with the setting sun, or perhaps the knowledge of the swiftness of the dusk, like the swift snuffing-out of a life in its prime ...

She was letting her mind wander when something fell from the bible. She bent to pick it up, and saw it was a small, embroidered bookmark, similar to the ones she had made as a child. The words, worked in gold and green, were simple and straightforward: God forgives all.

The book had fallen open at the place marked by Garnet obviously shortly before his death. Her eyes caught the names of King David, Bathsheba and Uriah. A thought began to form in her mind becoming an uncomfortable suspicion. Garnet had read this passage before he died, and possibly many times before that. She remembered the story of David which she had loved as a child, thinking him brave and exciting, and wicked. In her secret heart she had admired Bathsheba, the beautiful wife of the soldier Uriah. Bathsheba had caught the attention of Kind David who had taken her during the Siege of Rabbath. David had sent Bathsheba's husband into the forefront of the battle where he would be killed so that Bathsheba would be his. She shut her eyes in sudden terror, not daring to move.

Garnet had sent Buck and a handful of Hottentots into certain danger in the Bama Pass ... If Lungelo had wished, or if he had thought they would be followed almost immediately by the main troop, he would have killed the reconnoitering party. In that way, Lungelo could have held up the troop, which would have been forced to clear the bodies away and by that time, the warriors could have escaped, evading the troop altogether. But Lungelo had been even cleverer than that. He had patiently waited and let them through, deceiving the main party into believing that the way was clear.

It was only a suspicion that could never be proved, but in her heart she felt a sinister certainty that it was true. She remembered now all the things he had said about Buck before he left that last time, and she understood so clearly how his deep, frustrated and humiliated love for her had turned his admiration and respect for Buck into overriding jealousy and hatred. She wondered when he had begun to suspect the truth. Was it that day in court? Did the birth of her daughter deepen the suspicion already there, especially as she so closely resembled her father?

It was all because of her. She had been at the centre of it all. And Buck had been so distressed at Garnet's death. He had been unaware of Garnet's intentions and carried out orders as usual, not realizing what vengeance filled the other man's mind.

After a moment or two she opened her eyes. She knew then that if she lived to be a hundred she would never forget what she had discovered. Buck Jones knew nothing of it; he did not even know that the child with the Fitzwilliam name was his. He had not known about the farce of her marriage, and he never knew how much Garnet had come to hate him.

She felt strangely and savagely angry that he could have done it, and left her with a child to raise alone. Where King David had succeeded, Garnet had failed and had been forced to pay the cruel and immediate price.

She wished that she could die too, and end it all. It seemed to her the end of everything. There was nothing left. Grief, rage and bewilderment continued to build up inside her. Now, after her discovery, she could not fight off the dreadful dejection and the sorrow. She thought of her father then, the strong rock who had always been in her life, and her teasing, quick-tempered Uncle Cady — and dear easy-going Sam.

I want to go back to Dwyers' Cross, she thought for the first time in months. Oh, dear Heaven, I would give anything to be back there now.

PART TWO
1826–1834

CHAPTER
Twenty One

Esther could hardly believe it. She stood mute in the kitchen at Dwyers' Cross, looking down at the letter in her hand marked with the English frank. It had just arrived from Lady Caroline Fitzwilliam.

It was a cry of horror at her son Garnet's dreadful death a year previously, and an accusation so terrible that the griefstricken, bitter words seemed to burn the paper on which it had been written. And the words would be branded on Esther's brain for as long as she lived.

The letter stated cruelly how the family had tried to dissuade Garnet from marrying her, a woman they regarded as a penniless schemer. It described how his mother had prevailed upon him in letter after letter not to marry below his station to an Irish girl with no dowry, gentlewoman though she may be. Lady Fitzwilliam had wanted a brilliant marriage for her favourite and cleverest son into some well-connected, old English family. As a younger son she thought it most important that he marry money and position. When his father died after the shock of the Lightfoot murder case, in which Esther was implicated, it was discovered that he had cut Garnet from his will and bequeathed the Dorset property intended for him to his younger brother Arthur. Thus Garnet had been forced to fall back on his army salary as his allowance ended on the day of his father's death.

She blamed Esther for everything: for her son losing his inheritance; for his early death, underlining the fact that a wealthy wife's inheritance would have set him up for life when added to the worth of the Dorset property to which he would have returned, selling his commission in Africa, and the handsome inheritance which was his due. In order that Garnet's unsavoury wife would not

215

get her hands on his money, his father had revised his will, cutting his son off without an extra penny to his name.

Slowly Esther put down the letter on the kitchen table and pushed back a tendril of damp hair. The smell of freshly-baked bread filled the room, and rough lumps of dough stood nearby, ready to be baked in the anthill oven not far from the house. The iron kettle began to steam and whistle from its hook over the fire. She took the kettle from its cradle, her face suffused with anger. She was so choked with emotion she could hardly think, she could see nothing as fast tears blinded her eyes.

Everything became clearer as she wiped them away with the tip of her pinafore. It all began to fall into place — now she understood: Garnet had suffered the pain of knowing his parents were against their marriage, yet, he had gone ahead without telling her, and seen it through only to discover he had been deceived. She remembered how determined he had been to keep the matter quiet, even the child's existence, because he had known he would be cut off without a penny and he had agreed to support her and Aurora.

She also remembered the letter he had received a month before he died, announcing his father's death. It must have told him that he had been disinherited, because after that his whole attitude towards her had grown worse, until she unwittingly drove him to thoughts of revenge and his own untimely death.

There was a box somewhere containing all Garnet's letters and papers. Up until then, she had not been able to bring herself to look through them. Everything he had kept from her, all his family's feelings, would be there. If only she had known before. Swiftly she walked upstairs to her bedroom where Aurora slept peacefully in her cot, and fetched the box down from the cupboard where she had put it, out of sight. Riffling through the contents, she came upon a bundle tied with black string addressed in the same unmistakable handwriting of his mother. Drawing a deep breath, she pulled them out and ran back downstairs.

Pouring a cup of tea, she sat down at the table and began to open the letters one by one. What she read shocked her, but she forced herself to read them all. They revealed that his mother had been against Esther not only because she was poor, but because she was Irish — not even Anglo-Irish, but full-blooded Irish. She stated that despite the union of the two countries in 1800 the English did not regard the Irish as equals, that they were a primitive and inferior species. And she begged him to reconsider and not marry 'that woman'. In another letter she stated that the Fitzwilliam fortunes were some of the largest in all Britain, and that on their father's death the eldest son, Jermyn, would inherit his father's title, the large main family estate and other properties, two Parliamentary seats and a considerable yearly income. The property in Dorset plus a handsome inheritance were to go to Garnet, and a property in the north to the youngest son, Arthur.

The letter revealing his father's death was bitter in the accusation that 'that woman' caused it and had brought the family's name into disrepute when the trial became known. She had been convinced that Esther had been behind the murder and had forced Buck to do it. The last letter he had received, shortly before his death, included a vicious lampoon about her and Buck Jones. It stated that stinging debates had started about the trial in the House of Commons, and heated controversy in the coffee-shops. Buck Jones with his red-haired fiend had alternately become a villain and a hero.

She rose and walked slowly to the stable-door, the top half standing open to the hot, January day. For a long time the green leaves of summer had flourished. The gardens beyond the homestead were a riot of flowers, orchards, vineyards, bubbling weirs and water furrows. She could see, all about her, the wonderful work of reconstruction that her father, Uncle Cady and Sam had done to the farm. Her eyes travelled to the new barn standing to one side of the yard and beyond, the orchards of small fruit trees, their young leaves shimmering as they trembled lightly in the hot bergwind. The serried ranks of young, trellised vines, sturdy and gnarled and surrounded by a quince hedge, bore the new crop of grapes, replacing those that had perished in the flood.

The turning point had come at last to the frontier as it began to prosper and improve. The hated government-owned Somerset Farm had been scrapped and there was no more competition for produce. The settlement was now established on sound foundations.

Although she felt angry and humiliated by the letters, an excrutiating remorse had wracked her for months and that cushioned the effect somewhat. She was still slowly recovering from the shock of Garnet's death, accepting it almost as a punishment for marrying him more for what he could do for her and her child, than for himself. She had reached an emotional turning point in her life, and she knew she would never be the same again.

Buck Jones had left the army soon after Garnet's death to become an elephant hunter and she had not seen him again. He had quit the colony a year before for the newly-established outpost of Port Natal in the land of the fierce warlike Zulus, and nothing had been heard of him since. She could shut him out of her mind until she thought of Aurora. He had been renewed in the perfection of the tiny fingers and toes, the soft fringes of dark eyelashes covering intensely-bright blue eyes so like his, and in the soft fluffy brown curls misting the small head. Although the child could not sit up or crawl at nineteen months, the appearance of her did much to arouse the protectiveness of her father, uncle and Sam.

Aurora aroused a fierce protective love in Esther such as she had never experienced and for all her fiery, impulsive ways, she found an unexpected streak of stoical self-control that had only recently begun to surface. The growing fears that the small child was not the same as other children of her age, that she was backward, haunted her. And the guilt that her daughter had been given to her imperfect because of her sin with Buck Jones lived with her, day in and day out. And yet little Aurora had been the fruit of her love for Buck, and whatever was the matter with her she was his child — and the only part of him that Esther would ever have.

She could hear the sound of voices under the mimosa trees. The hard ring and clang of chopping wood came from the edge of the clearing, and her eyes caught the darting movement of a small, bat-eared fox disappearing into the long grass bordering the orchards. She stood for a moment gazing at the steady flight of a flock of quail, and the bright, vivid flash of a sunbird alighting on a bush where cicadeas shrilled. She breathed in the fresh country air, surrounded by the determined efforts of the handful of men left at Dwyers' Cross that had made it one of the finest farms in Albany.

She had returned to the farm after Garnet's funeral, in great need of her kinsmen. Garnet's will, lodged with his lawyer, Mr Aron Pearce in Cape Town, had been brought by that gentleman to the farm. She had been astonished to learn that Garnet's possessions were far less than she had imagined. Now, from the letters she knew the reason. She had Glendower Park and its contents but very little else. Most of his money had been sunk into the estate, the rest being eaten up in rising costs and death duties.

She had been forced to sell the estate and most of its contents to a wealthy barrister, the proceeds being divided between Aurora and herself. Under the guidance of Mr Pearce and her father, she had set aside a good sum to be kept in trust for Aurora in the Lombard Bank in Cape Town until she attained the age of eighteen. The rest she had used to pay her way at Dwyers' Cross, a share of it being loaned to her father for improvements to the farm. By cajoling and bullying she had forced him to accept, to help him pay off a large loan obtained from the bank with Garnet's help on arrival at the Cape six years before. Finally, he had accepted only on condition that he would pay it all back as soon as possible. The portion loaned had helped him to repair much of the damage of the flood.

In the settlement, where the smallest ripple was felt all along the grapevine, Garnet's death had cast such a shadow that it seemed every corner of it was in some way affected. The news of it seemed to subdue the atmosphere, push back hope of peace for a while.

Then her anger reasserted itself and the bitterness, especially against Lady Fitzwilliam, burned inside her. She decided not to tell anyone of the contents of the letter. She would burn it, destroy the hateful, damning contents forever. She was grimly determined that the Fitzwilliams would never know of Aurora's existence. If they found out about the child, it would lead to the discovery that she was not Garnet's flesh and blood and questions would be asked. She could never go through all that, not after the trauma of the trial and its side-effects. She wondered what would happen if they knew of Aurora's presence — would they try to take her away as Garnet's child, or spurn her as the offspring of 'that Irish witch'? Whichever way it turned out, both she and her daughter would suffer the consequences.

She made a silent and desperate vow. Never would she reveal the truth about Aurora, not even to the child herself, and she would destroy all traces of the Fitzwilliams from her life — she would burn all the condemning letters, every one.

Aurora belonged to her, she had conceived and borne her in great anguish and shame, and she would use every means she knew to keep the reputation of her child untarnished.

CHAPTER
Twenty Two

Esther laughed, pulling the ends of her thin, knitted shawl about her shoulders as the wind caught her hair, whipping it madly about her face and stinging her eyes. She stood beside Joshua, watching two recently-employed Hottentot labourers run through the fields waving sticks at a large ursine baboon fleeing through the patch kept for Indian corn.

The settlers were now allowed to employ Hottentot servants, and the two disappeared into the long grass edging the fields stretching out before them. Greying clouds scudded across the sky, chased by a strong wind. To the east the Kap River threaded a tortuous path through the wooded hillsides towards the Fish River. Behind them a new, rough road clawed its way around the low shoulder of hill and fell away through the valley to the west. Their horses were knee-haltered and let loose nearby.

A shot rang out as one of the hired men rushed up and fired at the disappearing animal's head. Small lizards scattered over the hot stones and a flock of hadedas rose in disturbed flight. The baboon cried out like a beaten child as it stumbled wildly through the grass. It was carrying one of its young on its back to the safety of the thickets near the river. They could see it clearly now — the great, dog-faced animal, its hideous jaws gaping to expose the formidable canine teeth nearly an inch long.

Esther winced at the sound of the screaming animal. It was too similar a scream to that of a human being, and after all these months in the bush she was still not used to it. It was the same all year round. These animals continued to wreak tremendous damage on whatever crops there were at the time. This one had dared venture up as far as the vegetable garden.

The hired hand ran up to the thickets in pursuit and loaded his musket for another shot which he pumped into the baboon as it appeared briefly before his range of vision. Before long it was carried lifeless from the grass by the two Hottentots who captured the baby baboon and took it up to the huts.

For some reason the experience unnerved Esther. She knew the baboons were wild creatures and dangerous, and she had always detested them. But this one had been a mother escaping with a helpless baby, and quite unexpectedly she felt sympathy for the dead beast and its young. She could not understand herself. A year ago she would have been unmoved by the suffering of a wild animal. She would have been afraid of its ferocity and ugliness, but something had indefinably changed inside her, and all she could experience now was its pain.

Joshua knitted his brows fiercely. He looked out over the rolling hills, and smiled. 'Can you believe that all this raw earth is now ours, Esther Mary?'

He watched the wind sweep the crests of the milkwood trees and billow out the loose creepers hanging along the branches. 'After all we've been through here, wrestling with this dragon of a land, we are finally succeeding. I can tell you now that there have been moments when I hardly thought it would be possible.' He chuckled, looking at some scuttling fieldmice vanish into the shadows of the grass. 'To be sure, my girl, at the heart of the Irish soul is land — something you can get your hands on, something permanent in the midst of the chaos of life. It is there when all else passes away. Something durable to hand down to your children and grandchildren.'

Esther raised her eyes to the severe dignity of her father's face, now showing the signs of advancing age. He was one year off sixty, a good age for those days, but his spirit was as fierce as ever. She looked down at the upturned clods waiting for new seeds, the soft sweet odour of the moist, ploughed-up earth in her nostrils.

'But will it ever be enough for you, Papa — this land?'

'Damn it, girl,' he replied forcefully, 'Never will there be enough for any full-blooded, hard-working man. Nothing is ever enough for the human spirit, and that is what we call progress. Dissatisfaction leads the way to improvement, it always has. Who the devil wants to stop now? Look about you.' He stretched out an arm about him.

'Look what we've done already. The strong have survived in face of great obstacles, and this is only the beginning of what we can do in the future. There are hundred of acres of virgin soil out there waiting to be tamed and cultivated.' He paused, sighing deeply. 'I only hope that I can be spared long enough to see it happen, because happen it will.'

Esther swept a long, loose strand of red hair from her face, smiling. She had not seen her father so alive, so enthusiastic for a long time.

'Come on, Papa, you'll outlive us all and still push your grandchildren before you.'

A smile tugged at the corners of Joshua's mouth as he placed an affectionate arm about her, giving her a quick squeeze as he used to do when she was a child.

'That would be my wish, my dear. It's good to have you back at Dwyers' Cross with that dear, young granddaughter,' he said simply, savouring the thought. 'Pity Garnet could not have been spared to see her grow into the lovely young woman she promises to be.'

There was an uneasy pause in which Esther stiffened ever so slightly. A troubled frown knit her brow. Somewhere in the recesses of her mind a warning light flickered. Whatever would her father do if he found out the truth about Aurora? Especially as her natural father had been Joshua's strongest opponent regarding the frontier defence system.

Esther was neither awed nor intimidated by her father. She regarded the fierce, lined face, beaked and stern, as calmly as she would have regarded her late brother. The strong, jutting chin did not alarm her, nor the alert and penetrating grey-green eyes set under thick, grey brows. But now an unforeseen threat to this bond of new-found comfort and closeness between them touched her like a small, grey shadow across the sun. She shivered, folding her arms across her chest.

'It's a dirty wind out today, Papa, I'd best be getting back to that darling child before she screams blue murder from starvation.'

He peered at her, suddenly anxious. 'You know, Esther my dear, it would be well for you to consider marrying again — to some decent fellow who can take care of you and Aurora. Your uncle and I are neither of us getting any younger, and I worry about what will happen to you when we are gone. I would like to know that you are provided for, like your sister Laree.'

222

Her face clouded, then lightened as she looked up at his familiar and beloved face. He relied so much on her these days, though he would never admit it, and she could now give more, having been through so much herself. She could understand more. She smiled, a renewed feeling of love for him rising in her.

'Don't worry about me, Papa, I can take care of myself very well.'

'It's a hard world for a woman alone with a child to raise, Esther Mary. Promise me you will think about marriage again. There are several fine young men in Albany.'

But not for me, she thought, scuffing her shoe in the dust. Pursing her lips, she nodded reluctantly. 'I will give it some thought, Papa — now don't be late back for dinner or you'll spoil your favourite dish.'

He chuckled. 'It's just an excuse to avoid my suggestion.' She waved gaily as she mounted her horse and rode back through the long grass blowing before the wind. He hair streamed out behind her like a vivid scarlet flame as the wind took it and snatched it away, the glint of a musket lying across her shapely shoulders.

Now she could see the farmhouse send up a fresh blue feather of smoke, and smell the woodsmoke from the chimney.

It had been with great relief that she had heard of Lady Caroline Fitzwilliam's death soon after receiving her last letter. The fear of losing Aurora to her, or being exposed, had vanished. She was sure that the rest of the family would be only too glad to forget the whole affair as if it had never existed. Surprisingly, she had received a letter from Garnet's eldest brother, Sir Jermyn, telling her of his mother's death and of his knowledge that she had a child. He had wished her well under the circumstances, implying that the matter was closed and he had no desire to pursue it further. Secretly Esther assumed that it would be to his advantage to forget about any child of Garnet's thus lessening the chance of the child as a future contender for any part of his inheritance, there being several grandchildren already.

Now only one tiny, dark shadow flitted across her mind as she rode towards the house. She had to keep the identity of the child's father from her father and uncle, and from the world. The warning light flickered once more before it died. There was no one who could find out — except the father himself, and he was miles away. She was conscious of still being young and alive, and her resolution for ultimate freedom became stronger by the minute as she cantered into the yard. It was only at night, when she slept alone, that she suffered torments of yearning and her tears would wet her pillows.

Soon she was back in the kitchen, scolding one of the men for spilling water on the floor. The household had subtly changed since her return over a year ago. Her exuberant manner and the affection she bestowed almost carelessly on those she liked were appealing, while the sharpness of her barbs and thrusts keenly pierced those she disliked and scorned. It was good to have her back and this afternoon the steamy, savoury smells of mutton stew drifted through the kitchen, lifting the senses and spirits of all those in the yard.

Esther lived fully and zestfully and those about her were caught in her enthusiasm, not knowing the full extent of her moments of grief and remorse. Her father was right, it was hard for a woman without a husband in society. A widow had more status than a single woman but it was not the same as being married. It was this daunting prospect that faced Esther, but she could not bear the thought of subjecting herself to any of the men she knew, her fierce will subdued. It was against this background of insecurity that she made her plans. She would succeed on her own in the face of all opposition. She would not be a prisoner of this valley, she would stay because she wanted to stay, and because her father needed her. She would create her own happiness. No one would trap her into any arrangement she did not want; she had been through quite enough already.

The storm of agitation and protest that had been growing against Lord Charles Somerset for so long had gained considerable ground in England, especially after the Commissioners of Enquiry returned. Buck's sensational trial had also played its part in bringing the corruption and inefficiency to the notice of the British public. Lord Charles was forced to return to Britain to defend himself against the attacks made by the settlers. Major-General Bourke was sent out as Acting Governor, accompanied by his wife and three daughters.

Esther felt a touch of sad affection for the weary Lord Charles who had been kind to her during her stay in Cape Town. He had been one of the few who had believed in her innocence during the trial, which all seemed now so very far away. She wondered what would happen to him.

The days passed in a welter of hot sunshine and bergwinds, and all the time the tide was turning for the Albany elite like the Dwyers, men of old background and tradition. They were slowly being challenged for the leadership of the settlement by the rising new commerical class of self-made men. It was their voices that were getting ready to be heard.

Esther, a dark cape about her shoulders, stood on a small promontory overlooking the west bank of the Keiskamma River, early one morning at the end of February. She was waiting for the gun to boom from Fort Willshire opening the trade fair with the Xhosas stationed on the opposite bank.

It was only minutes before eight o'clock and there was much activity and restlessness among the colonial traders assembling their wares and packing out the last goods for bartering from their wagons. The myriad of campfires on the Xhosa side of the river had twinkled and glowed all night as a few thousand tribesmen and their women had gathered from all over Xhosaland.

Fairs were now held regularly every Wednesday, Thursday and Friday in an attempt to control trading between the two races and to prevent the illegal gun-running and black market which was still taking place. No trade was allowed in cattle, guns, ammunition or alcohol. Cady had obtained the special trading licence necessary and Esther had finally managed to persuade him and Sam to let her join them on this trip, leaving Aurora in the care of Hannah Byrne.

Looking down and across the river shimmering in the early light, she wondered what the day would bring. She could see the collection of Xhosas assembling their goods in bundles as they waited for the signal, looking like so many ants swarming on the river banks. She had never seen so many black men before, at such close quarters.

It was a seemingly peaceful scene, the wooded gullies studded with aloes, euphorbias and cycads falling away down the hillsides, and opening out across the river into wide, flat, open countryside. It was there that hartebeest and many of the larger antelope no longer seen elsewhere now roamed with the great herds of elephant, rhino and buffalo. The plains near the kraals of the Chieftain Mazwi had become the home of the shy quagga, whose flesh was carrion, and who, since the coming of the settlers, was hunted purely for sport.

Esther had never been this far on the border and she felt that wonderful quickening of delight at the beauty and strength of the countryside, the wildness of it which pulsed with power and life.

'Good morning to you, Esther — please come help with some of these baubles, will you?' Cady said, his arms spilling bric-a-brac.

Before she could answer Sam reached out to take some of the large fish-hooks, shiny shoe-buckles and great, gilt buttons.

'See here, Mr Cady, how you came by all these trinkets and such is beyond me,' Sam said, raising a quizzical eyebrow.

Cady only shrugged, his eyes more green than hazel under their thick, copper lashes. 'Don't go on at me, lad, so early in the morning. I begged and borrowed the lot, but never stole as much as one. Ask Esther — she's to blame for the whole glittering lot.' He gave Sam a sly wink, handing him the overflow from his arms.

He buttoned up his brown skin jacket and looked out across the river. 'Believe it or not, out of this uncompromising, small world of rocky hills and dark shadows come men of purpose, decision, whose power and greatness of heart shall lie across the face of this land yet, mark my words.'

Esther put a hand on her hip, her head cocked to one side. 'Glory be, Uncle Cady, you do wax lyrical at times. Greatness of heart or not, let's get all this stuff into proper order before the gun goes off. I would really like to know just what you menfolk would do without us women.'

Sam chuckled, the bright specks of his black eyes reflecting the sunlight, his wiry, iron-hard arms showing from a much-patched, blue-check shirt as he grappled with the awkwardness of his load. 'Well, you could start showing us, Miss Esther, by giving us a hand with these wares. True as bob, I didn't know we had so much. There goes the gun — those devils will be across the river in less time than it takes a vulture to skin a carcass.'

The articles were laid out on a linen sheet. His expression hidden, Cady looked down at the display of everything from fishing lines, earrings and tinder boxes to red clay and, most prized of all, beads. Then he laughed and clapped Sam on the shoulders, his copper hair now touched generously with silver.

For all the roughness of his skin trousers and home-made jacket, there was still the mark of birth and breeding in his weathered, lined face, and he still carried himself like the ageing warrior he was, his proud face as always set for battle. He was fifty-one with only the family name and his memories of Ireland left, but he would never give in, that Esther knew as she watched him. She knew that once he, like her father, had made up his mind there was no going back, no running away, not because of what he thought, but because he was a

226

Dwyer, perverse, stubborn, Irish. This she knew was both a strength and a weakness in him, fed by his unflagging pride and a deep unrest. In that moment she felt proud too, that he and she belonged to the same blood.

He looked at her, a wry glint in his eyes. 'What we need now, Esther Mary, is the patience of Job and the wisdom of Solomon to do business with these wily savages, who drive white men to madness with their haggling.'

The Xhosas moved over the western bank, clustering themselves opposite the traders where they arrayed before them all the treasures of the bush. Collections of ivory, wild animal skins, karosses, all types of birds, young buck, parrots, monkeys, baskets, mats, phoenix palm hats and rhino sjamboks covered the ground, and the long leisurely business of bargaining began. The background was peppered with scarlet as the redcoats from the Fort wandered in and out of the milling crowds on the lookout for any sign of trouble. For a brief second Esther's heart skipped a beat at the sight of a tall redcoat, then her excitement faded. It was not Buck Jones, and never would be. He was no longer a redcoat. She felt unusually let-down and empty. Why she should have thought of him then, she did not know, except that it seemed a fitting place for a hunter to be with its restless activity and strange undercurrents.

So many small things reminded her of him today: a soldier's easy, determined stride, the arrogant angle of another's head, the husky tones of yet a third. He seemed to be all of them, and yet fully none. It was as though he had become a distant shadow in her life, and the clearest memories she had of him was that brooding, white anger in his face on the day he told her of Garnet's death.

The wiry, old man facing Cady threw down a necklace of paste beads, disgust written all over his wizened face. He shook his head, the bright, dark eyes shrewdly raking the face of the white man opposite him. His grizzled, woolly cap of crimped hair was white and he wore about his thin hunched shoulders, a skin kaross.

Cady threw up his hands in growing impatience, glaring at the old man, who returned his stare with quiet impassiveness. Cady scrubbed the back of his head, a movement of extreme exasperation. 'Hell's damnation! What is wrong with those beads? This old prune's been haggling for hours and he's refused everything so far. What the devil is wrong with him?' he snorted, thrusting his quivering jaw

227

almost into the old tribesman's face.

'The old man's no fool, Mr Dwyer — paste beads break too easy, he knows that. He's trying to tell you by throwing them back.'

Esther whirled round at that familiar husky voice expecting to be deceived once more, unable to believe that it was really Buck Jones this time. Her heart set up a wild thumping as she realized it was him, grinning from ear to ear, blue eyes brilliant as sapphires.

He wore a full, sun-streaked beard and was dressed in the skin trousers and jacket of a frontiersman, a low brimmed Phoenix Palm hat on his head. He looked a little older than when she had last seen him, and there seemed some indefinable difference, but otherwise he radiated the same strong, masculine appeal. She watched him as he doffed his hat to her, experiencing again the depth to which her mind and body was stirred whenever she was in his presence. He still had that power over her, and resolutely she tried to fight it off.

He bowed, smiling at her, exposing even white teeth. 'I didn't expect to meet you at such a gathering, Ma'am,' he said, his expression unreadable. His head, a tumble of brown curls, cocked characteristically, but his eyes narrowed against the light, the net of crow's-feet wrinkles at their corners.

The remembrance of their last meeting, of what had been a bitter experience touched her deeply. Thoughtfully she laced her fingers with elaborate care, somehow managing to hide her disappointment at his reserve, as he knelt beside Sam and the old man. He picked up the necklace of coral and transparent beads in turn. Rubbing them through his fingers he looked up, surprising the superior gleam that lingered in Cady's eyes. He spoke in the soft, clicking Xhosa tongue to the old man, who answered him gesticulating and nodding his head vigorously. Buck suppressed a glint of mirth and Esther wondered what the old man had said.

Quickly he turned to Cady, his voice easy but subtly veiled with scorn. 'Old Dantalasele here says the coral beads look too much like certain seeds found in these parts, so they are worthless to him. The transparents are out of fashion with the dusky wenches over the border. Goes to show that these so-called savages have their fashions like the rest of us.

'He also cannot understand the impatience of the white man which he says is like a disease.' He ignored Cady's expression of acute annoyance, and held up a necklace of turquoise stones. 'You can bet your sweet life these will sell.'

Buck cocked an eye at the old man who was watching him closely, and showed him the beads, speaking again in Xhosa. The tribesman grinned, showing gums of broken teeth, blackened by the smoking of long African pipes for many years. He clapped his skinny hands with delight.

With a brief smile, Buck rose. 'He'll take 'em, Mr Dwyer — in exchange for ivory. Those beads will be the pride of some black maiden across the Keiskamma by daylight tomorrow — they call 'em *tamboos*. Beads are used for just about everything in Xhosaland, and for money further inland, and you can't go wrong with the ones in fashion,' he said in an expressionless voice. 'It's a good thing to know a man's language and his customs — you can get through to him better that way.'

Cady studied him minutely, a glow of anger stealing over his face. 'You and those missionaries led by that rogue Dr John Philip, you think you know everything about frontier affairs because you happen to speak the language of the savage. You think we are the cause of all the trouble, that we whitemen are the villains of the piece and the Xhosas are pure and noble. Mark my words, Mr Jones, you will end up speared by your own liberal stupidity.'

Buck shrugged broad shoulders as he stood before them. Behind him the Union Jack fluttered softly from its flagstaff at the Fort.

'There is one important difference between Dr Philip and myself, Mr Dwyer — a difference I think you should know. Dr Philip knows less about the Xhosas than I do, and he is less interested in them. His work lies with the half-breed clan of Griquas. I want justice for both black and white races on this frontier.'

'And what gives you the arrogance to think you know it all?' Cady snapped, fierce fire in his eyes.

Buck stole a glance at Esther, then turned again to her uncle. 'I have freshly returned from Port Natal, Mr Dwyer, after a long absence from the colony. I have seen the disturbance and the chaos caused by the Zulu Chief Shaka and his followers among the tribes along the eastern seaboard and further afield. The Zulus press dangerously on the northern flank of the Ama-Xhosa who need land where there is no more for them. The Xhosa are hemmed in by the Zulu on one side and the whiteman on the other. The situation is fraught with tension and all over Xhosaland there are plots and counter-plots, black man against black man, black against white.'

He leaned forward, biting back a trace of impatience. 'Anything could spark the tension across the border, Mr Dwyer. It is like a tinderbox. It is we who have the terrible responsibility of keeping the balance between the races, because we have the power,' he said, speaking now with a deliberateness brought about by his own knowledge of the situation.

Cady's eyes sparkled with suppressed rage. He peered at Buck, his eyes almost hidden as they narrowed in contempt. 'No white man can ever speak with these savages, Mr Jones. There is not an honest man among them. They already think we are weak because of our ineffective defence of the border. We must show 'em we are strong and determined, and not gullible fools before their treachery.'

Buck watched him keenly. He did not answer immediately, his eyes turning towards a young Xhosa man walking agilely some yards away. He was six feet in height, as handsome and as strong as a black Apollo, with a wide, grinning smile and the bearing of a prince. Buck held the open, direct gaze of the beautiful, gleaming, young Xhosa, and when he spoke again, his voice was angry, sarcastic.

'There is Nyzei, the heir to the old chieftain, Mazwi. His father is one of your strongest allies — unlike that deceptive Gaika who changes his colour when it suits his purpose. Old Mazwi is weary of strife. He desires peace and he is willing to work with us to gain it, if we let him.'

Cady's lips drew back in a snarl, his eyes narrowed to two green points of hatred. 'I spit on his help! It is his people who have caused the most suffering at Dwyers' Cross, who trespass on our land and steal our cattle — his son, Lungelo, who killed Garnet Fitzwilliam and left my niece a widow with a child to raise on her own. It jars me to share the same space as these murderers and thieves. You trust a man where there is no trust. He plays us all for fools.'

Buck inclined his head towards Esther. 'I beg your pardon, Ma'am, I'm sorry to mention facts that could open up a wound.' He looked at her suddenly-strained face, the expression on his own enigmatic.

She stiffened, embarrassed, aware of her pounding head and thudding heart. As the world seemed to dwindle to just him and herself, Cady's voice cut between them.

'Never, never will there be peace on this border while that snake

230

Mazwi draws breath.'

Buck answered with cool directness. 'The problem is not Mazwi, Mr Dwyer — but Nyezi's half-brother, Lungelo, who is restless for power. He is older than Nyezi, more experienced. He wants to take the rightful inheritance from him. He has been outcast by his father this past year after the massacre at Bama Pass. Mazwi was upset by the whole affair. Lungelo is ripe for trouble, and it is he you court by the ignorance of the tribes, of him, of his father. Mazwi himself has likened his two sons to the white and red mabele grains — Nyezi is good, but young, too trusting, impetuous. He is the son of Mazwi's eldest and most important wife who bore him late in her life. He is no match for that fire-eater Lungelo who is bold, arrogant and bitterly jealous of him.'

He stopped, every now and then his blue eyes glanced at the tense young woman with the red hair opposite him. Then he turned his head away and gave a low whistle. 'Speak of the devil — there is Lungelo now. He faces his father's wrath to be here.'

All eyes followed his to watch Lungelo as he spoke to Nyezi. They could not hear their voices but Lungelo's face told a story. He drew his thick, black brows together above his broad nose, the nostrils distended. He straightened his strong shoulders, bringing up a hand to flick away a fly from his face, the bangles on his wrists jangling together angrily. He was the eldest of all Mazwi's sons, and yet he could not earn the right to be chieftain in his father's place because his mother was not as important as Nyezi's. But he regarded himself as the rightful heir.

And this was the man who had helped to cause Garnet's death, who could have caused that of Buck and the Hottentots. Esther suddenly felt sick. She wished she had not come. Seeing Garnet's murderer so suddenly for the first time was disconcerting; it had brought back the suspicion of what Garnet had tried to do to Buck, and she had had no time to prepare herself. She wondered what Buck thought. She risked a quick glance in his direction and found him looking at her. Immediately, as though he had touched her, she felt emotion flash like little needles under her skin. She looked away swiftly, again incredibly aware of his presence.

Lungelo spat on the ground venomously and strode away. Esther, watching him, shivered, feeling a sinister, ill-omened shadow flit over her mind.

231

A cold anger spread through Cady then. 'We will fight them all, Mr Jones — they all have the same black heart. We will fight them until we triumph or die in the attempt,' he hissed.

Esther knew the pain in her uncle's heart, she could feel it almost as a tangible thing. Cady had been wrong in his judgement of the Mazwis. Their entry to the clay pits had not been trespassing as he had thought, but a ritual return to an old and traditional place for their ceremonial clay. Orders to stay away from it were meaningless. It was a place to which they belonged. The Xhosa simply saw the pits and the Dwyers' land as theirs, a part of their existence, a symbol of themselves and their tribal religion. Esther and her people were in this land, but not of it. Its secrets were lost to them and they walked it as strangers.

For all that, she was moved by her uncle's frustration and bitterness. She knew how angry he felt towards Lungelo, Garnet's murderer, and she could see how he restrained himself with great difficulty from attempting to kill him there and then. But she was also impressed by Buck's fierce intensity, by his knowledge of the situation. His husky voice broke her thoughts.

'I know you will continue to fight them, Mr Dwyer, but it would do well to remember that there are the innocent and the guilty on both sides of the border — the red and white mabele grains among us all.

'Good-day, ma'am.' He bowed slightly to her, replaced his hat on his head, and sauntered away through the crowd.

In the silence that followed, Buck's words lived on in Esther's mind, filling her with the restlessness of many questions. She was moved by her admiration of him, by what he said, and disconcerted by the sudden violence of her feelings. He interested her, intrigued her more deeply than she ever cared to acknowledge. Staring after him, she felt oddly disappointed that he had gone.

If we had met in other times, she thought, and not as the two people we are, perhaps then things between us would have been different.

Her eyes met the guarded face of her uncle, encountering his unusually cold expression. A silent challenge flared between them then. Her eyes, full on him, matched the icy disapproval of his tightly compressed lips. He is warning me off, she thought. He had clearly divined all her thoughts and his mouth formed a bitter line.

'Esther Mary, that arrogant elephant hunter is walking down the wrong road, and some fine day he is going to pay the price and those on his side with him. How in hell's name can we come to terms with the black men when we whites cannot agree among ourselves, I ask you that?'

He broke off abruptly, unaware in the long, silent moments that followed, of how the course of his life and that of his niece were subtly changing.

CHAPTER
Twenty Three

By 1826 the frontier was seething with unrest and the whole colony was almost bankrupt. It still suffered from unsettled government, and soon the Cape Corps would become the Cape Mounted Rifles, to be run more economically with less men, further reducing the defence of the borders against the Xhosa inroads.

But these matters were always conveniently thrust aside for the favourite entertainments of the day. One such was racing, which had reached the frontier and caused many dramatic crises. Various tactless confrontations occurred on the racecourse between soldiers and gentlemen who believed they had been insulted by the other in certain ways. The new Landdrost, Major Dundas, and his goodlooking wife, withheld their patronage from the sport, pleasing those settlers who disliked it, and regarded good-humouredly by those who did.

It was at one of the race meetings in the early autumn that Esther accompanied Laree and Roydon on the first social occasion she had attended since Garnet's death. It was a Saturday and the course overlooking Grahamstown was a bustle of activity. Joshua was one of the stewards and Cady was racing his new horse against some of the finest riders in Albany.

Esther sat with Laree in the Wilson's curricle in the half-shade of the mimosa trees. The day was warm yet, the ghost of summer still drifting here and there like the fragments of some nostalgic, old tune. Shreds of clouds scudded across the sky, dappling the fields and hills with small moving shadows. Across the rolling acres of bush, the kloofs were bright with spiked aloe flames, orange and mauve strelitzias and a riot of succulents spilling down the rocks, and flowering in moss-covered crevices.

The riders and male spectators moved restlessly about before the start of the first race, while the women paraded about like peacocks in all their latest finery. Esther was still in mourning and her gown of black silk, with a double row of ruffles at the neck and at the wrists, cool and smooth against her skin, created a striking effect, contrasting with her luminous, creamy complexion. A small mourning hat, lined with black velvet, covered her dark red curls.

She looked in the direction of the laughter following Cady as he regaled a group of spectators with some droll joke at his opponent's expense in his inimical style. As the riders prepared for the next race Esther's gaze was drawn to one of them, rising above the others. His coal-black charger restlessly pawed the ground as his rider raised his head.

She was aware in that instant of a sudden pang in her breast, a familiar, wild, uncontrollable thumping. The suddenness of recognition made her body feel weak. It was Buck Jones, sitting magnificently astride his horse, leather jacketed, skin breeched, right in the midst of them.

He turned and looked at her, and she remembered every detail of that bronzed, strong face, now alive with the challenge of the race. Something in those brilliant, blue eyes made her catch her breath. She felt once more her body heat with passion, and for once she did not care. She had so long been denied intimacy with a man, and had determinedly kept her mind from any such feelings, that she now recklessly welcomed it. She could not stop thinking about him since their meeting at the Fort Willshire fair, nor altogether hide her delight at seeing him again.

He had become a well-known and excellent elephant hunter, and through the grapevine she had heard that the ivory he hunted was fetching good prices on the Ivory Floor in London. There was talk that he was becoming a fairly wealthy man, that he had returned to buy one of the farms vacated by a settler who had moved to town. He had, it appeared, banded together a small group of men to work the farm near Port Frances, and was in and out of the colony on hunting trips to the interiors, a familiar figure among the traders at Port Natal.

Boldly Esther returned his gaze. Her lips curling a little, she inclined her head in acknowledgement of his presence. He raised his riding crop in greeting, his eyes moving over her easily and familiarly as she sat back in the carriage against the cushions, the picture of complete seductive femininity. She flushed furiously, the gold mourning ring flashing on her finger as she moved her hands restlessly in the dappled sunlight falling between the trees. She looked away as a stream of gay spectators flowed between the mounted horseman and herself. When she looked back, he was gone, and she felt a sense of loss.

Laree glanced at her, puzzled, as Esther's impatient eyes raked through the crowd for a glimpse of him. One dainty, black leather slipper tapped on the floor of the carriage until she discovered him at the far end of the line of riders.

The atmosphere was heavy with tension and excitement as the second race began. 'They're off!'

Holding her breath, Esther watched Buck surge forward with the rest. Caught up in the general excitement, she raised her spy glass and saw him kick his horse into a gallop, speeding down the course towards the finishing line.

With every stride his horse overtook the others, carrying him past them until he was fighting it out with her Uncle Cady. Cady sped up beside him, taut with tension and grim-faced.

'C'mon there! C'mon!' The roar of encouragement from the crowd floated out over the course. Through the glass Esther could see Cady urging on his horse. For an instant the ragged group of horsemen passed in front of her, then with a dig of spurs, they leapt away, riding for their lives. For a moment, she lost sight of Buck and her uncle, then she picked them up again flashing out of a dust cloud, with Gert Venter's son Arend closing in behind them.

Laree's voice was full of excitement. 'It's Mr Jones' horse. He's giving Uncle Cady a real good race!'

Buck and Cady were level with each other, there was nothing to choose between them. The turf flew and scattered in all directions amidst the roar of fierce shouting from the male spectators, jostling to get a better view of the finish. The air was electric as the three horses out in front raced madly towards the finishing post. Suddenly, like a streak of lightning, Buck's horse shot forward. There was neither elation nor disappointment on Esther's face as he managed to beat her uncle and Arend by a hair's breadth past the winning post. A great cheer rose into the air from the spectators.

But Esther had eyes only for Buck as she watched him cut his

236

speed on the edge of the course and bring his horse to a shuddering stop. Then he wheeled about, and trotted back to the disorganized knot of men at the start. She saw him receive more applause from the crowd, then she lost him as her uncle rode up, and there were congratulations all around for his magnificent performance. He took it all in good spirit, but Esther knew that he was peeked and annoyed at being beaten so narrowly by his arch rival. Buck was one of the finest riders she had seen in a long time, and her uncle had always been one of the best. Even now, at his age, he was still very hard to beat.

After the excitement, a small group of admirers gathered about the curricle to talk to her, and she lost Buck once more in the crowd. He disappeared and she never saw him again that day. She rallied as best she could, hiding her sharp disappointment. Deep down for her, something had gone from the gathering, something elusive, exciting and vital. She knew there were whisperings about her and the young men gathered about the carriage, and she deliberately ignored the speculative murmurings, her mind far away on other matters.

Laree put out a gentle hand and laid it on her sister's arm. Esther turned and looked at the younger woman who was reading her face so clearly.

'How I wish it wasn't only in books that princesses married herdboys, my dear Esther, or that Papa would condone such a thing. I am exaggerating, of course, but it is the only way I can explain myself,' Laree said, her understanding of the situation complete.

She seemed to know it all — Esther's grief, her emptiness, the restlessness that was always there at the back of her mind. She never ceased to amaze Esther, showing aspects of her nature hitherto unguessed. Laree, softly spoken, gentle and hesitant, had an unexpectedly determined will, and wisdom far beyond her years. Esther studied her with the relief of one who does not have to explain anything. The large, blue eyes edged by thick brown lashes that usually appeared doe-like in the heart-shaped face, now had a certain stubborn glint in them.

'And oh, how I do approve of your choice, dear Esther — now he is just the man for you. But dear me, how very snobbish and unbending is the background from which we come, which is the greatest pity of all sometimes.' She spoke so softly that it seemed as if she was talking to herself.

237

Esther winced. She had heard every word, and the pain of it filled her again. He was all wrong for her — his background, his station, his reputation, everything. But he was so special, so unique, and he was the father of her child. If only she could tell Laree everything, could confide in her. She bit her lip, overcoming her momentary weakness.

She thought of Aurora, with his eyes and dimples. She seemed a slow, bland child, backward. Esther had tried not to focus on the difference of her child from other children, but increasingly as time passed, that difference was becoming more evident. She sighed, trying to bring herself back to her present surroundings, wishing that Buck was still there.

Joshua, Cady and their guests, Arthur and Roydon Wilson, lifted their heads from the huge beef pies before them. Sam, cutting a chunk of fresh bread stopped to listen, his knife in mid-air. It was some weeks after the race meeting and Arthur and Roydon were on a brief visit to Dwyers' Cross.

They all stopped to listen as the sound of a galloping horse broke into the noon stillness. Esther turned from the fire to see Cady on his feet, springing past her as he raced from the room. The flying hooves had reached the top of the dusty path leading to the house.

A scatter of small stones flew up as the horse was brought to a sharp halt. The rider was Michael Byrne, breathless, dishevelled, his shirt caked with blood. The men from the house were soon crowding around him as he dismounted.

'It's Dougherty, sir — 'e's been killed by the Caffres at Trompetter's Drift. The devels 'ave taken your cows as well,' he cried hoarsely, struggling for breath.

Anger flared in Joshua's eyes, his square jaw set taut. 'And what in the devil's name was Dougherty doing at the Drift, Byrne?'

Byrne looked at him, his face pale and strained. Sweat-matted locks of hair fell over his forehead. ''E was trading with the Caffres, sir — 'e and Penny, sir — bartering beads and buttons for ivory and cattle, they were. Dougherty had the ivory on 'im when I found 'im.'

Joshua swore. 'Damn it, Byrne! I trusted Dougherty. How long has this smuggling been going on? He had no licence, nor had Penny.'

Byrne shrugged. 'I don't rightly know, sir — Penny is in Grahamstown gaol right now.'

'You had better tell us all about it, Michael Byrne,' Cady said, as

238

the others clustered closer around him.

Byrne took a deep breath, his eyes darting from one man to another. 'Well, as far as I know, sir, they 'ad finished trading, or so Penny said. They were on their way back when they passed a party of Cape Cavalry near Fraser's Camp. The 'ottentot soldiers tried to arrest 'em and take away the cattle and ivory. Dougherty escaped and Penny was taken back to Grahamstown. 'E was on 'is way there when I met 'em.' He paused, licking dry lips.

'I then went back to the Drift and found Dougherty's tracks all over the place. There were cattle spoors leading into the deep kloof not far away. Seems he was surprised and murdered by the tribesmen, sir. I found 'is horse tied to a tree, the stirrup irons cut from the saddle. 'E was dead when I got there — with an assegaai in his neck. I was on my way back here to tell you, sir, when I met Mr Buck Jones and two of his men. They are bringing the body over here on a stretcher.'

'Damn them all to hell's flames!' Cady burst out savagely. 'Will those wild savages never leave us alone?'

'We'd better look into this matter, Cady,' Joshua said, nodding sharply in Byrne's direction.

There had been several instances recently of bloodshed between the Xhosas and the farmers, and now there was Murtagh Dougherty from Baltinglas. He had left O'Reilly's party and joined the men of Dwyers' Cross years ago, and ever since he had been one of their most loyal supporters. He had refused to leave the farm when most of the men had gone to the towns.

Noon slid into late afternoon before Buck Jones and his two men arrived with a cart carrying Dougherty's body. Their dark shadows fluttered briefly over the patches of grass, disappearing to reappear on the next as they moved forward. Apart from the harnesses and spurs jangling, and the dull rumble of the cart wheels trailing pale clouds of dust, nothing but a vast, empty silence lay about them.

'This is not the end of it,' Joshua thundered as he went out to meet them. 'Those Xhosas know the weakness of our frontier defence — of the delay in getting permission from Grahamstown headquarters for military aid. We are forced to take matters into our own hands. A man has been wilfully murdered, albeit trading illegally. Another life has been taken and our cattle stolen. We are calling out a commando immediately to get our cattle back, and to avenge this man's life.'

Esther's heart leapt as she saw the tall, strapping figure of Buck Jones. He was clean-shaven and wore his low-brimmed hat pushed casually to the back of his head. He dismounted, wiping the sweat from his eyes, his imposing figure blocking out the trees behind.

Since his return, this man had become a thorn in her kinsmen's sides. He questioned their aggressive actions against the Xhosas at the pits, and had opposing views about the reprisal system, an arrangement well-known and recognized in Xhosa law whereby commandos led by an officer had been allowed into Xhosaland to retrieve stolen cattle.

Buck believed that some system of reprisal was necessary, but he was against the way it had been carried out. He believed that innocent Xhosas had suffered for the actions of the guilty, as cattle had been indiscriminately taken by redcoat and colonist alike. And there had been several cases of colonists taking more cattle than had been stolen as the settlers' cattle was now of a higher quality than that of the Xhosas.

The Acting Governor, Major-General Bourke, had abolished the reprisal system stating that no invasions were allowed into Xhosaland, even for the recovery of stolen cattle. The colonists had to apply for military aid which usually was a long time coming, on purpose in most cases.

Esther watched Buck now and saw the steady, intelligent eyes never waver. She knew he was going to oppose her father yet again.

'I warn you, Mr Dwyer,' he said, 'that if you plan a secret commando into Xhosaland you will cause retaliation raids. There is no excuse for provoking the tribes and possibly causing a large-scale raid over the border. What your man did was illegal.'

There were muted mutterings from the men who had gathered about Joshua, Cady and their guests.

'Those savages are out there, waiting their chance, intent on harm. Do you expect us to ignore this wilful murder for whatever reason, and to show the weakness again on our side?' Joshua said sharply, his lips in one hard line.

Buck's startling blue eyes were cold. 'Your men were acting outside the law whether it is right or wrong, Mr Dwyer. They have reaped their own bitter harvest. They knew full well what they were doing, and the consequences. Punitive raids such as you intend will fan the flames until the whole settlement goes up in one mighty conflagration, another war more bloody than the last.'

Joshua regarded him angrily. 'We have no effective defence, Mr Jones, and it's worse since the Albany Levy was disbanded last year. We are forced by the restrictions placed on our defence by the Acting Governor to return to the system of our own commandos and punitive raiding-parties. I know those men were acting illegally, but a life is a life, and Dougherty was one of my best men. He stuck with me through the worst, and we will not desert his memory now. Most grievous of all, we are up against administrative incompetence not of our making. No, Mr Jones, we go our own way and take the law into our own hands on occasion, like the Boers on the northern borders.'

There were grunts of approval at his words. Buck's eyes were contemptuous, his Sussex burr more rounded and strong. 'We are a small cluster of British and Boer, Mr Dwyer, holding back a sea of black tribesmen behind some thirty miles of Ceded Territory, bordered on two sides by fordable rivers and impenetrable bush.'

He looked from one face to the next, pinpricks of anger in the blue ice of his eyes. 'There are so many holes, so many crumbling stones in our living, white wall that the reprisal system of patrols as we have used them cannot and will never work effectively.' His voice rose, his lips hard, the strong jaw stubborn. 'The border itself, Mr Dwyer, is indefensible.'

'And what is your answer to the problem we face, Jones? How do you intend us to build up these crumbling stones you so rightly describe?' Cady blazed, stabbing the air with his musket. 'We are settled here by Governmental authority, rightly or wrongly. We've inherited this mess, this whirlpool of violence and conflict, and we have to deal with it one way or the other.'

Buck threw a calculating look at the men, standing now uneasily before them. He looked down the row, ranged in a ragged line, all sullen faced and resentful. 'It is time, Mr Dwyer, for the two races to learn the ways of each other before it is too late. The only way is to bring the black man in among us so that he can learn our skills, civilize himself, become a productive part of our society. And in turn we must learn what he has to give us — the give and take of character and skills from both sides of the border.'

Cady laughed derisively. 'How interesting, Jones! Left to you we'd all become fine white tribesmen, one and all.' His laughter was accompanied by that of the men.

Buck ignored his remark. 'We cannot separate the two races forever — there is not enough land for either. There is trouble in Xhosaland — the sounds of unrest are heard throughout its length and breadth and echo on our borders for those wise enough to listen,' he said in a hard, though not hostile, tone.

Cady exploded, his face locked into lines of harsh bitterness. 'Go back to your cursed wilderness, Jones, and take your fine ideas with you. You want to break the living wall, not fortify it more strongly.'

A deep silence fell as the sun began to fall behind the hills and the shadows lengthened across the fields. The screech of hadedas filled the air as they rose from the thickets searching for beetles.

Two of Buck's men unloaded the body of Murtagh Dougherty and laid it on the ground. 'Take the body of your man,' Buck said in a voice of steel. 'If you are still hell-bent on your reckless actions, we can only hope that there'll be land left for your people to protect.'

Buck called to his men and strode to his horse. As the cart started to move forward, he vaulted on to his mount. He wheeled it about in time to catch Esther's eye. There was a sudden duel of glances as his eyes invaded hers, drawing her to him, and she felt again the sudden heat of suppressed passion. He sat some paces from her, yet, in some strange way they seemed joined together.

Then his face darkened abruptly, a dangerous spark in his expression. She was instantly alarmed by the hard set to his face, as if her kinsmen's hostility had distanced them.

'I hope in all earnest, ma'am,' he said, his words clipped, 'that by the time your kinsmen have done their foolish deeds, there will be a patch of land for you and your child to call your own.'

She clenched her fists so hard that the nails bit into her flesh as she watched how, with a dig of his spurs, he urged his horse on to take the lead past the cart. The stallion broke into a gallop and fronted the bushes, Buck's leather jacket a brown flash before it disappeared into the trees.

As her father stumped back to the house, Cady stood straddle-legged, hands clasped behind him, barking orders to the men to carry the body up to the yard. When Cady finally left the men the silence among them shattered as they gesticulated and cursed, raising their voices roughly in anger and bitter disillusionment. As the night crept up the hills from the fields below, Esther heard them from the kitchen, and turned her back, her heart like a lead weight.

Hearing a sound in the doorway to the sitting-room, she turned. It was Roydon, his pale skin flushed. 'I beg your pardon, Esther, if I startled you.' He cleared his throat.

'Have a care, Roydon Wilson,' she said, 'you're enough to frighten the wits from anybody with your quiet shuffling.' She smiled wearily. 'If it's any comfort I am making a dish of tea. Would you care to join me?'

'I would that,' he said gruffly, and approached the table. 'But you need a spare bit of muscle to get that fire to full strength once more.' He smiled at her. 'Let me help.'

All around them, kitchen utensils winked and glittered in the light of freshly-lit candles. He piled fresh billets of wood on the fire and set to work with bellows to work up a new blaze. The fire flared up into rosy sparks, rushing and roaring up he chimney. He sat back on his heels, grinning with satisfaction. Rising, he seated himself at the large yellowwood table and pushed aside a big, bronze skillet pan at his elbow.

He eyed her soberly for a moment as she drew forth a canister of tea and a white and blue china teapot in the warm silence.

'How is it you can be so calm in the face of a man's death, Esther, and his body hardly cold?' he asked at last, as she turned to face him.

Esther pursed her full, generous lips. Years ago she had scoffed at this man, who was now the father of three children. There was some kind of strength about him, unsuspected by her until some time after his marriage to her sister. She drew a deep breath.

'I am not as calm as I look, Roydon, only better able to hide it.' She swallowed hard. 'But it doesn't do to weaken and let go, I've learned that the hard way. We must press on, and work helps — cooking and such, the little daily chores that give some kind of continuity to things. No one deserves the death of Murtagh Dougherty, but I am weary of all this fighting and bitterness.'

A silence fell and she wished she had not spoken. There was the warm hiss of the kettle over the fire, and the smell of guttering tallow candles. She busied her hands with the kettle.

At last he broke the silence, his slow, steady Devonian voice falling on the quiet room. 'I think we speak the same language, Esther. Ever since Mr Jones left I've got to thinking that maybe he is right. He speaks the Xhosa language, he knows Xhosaland and beyond.

Perhaps we should heed his warnings. I do not think I will join your Uncle Cady on his raiding party tonight — not because of fear but because I agree with Mr Jones that it will lead to trouble we can ill afford at this time.'

Esther turned to him, surprise in her fine, dark blue eyes. 'Perhaps you are right, Roydon, but very few will agree with you or with Mr Jones, and never my father or yours.'

He looked at her candidly. 'What you say is true, but I have made up my mind. Your uncle is getting a party together to leave under the cover of darkness.' His voice was unusually sharp. Esther turned away and went to the fire to fill the teapot from the kettle.

He watched her. She seemed more thoughtful lately, to have changed from a sparkling, boisterous young girl to a woman, more beautiful, but who laughed and mocked without the glee of childhood as she had done before Garnet's death. She seemed troubled, as if she were tangled in some darkness and was struggling within herself.

He was silent for a long time, then he cleared his throat. 'There is only one important fact as I see it, and that is what we believe is right. It does not matter what others say or think. And that is the whole truth of it.'

She spread her hands, her face strained. The light had gone from her eyes. A small muscle worked in her cheek and her hands trembled slightly. She looked full into his face, a new-found respect in the depths of her eyes.

'The wildness of this place has changed us all, Roydon — even you. It has brought out strengths and weaknesses that none of us knew we had. And it will go on testing us until the day we go to our graves, spent and burnt out.'

She was smiling now, but it was a brave, tired smile. Roydon suddenly grinned boyishly. 'It has done that for sure, Esther, but we are not defeated yet, not by a long way.'

She felt the tears gathering in her eyes and kept her head bent over the teapot in the table. Roydon smiled, taking the cup she offered. Cold dread filled her heart as she sank down on the bench opposite him. 'I only hope you are right, Roydon Wilson — I only hope you're right.'

She drank the liquid in her cup, her face rigid, her lips pressed tightly together. A dog barked suddenly and she heard the men enter the house, their muted voices planning the raid for that night. Would it never end, she thought, cradling the cup of steaming hot tea between her hands, all this violence and death?

They waited hours that long cold night for news of Cady's raiding party. A fire had been laid in the stone fireplace, the leaping flames throwing irregular patterns across the faces of the four people in the sitting-room. Joshua and Arthur Wilson sat smoking, speaking now and then as they puffed away. Esther sat in one corner thonging a hide jerkin beside a wavering, guttering candle. She felt depressed and increasingly anxious.

Roydon stood at the fireplace, looking deeply into the flames, then he turned, his usually good-natured face flushed with anger. 'It was a wild thing to do — going on this raid. Now we bring all the bitterness of the Xhosas down upon us, man, woman and child.'

'Oh, Roydon lad, do be silent,' Arthur Wilson said irritably. He raised his quizzing-glass to peer at his son, then shifted painfully in his chair, the rheumatism in his joints sending sharp pains through his limbs. 'What's done is done. If nothing had been done, it would only have made matters worse, not better. We cannot sit by and condone this kind of senseless murder, for whatever the reason.'

He reached beside him for the pewter mug of porter now brewed by licence on the farm. Joshua extracted a blazing faggot from the fire with finger and thumb, and relit his black clay pipe with great deliberation. The wind that had risen outside was muted by the crackle of the flames and the voices of the men.

'Mr Jones said it could cause a large-scale raid and worse trouble than we know,' Roydon persisted, thumping a fist on the mantlepiece.

'That man Jones is an unprincipled adventurer, Roydon,' Joshua said. 'He is the mouthpiece of those interfering missionaries, led by that infernal Dr Philip, who can see no wrong in the black man and no right in the white. Be sensible, lad, they will bring us great trouble yet, mark my words.'

Roydon frowned, trying to control his temper. 'If I may say so, sir, Mr Jones cannot be a mouthpiece for anyone. He is too independent of spirit. As he said, he favours no side over the other, but wants peace for both. And he seems to be right in one thing — we cannot hold back the black tide against us indefinitely.'

Esther looked up quickly. She had ceased being surprised by Roydon, but she knew that he was only adding to the bitterness that the older men harboured against Buck Jones.

Joshua coughed, his eyes contemplating the smoke curling lazily up from his pipe. 'That elephant hunter is an uneducated man, Roydon — what formal learning has he had? Only what he has gleaned and borrowed from other minds. Granted he is quick to learn, but he has not the background to put that learning to good use. He stirs up trouble, seeing problems where they do not exist, making them bigger than they really are. I wouldn't listen to him, boy — there is no authority whatsoever behind what he says.'

'Garnet believed in him — God rest his soul — he thought the man knew what he was talking about. If you remember, sir, it was Buck Jones who went along as interpreter when His Excellency Lord Charles finally visited the Xhosa chiefs with Henry Somerset. If I recall rightly, they even had word sent to him in Port Natal to help them out.'

'Be that as it may, Roydon, I still have no faith in the opinions of an unlearned man with no background and a notorious reputation. He knows the Xhosa language, that is the only reason why he was asked to interpret, nothing more, nothing less,' Joshua said with finality.

The division of opinion inevitably resulted with Roydon silenced heavily. Buck Jones had caused a conflict of ideas in the fight over the land between black and white. Esther kept her growing anxiety hugged to herself as the orange sun lifted slowly from the rim of the hills, melting away the vapours of mist drifting up between the tangled thorn trees, lying thick in the deep hollows.

Another day and night passed, the tension mounting with every passing hour. The following night, Esther sat in her corner without moving, held fast in the grip of rising fear, while the wind moaned outside. Roydon sat on the floor of the sitting-room with his head resting against the wall, his light grey eyes staring unseeing into space. Cady's grey hunting dog lay beside him on the floor. His father sat dozing alongside the fire, emitting gentle rumbling snores, his plump legs stretched out painfully before him. Joshua remained in his chair reading, his pipe clenched between his teeth. The wind died towards midnight and a deep, impenetrable silence blanketed the land. But there was no ease in that silence. The air was fraught with tension. Esther could feel it, and the longer they sat in the quiet room, the more she felt like screaming and the tighter her nerves stretched.

Everything was centred on the success of Cady's commando. Her mind began to reel as the screws of her imagination tightened her heart. This horror of bloodshed, violence and danger dogged their steps at every turn. She wished it was a dream from which she would wake and find it was not true. But she knew, as always, that she must face up to it all, in all its brutal ruthlessness and savagery.

The dawn came with a hint of grey-green behind the hills where a cold wind was rising once more. Cady's dog whined uneasily beside Roydon, and then lay down. After some seconds it growled and padded about the room with its ears flat against its head. All eyes watched the dog with heightened alertness. He lay down before the door, waiting.

Not long afterwards, they heard men's voices, and heavy footsteps sounded on the gravel outside. Joshua was already at the door, pulling it open, the wind howling through it. Cady entered at the head of a tired group of straggling men stumping through the door. Esther and Roydon stood on the edge of the small knot of grim-faced men, not daring to breathe as they tried to read success or failure in their faces.

'It was a disaster,' Cady said, rage fighting the humiliation on his face.

'By all the saints, Cady! What do you mean — a disaster?' Joshua demanded, his face unmasked by complete and utter disbelief.

'It was through no fault of Mr Cady's, sir,' Sam burst out. 'Our guides led us to the wrong kraals and we attacked before learning of our mistake.'

Cady raised a forestalling hand. 'Enough, Samuel, enough.' He cleared his throat. 'It is as Samuel has said. We opened fire and killed a large number of tribesmen before we discovered our mistake. The worst of it is — and I hate and despise myself for having to say this — there were women and children among them, to our eternal shame.'

Sick horror froze the air, paralysing the four who had waited so long to hear the outcome. Then Esther cried out, 'No — by merciful heavens, it can't be true.'

Cady's shoulders slumped heavily as he punched a fist through the hat in his hand. 'It's all too true, Esther Mary, there's no denying the fact. We had to fire to show that we meant business.' He turned to

Joshua. 'We captured two hundred head of cattle — but by the time we realized our terrible mistake, the real thieves had escaped. We were pursued for miles by enraged Mazwis, and two of the men from Barber's farm were murdered while searching for a horse near the Drift.'

Arthur Wilson, watching him, said grimily, 'As dreadful as it may sound, Cady, it was one of the hazards of the border conflict. In the heat of the moment some regrettable things happen. It only equalizes what the Xhosas have done to us in the end — all those innocent herdboys we have lost, murdered for no real good reason. Don't forget James Coffee, Murtagh Dougherty and all the rest. Life has its own way of retribution, whether we like it or not.'

'Two wrongs never make a right, Father,' Roydon cried suddenly, incensed beyond reason. 'Mr Dwyer and his commando killed innocent women and children — and innocent men, too! Up till now, no Xhosa warrior has ever laid hands on one of our women or small children. These men have the blood of those innocent Xhosas on their hands. This will probably cause a large-scale counter-raid on our farms and then the mistakes of the guides on the commando will lie heavy when still more lives are lost.' He stormed towards the door, opening and closing it with a bang. There was a profound, ominous silence as the men left the house to talk quietly among themselves. The news of the disaster began to sound in all parts of Albany, the small ripples becoming great waves that came crashing down on all those at Dwyers' Cross.

A storm of bitter disapproval broke out. Public opinion flamed into public condemnation and the raid was called the 'blundering commando'. Many were of the opinion that if Cady had the good of Albany at heart, he would have managed the affair more efficiently, that he deserved no thanks for the attempted action or forgiveness for the mistakes of his guides.

Its failure aroused the hottest critics among the settlers who bitterly resented the attack and felt that the bungling would cause worse conflict on the border. Ironically, however, Cady still felt he knew his fellowmen and neighbours well enough to know that had the raid been a success the commando would not have been abused.

As early winter arrived, Murtagh Dougherty was laid to rest beside James Coffee and John Tobias.

CHAPTER
Twenty Four

In the soft, pearly-grey light of pre-dawn that hazed the surrounding line of hills and bare fields, Esther walked to the barn across the yard. It was still very quiet as she washed the udders of the cows. Gently she began to squeeze and tried to stay in rhythm to prevent an almighty kick from the great back legs. She still did the milking as she had done when the labour was scarce and none of the men could be freed from other farmwork to do it. She had elected to do it because it helped to take her mind off her sorrows, especially in the very early morning before the other work of the day began.

The barn was very warm from the heat of the animals' bodies, and homely, a perfect place to quieten her mind, to get back to the unhurried rhythms of nature after a restless night. She liked its warmth and the muted noise of the animals. At the far end of the barn, the black Mantatee stableboy plied a currycomb and straw wisps to rub down the winter coats of the four horses.

There was an emptiness inside Esther still, but she was often too tired to think much about it. The worst time was in the very early morning while the house still slept. These were the hours she could not conquer, as she tossed in her bed restlessly, tortured again and again with the past. She could hold down those feelings as she worked during the day, but this morning she felt sick of the endless tasks. Her undressed hair was lank and fell in wisps about her face, spilling from under the scarf she had tied about her head. As she looked at her rough and chapped hands, she longingly thought of sweet-smelling perfumes, elegantly dressed and pomaded gentlemen, and hot baths drawn for her by her maid at Glendower Park. Now she could only smell cow dung and animal smells until she thought she would never smell anything sweeter again.

Some disturbing sense made her keep glancing over her shoulder. The animals showed an unusual uneasiness, and she wondered if there was a snake in the barn or a hyena or wild dog nearby. The pale square of the stable-door let in some light, but she could see nothing in the shadows. Her glance stole towards the barrel standing near the door, filled with salted beans, and the pounds of quince, fig and peach preserve which were stacked in one dark corner, away from the animals. There was nothing there as far as she could see.

Something made her stop and turn again in surprise. She called to the Mantatee boy who came over to pick up the pail of milk beside her on the floor. As he walked off, she rose and followed him to the door. He disappeared across the yard and she stood at the door, looking about her.

The sky was just beginning to blush pink. Very soon her father and uncle would rise and be away, overseeing the lands. And the men would wake with plenty of noise. But now all was silent, nothing human moved. Cady's dog and the other dogs were nowhere to be seen. Her eyes took in the whole scene. Where the milkwoods ended, open land stretched behind the house, dotted with small islands of acacia trees and thickets of thorny, olive-green wag-'n-bietjie bushes — the rest a carpet of tall, coarse grass. The men's huts clustered together behind the orchards of fruit trees to one side of the yard.

A morning wind was stirring, clearing the cool, pale sky of cloud and making a brittle sound in the tops of the milkwoods. The dense vegetation around the farmstead had at first given a sense of security to those who lived there. But Esther had learned from experience that this was not so. Who knew what or who could be out there watching and waiting?

The clucking of the poultry reached her from their pens surrounded by renoster bush under the trees. The rooster crowed into the air, full-throated and loud. Then it stopped.

She felt a shiver of apprehension as surprise turned to the familiar feeling of fear twisting her nerves. She heard a bird give a sharp cry near the edge of the milkwoods, and for a moment she was deceived.

Then she froze. Her eyes widened as she saw them, vague outlines emerging stealthily from the deep shadows of the long grass near the trees. It was a band of Xhosas, their faces daubed with red clay, assegaais glinting in the pale grey light. She felt helpless. Her legs could not move. All she could do was stand there, her heart pounding as sick fear pierced her.

She no longer had words to pray, nor resources to turn and hide. There was no time to run to the house, no time to warn her father or the men. She knew that she now had to face something she had never faced before. She fought down a wave of sickness and stared at them. Her throat suddenly turned dry as she watched them move silently towards the yard. Panic shrieked through her nerves as she caught sight of them drawing nearer. She had heard that Xhosas did not kill women and children, but after her uncle's disastrous commando she was not going to take that chance.

Time was short. They were closer now, unmistakable. They seemed so sinister with their silent, frightening way of melting into the countryside around them. Without another thought she quietly ran inside the barn to where she had left her musket propped up against the barrel of beans. White with terror, she snatched it up, waiting in the shadows, every sense strained to catch the slightest sound outside. She prayed desperately that the Mantatee boy would not come back or else he would surely be killed.

Then it came. A quiet padding of feet. She felt the strength drain out of her legs, but managed to stumble to the door, seeking a chink in the knotted wood. Finding one, she screwed up her eyes and looked out. The black men silently ghosted towards the barn and the cows, still dark in the half light.

Her nerves stretched to breaking point as she observed their stealthy progress. A sickness once more rose in her stomach and there was a burning behind her eyes. The men vanished for a moment in the dark shadows of the large water barrels at the side of the barn. She drew a deep breath, trying frantically to calm herself.

The first panic passed and she began to seethe with fury. How dare they come here to the farmhouse that had been built by many months of struggle and hard work. And now they were arrogantly coming to steal the cattle in the barn, to spirit them away and take them into the depths of Xhosaland. She closed her eyes to build up her courage, then before she could think too much, she flung back the door in one bold, angry gesture of defiance.

She stood facing them in the pale light of an early June day, staring at the advancing figures with an ashen face. Her gaze hardened as she aimed the long-barrelled gun into their midst.

251

'Stop!' she said, her voice shrill with anger and fear. She knew they could not understand her so she made her gestures very defiant, wishing desperately she could speak their language. 'Stop, or I'll shoot!'

In total amazement the men slowed their pace, all eyes turned warily towards her. Her message was clear enough as she waved her firestick towards them. The atmosphere was taut with tension. Her eyes never left them, the resolve growing in her heart that if they refused to stop, she would shoot to kill the man who was their leader. And if the worst came to the worst, she would die fighting. Backing up against the barn she was determined to protect the cattle of Dwyers' Cross.

The leading man stopped as she pointed the gun at his heart. He held up his hand, motioning the others to do likewise. He was tall and lean, a handsome black kaross, soft as velvet, hanging over his shoulders to his knees, his arm loaded with copper bracelets, bone pendants in his ears. As his daubed face stared at her without flinching, she recognized with a start that he was Lungelo, the arch enemy of the men at Dwyers' Cross, and the murderer of Garnet. She would know that face and that arrogant bearing anywhere for, once seen, Lungelo was hard to forget.

Behind him, his warriors stood, staring at her with proud, inscrutable eyes. Then he shook his assegaai at her, shouting alien, menacing words. Trying to steady herself, Esther saw more than a flash of anger in his dark eyes. A sharp coil of vicious fear tightened her stomach as she saw livid outrage on his face, a terrible hatred seeming to flow from the black man's soul.

She blinked briefly, feeling the cold sweat prickling her skin beneath her clothes. Then she lifted her head, determined not to back down, even though she knew full well that it was the women, children and innocent men of Lungelo's people that her uncle's commando had killed. Her only power was in her determination, and her gun. She saw a blur of black bodies, the shining assegaais, aware of the brooding menace around her.

The daubed faces watched her tensely as she waited with her heart in her mouth for them to rush her all at once. Would Lungelo's hatred of her people cause him to forget she was a woman and kill her in revenge for what her uncle's commando had done? For surely that was the reason he was here now. She took a step forward, still aiming

252

at his heart. Whatever this man was, he was no coward, she saw that as he faced her with hostile courage.

Suddenly he nodded abruptly, still glowering, and gave an order to his men. They all looked at him, and then back at her, gesticulating with their assegaais. They were obviously not in total agreement with him about leaving the cows in the barn behind her. He spoke to them again, brusquely and harshly, pointing back towards the clearing. He spat venomously on the ground at her feet, his eyes boring into her as she shrank back, trying her utmost to keep her composure in the face of his overpowering hatred. Then he turned on his heel, motioning the others to follow him. They all gave her a last accusing look and silently retreated the way they had come, melting effortlessly into the long grass.

Shaking violently with relief, Esther ran into the barn and put the musket down. The Mantatee stableboy together with the herdboy came running towards her, shaking with fear. As best she could with the disadvantage of the language barrier, she calmed them down, assuring them that the warriors would not be back that day, that they were safe and so were the cows. Then, slinging her gun across her shoulders she ran towards the house. She had saved them this time, she had saved her kinsmen's cows. But for how long could they continue to live in this way? For how long would they be spared in the bitter conflict mounting between both sides with only thirty miles of what was now called Ceded Territory to separate them? And since Acting Governor Bourke had allowed friendly tribes to re-occupy that territory, other chieftains had crept back on sufferance closing the gap between black and white still further — one of them Lungelo's crafty uncle, Mavile, with whom Lungelo now lived.

It was this old man who schemed and plotted for the time when Mazwi died, to overthrow the young Nyezi and to set up his half-brother Lungelo in his place. If and when this happened, Esther wondered, how much longer could they exist here so close to them?

Twenty Five

For some time they had been expecting a Xhosa attack, ever since Esther had thwarted Lungelo's cattle-raid, but they were still caught unawares.

A single raucous bark had been heard first, then a cacophony of barks as the watchdogs raced down the fields. The door crashed open, the ruby light of the last glow of sunset shooting across the kitchen. Sam, his fingers clenched round his musket, announced that the Xhosas were on their way to attack the house. Joshua rose from the table, his tired face white, and nodded towards Cady who was already pulling a brace of pistols from the wall.

Joshua ordered everyone to vacate the house and huts and to run for cover of the thickets bordering the clearing at the back of the house. Esther took Aurora, already asleep in her cot, and urged Hannah Byrne and her small son and daughter to follow while the men mustered for some kind of defence. There were so few of them in comparison with the band of warriors fast approaching. The Hottentots and Mantatees were posted at significant points under the cover of trees.

'We'd best keep cover until the Xhosas are massed,' Cady said. 'Then we'll set up some kind of charge, all guns firing to frighten them. There are too few of us, too many of them. We must save our reserves until the right moment.' He called his dog and disappeared.

The rest of the dogs who had been barking near the river, now fell silent, and it was suspected that either they had been killed or else fobbed off with chunks of raw meat.

Fear clamped its cold hand on Esther's heart as she pushed her way through the thickets of low-growing bush crowded together at the edge of the clearing. There she lay, hardly daring to breathe, with

Aurora, Hannah and the young Byrne children beside her. It was damp, the rain that had fallen in the last few days had stopped and the air still smelt sweet. Leaves rustled underfoot, a few twigs cracked among the thick palisade of bushes and black shadows. The air was strangely still; not even a breath of a small breeze stirred the leaves. Esther's ears strained for the slightest sound. The warriors would be close to the fields by now, or even beyond. What seemed like hours of waiting was in reality only minutes. She was shocked into full alertness as she held her small daughter close to the ground, as though the tiny frame was a warm and comforting lifeline.

There was a low throbbing across the earth, the ominous drumming of feet, and then the trees bled men. A large band of warriors surrounded the homestead with blood-curdling yells, brandishing assegaais wrapped in blazing grass. Frightened by the noise, a flock of birds, red-gold in the fading sunlight, rose from the fields in great circles, squawking with alarm. Esther listened with dread as she tried to peer through the screen of bushes towards the horrifying chaos of sound.

The handful of men burst from their cover in a bold, final gesture, all their firearms blazing. The warriors were checked by this unexpected attack and some of them fled. The rest stood their ground with fearless, wild courage in the face of the withering fire. They hurled their flaming assegaais on to the roof of the barn. Flames broke loose, snaking up and out and spreading as they leapt high against the skyline. The roof of the barn stood out as the darting, hungry flames swept through the wood. The deafening cries of the frightened animals rose above the confusion as the fire raged around them. Men were shouting as smoke billowed and stung their eyes. The Xhosas yelled as the shots tore past them, and eventually they were driven off.

Pails and casks of water were carried from the large water barrels near the barn. Sand was gathered to smother the flames, along with blankets, quilts and anything they could find. It was all happening so fast. A large column of orange flame wrapped in thick, black smoke rose straight to the sky, heavy curls billowing upwards with the splintering of timbers, the snapping of wood.

The fire devoured the barn and the roof broke away, still burning. Aurora began to cry as another surge of flame roared up, blotting out the sky as the barn curled back and buckled, the red-hot timbers falling inwards. The heat pouring from it made everything above and about appear to dance and shimmer in the darkness.

Esther ran from the cover of the thickets clutching Aurora to her, the sheer horror of it all shrieking through her head. Burning embers dropped from the sky all around, and the light of the fire was so strong that she had to shield her face from its overpowering glare. Men were running about in all directions and there was the splash of water being poured into pails. Urgent shouts for more pails and for sticks wrapped in cloth, sounded through the smoke. The greatest fear was that the roof of the house would also catch alight.

'There are truly times when I wish we'd built closer to the river,' Cady said to Esther, as he hurried up, exhausted with effort. He wiped the soot from his eyes. 'That water in the barrels is just about all used up.'

'There's no protection near the river, Uncle Cady, you know that. Imagine what would have happened if we had been there, with no time to escape the house.'

Esther tried to comfort Aurora who was clinging to her with the desperation born of enormous fear.

'True, niece, true — we need another pair of hands if you don't mind.' Cady strode on back into the smoke.

'Here, Hannah, take Aurora and your children. Look after them until I get back. I must help with beating the flames before it reaches the house.'

It seemed like hours that she beat the flames with a cloth-covered stick. Her arms arched, her face was blackened by the falling ashes. Fatigue had reached such a high intensity that she and everyone else moved in a nightmare of shadowy figures, the only reality being the terrible weariness and ache in every bone.

Sam had managed to save most of the animals with his small band of Hottentots, but nothing remained of the barn. The gaunt, fire-blackened ruins still smouldered, crumbled and charred as the dreadful night passed into an uncertain dawn.

They all stared out at the rising sun in deep, black depression. Esther saw her father's bitter eyes follow the crumbled line of the barn where the dying embers still glowed through the thin layers of smoke. His bitterness instantly turned to anger as he wiped away the soot-stained sweat streaking his face. Suddenly he looked so old. His fierce eyes fixed relentlessly on the ruins, and she watched him rally the men.

She herself felt tired, wearied beyond all reason. Licking lips caked with soot, she pushed a hand through hair singed by the heat that had poured from the fire. Her smoke-blackened face turned towards her father as she listened to him speaking to the men, his words reaching out through the cool, quiet dawn. Quilted clouds drifted across the sky, obscuring then revealing a few pale stars.

'We are not defeated yet, and that fool of a governor will know it before too long, if he returns to this colony. Had we a better defence system this would never have happened. But we are not finished yet. We've gone through drought, flood, rust, impoverishment and government incompetence, and we can rally now under the burdens of the heavy crosses we have been forced to bear. Change will come, men, we will see to that. This land is ours and we will win this power struggle over it with the Xhosas.'

There still clung about him an air of strength and purpose, slowly reaching those around him. It held them in its firm grip, denying them the end of hope and confidence. But for the very first time in her life, Esther did not believe him. His towering strength did not reach her and warm her heart as it had done so often in the past. She hid the growing heaviness of spirit within herself, and began to organize the kitchen without further delay. There were meals to be cooked and served, duties to be performed if they were all to get through that awful day.

With dead, lifeless eyes, she gazed at the dark ruins across the yard, and cursed herself for her self-pity. Yet again, they had all been overtaken by hardship and violence, and they would be again and again. Whenever she tried to see beyond it she could find nothing — just another battle, more risks, more bitterness, and less time in their favour. She thought of what Buck Jones had said about the smouldering fires of conflict on the border and in Xhosaland itself, of the vengeance, the bitterness and congestion, the lack of land. He was the only one who could help them. He knew the frontier better than most and he spoke the Xhosa language. He also knew the chieftains, their customs, their ways.

She formed her thoughts, and waited for her father to return to the house for midday dinner.

'Papa — there is someone who can help us, someone who can

257

speak to the Xhosas, get them to stop their plundering,' she said, holding her breath.

Joshua seated himself at the table. 'And who is this saviour of us all, my dear?' he said testily, lowering his craggy eyebrows.

She steadied herself by taking one very deep breath. 'Mr Buck Jones, Papa — he's the only one who knows the Xhosa well enough. He can speak to them for you, for the men.'

'By all the saints, Esther! Have you taken leave of all your senses?' Joshua narrowed his eyes, his nostrils dilating with instant anger. 'That man spells trouble! I would never ask for his help for any reason whatever. Our lives do not depend on that disreputable individual, and that's that.'

Esther stood her ground, her face as stubborn and angry as his. 'You are a stubborn man, Papa, and because of it you will bring ruin on us all. I have a child and I will not see her harmed. Mr Jones understands this frontier, he understands the Xhosa people. He wants peace as much as we do. I know he will help us.'

'That is quite enough, Esther — you keep out of the affairs of men. Although you think it, you do not understand one half of the problems! Now let me be.' His harsh voice jabbed furiously at her. 'I do not want that man's name mentioned in this house, is that quite clear? Besides, who knows, if he had got back to the Bama Pass sooner, he may have been able to save Garnet and the rest of the men! Until I know the truth of that affair I will never forgive him. Reconnaisance indeed!'

Esther was appalled. It was the first time her father had ever admitted that he was bitter about Garnet's death, or that he blamed Buck Jones for it. She saw now that he was bitter because it had been her husband, and not the other man, who had never come back.

'That's not true — that's just not true. Mr Jones was doing his duty.' She felt very angry, but she knew she could not reach him now. Too much had happened to him, to her. His face was hard, severe, shut off from her — his mouth drawn into a thin, inflexible line. He blamed Buck Jones for being alive while Garnet was dead. She had never believed it possible.

Joshua motioned with his hand. 'I have seen you suffer, my child, and I do not want it to continue. These ruins out there are not our right, and I will see that it is never allowed to happen again. I am off to see Major Dundas tomorrow to demand magisterial permission to send another commando after those savages. If permission is refused, which it invariably is, then the matter shall be carried to Acting Governor Bourke himself. That is all you need to know, nothing else concerns you,' he curtly dismissed her.

A coldness closed on Esther's face. 'What has happened to you, Papa? You were always a man of peace. You abhorred violence. You — a Justice of the Peace in Cloyne, used to solving conficts, not making them. Now it is you who advocates force. Strange that Mr Jones, a former soldier, a man of war, has now turned to be a man of peace. It seems as if you have both changed sides.'

Joshua's hard, weathered hand beat the air. 'Time and circumstances change us all. I want no more talk of Jones, he is most certainly not a man of peace.'

With growing dismay Esther left the kitchen. May God help us all, she thought.

Esther's mouth felt suddenly dry as the wagon, driven moodily by Sam, drew nearer to Eden, the farm belonging to Buck Jones. She wondered if she was right, secretly visiting the man she had tried so hard to forget, to cut from her life — and the man so bitterly opposed by her kinsmen. She had niggling doubts, now they were so close, that he may refuse to help her, but she also had the characteristic self-confidence in her ability to win him over.

She was on a self-appointed mission to ask his aid in speaking to the Xhosa chieftain, Mazwi, on behalf of her father and uncle. She knew that if her father or uncle ever found out they would be furious.

She stole a glance at Sam, slumped beside her unhappily on the driver's box, as the wagon jolted over the ruts and stones in its path. She had wrestled for many agonising days with the idea of approaching Buck Jones after the Xhosa attack on the farm, and now she felt the slightest twinge of guilt as she glanced at Sam out of the corner of her eye. She had tricked him; deceived him into bringing her here by pretending she wanted to accompany him to the market in Grahamstown. She had left Aurora with Hannah, her devious plans quite clear in her mind. As they drew near to the turn-off to Bathurst she had revealed her plan to Sam. She had asked him to make a detour to Buck's farm and explained her reason.

Sam had refused. He had stopped the wagon and argued with her, threatening to tell her father. Finally, she had resorted to blackmail, saying that if he did what she asked, and told no one, she would not tell her father about Sam's secret peach-brandy making which he sold to augment his income so that he could marry the late Gert Venter's beautiful, young, blonde widow, Helena. They both knew that her father drank very little, for an Irishman, and that he loathed the selling of the potent peach-brandy known as Cape Smoke. He himself had set up a brewery for porter, but he never would condone anything else.

Sam sullenly saw her point, surprised that she knew so much about his activities and his longtime, silent love for Helena Venter, which had endured through his feelings for Laree. He agreed, but refused to speak to her for the rest of the journey. All he was willing to say was that Buck Jones would refuse to help her because her kinsmen were so actively opposed to him.

Esther thought she could overcome that opposition if it arose, and was willing to cross that bridge when she came to it. She had retired into the wagon to change into more suitable visiting apparel, much to Sam's visible disapproval. Now she looked down at the apple green pelisse, buttoned down the front and cut short enough to reveal the pale green and white sprigged muslin underneath. A narrow-brimmed, green hat covered her red curls, surmounted with a spray of white ostrich feathers.

Nervously she opened her reticule and took out a timepiece. It was mid morning, and she wondered, for the first time, if he would be at home. She looked down at her hands, grateful for the gloves that hid their rough and chapped condition. Faint pink tinged her cheeks, for she knew it was more than his help she wanted. That was very important, and had been the first reason for her decision, but as time passed she wanted to see him again. She hoped that Sam, with his amazing astuteness, would not guess at the underlying reason for her visit.

She looked about her. The countryside was alive with spring, the wild, brilliant kaffir-booms showered with scarlet blooms. Ribboning the valley were the long, broad, swift reaches of the Kowie River alternating with narrow stretches, looping back and forth into the surrounding countryside, its banks richly draped with red, climbing-aloes. There was the drowsy, murmuring hum of bees among the great twisted trunks of boerbome and milkwoods whiskered with lichen and moss. She watched two sunbirds alight on a bush, their cries high and chattering, wings swirling sun-pierced colour. The rich perfume of African jasmine drifted on the air, rocks and gnarled trees pearled with white blossom. Tiny, long-tailed sugar-birds fluttered like insects among the first, faint lilac-misting of spekboom flowers. It was warm. Small clouds scudded overhead, flecking the sunlight falling on hill and valley.

Esther's thoughts returned to her father. She could no longer submit to his opinions as a matter of course. She was beginning to understand that men like Buck Jones had their own heritage of suffering in a world of class and privilege. She realized clearly now how he had been forced to claw his way to where he was by the strength, intelligence and unique determination that was his alone.

Physically, she had been a woman for a long time; mentally she was only just becoming an adult, with opinions of her own in a world where women listened to the views of their menfolk. She was learning to understand Buck Jones and his kind, but the fact that she did not always agree with her father did not mean that she did not love him. She would always love her father and nothing would ever change that.

Her heart began pounding as they drew towards a line of tall, bright, yellow-tufted mimosa trees on either side of a dusty track, planted years ago by the first owner of the farm. She wished Sam would speak to her as they proceeded in the direction of the farmhouse still hidden behind the trees. She wished he would say anything to take her mind off the matter now staring her starkly in the face, and from which she could not run away.

Quite suddenly, another cluster of mimosa trees came into view and the corner of a rough, white-plastered building. The cottage gradually became visible through the trees, a solid block of whitewashed stone set in a small clearing. Sam reined in the oxen and stopped.

'You're on your own from now, Miss Esther, my part of the bargain is done. I'll wait for you here — and don't dally. We should have been on the road to Grahamstown hours ago.'

He watched every line of her face, every fleeting expression, every uncontrolled muscle. Nothing escaped those bright, black eyes. Esther bit back a sharp retort, her heart jumping violently against her ribs. Suddenly she wished she had not come. She could not face Buck Jones alone. If only she could turn back and go on to

261

Grahamstown with Sam right now. But her old pride would not let her back down before Sam's merciless eyes, and she could just imagine how very angry he would be if he could read her thoughts.

She smiled as sweetly as she could while he helped her down from the wagon, a mask of bravado hiding her true feelings. Perhaps Buck was not there, then she could gracefully back out, with her pride intact. But she was here now, so she had better make the best of it. Lifting her head proudly, she began to walk towards the cottage without a backward glance.

The rough facade of the cottage fitted in well with the rugged landscape, its walls catching the warmth the sun offered. It had none of the attractive refinements of Dwyers' Cross, nor any of its mellowing softness. It looked what it was, a man's house, filled and lived in by men. A sprawl of low, labourers' buildings stood to one side, near a barn and several rough and practical outhouses. There was a wheelwright's shop and forge towards the back, and beyond them, green fields and hills. The garden was a weed-choked tangle of wild flowers and peach trees, a froth of pink blossom. The air was filled with the smell of fecund earth and the ripeness of the new season as she walked up towards the cottage. A line of oxen stood not far from the front door, coupled and inspanned to a load wagon, either ready for a journey, or just returned. A few sheep and goats cropped the grass growing in thick tufts among the blackened, mouldering ruins of an old Boer farmhouse further away. Apart from the wagon, everything looked deserted, the cottage unwelcoming with no curtains lacing the windows that stared out blankly across the land.

Esther felt alarmed that Buck might be away on one of his hunting trips when she heard a bellow of laughter from somewhere at the back of the cottage. Nervously shaking her skirts free of dust, she adjusted her bonnet and walked to the front door, her slippers sending little puffs of dust into the air.

The door opened before she knocked. Holding back her surprise, she stared at the short, wiry man standing in the doorway. He had bandy legs and a weathered face with an old sword scar running down the left side. He rubbed one gnarled hand down the side of rough skin breeches, his brown leather jerkin hanging open to reveal a soiled checked shirt and the ragged ends of a red neckcloth.

Esther lifted her chin the merest fraction, returning his stare with eyes as hard as dark blue stones. 'I wish to speak to Mr Jones on a matter of the gravest urgency, and at once,' she said, surprised at the tartness of her tone.

There was a pause as he weighed her up with shrewd eyes. 'And who may I say is calling, ma'am?' he spoke with a strong North Country accent, and she felt herself grow tense under his scrutiny.

'Are we going to stand here all day staring at each other, Mr . . .? I would like to see Mr Jones if he is here.'

He raised one untidy eyebrow. 'No need to get hoity-toity, ma'am. 'E's 'ere all right, but only just. Came in from a huntin' trip not more than half an hour ago. 'E's out in the back just about ready for a wash. The cleanest man I know is the Sergeant. I still call 'im the Sergeant, 'ave done for years. Can you tell me who is calling, ma'am?'

Esther looked at him thoughtfully. 'Mrs Esther Fitzwilliam.' He nodded unexpectedly. 'Mrs Fitzwilliam? Mrs Garnet Fitzwilliam by any chance, ma'am? I served under the late Captain all my years here on this frontier. One of the best men I ever served. Private Marsden Pike at your service, ma'am. Now if you will follow me inside, I will go and call the Sergeant before he has his wash.'

He motioned her inside respectfully, and Esther, feeling calmer now, looked around with interest. The sitting-room was long, and bright from the sunlight streaming sideways through the tall windows. At one end there was a large, open fireplace decorated above on either side with two magnificent ivory tusks. Under the windows was a rough yellowwood table and several riempie-backed chairs. Open rafters stretched across the room showing the triangle of roof above. The skins of several beautiful leopard, lion and antelope were scattered about the floor.

She walked over to the opposite wall and studied the powder horns nailed to the wall, a musket hanging by its sling against it. Alongside there was a set of surprisingly well-crafted firearms suspended in brackets: a few more muskets, a brace of small, bell-mouthed flintlock pistols with brass barrels and another small flintlock pistol. A bullet mould stood on a small chest near the kitchen door.

With strange satisfaction she noted that there was nothing here that was soft and feminine. There was no sign that any woman or women lived here. It had a certain rude, masculine comfort, sparse and spartan, and smelling strongly of leather and tobacco. As the sun

263

stole noiselessly across the floor of beaten earth, she walked through to the kitchen where thick tumblers and pewter plates cluttered a rough table, with the leftovers from the last meal. Her eyes travelled to dip-candles in their tin holders about the room, a piece of coarse soap cut from a bar, lying congealed on a tin plate beside a large washtub. There was a kettle filled with water singing over the fire, and a large pail standing waiting. It was hardly a woman's dream, she thought distastefully, but a woman could make it into a home.

She frowned as she turned the mourning ring on her finger, the gold burning bright in the light as the unsettling problem of what exactly to say to Buck Jones took shape in her mind. She had nothing to offer him in return, and she wondered if he would accept that.

She moved over to the window where she could see a strong stockade built some distance away, the muted tones of masculine voices reaching her from across the yard. Waiting in an agony of indecision, her eyes fell on the kegs of brandy stacked against an outside wall. A dog barked in the stables across the yard from where she could hear the whinney of horses. Voices sounded closer outside. She froze, the desire to flee overwhelmingly strong. Running back to the sitting-room she thought of Sam waiting restlessly for her. She had been wrong to come.

He entered so suddenly that she was left in a state of total bewilderment. He stood in the front doorway, the blue-bronze daylight behind him, his shadow stretching across the room. There was a brief silence, then he was striding forward, tousled, curly brown hair curling into his neck and outlining his tanned cheeks, the same magnetism in his blue eyes. The room jumped to life about him as his presence filled it, infusing it with his own energy and vigour.

He lifted one eyebrow. 'Well I'll be darned!' he exclaimed, the surprise unmistakable in his voice. 'I never did believe Pike when he told me you were gracing us with your presence, ma'am. Who brought you here? Did you come alone?'

'I came with Samuel Pettigrew.'

'Ah yes, Pettigrew — a good man.' He stood still across the room, his eyes running over her swiftly, and there was something in their depths she could not fathom. 'And what brings you into the house of the enemy with such urgency, Mrs Fitzwilliam?'

She stared at him, the rush of familiar excitement causing her to

264

become tongue-tied, affected strongly as she was by the force of his presence. Studying him, she was all too aware of the strong arms where the shirt had been rolled up to the elbows, of the small area of chest exposed by the open neck of the hastily-buttoned shirt. Emotions swept over her and two spots of high colour touched her cheeks as she remembered the intense passion they had once shared. Sometimes, at night, she imagined him in her bed, and would sweat, both to her disgust and rising passion. Her thoughts now were in disarray, desire and reason conflicting.

Then she shivered imperceptibly. It was as though the ghost of Lady Amanda Lightfoot stood between them. The picture of that witty, sophisticated woman in his arms continued to haunt her, those well-remembered, amber eyes daring her to fall into the same dangerous trap in which she had allowed herself to be ensnared, all those years ago — causing her to lose her self-respect and her sanity. Understanding how Amanda had been bewitched, she pitied the memory of her, as she feared for herself.

She chose directness, calming herself and saying, 'I have come here on a matter of greatest importance to Dwyers' Cross.' There was a small silence as she paused, then continued, 'You are the only person I can think of who can help us.'

'Us, ma'am?' She could sense he was wary, that his guard had not dropped. There was still a distance between her and this man which might never be closed. The startling blue eyes rested on her ironically. 'Of what help could I possibly be to Dwyers' Cross? Did your father send you here to use your pretty wiles, while he hides behind your skirts, with Pettigrew your partner-in-crime so to speak?' His husky voice was instantly terse.

She controlled a tremor of temper as his tall, powerful frame moved to the fireplace, where he turned and stood, arms akimbo, watching her. He had not invited her to a seat, and she knew he was deliberately keeping her on tenterhooks until he found out the full reason for her visit.

He was also treating her as if there had been nothing between them, as if they had never shared the intense passion between a man and a woman, as if she had never appeared in court to defend him, however slight it may have been, in a scandal that had not only rocked the colonial system but the House of Commons too. And that upset her the most. It was incredible to her that those firm lips had kissed her, that those hands had caressed and fondled her and given her such delight. It was this incredulity rather than resentment which held her silent for the moment.

Then, coldly, she said, 'My father knows nothing of this visit. It concerns only me. If he ever found out he would dearly like to draw and quarter me for sure.'

A muscle twitched in his cheek. Then his lashes flickered down, hiding his expression. He motioned her to a seat. 'What is it that only I can do to help you, ma'am? My curiosity is aroused as to why you have come all this way without your father's knowledge, to visit a man he hates.'

She drew a breath, steeling herself against his reaction. Trying to sort out her words, she remained silent. He leaned forward suddenly, his eyes still studying her. Then he smiled, his face lighting up with such radiance that her heart stopped for a second.

'I detect a certain recklessness in you, ma'am. If I know anything of feminine vanity it will be some rare ornament or trinket you fancy from the wilds that you think only I can bring you, that your father considers a senseless indulgence, a waste of time. Or perhaps it's ivory you're after — or a leopard skin for the ball to be held by Colonel Somerset to heal the breach between your kinsmen and Major Dundas — on account of a trifling commando mistake.' He chuckled. 'You would cause a sensation, ma'am, in a skin kaross amidst the finery of the ladies of Albany — start a new fashion, or a revolution.'

Her face was flushed as she realized she had never felt so unsure of herself. 'I have come to ask you to speak with Chief Mazwi — to explain to him that my kinsmen do not understand the customs of his tribesmen, to ask him to see that his warriors leave our land and our cattle alone. I have faced Lungelo once with no support other than a musket. He was coming to steal out cattle. Our barn has now been destroyed. He is bent on revenge for what my uncle's commando did to his people, of that I'm sure. The next time it will be far, far worse.'

His eyes flashed unexpectedly. 'I have heard of your misfortunes, ma'am — of how you faced the warriors, single-handed. A brave action it was, and to be commended. And I know about the barn. You ooom not to agree with the actions of your kinsmen?'

Hope sprang into her heart. He was looking at her strangely, and not unkindly. There was still a chance she would win him over, but

266

she had to be honest with him. He would see through any deception immediately.

'I do not know what I think — yet.'

He nodded, and after a pause he said, 'You want me to do the impossible, ma'am. You are asking to go behind the backs of your kinsmen to ask the Chief to stop his people from visiting the clay pits and venturing on to your lands. The Xhosas have always gone to the pits for ceremonial clay, you know that as well as I. They are entitled there. Even if I asked the Chief to stop his warriors from venturing on to your lands while collecting clay, your kinsmen will continue to chase them away and treat them with open hostility.'

Fire sprang into her eyes. She clenched her hands tightly in her lap. 'I am asking you to help keep the peace on the border near the farms, Mr Jones. The Mazwis do not understand the men of Dwyers' Cross any more than the men understand them. You are fortunate enough to understand both. I am asking you to mediate between the two.' Behind her words lay the shadow of a struggle. Her objective had one minute looked close within her reach and the next as remote as ever.

For a moment he looked at her in silence. His light-coloured shirt emphasised the breadth of his shoulders and the tan of his complexion. There was a glint in his eyes. 'Lud, I cannot believe you came all this way to ask this one mad, impossible thing. Your father opposes me with too bitter a force.'

Esther felt a wave of desperation as she strove for control and to calm her mounting fears. 'Yes, that is true, mad and impossible as it seems!' she exploded, eyes bright with anger. 'If you don't speak with the Chief we will all be murdered and lose our lands!'

With surprise she was conscious that he now was studying her with a different interest. She sat and returned his look. His expression did not alter, and yet she felt the air between them charged with emotion, as if he were reaching out to her, drawing her to him by some irresistible force, and she was longing for the empty past months to be filled. There was that indefinable quality about him that spoke to her for all her anger, and she knew, for the first time in her life, she was really in love.

At last, she forced herself to face him. 'You have to help us, Mr Jones — for without your help we are doomed.' Now she felt anguish. What was she to do if he refused?

He cocked an eye at her and for a moment it seemed as if he would agree, then he looked away and into the fireplace, staring into it almost moodily.

'I'm sorry, ma'am, I cannot help you. I cannot make rash promises to old Mazwi on behalf of people who will never keep them — for men who'll damn me for doing it. That would only cause more distrust and bitterness on both sides. Your father favours force — he will never agree to my ideas.' He watched her expressive face, then he shrugged, a note of exasperation in his voice. 'The sad thing about force is that in winning for a time, it also loses. I respect your kinsmen's courage — I could have liked them both — but I threaten their ways, their position, and so we oppose each other. That, ma'am, is the tragedy of the struggle for survival — it creates deep feelings and makes no friends.'

Confused, she stared at him. A great wave of disappointment filled her heart. The red blushes on her cheeks faded. He caught her eye and the silence between them was again charged with tension. Desire once more struck her like a knife. She remained transfixed by the subtle magic of his eyes. She had a lively conscience, but she had learnt, to her cost, that when a woman desires a man she has no conscience at all, only awareness of her appetites. She wanted him, simply and fiercely as she had ever wanted anything in her whole life.

She stiffened, trying to appear at ease as she thought she detected the faintest of smiles on his lips, but it was gone in an instant. She wondered how long she would be able to fight off the deep magnetic attraction between them that had always been there, and had spoilt other men for her.

This had been the real reason for her visit, she no longer denied it, and she wondered if he guessed. 'You refuse to help me,' she said, with a rush of emotion. 'You don't care a fig for anyone but yourself, Mr Jones.' She bent down and picked up her reticule lying on the chair. Her eyes once more shot to his face. 'We can all rot and be murdered for all you care and you won't even lift a finger — not one miserable finger — to help us!' Imperiously she stamped her foot, her eyes blazing though she realized she was being unfair to the man who had tried to stop her father before today.

'Spare me your temper, Mrs Fitzwilliam,' he said, his voice clipped, his anger matching hers. 'No one can help your kinsmen until they decide they want to be helped. It would be useless to try.

They are the most pig-headed Irishmen I have ever met — they will listen to no sense, and they are not the only ones.'

Esther stopped in her tracks, stung by his remark. She had overstepped the mark, she knew it. She opened her mouth to say something, then closed it again. 'I was a fool to come,' she said at last, her voice stiff and taut, but the expression in her eyes still not subdued.

He looked at her with that straight, disconcerting gaze of his. 'I cannot fight your father's battles for him.' The line of his lips was grim and hard. 'More's the pity that innocent women and children will have to suffer the consequences of their hot-headed menfolk — for suffer they will, in some way or other.'

His coolness made her rage vanish. 'I suppose there is nothing I can say that will change your mind?' she said in a colourless voice, flooded by renewed despair.

'There's nothing,' he said, 'But, ma'am, let's look on the more cheerful side — the Xhosas have a limited sense of warfare. They never attack women and children. The Zulus, on the other hand, have a different system. But you won't ever have to worry about 'em.' Strangely enough he was not smiling.

'That was unjustly cruel — to make fun of us being attacked by the Xhosas!' Her voice was vibrant, shaking with emotion as she writhed at his words and before the directness of his brilliant eyes. 'I do not know why I bothered to visit you.'

A dazzling smile creased his face. 'Perhaps because I am a puzzling and fascinating character, ma'am,' he said disarmingly, his eyes teasing. 'And because I seem to be the gift to the frontier to anything in trouble, with a rare understanding, as you so rightly said, of the human state both black and white.'

There was enough truth behind his words to cause a flush to creep up her neck and tinge her cheeks once more. 'I will not be troubling you again, Mr Jones,' she answered as coolly as she could manage.

Turning, she disappeared through the open doorway retracing her steps back to Sam. Before the trees hid the cottage from view she looked back for the last time. He was standing outside the door staring after her. She caught her breath, but he walked away and vanished from her sight behind the cottage.

Hopelessly, she hurried back to Sam. It had been such an unexpectedly deflating response that she arrived at the wagon in a fever of indignation and hurt pride. Sam was caught napping, stretched out full length, and snoring softly in the deep shade of a mimosa tree. Her impatient voice awakened him smartly. He jumped up startled and looked about with a rather blank stare, coming to his senses after a second, and brushed off his clothes. He looked at her, his head to one side and wagged a long, bony finger.

'Told you it would be no good, Miss Esther. I can see by your face that Mr Jones was unmoved by your charms.' He shook his head. 'That elephant hunter is nobody's fool.'

'Oh hush, Sam!' she snapped, throwing herself up on to the driver's seat. 'It's none of your business.'

'Well then, Miss Esther,' Sam sighed, shrugging nonchalantly, 'you'd better change again — it's mighty dusty on the way to Grahamstown, and we've a lot of time to make up.'

Oh damn you, Buck Jones, Esther thought in helpless rage. I never want to think of you again. But she knew that she would not be able to stop thinking of him all the way to Grahamstown. He would not help her. She had no power over him. Everything had all been so disastrously snatched away from her. She was trapped by her own nature, when all hope was gone, and her vitality ebbed away. Tears came to her eyes, beading on her thick lashes, and trembled without falling.

CHAPTER
Twenty Six

The spring of 1826 flowed into summer on clouds of bloom. The drifts of pink and white blossoms in the orchards at Dwyers' Cross were replaced by light greenery hiding the first crop of ripening fruit. Bouquets of right red geraniums blazed in the garden and the white candles of bushman's-pipe spilled over the wattle fences with green lattices of jasmine leaves.

The reconciliatory ball at Oatlands Park, arranged by the Somersets to bring Major Dundas and the Dwyers together again, had come and gone and it was early one night at the beginning of December. In the deep quiet of the country stillness, glowing fireflies lit up the darkness lying about the homestead at Dwyers' Cross.

Joshua, Cady and Sam stretched out in their chairs in the sitting-room, glasses of porter beside them. The light of two candles fluttered gently on the mantlepiece, throwing the figures into enormous weird shadows against the walls. A bundle of wheat bags lay in a discarded pile near the door, evidence of the harvest failure that had hit the whole colony.

In the kitchen Esther picked up a candlestick and slowly made her way to the stairs. As she passed the door of the sitting-room she stopped. Her Uncle Cady was talking, she could hear his words quite clearly.

'By Jove, Joshua, it is most heartening to observe that the Xhosas have kept away from our cattle these past two months. Perhaps they have learnt their lesson. Somerset seems to have been proved correct when he said, 'a watchful eye persistently kept and strong reaction is the key'. I can only hope that they are not planning some unpleasant surprise and seek to lull us into a false sense of security.'

Joshua chuckled. 'It has given us a breathing space, Cady, though why exactly they should leave us alone at this particular time escapes me, especially as that Lungelo fellow and his uncle, Mavile, now live under sufferance in the Ceded Territory. I cannot really understand it.'

Esther stiffened, all her feelings heightened. She remained quite still, fascinated as the talk flowed on in the same vein for some time, before turning to the restlessness of the men after the harvest failure. A faint hope began to rise. Buck Jones must have spoken with Chief Mazwi after all. It seemed too much of a coincidence that after two attacks on the farm the Xhosas had not come near their land except to fetch their clay.

The more she thought about it, the more it seemed the only plausible explanation. Perhaps it was a coincidence that Lungelo had not come back, but she did not believe it was when it concerned the people living with Mazwi. But why had Buck refused her so definitely? She could only think that he had thought about her plea and changed his mind. If he had gone to Mazwi, he had done it, not for her father and uncle, but for her. He would never admit it, she knew. But the fact remained that he had done it at her request.

It seemed to her then that Buck Jones had been a consistent thread in her life for six years, his presence flickering across its events. He seemed always to have been there. She now wanted him to be there always in the future, too. She only had to think a minute and she could see his whole farmstead laid out like a picture, and his presence there, strong and vital and real.

The mumble of voices dimmed as she tiptoed quietly up the stairs to the bedroom she shared with her small daughter who lay peacefully asleep, the sound of her even, gentle breathing soft in the stillness of the dark room.

Esther put down the candlestick beside her bed and stared at the window framing a sky full of stars. A nightjar shrieked, the harsh notes whickering and echoing across the valley and out into the remote silence beyond.

She looked around the room and at everything in it, suddenly feeling lost and lonely, for it represented a way of life that kept her from him. She wanted more from him than brief, haphazard moments, unexpected meetings here and there. She wanted more of his time, his life, himself.

Feeling more relaxed, her hands stopped their trembling. She had made her decision and would throw every caution to the wind, even if it meant a confrontation with her father. She had always wanted Buck, and now she not only needed him but she felt that finally she was ready for him. And the thought suddenly invigorated her beyond all reason.

Laree and Roydon had arrived with their children at Dwyers' Cross for Christmas, to be followed later by Arthur and Charity Wilson accompanied by Joshua on his return from Bathurst.

Even though the wheat harvest had failed, and the echoes of bankruptcy were again beginning to be felt throughout the colony, fortunately at the farm, the fruit and vegetables flourished, and everyone had worked together to make a celebration worth remembering.

In Josua's absence the kitchen was a hive of activity, redolent with the smells of plum pudding, mince pies, spiced beef and pork, for the following day. Esther had spent the entire past week cutting up a pig for the great occasion. Apart from this one centre in the house, all other work seemed to have stopped, and lively, confused excitement reigned everywhere else.

Across the yard, near the forge, the Wilson children and small, slow and clumsy Aurora watched the group of Hottentots playing knucklebones in the dust with raucous laughter. From the men's huts came the rumble of voices broken by gusts of mirth, and now and then a lusty oath.

Back in the kitchen Laree was goffering a frill with a heated iron, trying to ignore the sounds of merriment from across the yard, while Esther stirred the large plum pudding over the fire. Rich, delicious flavours filled the room, floating under the door and through the window to where Sam sat outside, close to the wall, as he busily carved a fiddle of wood-green collected from the thickets.

Laree raised her pretty, gentle face, startled, as if she had seen a disturbing vision. Cady came into the room, bleary-eyed and unshaven, his neckcloth askew. Abstemious enough for the standard of the day and for his own race, he had made up for his abstinence throughout the year by drinking himself into a state of absurdity from early morning.

Now Esther turned from the fire, a baleful expression on her face, as he pouted and weaved his way towards the door. He glanced at her warily, to see her reaction, as he pulled it open, letting in vicious little gusts of wind. She wiped her hands and looked up in exasperation.

'In your condition you will be knocked down by the first gust of wind,' she said.

Pettishly Cady ignored her, and after a fight with the door, he stumped out, as Esther clattered mince pies behind him. The door slammed shut. He was caught by a fierce sweep of air and lost his balance, nearly upsetting Sam, and stepped into the tub for washing dishes outside the door, waiting to the emptied.

For a moment he lost his bearings and sat there half-submerged. Then he turned on the gaping Sam. 'Get this thing removed at once — should 'ave been done hours ago — damned slackness on this farm, disorder everywhere, that's the trouble.'

Sam took one look at Cady's face as he was climbing out of the tub, and agreed at once. He rose, striding with great purpose to give the order. Cady tried to steady himself, all his movements clumsy and making an enormous amount of noise, before he fell to lie beside his dog. By this time everyone in the yard had been drawn towards the noisy focal point, including Esther and Laree. They stood in the doorway, their mouths twitching with mirth as the Hottentots and the children guffawed at Cady's antics. The sound of merriment reached a crescendo until Sam, straightening his face severely, strode up and robustly ordered the wash-tub's removal.

Cady stood up in a flood of brandy and self-pity and made his way back to the kitchen with much difficulty in the strong wind. Having successfully negotiated the door before it banged shut once more, he proceeded into the room. Esther looked up and saw a dripping figure advancing in front of the table, water following him in a trail across the floor. She fell silent at the glare on his face and bit her lip, trying not to laugh, as he disappeared into the merciful silence of the sitting-room beyond.

The sound of horse's hooves beat through the wind as a lone horseman galloped out of the milkwoods and across the clearing. Cady's dog barked and all eyes in the yard turned in the direction of the approaching horse. There was a sudden silence, then a heated jabbering broke out. Esther lifted her head and threw open the top half of the stable-door, holding it back with one hand. She looked towards the clearing and saw the rider reining in his horse, and

274

reining it in strongly. She knew then that something was wrong, terribly wrong.

It was Buck Jones. He walked his horse forward, stopped, leaned on his pommel and gazed harshly at the knot of men advancing on him. Laree called to Cady as Esther pulled open the bottom half of the door. The door opened and banged closed as she and her uncle ran out and pushed their way through the small group of wary, guarded men.

Still wet, Cady thrust his face upward, his unshaven chin stubbled and coarse. 'And what in devil's name brings you to spoil our Christmas, Jones?' he roared, his words slurred but angry. 'You always are the harbinger of black news and never have I known it different.'

Buck's eyes were hard and Esther saw the disgust in his face, the instinctive recoil. She wanted to die of shame.

'I bring you a Christmas gift, Mr Dwyer — the body of one of your men, Seamus O'Connor. He was murdered at Kaffir Drift by coloured bandits — the Bergenaars.'

Esther caught her breath, an eerie shiver slithering down her spine. There seemed to be no solace, no peace anywhere for them.

'Will your people never learn?' Buck's voice was terse, angry. 'O'Connor was supplying those desperadoes with guns and ammunitions in return for their cattle or perhaps a comely black wench from one of the slaughtered tribes in those parts.'

He dismounted, his clothes caked with dust. 'After one stint in gaol, I would have thought he had learnt his lesson. He would be alive today if he hadn't got mixed up with that tribe of half-breeds living in the mountains of the Ceded Territory.'

He stood back, parting the group to reveal the mutilated, blood-caked body of O'Connor slung over the back of his horse, the arms and legs dangling lifelessly over the side. There was a moment's stunned silence as if, although the men knew the truth, the mere statement had shocked and quietened them all.

Cady stepped forward, instantly blackly sober. 'I cannot believe such a thing of O'Connor, for all his past smuggling with the Xhosas. Where's your evidence, Jones — the guns, ammunition — for without them there is no proof that he was involved in the crime you have convicted him of. Well? Show me one piece of concrete evidence as to what he was doing or else I will strengthen my own belief that you are hell-bent on causing trouble at Dwyers' Cross to prove your case against us.'

Buck's cold gaze fell on him. 'Most of the guns and ammunition were stolen along with any valuables on him. There is only one small cache left behind in the wagon he used — I hid it in the bushes near the Drift. If you doubt my word, I have a Xhosa tracker who saw it all. Even though he cannot speak our language he can witness for me.'

Esther felt numb, utterly shattered. She could only guess at the intensity of his feelings from the way his strong fists bunched and unbunched at his sides.

'Lord alone knows how much cattle they got from that band of renegades, to be traded elsewhere for rixdollars,' Buck continued, his voice chill and deliberate. 'That tribe is the most dangerous of cut-throats to ride the African plains. O'Connor must have been mad to get mixed up with 'em.' His lips curling angrily, he strode over to the body, untied the thongs tying it to the horse, and lowered it to the ground. 'This is the last body I bring back to Dwyers' Cross. The cache is your problem. You can fetch it when and as you will. For your information, it was these same renegades who forced the Bechuana tribes to run starving into the colony only weeks past — and it was your man and his accomplices who encouraged 'em. Do you realize that these undercover activities of the black market traders weaken the usefulness of the weekly legitimate fairs with the Xhosa that are controlled by the military?'

Cady's face quivered with rage. 'And do you realize that if there were free trade in cattle between the races this would not happen?' There was a pause as he shook his angry fist in the air. 'There are too many restrictions on our trade, and until they are removed this state of affairs will continue.'

'True enough — but smuggling is not the solution to a tricky and inadequate system. In fact, traders harm the relations between black and white by using unscrupulous methods, Mr Dwyer, in their dealings with the Xhosa. And this is apart from smuggling of guns and shot into Xhosaland. They give the Xhosa and the renegades a very low opinion of the white man and prepare the way for future wars. It is your men and others like 'em that are to blame.'

'Just you get off this land!' Cady shouted furiously. 'Get off and don't ever come back.'

Buck wheeled and turned his horse about. He led him from the yard, leaving an excited outbreak of noise behind him. Esther stared at the men around the body, that agonisingly sick feeling in her stomach. Then her eyes lifted and gazed after Buck's retreating figure as it disappeared out of the yard, a string of Irish curses floating in the wind after him.

He had not looked at her once during the entire argument, not once acknowledged her presence in any way.

The agitated crowd began to break up. After a moment's hesitation she picked up the skirts of her faded blue cotton dress and, clapping a quick hand to her housecap as the wind blew, she ran across the yard after him.

Once out of sight of the yard, Esther pulled off the cap and raced as fast as her legs could carry her, her heart beating wildly with the fear that she may have already missed him. With a great surge of relief she saw that he had stopped to give his horse a drink at a weir where a water trench had been dug deeply into the earth, leading into the fields.

The horse was knee-haltered, and having a good roll in the sand to cool itself, and Buck was kneeling at the water's edge, his gun lying on the ground beside him. He cupped his hands and swept up the diamond drops as she came forward, gasping for breath.

Behind him the low hills arched their backs against the sky, blue-green mottled sweeps of rock. He rose at the sound of her footsteps, his gaze immediately falling on her flushed cheeks and dishevelled appearance. He watched her in silence until she reached him. As the wind brushed her face and caught her hair, she could hear the high-pitched whistles of Cape teals reverberating across the fields as a small flock flew from a thicket, dived and settled at a safe distance a little way off.

'You can't go like this, Buck Jones,' she burst out breathlessly, standing tall and strong beside him.

He raised a brown eyebrow. 'And what exactly do you mean by that, ma'am?' Arms folded across his broad chest, he eyed her blandly. There were lines at the corners of his mouth, but his gaze was steady. Behind him she saw the tall milkwoods running up to the sky as blue as his eyes.

She looked at him, conscious, as always, of an unwitting excitement. Flushing hotly, she bent her head abruptly, the movement sending a shiver of sunlight over her bright red head.

277

Then raising her head, she met his look with a little frown, her body taut, every muscle stretched against the invisible pull between them.

'I mean — it seems so impolite for you to go off like this without one word of thanks for bringing back O'Connor's body. And there is something else — I know what you did for us by speaking with Chief Mazwi — I know it was you, and I want to thank you myself.'

He uncrossed his arms and stared down at the riding crop he had pulled from his boot, then he nodded. 'I see,' he said, his husky voice soft, 'that it takes a lot to deceive you. What is it you want from me this time?'

The atmosphere had grown more tense. Esther tightly controlled a small shiver of irritation and hurt pride. She managed a faint smile. Fleetingly there was in her face all the uncertainty and forlorn beauty he had seen that day long ago when she had tried to defend him in the courthouse in Cape Town.

'I want nothing from you, Buck — I only wanted to thank you. I appreciate what you did if no one else does. They don't know about it, but I also want to apologize for my uncle's behaviour.'

She pushed away a strand of her hair as she watched the throbbing of his tanned throat, trying to hide the pain in her heart, to forget what lay between them.

He turned his whip over in his strong, broad hands and glanced at her, a glint of approval kindling his eyes, then it was gone.

'Your apology is accepted, ma'am. Now if you will excuse me, I still have a long way to go.'

She stood there, lost, the wind billowing the skirts of her pinafore and the blue dress beneath. Alarm rose in her again, as if something infinitely special, something elusive, was escaping her. If I lose him, now, I will wither and die, she thought wildly. She felt the scalding tears spring under her eyelids so that he and everything around him grew indistinct. Resolutely she fought them back. In a terrible stabbing moment of perception, she knew a sense of loss so strong it seemed to squeeze the breath from her body. Panic seized her. She felt she was going mad, that she wanted to hold him back from passing down the track. That somehow, in passing down she would lose him forever.

He was about to call his horse when he turned and eyed her keenly, his brow slightly puckered. 'Is something ailing you, ma'am?'

The vivacity had gone from her face, and some of the colour. She saw his eyes brighten as if his thoughts were lifted in some eager anticipation. The steady eyes, the resolute, beautiful mouth had not for a long time been so close. She remained still, drawn into those eyes.

I must have him, this adventurer and bastard. She took a step forward — across the chasm of birth and station. 'Help me,' she whispered fiercely. 'Help me against all this violence and uncertainty at Dwyers' Cross.' She laid a restraining hand on his arm, the thick skin of his jacket sleeve rough under her fingers.

His wariness, his distant, cool manner was now ripped away. His eyes held her in one long, compelling look, holding all her frustrated longings, her unfulfilled desires, everything that was between them. 'Shameless little fool!' he murmured, putting his riding crop into his boot and suddenly closing his arms about her.

The restraints she had forced on her nature for so long broke, as she felt again the fierce thrill of being in his arms, overcome by her passionate desire to surrender herself to him once more. As his lips touched hers, a sharp intake of breath betrayed her longing for him. The force between them had grown powerful and impatient in its long captivity, and the awful longing could no longer be denied. He kissed her with ardour and passion and she could think of nothing but the exciting urgency of his mouth and the warmth of his breath, the feel of the strong muscled legs against her own. She quickened with the sweetness of overpowering surrender, that immense and incredible remembered joy. The blood beating in her throat and temples obliterated all will and reason as her whole being burst into one glorious flame threatening to submerge her.

Lost in that wild and beautiful madness she undid the buttons of his shirt and put her hands underneath, touching the hard, muscular chest. 'I don't know why,' she whispered against his mouth, 'but I love you as I have never loved any man before.'

With iron control, Buck straightened his body, and through the haze of heated passion she was aware of his strong and surprisingly gentle hands taking hers and drawing them away. That one kiss had been too much and too little, leaving both souls hungering and aching.

'Easy, easy,' he urged softly, 'I have wanted to do that again for a very long time, ever since that first time at Port Frances — and you do not know how hard you make it for me to resist you.'

'You do not have to resist me, Buck — take me with you,' she breathed urgently. 'I want you to take me with you.'

He smiled, looking directly into her eyes, and tipped her face. He drew his fingers over the nape of her neck under the windblown, tousled red curls and said, 'I do believe this to be some outrageous proposal of marriage, or worse. You really are the most unprincipled young woman, Esther Fitzwilliam.'

'Yes, as far as you are concerned, I am. You made me like that long ago. I want to be with you always — even against my father's wishes.' Her voice was desperate, pleading, urgent.

He was watching her intently. Then he released her with a troubled face, and let her go. 'That cannot be, Esther,' he said, 'I only wish to heaven it could. There are too many differences between us.'

'I don't care about differences between us — they don't matter anymore. Circumstances have changed all that, can't you see?'

He was silent, a deep crease between his brows. When he spoke, it was with a little difficulty. 'They do matter, sweetheart — to your kinsmen and the people of your special world. Dwyers' Cross is your home, its people are yours — your life is here with them, not with me.'

He picked up the reins of his horse. She wanted to dash herself against him and scream. She thought of him married to another, of the bonds and vows binding them tightly together for years, of another woman bearing his children, for she could not see him unmarried for much longer. Her eyes darkened with pain, the tears held back for so long spilled freely as jealousy tore at her. She would rather have that much of him without background and privilege than what she had now.

'I want you. Will you never understand that? Nothing else matters beside that. I would gladly give it all up to be with you.'

He sighed. 'Sweetheart,' he said, with unexpected gentleness, 'we live in different worlds, you and I — as apart as if we lived on two different continents. It could never work out.'

She felt the rage from weeks, months unleashed as she bunched her hands into fists and beat them against his chest. 'How I hate you, Buck Jones! You play with women, make them fall in love with you, then you tell them you have no need for them — for that is what you are telling me now. You play with feelings, like those of Amanda Lightfoot who loved you so desperately. You did it to me that first time, and now you are doing it to me again.'

He succeeded in overpowering her, clamping both her hands fast behind her back. His face darkened for an instant as he strove for control. Then in sober silence he let go her hands and lifted her face, soaked with tears, cradling it between his fingers, his eyes holding hers.

'Listen to me, Esther, believe me when I say that if I thought we had a chance of happiness together, I'd take it. I've lived all my life taking chances, but not this one.'

Her face crumpled as she looked up at him for one dizzy moment. 'You are really saying that you don't love me — that I mean absolutely nothing to you — just as you didn't love Amanda.'

He stiffened, then relaxed. 'There you are wrong — I do love you, and have done for a very long time, that is my misfortune. I have had to live with that knowledge — to see you as unattainable as ever, married to someone else, sharing his life. That is why I don't want to hurt you. Yes, I went to old Mazwi for you, and I hate seeing you mixed up in all this violence and hatred at the pits, but I am a rough fellow, sweetheart, a self-made man.' His eyes were almost playful, almost teasing. 'Your background shelters you from many harsh realities — I have no such shield for you. It has taken me the best part of my life to build my own — and I cannot ask you to share that kind of life, even though it tears me apart to let you go.' He sighed, stroking her hair. 'Besides, by making that choice, you would cut yourself off from your kinsmen, from everything you've known all your life. I cannot ask that of you, and I never would.'

She was about to flare up in a temper of despair when she saw the expression on his face was unusually compassionate.

'Of all the women I have known, Esther, none has possessed the fire of heart and mind of you. You are a beautiful witch, a temptress, not fully awakened to your powers as yet. You could kill the man who loves you — drive a knife right through his heart and never know it. Be sensible, wench — find yourself another prince like Major Fitzwilliam and make a respectable life for yourself and his daughter. You owe her that one thing, for life can be punishing hard without it.'

He bent down and swung his gun easily on to his shoulders, then he started to move away and she choked back a cry of a wild anguish so terrible it shook her. She wanted then so desperately to tell him that Aurora was not Garnet's daughter, but his, that her marriage to Garnet had been respectable and nothing else, that Garnet had tried

281

to kill him, but lost his own life instead.

The sound of a galloping horse from the direction of the homestead beat on the air. They both looked up to see Cady charge towards them, clouds of billowing dust behind him.

'Here come trouble on hot wings, sweetheart. You'd best return to the house and forget that I ever existed,' Buck said, crinkling up his eyes against the sun.

Cady drew up sharply in a shower of stones, rage and fury on his face. 'Return to the house this instant, Esther Mary! You have no right to be out here with this man unattended. Your father will be furious when he returns and finds out about your scandalous behaviour.' He turned to Buck. 'And if you ever set foot on this land again, Jones, I will not be responsible for my actions, so help me. And I bandy no idle threats.'

'You have no need to fear me any longer, Mr Dwyer,' Buck said, his eyes hard as stones. 'I will not come back. Your niece is in no danger.' He regarded Cady with a cold, enigmatic expression. 'But do not threaten me — it may go ill with you if you were ever forced to carry out your threats.'

Cady angrily intercepted a look between him and Esther, and as their look held for the briefest of seconds, Esther felt her spirit soar and burst free, rising for a precious, transient moment like some exalted bird into the skies, then it vanished.

Tossing her head, she turned away and marched back to the house, straight-backed and rigid. She never once looked back. She ached for the warmth and strength of him, but instead she heard the pound of his horses' hooves, and continued to hear their echo long after he had gone. All she knew was that her world was collapsing about her in some horrible, inexplicable way. Buck had taken with him all the vitality, all the colour from her life, and there was nothing but emptiness everywhere, on the land, in her heart.

CHAPTER
Twenty Seven

Joshua leaned forward in his chair before the empty sitting-room fireplace, puffing the bowl of his pipe into life, a mug of porter on the small table beside him. The light of the candles cast a soft glow about the room, an oasis of warmth and comfort.

It was mid-January, a month after Buck had brought back O'Connor's body. 1827 had dawned on depressed circumstances once more. The whole colony was feeling at last the effects of bankruptcy and the unsettled state of government. The currency had been converted to English coinage with great loss to all, and only English was used in the law courts. The harvests had failed and all classes of the population were again poverty-stricken.

Esther had carried Aurora to bed after the small girl had fallen asleep on the skin rug, and now she eyed her father thoughtfully. Staring at his face, she wondered if she still possessed the power to cajole him as she had done so successfully in the past. She had cooked him a good meal and hoped that he was feeling more mellow.

He had changed so much in the last few years, twisted by griefs and bitterness which he bore alone, allowing no one to come too close to him. It was as though in trying to fill the void of her mother's death, he had tried to replace her by building this house, cultivating the land — something he could call his own once more, and work for, something larger than himself.

He smiled up at her, puffing at his pipe, content to let the minutes pass in the quiet, homely room. As if echoing her thoughts, he said, 'I have grown fond of this house, Esther Mary, every stone, every post has been built by us. It is ours. I do not think I will ever want to change it, I'm too old. And even though we have recently lost most of our men because of the sorry state of the colony, I will stay here.'

She looked at his face, a little drawn, with the hint of tiredness, the signs of a fleshiness beginning to fight against the weathered hardness of it, showing his advancing age. He still looked well for his years though and it was she, at twenty-four, who felt the weight of age just then.

Oh Papa, why do you make it all so difficult, her mind screamed. Why must you be so beloved to me? And I am about to hurt you so very deeply. I cannot bear to think about the pain I am about to cause you, and especially in these bad times. She twisted her hands tightly behind her back, looking down at her slippers. Why was there never anyone older and wiser to help her, to shield her? She had helped so many in times of crisis — her sister Laree, Hannah, others. But there was never anyone to help her. All she had was her own fallible strength.

She cleared her throat, a cold sweat breaking out on her brow. This was the hardest thing she had ever done, but it was now or never.

'I have something to tell you, Papa,' she said finally, blurting it out.

Her eyes met his, suddenly sharp, questioning regard and she quailed inside. She wondered what she should say, then decided to say it straight out.

'Papa — I want to marry Buck Jones.'

It was done and nothing in the world could now undo her words. An uncomfortable silence fell, and she wished she had not spoken. She bent her head, the rich braids of her hair sparking in the candlelight.

His face was shadowed as he looked at her incredulously. 'You want to — what?' he exclaimed, finding his tongue. 'Have you lost your senses, Esther? Do you know the full import of what you have said?' His mouth twisted into a grim line. 'Whatever possessed you to say such an outrageous thing? If it was not so serious, it would be laughable. Explain yourself, child.'

Esther raised her head and looked directly at him. 'I am in love with Buck Jones, Papa — and he is in love with me. I want to marry him with your blessing.'

'You'll get no blessing from me for anything as-as-as-that. You cannot be serious,' he said, his face tight with bitterness. 'That man has got round you in some unscrupulous way. He has not seduced you, has he? Got you in the family way? God forbid!'

Esther was forced to smile mirthlessly. 'No, Papa, nothing like that. And Mr Jones has not got round me as you put it. It is entirely my idea. It is what I want with all my heart.'

'What you say does not make sense, Esther, you come from a proud old Irish family with background and tradition, and respectability. You cannot harbour thoughts of throwing yourself away on a baseborn man who does not know who fathered him! You have your choice from a string of suitors in Albany — even Cape Town, if you so wish. When we are on our feet again I will get Charity Wilson to help arrange dinners, dances, here — and you will choose someone of your own station. I will not have you degrading yourself with a man like Jones, and that's that — not now, not ever!' He thumped a fist fiercely on the arm of the chair, spilling the mug of porter.

'Papa, I have as much right to happiness in this wild place as anyone else. Everything in our lives has changed — this place has done it. The class system is falling away — and if you don't believe me, look around you — men who had nothing, who were nobodies, are making money even now in these bad times, and living in good style, better by far than we are, men you would hardly have passed the time of day with, back in Ireland. Those days are over, Papa.'

'Not for me they aren't,' her father thundered, his face purple with rage. 'Once the class system goes, everything of value goes. Why do you think there is such a thing?'

'I truly love this man, Papa. I have grown to know what he is — a real man, one of nature's gentlemen. Never has he been rough or rude to me and that is more than I can say for some of the quality folk in this settlement.' She lifted her chin stubbornly, her voice rising with heightened emotion as she strove to keep her temper in check. His reaction only made her more determined to have her way.

'How can you stand there and say those things to me!' Joshua's voice was sharp as a dagger, his eyes the colour of grey smoke, flecked with green fire. 'That devil has got to you — he will pull you down to his own miserable level, and my granddaughter, the daughter of noble blood, with you! You will throw your heritage into the dust. He only wants you so that he can live on the respectability of your background. Esther, do not do this thing — it will be your greatest humiliation, and ours too.'

285

That beloved grandchild has his blood in her veins, she silently screamed at him.

She stared at him, her eyes burning in her head, blazing with sudden, deep rage. 'Buck Jones has not asked me to marry him — he won't allow himself to put me in the position you describe. But I know it won't do that to me; he is a finer man than most I know. He'll pull me up instead with his own generosity and greatness of mind and heart.'

'You are of age and a widow — I can't stop you doing this foolish thing. But if you do, you will not get my acceptance or your uncle Cady's. I will be forced to cut you off from your family and our connections. When the financial situation changes I will pay you back every penny of the loan you gave me — but not a thing more, is that quite clear? You will be cut off from everything.'

She tossed back her head. 'I have a right to choose my own life, Papa.'

'Choice you have, girl,' he hissed venomously at her, 'you have always had it, but the choice to do the right thing.'

His fingers wound themselves tightly around the stem of his pipe. His expression darkened as he regarded her, facing him mutinously. He had made his decision in his habitual, swift way and she knew there was no way in which he would ever change it.

'You leave this property to marry that man, Esther, and you will never return here. We will have nothing to do with you.'

She spread her hands, her face strained, the light gone from her eyes. Something burst in her. 'I don't want to hear what you are saying! Don't dare tell me that! You throw me out because we measure everyone by the clothes they wear, who their parents are, their wealth, and because I have discarded those measures and have dared to measure a man by his individual dignity and worth as a human being! I am sick to death of the stifling rules of etiquette, the endless bargaining about things that concern two human beings, as if love can be bought and sold!' Her voice was high, taut, strangled. She ran from the room and up the stairs to her bedroom, the homely quiet of only moments before shattered.

'You go to that worthless elephant hunter, Esther, and you will never set foot in this house or on these lands again,' she heard her father roar after her.

She slammed the door and threw herself on the bed, but there was no relief against the stifling fury in her. The pain was alive, a white-hot blade of anguish, probing, screaming through her veins and she could not break it. She remained there for some minutes, her tortured mind trying to find some way out of the terrible darkness assailing her.

The distant barking of a pack of wild dogs sounded in the kloofs somewhere. Africa was about its business of life and death. In a fit of temper Esther rose and hurled her silver-handled hair-brush at the door of the darkened room, relieved that it did not awaken Aurora. Fists clenched, she walked to the window, tears of frustration stinging her eyes. Then she turned in the darkness and sat down again on the bed, her throat aching from holding back the tears.

Finally, long before dawn, she made her decision, knowing she could never go back on it once she had made it. She would have to live it through for the rest of her life. If Buck could not come to her, if he was forbidden to enter the lands of Dwyers' Cross, and she did not want to live unmarried or married to someone else, then she would go to him and beg him to take her in with Aurora. She would throw herself on his mercy. She felt a rush of fear and relief at once. The full-blooded passion inside her had won, and changed her whole future.

There was no sound from the kitchen as the house roused itself from its slumbers at dawn. No busy clattering of pots and pans, no delicious cooking smells greeted its occupants. There was only a deep, puzzling silence.

Esther's bedroom was empty. Most of her belongings had vanished and so had little Aurora. In the yard there was no sign of her Cape cart and her mare was missing. The cooing of the turtledoves and the shriek of hadedas filled the wooded copses. The rooster crowed loudly from his perch under the trees in the yard. Above was the limitless sky, the folds of the hills rolling away. Only Joshua knew where she had gone, and his strong, terrible pride, as strong and terrible as hers, would never allow him to send anyone to fetch her back.

Esther would have to pay — and pay dearly for what she had done to herself and to the family. She would be cut off from all communication and security of her family. The money she had lent would in time be paid back, penny for penny, but nothing more. There would be nothing for Buck Jones to lay his hands on. Joshua would salvage as much self-respect as he could from the wreckage she had caused, he would make very sure of that.

Twenty Eight

There was a tightness around Esther's throat, a hollow in the pit of her stomach, as she whipped the reins over the flank of the mare pulling the Cape cart. She sat on the shallow driver's box, a musket edged in beside her, ready for use. Behind her in the cart sat two-and-a-half-year-old Aurora, content against the soft cushion of piled-up blankets. The brass-studded, wooden chest containing their worldly belongings, was up on its stern at the back of the cart. Expediency had lent unexpected strength to help Esther drag it up there, and she still wondered at her success.

She was unsure that everything would go as she had planned, but she could not turn back. The cart wound its way through the tangled greenery, past enormous euphorbias lifting their candelabra-heads far above the other shrubs. The hills of the west were still purple with night, but the sun made little ponds of light on the flanks of the hills to the east. The trail carried them round a hillside with rising ground on either side. The cart moved in a cloud of dust into the deep quiet among the hills festooned with bright aloes, thorny acacia and euphorbia.

Slowly the steamy mist was sucked upwards in patches from the Kowie River, thinning and disappearing fast in the growing warmth of the sun. A small breeze had lifted it very slightly above the water like a canopy, impregnating the air with the damp smell of the sea.

Now grey, twisted barks of trees flashed silver in the light, monkey ropes like grey cobwebs clustering about the branches. Flocks of brown sparrows took off some way beyond the trees. A covey of startled, slate-coloured guinea-fowl flew out from the grass, squawking as the cart approached. The trees thinned out on either side, like a forest of wraiths, the cartwheels brushing huge spiders' webs glistening with dew.

A sudden shot rang out from a nearby clearing. Aurora cried out as Esther spun round with instant alarm and grabbed her gun. She stopped the cart and waited as she heard another shot hit the air, the echoes reverberating about the surrounding hills. Then there was a silence, followed by the roar of an enraged lion. Esther was startled. As most of the large game had left the colony for Xhosaland after the arrival of the settlers, she had not expected to hear the roar of a lion, especially in this area, so far from its usual hunting grounds. A spotted hyena that she had noticed before, darted through the grass in the direction of a third shot, and a group of vultures flew down one by one and settled on trees nearer by. The silence became frightening. Esther shivered, turning her head towards the bushes, her eyes fastening on the deep green drifts of shining leaves.

A dreadful roar rent the air. The mare shied, whinnying nervously and she had difficulty calming her. Gripping the reins until her knuckles were white, she glanced apprehensively about her, but nothing moved. A coldness spread throughout her body as she forced the mare slowly on. She knew that someone, or some animal was out there in the bush. She was about to speak to Aurora when a shape detached itself from the trees, and a man dressed in skin trousers and jacket appeared before the cart and stopped dead in his tracks, a heavy-barrelled gun in his hands.

Esther picked up her own gun and pointed it at his heart, her eyes steady, her aim accurate. He held up a hand, the muzzle of his own firearm flashing in the great bands of light striking through the trees.

'Well, ma'am — and what would you be doing in these lonely parts, alone and unattended?' His voice was rich with a north-country accent.

She waved her gun at him, her voice sharp. 'Don't you come any closer or I'll shoot to maim. I am on my way to Eden, the farm of Mr Buck Jones, but I seem to have lost my way.' She felt a feeling of desolation and loneliness as Aurora started to cry again.

The man studied her, then nodded, staying where he was. He was lean, wiry and tough. 'You look after your child, ma'am. I mean you no harm. Eden is where I'm headin' — seeing as I live there with the

Sergeant. Me and my mate, Egmont Moss, just killed a black-maned lion back there. That beast did eat my horse last night while we slept in the bushes. Old Egmont, he's bringing back the carcass on his horse to the farm. If you trust me enough, and give me a lift, I can direct you the rest of the way.'

Esther hesitated. She was tired, having travelled a day and a night and been forced once or twice to ask her way at lonely farmhouses.

'My name's Moses Higgins, ma'am — formerly from the Midlands. I served in the army with Sergeant Jones as a private until the Cape Corps was reduced drastic-like, and now I be a carpenter and farmer by trade and inclinations.'

Esther decided she could trust him and agreed to give him a lift. He jumped up beside her. There was no way out of the course of action she had begun, so she let him direct her, setting her mind against the terrible sense of panic starting inside her at what she had done. There was a hollow in the pit of her stomach as she picked up the reins. Higgins was affable and shrewd, and he had a puckish sense of humour which did much to relieve the tension mounting in her as they approached the farm. If he was curious as to her reason for visiting the farm alone and unattended, he kept it to himself.

She knew with rising dread that no one could push Buck into any decision not of his own making, and for the first time in her life Esther knew the real meaning of isolation and the icy coldness of its grip. It was as if, without warning, she had been swept off her feet by a strong current, borne along by a great, silent force over which she had no control. As they travelled on she caught glimpses of the rough, winding tracks leading to a farm here and there. On the skyline she could see a man and a boy with a team of oxen and a home-made plough. Clouds scudded above, their great, grey underbellies holding the promise of rain.

Her throat was dry as the long avenue of mimosa trees swung into view. She had burnt all her bridges behind her and she was forced now to build new ones or drown. She knew that by now she would be regarded as a fallen woman in the eyes of the community and that if Buck refused to have her and her child, there was nowhere else to go. She had gambled everything on persuading him to take her and Aurora into the shelter of his home. Quite suddenly and painfully, she was learning that once one broke with convention, one could never crawl back to its comforting shell again. She understood now what Buck had meant when he had talked of the protective shield of her family background. She and Aurora were alone — cut off from the past and all its connections. The realization was both chilling and daunting but she would not, could not, turn back.

Trundling over the ruts, and dipping up and down on the dusty track, they made their way towards the homestead. With fierce determination Esther threw out her disturbing thoughts as the corner of the rough, whitewashed cottage came slowly into view through its screen of mimosa trees. A dog crouched in the ruins of the old Boer farmhouse, his eyes fixed on the cart, following its every move. The next second, at the sound of Higgins' voice, it bounded towards them. Smoke curled from the chimney, and in the still air she could hear rough, male voices and the muted clatter of some activity from the yard at the back.

She risked a quick glance at Higgins and wished she had not done so. The sombre expression on his face was too unsettling, almost as if her presence was about to cause some kind of complication.

'I see that old worm-eaten Pike has got the fire going, ma'am — and it sounds like the men are in the stockade. We been trying to break a wild mare, a beauty of a beast, but vicious as they come, for a week. It'll be for the Sergeant to have a go — he broke in army horses, y'know. Goddamned good too. I need a horse to replace the one lost to that grizzly, stinkin' lion back there. But I don't want no wild unpredictable mare.'

He braced himself and jumped down from the cart, then he turned and faced Esther. 'I'll give you a hand, ma'am, when you get to the cottage. We'll have to go round the back — that'll be where the Sergeant is of a certainty.'

The dog gave an excited bark and loped ahead after him as he started to walk towards the cottage, leading the mare. Esther caught her breath and prepared herself. For one blind second she wanted to flee from this alien, male world. Aurora shrank back against the blankets, clutching a china-faced doll, afraid, with a child's keen sense of atmosphere. Esther wondered suddenly what she was doing, bringing her child into this frightening new place, away from all those she knew and loved. Perhaps her father had been right after all.

The mare walked slowly forward, following Higgins around to the yard and the stockade, whence the cries rang out more loudly.

Esther's blood seemed to freeze in her veins. The broad, male humour rang around her and she knew all at once that she and Aurora were out of place. She had not quite imagined it was like this, for on her first visit it had been quieter, and she had only seen Marsden Pike and Buck. Now the place seemed filled with men.

The cart drew up, and leaning over she drew out the protesting child, carrying her on her hip. Higgins rubbed his stubbled chin. 'You'd best come over to the stockade, ma'am, there's no knowing how long the Sergeant will be.'

Esther searched his face for any mockery, but finding none she followed him, her dark blue pelisse swirling about her ankles, her small, matching bonnet slightly askew.

Only three men crowded into the entrance of the stockade — not as many as she had expected. On seeing Esther with Higgins and the child, they drew back in amazement and stared at the trio curiously as they took their places inside.

The air was thick with horse and leather smells. The mare was a remount which had arrived with the first consignment of merino ewes, a new experiment in the colony. Although the mare had submitted to be saddled and bridled, she had refused to be mounted, and in one week she had thrown all the men so far, except Buck. She had broken one of the men's ribs in the process, and he was at that moment recovering in his hut.

The horse was dancing on her hind legs. Two men were trying to bring her front feet down to earth, using headropes. Her nostrils flared and her eyes rolled sidelong; she reared her head. The horse was one of the most beautiful animals Esther had ever seen. She was a chestnut — a shining copper with a white blaze. Her chest was broad, the neck arched, and the mane long, strong and silky.

Buck was standing quite close to the animal, so intent on her that he had not yet noticed Esther. He was gleaming with sweat, sleeves rolled up to the elbows, shirt open at the neck exposing the brown curls of hair rising from his chest.

'The only thing to do with this vicious creature is to shoot her, sir, before she kills somebody,' cursed the big man holding the rope, as he gave her a vicious crack across her wide, firm back with his long, oxhide whip. The mare gave a squeal, forced up her head, and pawed the air. Then she backed, rolling her eyes, quivering with rage.

'Not so fast, Parker,' Buck said briskly. 'She's had a good week of

292

it; what she needs now is a different kind of handling. When I whistle let go those ropes.'

Parker, a man as big as Buck, dark and swarthy with a thick, black beard, nodded, then he and the Hottentot who held the other rope stood waiting.

Esther watched Buck in fascination, how the strong fingers tightened at his sides, and again she was forcefully aware of his ability to take command of a situation. A silence had fallen over the men as he whistled sharply. Parker and the Hottentot sprang away on either side and the mare moved her ears backwards and forwards as Buck went up to her. He unfastened the rope halters, letting out two links of the curb chain simultaneously.

'Now my pretty, steady on and let's show 'em just what you really can do,' he said softly. The horse's ears pricked up. At the sound of the voice she became still. Then she snorted, and pawed the ground warningly. The men were silent, waiting for her to savagely swerve out of his way.

Gathering the reins Buck swiftly swung himself up into the saddle before the mare realized what he was doing. She gave a violent start, swerved and lashed out, missing Parker by inches. With ears flat on her back, she bounded half her weight into the air and came down on four stiff legs. There was a hum of surprise as Buck kept his balance as she strained forward, snorting.

Esther glanced around, seeing that everyone was staring at Buck: the five men, and the handful of Hottentots. The big man, Parker, had stepped before the others, tense and stiff. Her eyes returned to Buck.

He allowed the mare to hurt herself several times as she bucked against the palisade of wooden poles in her wild frenzy, and once he hit her between the ears with the flat of his hand, but all the time he was quietly whispering to her, over and over again. He kept his seat with an iron grip and a balance that amazed Esther, who had been holding her breath anxiously, expecting the mare to throw him at any time. She patted Aurora who had buried her small face in her neck, but her own eyes were still riveted on the mare.

After about twenty minutes, Buck looked over the back of the animal and called, 'I think she's about done in, Parker.'

The mare blew and shook her bridle, giving up the unequal struggle, and neighed loudly in defeat. She slowed to a walk, allowing herself to be mastered by her rider. A loud cheer broke out from the men as Buck cantered around the stockade and reined her in before them at the entrance. Noisy laughter and ribald comments greeted him, the men forgetting for a moment Esther's presence.

Then they fell silent, wary eyes glancing at her as Buck stopped, catching sight of her. His firm mouth curled slightly at the corners, his eyes suddenly alive with interest. Then his gaze moved to the small girl curled into her mother's arm. He took in the gay little bonnet, nestling against the brown ringlets of her hair, the trim, tiny kid slippers tied with velvet ribbons, and the bright dress, sprigged with primroses.

Esther could feel the crimson of embarrassment creep from her neck up to her face. The sunlight gilded a rim around the bounce of red ringlets and cast a shadow across her face under the dark blue bonnet. She was suddenly conscious of his nearness, of every detail about him once more, and the energy that radiated from him.

He puckered his eyes, looking away, and then the light illuminated his face again; it had a shuttered look, his eyes staring ahead for a second or two. All was quiet in the stockade when he dismounted, patting the mare's head, and talked to her soothingly. The very way he spoke to the horse, the gentle touch and complete absorption in the mare, spoke of his love for animals. He left the horse as the men dispersed. The stockade entrance was closed, and Buck and Esther stood facing each other in the bright sunlight.

She looked at him, the black wave of apprehension lifting a little.

'What brings you back to Eden?' he said, his eyes crinkling against the light, flushed from work, tousled and smelling of horse.

'I'd rather not say — out here,' she said softly, averting her gaze from the men grouped together curiously, not far away.

Buck's eyes glanced at the men, then returned quickly to her. He pursed his mouth, the dimples playing about his cheeks, noting her wide-spaced eyes, richly lashed under excellently marked eyebrows, and the way in which she looked at him. She suddenly looked so young and defenceless.

He relented. 'As you wish,' he said. 'But I have to wash first — I cannot remain in the company of a lady stinking to high heaven. There is a rough well-pump we fixed up in the yard — it won't take me long. Make yourself comfortable in the sitting-room.'

He turned to the men, calling Higgins to outspan the cart and water and feed the mare. He dismissed the others and led the way inside the cottage.

Esther was held back by Aurora who started crying again, and clinging to her.

'It's better not to force her,' Buck said with that gentleness that always surprised her at unexpected times. 'It's the same with any young thing in strange surroundings — like that wild mare out there. Take your time while I wash.'

He called to Pike to bring a glass of wine for the lady and some milk for the child. Then he strode towards the kitchen, his movements easy and relaxed, as Esther entered the sitting-room more slowly with Aurora held firmly against her hip.

She stood in the familiar, cool room, with its powder horns, guns and skins. She was surprised to notice a few books were now ranged high on a frame of stout poles over the two bedrooms, with lion and leopard skins stretched along the thatch above. Pike came in with two glasses of wine, a mug of milk and more than a suspicious glance at Esther and her child. Clean and glowing, Buck soon joined them. His eyes grew brighter, the lines about his mouth deepened the merest fraction as he motioned her to a seat. He picked up a glass and, settling himself on a chair near her, he lifted his glass. 'To you — and your daughter.' There was a smile about his lips as he leaned back in his chair, his booted legs stretched out before him, as if nothing she did anymore could surprise him.

Esther put her glass to her lips to stop them trembling as Aurora nestled closer into her lap.

'You have a beautiful daughter,' he said with undisguised admiration, looking at the little girl peeping at him from the shelter of her mother's arms. 'She has much of her mother about her, but not her eyes. Of her father I can see nothing yet.'

Esther stiffened, trying to keep calm. She did not want to talk of Aurora, of the fact that she could not walk or talk, although all Laree's children had done so at the same age. She could only crawl in a slow, clumsy fashion. The last thing she wanted to tell him was that she suspected something wrong with the child, and the terrible fear she had that it had been caused when Garnet raped her on their wedding night.

She picked her words carefully, not wanting to be thrown out before she had a chance to explain her position properly. 'Aurora and

I have left Dwyers' Cross for good, because I simply cannot live without you. We are asking you in all humility to take us into your home.'

'What?' he was incredulous. The startling blue eyes, so like Aurora's, swept over her face as she sipped her wine with controlled slowness, savouring its warmth.

Quickly, with a pathetic smile, she said, 'I have run away from Dwyers' Cross, from my father, my uncle — and we, the child and I, have literally nowhere else to go.'

He leaned forward. 'Well, if this isn't the darnest marriage proposal I have ever heard! You are throwing yourself at my mercy, in all humility? You could not be humble, Esther Fitzwilliam, if you tried — I find that very hard to believe. You are without a doubt, a most shameless and impulsive creature.' He was now amused.

She shot him a look, straightening her back. 'Please have the good sense to take me seriously, Buck Jones — there are those who haven't, to their cost. I am indeed at your mercy and the child with me. I cannot return, for my father has cut me off from all connection with my family because I dared come to you. If you will not have us — I won't go back, I won't!'

His eyes held hers in an enquiring glance. 'You really mean your pride won't let you return defeated. You never cease to amaze me.'

She bristled at his light, mocking tone. 'Even now, I am regarded as a fallen woman, and if you care about me as you said you did, you should care about that.'

There was a suggestion of mischief in his eyes. 'But you do not appear to care too much about that yourself, Esther. You are a saucy minx, no doubt about it. From now on you understand, the duel between your kinsmen and myself will become even more vicious. This does not bother you?'

She shook her head, swallowing the lump in her throat that made it difficult to answer him, having no way of knowing what his own thoughts were. 'I do care — I care very much. That must show you the extent of my feelings for you,' she said at last. 'We are, as you see, Aurora and I helpless and defenceless females.'

He stood up. 'Aurora is that for sure, but the hell you are, Esther. Helpless and defenceless be damned. A woman who can stand up to Lungelo and his warriors single-handedly, and who has gone through what you have and can still lift her head with fire in her eyes

296

is not one jot helpless — or defenceless.' He put down his glass on a wooden chest, unmistakable laughter bubbling through his voice, rich and infectious. 'No helpless female would dare to come all the way here, with a child alone, and only a musket between them for protection. You deserve a medal for sheer guts.'

She looked up into his eyes, trying to read his expression. There was a moment's silence, and Buck watched her face with a slightly cynical lift of his eyebrows.

'I salute your courage and your boldness, Esther Fitzwilliam. You are undeniably brave, beautiful and one hell of a reckless wench. This is your style — running away in the dead of night on some wild, exciting adventure, with very little thought of the consequences. That is what you have done all your life, I've seen it ever since your arrival in this colony. But I cannot for one moment believe that you have given up everything for — this.' He gestured about the room. 'Guns, skins — this just isn't your setting. You enjoy the chase, the wild thrill of the forbidden — but not as a permanent way of life, and you would hate me for giving it to you. You are being not a little selfish in throwing your desirable self at me, daring me to take advantage of you because it appeals to you to play with men. I love you, you know that — and you are here to play with fire. But I will not satisfy your wicked schemes, and I refuse to take advantage of you, though I would like to and you fully deserve it.'

The lights of horror appeared in her eyes. She felt paralysis set in at the unexpected cynicism and doubt in him. Could he not see she was sincere, that she had risked everything for him? That every step she had taken had been thought out, agonised over for hours? Did he understand nothing of her at all? Her eyes slid away from his, and a small, soundless sigh escaped her lips. Her expressive face revealed what she thought of his words. His glance flickered over her slim fitting pelisse with its small fur collar, part of the trousseau from her marriage.

'Every word I have said is true. I have burned all my boats in one final, wild gesture.' A different quality had crept into her voice. Her face looked drawn, a mask of profound sadness settling on her features. 'If you don't believe me, and you think all this is a silly reckless adventure to gain your attention, then there is nothing more I can say to convince you. I am desperate, an outcast from my family, and must suffer accordingly. And Aurora with me.' To her horror, her voice gave way completely.

He looked at her, alarmed, and sat down. 'Then you have landed yourself in one ugly mess.'

She heard the concern in his voice. Suddenly, looking at him through half-closed lashes, she felt hope dawn once more, and her horror receded. She had her last card to play, and she was forced to play it now. If she failed with this one, then she had gambled and lost everything, including her reputation, and that of her child.

'No more of an ugly mess than what you landed me in at Port Frances, Buck Jones. The result of that madness was — our daughter Aurora.'

Shock registered in his face. '*Our* daughter? Whatever are you talking about? Is this your final deception?'

Instantly the look of hope faded from her face. 'Aurora is not a Fitzwilliam at all. I married Garnet under false pretences — he did not know I was carrying your child, and he never forgave me when he found out.'

She heard his quick intake of breath. 'Then, if this is the truth, why did you not tell me before?'

Her face aflame, she said, 'Everything was against it. You were in prison, on trial for your life. If it had become known, I would have become a social outcast and the child with me. And you would have surely been condemned to death. It would have done no good.'

'Then you have suffered all this — alone? The Captain must have breathed hell-fire when he found out.' Again she heard the concern in his voice, and a preoccupied expression drew over his face showing that his mind was working swiftly.

'Garnet was — very angry. He — he forced himself upon me in a vicious and merciless manner, to punish and torture me for what I had done, for the deception I had played on him.' There were tears in her eyes and all at once it came flooding out, all the fears and the anxieties she had lived with for months. 'We agreed to play a charade so that his reputation and mine would remain untarnished before the world, but it was an unhappy marriage — and because of that one terrible night, I suspect something happened to our child — she — she is not as agile, as quick as children of her age.'

It was very quiet and the silence bit more keenly into her nerves than ever. 'I have been honest with you — you are the only person who knows what I have said. It is now your decision entirely. I

298

wronged Garnet and his death changed my life. If you agree to take us in, I will make up to *you* for all the years of pain I caused him. Otherwise I foresee a lonely widowhood, or marriage to someone I do not love — no doubt rightly deserved.'

Her hands were trembling as she looked away, and she frantically hoped that he would not notice. Then her eyes found his, and she spoke frankly once more, with much relief that someone else knew at last. 'I feel I could make you happy, if you will only give me the chance. Aurora needs her father, a strong man she can admire and trust, even if she is — backward.' Her face asked the question that she could not bring herself to frame.

Buck steepled his fingers together and leaned forward. His gaze travelled to Aurora, now sitting awkwardly on a skin rug at Esther's feet, his expression holding a rare look of softness and pleasure.

'You have indeed great courage, Esther, enduring the anger of another for what you and I had done — living with this between you day in and day out, suffering it all alone. You had the courage to face the twisted questions that day at court — and everything you have done has been because of me. Now you throw yourself at my feet in the biggest gamble of them all, trusting that your luck will hold.' He took a deep breath and sighed. 'I understand all that — for that is the way I have lived. You have thrown away everything for a love that burns so fiercely it cannot be denied.'

He looked at her, admiration and a growing respect mirrored in the blueness of his gaze, a look he had never given any other woman. He smiled. 'You have run me to earth sweetheart, and pierced me at my weakest spot — you and the child. How can I turn away such a lovely and defenceless small girl — my daughter. Maybe the rest of the world does not approve of Buckmaster Jones in your life, but it would seem time for us to prove them wrong.'

Esther stared at him, aware of a startling triumph that she had hardly dared to expect, but also aware of how nearly it still trembled in the balance. 'But the child — she — is not normal.'

He shrugged broad shoulders, a compassionate gleam in his eyes. 'Aurora is like a wounded animal, nothing more, nothing less. The other animals may not accept her, but there are some with, shall we say, superior intelligence, that see beyond all that to the real child within.' A kindly, teasing light was back in his face. His interest and feeling towards the little girl were obviously sincere. 'We must teach her with more patience, that is all. I have yet to find the animal that does not respond to love and affection.'

Esther's hands collapsed suddenly as though she had dropped an enormous, invisible load. He rose and came towards her, drawing her to her feet. She saw him through a curtain of unshed tears, and felt his warm, strong hands, rough with work, cup her face as he undid the ribbons of her bonnet, pushing it back from her head, revealing the unshadowed brilliance of her hair and eyes.

Esther's breath came a fraction faster. 'I don't know what to say,' she said, 'except that you are truly the most remarkable of men — and to take a wounded being is the most remarkable deed of all.'

'Hush,' he said, smoothing the hair from her brow. 'We, all of us, are wounded in some way or other. Life touches everyone with its hard hand, only some are able to hide it better than others, that is all. We are now in this together — now that you have so convincingly asked me to marry you — and face both your kinsmen and the world. Unequal odds have always suited me. We are two of a kind, sweetheart, and have the courage needed.'

A quick frown from Esther's brow. 'Aurora — Aurora must never be told she's not Garnet's daughter. It would cause her the greatest distress if she understood that she's — she's . . .'

'A bastard?' There was a deep note in his voice that compelled her to look up into his face. His sky-blue eyes met hers. In the sudden stillness that followed, she heard somewhere the melancholy cry of a bird. 'It is a state I know well. Never fear, she will remain in safe ignorance, my dearest Esther.'

He held an auburn ringlet of her hair at her cheek, watching the end curl round the heel of his hand. 'You know, I couldn't bear you marrying anyone else but me. I went through enough hell the first time — imagining you with the Captain, thinking of him making you happy, giving you the world.'

Then his firm lips were on hers. He was wide and solid, with a strength that wrapped her with a satisfying reassurance. All she was aware of was heat, a blaze of power, the pressure of hard muscles in a strong body, a complete blending of passion and tenderness, then it was over.

Aurora was crying and pulling at her skirts, and Pike was roaring from the kitchen announcing the midday meal.

'Come, Esther,' Buck said huskily, placing an arm about her

300

shoulders. 'Join us for the meal. It is not Government House style, but it will do.'

They interrupted a rather bellicose Parker declaring that the French Navy was quite right to kill Nelson at the Battle of Trafalgar because the British Empire was for the birds and the stinking rich, swaggering upper classes. Wiping the foaming milk off his upper lip, his large hands making the tumbler look like a thimble, he asserted that he did not care who heard him because it was men such as he who had built the ruddy Empire, with toil and sweat and bloody fighting in wars not of their choosing, and it was only the upper-class swags who had the money and the leisure to enjoy it all.

Buck tipped a warning look to the men sitting at the table, noisily wolfing down a loaf of bread, chunk by chunk, and sopping up the gravy from the stew on their plates with gusto and much slurping. Higgins looked up, a piece of bread poised in mid-air, halfway between the table and his mouth, a curious frown on his lean face. The others looked surprised, the silence that fell growing heavier as they stared at Buck with the two females.

They respected Buck, who in their eyes was not only a natural leader, but an educated man who possessed the valuable asset of being able to read and write passably well. Besides, he never tried to be too popular with them and they trusted him for that; it never worked if those of higher rank curried favour with their subordinates — a fact both he and they knew.

He motioned that they should rise in the presence of a lady, which reluctantly they did, benches creaking and feet shuffling noisily. Then Buck announced without ceremony: 'This lady has consented to be my wife. We will marry without much delay.' The atmosphere became subtly strained. The men resumed their seats and hurried through their meal, hacking the bread and spearing the pieces of stew meat with knives more suitable for some unmentionable task in a slaughtering shed, the rise and fall of their subdued voices falling about the table.

Esther felt that in some unspoken way she had become an unwelcome addition to their lives, that probably they regarded her as a restriction on their complete male freedom which they had enjoyed up until then. Buck was speaking to Higgins. She looked sideways at his self-contained, firm profile, and it was as if a persistent, obscuring mist was swept away, releasing her after all those years. She felt strong, ready for anything, sure that in the end she could get the men to accept her. She met his eyes as he inclined his head towards her. Her spirits lifted. Nothing mattered in the whole world anymore except this new joy inside her, making her past life seem like a state of deprivation.

After some brave stabs at the meat, she raised her eyes holding her head high in her victory and looked over the bent heads at the wild, untended garden and the threat of rain outside the window. She did not want to talk or think, she just wanted to stay there forever, knowing that Buck was there.

CHAPTER
Twenty-Nine

As there were only two bedrooms in the cottage Buck gave his up for Esther and Aurora. The other room belonged to Pike. Buck moved in with him until the following day when Esther would be taken to Grahamstown to stay with his friends, John and Elizabeth Rowlands, who owned the largest merchant store in the village. Higgins had already been despatched with a letter dictated by Buck, but written in Esther's flowing hand, explaining the position.

For hours the summer clouds had been gathering over the bush, and in the hills the crash of distant thunder boomed. A sudden flash of lightning flickered along the ridges of the low-lying hills. By the time night fell, there was a heavy deluge of rain.

It was hours later that Esther fell into the dreamless sleep of the utterly exhausted. She had spent the remainder of the afternoon cleaning the cottage and helping a grateful Pike with the supper. Buck, Parker and one of the others had gone in search of two of his merino ewes lost down one of the heavily-wooded gullies running down to the river, returning only at dinner-time.

Esther was awakened that night by a mighty din and the dog barking. There were raised voices outside and a crash on the front door. It soon transpired that there was a wreck outside the treacherous sandbar at Port Frances and every able-bodied man who could swim had been called out to help the nine seamen on board, only three of whom could swim and had made the shore.

Buck left with Parker and Egmont Moss. Esther watched with wry amusement as Pike's face wrinkled like a fan when Buck asked him to look after the two females in his absence. Then he was gone and the house became a silent, almost deserted shell.

Esther lay for hours, tossing and turning in the darkness. If anything happened to Buck now ... She did not want to think about it, could not think about it. Only he stood between her and insanity, between her and the outside world. She could not bear the thought of losing him when she had only just won him. The thought of loss was often with her since Garnet's death, and she tried to concentrate on her coming marriage.

The men returned near midnight. She heard them from her room and had to suppress the desire to rush out and see if Buck was all right. Fresh billets of wood were piled on the fire in the kitchen as she crept to the bedroom door and peered into the darkness of the sitting-room beyond which she could see some way into the kitchen. The leaping firelight threw into bold relief the rough-hewn faces of the small knot of men seated around it, their eyes ringed with fatigue. The storm had ended and now the moon flitted in and out of the silver clouds above the trees outside, drenching the landscape with mysterious, ghostly light. The bush was alive with crickets again, with the deep-throated croaking of bullfrogs and the screech of a nightjar as it soared away unseen through the summer night.

Only yards from the kitchen firelight, very little, apart from the eerie moonlight, was visible. Esther could make out Buck's profile as he sat beside the fire, raising a large pewter pot to his lips.

'Lud,' he groaned, wiping his mouth with his hand. 'As an experienced judge of grog, this stuff's rotgut.'

There was a hoot of mirth. Pike chuckled loudly, looming up in the darkness behind them. 'You should try Nagmaal wine, sir — rum good stuff, that.'

There was more rumbling laughter. 'So that's what old Pike does, visitin' Nagmaal with 'em Boer wenches. Steals their ruddy communion wine. How's that Annemarie near Salem, eh, Pike? She's a comely wench that one, built to accommodate a dozen like Pikes comfortably,' Parker roared, his large face shadowed by his bushy, black beard.

Hoarse laughter and bawdy comments drowned the rest of the talk. The voices drifted about the fire as Esther waited in a growing welter of impatience, anxious to know what happened. Finally, the men rose one by one, yawning and clutching their greatcoats, and left the cottage to Buck and Pike, the latter returning to his own room soon afterwards. She took a chance to slip through to the kitchen, her heart setting up a wild beating. He was still in his chair, his head thrown back, fast asleep. Stifling her disappointment, she gazed down at him. His shirt front was thrown open in careless disarray, exposing his bare torso to the waist. Her eyes travelled the familiar breadth of the wide shoulders, across the broad expanse of chest covered with brown curls of damp hair, down to the lean belly, ribbed and corded with muscle. He was truly as magnificent as she remembered, and never had she wanted him so much.

The dog, lying beside him, rose at her approach. She patted him as he fluttered his tail against her nightgown skirts. Satisfied he lay down and she went closer to Buck and knelt beside him. She stayed very still, to enjoy her silent, undisturbed possession. How she loved him in that moment. It was a feeling almost too full, too powerful to bear, as passion and a deeper longing stabbed through her like a piercing pain.

Then she stood, gazing at his naked torso, admiring him. Why had she misread him and not allowed herself to love him long ago? All those years ago. She had missed so much not being with him then, so much of his life. But then she had not been the person she was now, and she knew it would not have worked then. She had still *so* much to learn. In the past she could not have stood the pain of standing alone against her father and uncle, against the society she had known.

She returned to the bedroom to collect a blanket from the bed, resolving to spend every moment she could with him after they were married — to catch up on everything she had missed. As she arranged the blanket over him, she was only too conscious of the fact that she was arranging her whole life around this man, that Esther in her own right no longer seemed to exist. And so it had been with Amanda Lightfoot. What was it about him that made women such as they, do such wild things?

Whatever else she was, Esther had never been blind to her own weaknesses, and she was in full knowledge of what she had done. It was almost frightening, she thought, that two people could rouse so much feeling, so much passion in each other as she and he did.

Pike's voice broke through her thoughts. He came slowly through the door, fingering his nightcap and blinking in the light of the candle on the table. 'Sorry, Ma'am, I 'eard someone in the kitchen and came to investigate. Didn't mean to frighten you.'

His eyes flickered from her to Buck. 'The Sergeant's just about done in — 'e went into those treacherous rollers time and time again. Thanks to 'im all lives were saved, except for one poor blighter. 'E was lost overboard and the Sergeant could not find 'im. Parker says that the last time the Sergeant went in, 'e could hardly drag 'imself up on the beach. Conked out like, lost to the world for a while. Every time 'e went into the water, the men they kept 'im going with tots of brandy.'

Esther nodded. 'He has done more than most, Mr Pike, and he needs sleep more than anything else right now.'

Pike hesitated, fumbling with his tattered gown. He tapped his yellow teeth together. 'If you don't mind me sayin' so, ma'am, the Sergeant's a good man. 'E's 'ad a rough life, same as the rest of us. We're no fancy folk, ma'am, but 'e's never complained about 'is lot that I've 'eard. Gets cross at times, roars like a goddamned lion, then it's done with. 'E don't bear no grudges.'

He scrubbed at his stubbled chin in acute embarrassment. ''E needs a strong woman, ma'am — to look after 'im like. 'E would kill me for saying so, but 'e's that careless with 'isself and that powerful body of 'is — pushes 'imself beyond what's good for 'im, punishes 'imself and 'is strength.'

Esther smiled with reckless warmth. 'I will do all in my power to look after him, Mr Pike, you can depend on it. I won't let him down. He's been very good to me and my child.'

The sadness that had lurked somewhere in her eyes had gone and was replaced by an eagerness that gave a vitality and sparkle to her face. She left the room, listening to the wild singing in her heart. She was shrewd, practical and realistic, but she was also a Celt, and her innermost fibres vibrated to the silent music from that other world of dreams and ideals and fairy creatures. And it told her, beyond a shadow of a doubt, that from the moment she first met Buck, their marriage had been inevitable. After so many months of restless longing she was glad she was here at Eden, where she belonged.

306

Thirty

Early the following day Esther and Aurora set off with Pike for Grahamstown in the covered wagon Buck used for hunting expeditions. She did not see Buck as he was still sleeping after the hectic night, and so regretfully had to leave without saying goodbye.

He had promised to arrange a licence and get a preacher willing to marry them as soon as possible. After a day and a half of travelling, the wagon wound down one of the broad roads now fanning the countryside, towards the town. Grahamstown had become a larger, sprawling centre for wholesale merchants; a maze of long, wide streets bordered by thatched cottages behind long, narrow gardens, new stores, office buildings and one or two more inns. Here and there double-storied houses stood further back, set in wide lawns on the gently-sloping hill-sides.

The wagon rumbled over the stone bridge spanning the river and entered the town. The grey ramparts of Fort England towered over them, its Union Jack fluttering softly from the flagstaff. The street became more crowded nearer the bustling market square, a mosaic of wagons, carts and gaily coloured stalls, draped with piles of fresh goods and merchandise. The river water flowed down the sides of High Street, where each resident whose garden fronted on to it, would fill a bucket in strict rotation.

Pike stopped the wagon before the Rowlands General Store, one of the first to be set up after the flood. Esther turned and raised a fine eyebrow at him. He grinned. 'You'll be well cared for 'ere, ma'am — them's good folks, all seven of 'em.'

'Seven of them, Mr Pike?'

Pike screwed up his eyes, the jagged knife-scar down his cheeks more noticeable in the light. 'That's right ma'am — mother, father and five young 'uns — but two more's no trouble. The Sergeant's often stayed over 'ere with 'em on his trips to the village.'

Esther's questioning eyes met his. 'But will there be enough room for us, Mr Pike? I would hate to be any trouble to Mr and Mrs Rowlands, not knowing them at all.'

He shook his head, looking at her intently. 'The Sergeant would not have asked if he knew it would be too much trouble, ma'am — you worry too much.'

Pulling her paisley shawl around her shoulders, Esther climbed down from the wagon, lifting Aurora after her. She followed Pike into the store, carrying her daughter. No sooner had they entered when she stopped to look with curiosity. It was a large room filled with the mingled smells of spices, soap, candles and coffee beans.

There were two storerooms crammed with fat, wooden kegs of American flour, sugar and tea. Cheeses stood wrapped in coarse, white cloths on the counter and the shelves were filled with bolts of calico, muslin, gingham and cambric. There was merchandise from England and the East Indies — smoothing irons, saddles, China lutestring, Madras longcloth and, hanging from the rafters, pewter jugs, tankards, gentlemen's hessians and Wellingtons. Peppermint lozenges stood in large stoneware jars beside twilled bombaset and flasks of gunpowder. There were even a few dusty casks of wine at the back of one room. It was like a fairyland of different smells and exciting displays, varied and fascinating.

Soft, barred light fell through the windows out of a late morning sky, as a woman, small and very slim, in a plain blue homespun dress made her way to meet them from the back of the second storeroom, with a great bunch of keys and a timepiece jingling at her waist.

Her faded hair was untidy as she came swiftly forward, wiping dusty hands on her wide pinafore. There was a warm glint in her light brown eyes as she introduced herself as Elizabeth Rowlands. A tall, gangling boy of thirteen came up behind her, peering at them curiously.

'So, Mr Pike, you have brought the lady. Mrs Fitzwilliam, I have been waiting very impatiently and curiously to meet the one

308

woman who has at last captured the heart of Mr Buck Jones. I take it that the letter I received from Mr Higgins was in your hand, for though Buck writes passably well, his writing is not a patch on yours!'

She stopped and gazed up at Esther for a moment and at the small girl in Esther's arms. The warmth in Elizabeth's eyes gave way to a frank stare. 'Whatever I expected,' she said, 'I was never prepared for just how beautiful you are. And so tall — but then being so small myself everyone is tall to me. Buck could only have a tall woman.' The light brown eyes suddenly smiled out of her homely, freckled face. 'Very few women can match him, my dear, and we thought he was doomed to be a bachelor for life. I am so glad that you made him change his mind.'

Then she turned to the boy at her side and introduced him as her eldest son, Jonas.

'I hope that we are not putting you to too much trouble, Mrs Rowlands, descending on you at such short notice,' Esther said, glancing at Pike. His weathered face creased into a smile. He looked as if he had no cares in the world this morning.

'Like I said to Mrs Fitzwilliam, she worries too much,' he said to Elizabeth.

Elizabeth came forward, stretching out a hand to take Esther's, the bunch of keys jangling at her side. 'Of course you are no trouble, and please call me Elizabeth. A friend — or rather a wife-to-be of Buck's is a friend of ours. You are very fortunate to have such a man, Mrs — may I call you Esther?' She spoke openly in her gentle, Cornish lilt, though her words were quite unabashed and forthright.

'It will be a pleasure to have you with us until the wedding if you'll excuse a houseful of menfolk. You see, I never did produce any daughters.' A large smile broadened her lips. 'I have, as you know from the letter, the strictest instructions to make up a wedding gown fit for a princess, of your choice and at Buck's expense. Now, Mr Pike, if you will unload Mrs Fitzwilliam's chest, she and I will take the short walk to the house further down the street.'

Esther felt a sudden surge of warmth towards the small energetic woman who had welcomed her so easily in a way very few women had done before, always seeing her as a threat.

Elizabeth called a rotund man and asked him to tend the store awhile with Jonas, then she marched ahead to a comfortable eleven-roomed house on eight acres of ground, with its young orchard in full bloom.

'I don't serve in the store you understand — John thinks it most unladylike. I work in the back, sorting and checking. The counter is manned by Joseph back there, John or my son Jonas when he's not in trouble. John is away getting supplies in Port Elizabeth for now,' Elizabeth explained, as she strode purposefully into the long, narrow garden before her house.

She showed them to a small, clean room at the back of the house. The garden outside basked in the warm sunshine and there was a faint, delicious scent of flowers. Some distance off, the orchard sloped down to the river. Through the trees Esther could see the silvery gleam of water. Three young boys were playing on the grass nearer at hand, supervised by a Hottentot maid, their laughter high-pitched and mischievous.

Elizabeth glanced efficiently about the room. 'I hope it is all to your liking, Esther. Make yourself at home, won't you?'

Suddenly Esther could bear it no longer. She felt an absurd desire to fling her arms around her at the sheer relief of finding such warmth, such acceptance. But all she could bring herself to say was, 'I cannot begin to express my gratitude, Elizabeth. You don't know me and yet you take my child and me into your home so open-heartedly. Very few would do that.'

Elizabeth grinned, waving a small, impatient hand. 'I have no patience with those who are not what they seem. I know all about you, Esther, about your marriage to Major Fitzwilliam, that dreadful murder case and Buck's trial, the Major's death, your father and uncle, the blundering commando — all that. The Dwyers are well-known in this community, as you know. Nothing you do escapes notice, my dear. But you are what you are, you don't try to hide it and I like that. It is a matter now between you and Buck alone.' She moved back to the doorway. 'John and I have known Buck for three years. He's brought us much custom and he's helped us from time to time, and especially now that business is not too good. If it hadn't been for him last year we would have gone bankrupt. He's done well hunting and I suspect he will go far in this community yet.'

Her tone was matter-of-fact. She jiggled a key from the bunch in her hands, then went on, 'We like Buck — I would trust him with my life if I had to — and our five sons adore him. He loves children, did you know that? Forgive me for being blunt, but I have always hoped he would marry and have many children because he will be a wonderful father.'

Her eyes turned to Aurora staring shyly up at her. She watched the little face, her movements, her expressions. 'He'll be very good to your daughter, depend on that.'

All Esther felt before the scrutiny from the tiny woman was a soft glow of happy warmth. She sat down beside Aurora on the small, wooden bed, and smiled as she slipped off her pelisse. 'A thousand thanks, Elizabeth.'

Elizabeth turned to go. 'I have to return to the store. You rest yourselves here. I don't trust anybody in the store while John is away. Please excuse me — I'll be back in an hour to get you all a meal.' She stopped in the doorway and with a rustle of starched skirts she turned back. 'Make yourself some coffee or a pot of tea — there's wood on the fire in the kitchen. Be good to Buck, my dear, he deserves the best.'

She was watching Esther closely, then her smile reappeared. She turned and left, then came back again mischievously and poked her head around the door. 'If I was as beautiful as you and I did not have the kind of wonderful husband I have, I would have tried to capture Buck Jones for myself long ago.' With a naughty chuckle she vanished.

Esther smiled to herself. I will be good to him, she thought, I'll show them all, but most of all, I'll show him.

Her wide, uptilted eyes were unusually contemplative. So that astute, businesslike, no nonsense little Elizabeth had joined Esther as one of Bucks's mesmerised admirers. Then she had done the right thing after all, willingly cutting herself adrift from everyone she knew, everyone she had loved, and casting herself out on an island with a man she adored and admired, but about whom there was much she still had to learn.

She was now in another world, peopled by beings quite different from those she had known. Her family would not be at her wedding, none of her friends would be there to give her encouragement, no kind, supportive Laree. But for all this, she knew she had done the right thing. It seemed to her then, that all her life she had been waiting for this challenge, that all the past events had been moulding her and leading her to it.

The coming event was full-flavoured meat for the gossips, especially as both Esther and Buck were well-known for different reasons. The social life of the town was already badly disrupted by a bitter quarrel between Frances Somerset and the wife of the Landdrost, Mrs Dundas. Colonel Somerset was in disagreement with the Major over the policy regarding the border raids. Mrs Somerset had withdrawn herself so much from the town's social life that she virtually was isolated at her home, Oatlands Park, only seeing close friends and official guests.

In an isolated community, prone to petty quarrels and much backbiting, every scrap of scandal was pounced on and painted in dramatic overtones. And so it was with the Fitzwilliam-Jones union. Esther prepared herself for the coming event by ignoring the inevitable clouds of gossip and speculation collecting about her. There was even some rumour that she was shamelessly with child and forced to marry Buck. Buck, himself, maintained a detached silence about the malicious story, knowing that nothing he could do would quash it but that time would prove it to be untrue.

Within weeks he had, with his numerous contacts and resources, obtained a marriage licence without the normal formality of banns being published for the regulation fourteen days and managed to get a minister to perform the ceremony for a very high surplus fee. He also ordered a table and chairs, and some kitchen and bedroom furniture for Eden from a Boer living in the town. It was in this atmosphere of good-natured activity and excitement that Esther waited for her marriage day.

On a blustery day at the end of February Buck arrived at the Rowlands house with Pike in the Cape cart for the wedding. Esther, unable to wait, burst through the open doorway. For a few seconds both men remained stock-still and looked at her in such silence that even Pike, recovering from a hangover from the night before, sobered up immediately.

She was so vividly alive, so radiantly beautiful in a silk gown a shade deeper than the palest sherry. A pair of the daintiest

312

embroidered slippers peeped from the whirl of soft skirts and petticoats as she ran towards them. The rich red ringlets framed her face in bright showers under an elegant, small, pale-sherry-coloured bonnet, banded and beribboned in sherry and white.

'I thought you were never coming,' she announced running out towards them. 'You're so late. All the guests have been waiting for ages.' She stopped, her face wreathed in smiles, and gazed at her future husband. Never had she seen him look quite so striking and handsome as in his wedding clothes.

'Did you think I'd run out on you, sweetheart?' Buck asked. There was a new intensity in his voice. It was apparent in the blue gaze that seemed to scorch the air between them. 'If it hadn't been for Pike here, we should have arrived long ago.'

He climbed from the driver's box, giving her a gallant bow. Looking at him as he straightened up, Esther was seized with an impatient desire for him. She returned the long look he gave her, to be interrupted by Pike groaning loudly as he put his hand to his wilting brow.

'Me 'ead is poundin' so hard that I can't hear myself think. I feel dreadful and nobody cares. And never did I feel more like an overdressed cockerel in all this finery. It's not fair to make a body so uncomfortable when all I want is me old jerkin and leathers,' he grumbled. He looked down from the cart resentfully, as stiff as a poker, dressed in fawn frockcoat, grey waistcoat, cranberry breeches and puttees, the black, curled-up beaver hat squashed down on his head like a busby.

'It's all the Sergeant's fault, ma'am, that you find me in such a fine state! Trumpeting into my room at the inn like a ranting bear, throwing these dreadful garments on the bed and demanding that I put them on right away, with me 'ead sawing away like some great hammer. An' that's not all — then 'e takes the jug of the coldest water imaginable and pushes me 'ead into the basin, just like that — no respecter of finer feelin's, no sir. 'Tis a wonder I've survived at all, I tell you.'

'It's fellows like old Pike who keep the taprooms of this village in business,' Buck said, throwing Esther a wink. He gave the bandy-legged man a voracious smile. 'Now just a word of warning, Mr Pike — and it would do you well to heed it, my friend — keep your breath to yourself at all times, the very smell of it will make

313

the wedding party drunk as lords. Come now, we have kept the bride waiting long enough.'

Peals of laughter escaped Esther's lips as Buck's brow wrinkled into mock disgust. Pike decanted himself heavily from the cart and stood in the gusty wind, bleary-eyed and not a little sorry for himself, his breath fumigating the air around him for some way.

'Come now, Pike, it's not so bad, after all it's not you who is taking the fateful step. Cheer up, for afterwards you can get back to drinking and making merry at my expense,' Buck said expansively, taking Esther's arm. 'And if we don't hurry up I stand to lose the bride as well.'

Pike brightened considerably at the mention of drinking and strutted past them and up the path to the house overflowing with guests. They were a mixture of Buck's ex-comrades from the new barracks, the men from Eden and a handful of friends, both British and Boer. They surged from the door to draw them into the simple sitting-room with impatient excitement and then stood back, waiting as Buck and his bride walked into the room where the rosy-faced Reverend Gatehouse awaited them.

Elizabeth suddenly became businesslike as the guests assembled in the room. She looked across at the preacher as the marriage ceremony was read in sepulchral tones in the hushed silence. Afterwards the voices swept in warm gusts about the bride and groom enjoying a wedding feast which had been prepared by Elizabeth, Esther and some of the women present. Choice wine in dusty casks was brought in, and Esther raised her goblet to Buck, the light dancing in the cool, white wine.

The room hummed, laughter coiling itself warmly about them as she and Buck stood at the long, wooden trestle-table laid out with tasty English and Boer fare. There were huge beef pies poured over with cream, goose, spiced sausage, chicken pies, deliciously flavoured vegetables and large cakes. Home-brewed porter, port and wine flowed as the warmth and gaiety rose.

With a sense of returning security, Esther looked down at the golden chicken-pie on her plate and eagerly bit into the crisp pastry. Buck put his hand over hers, covering the delicate engagement ring. It was fashioned in a small flower made up of tiny diamonds set on its slender band beside the new wedding ring winking on her finger. He looked deeply into her eyes and she felt

314

her heart turn over. Never before had she seen such a tender expression on his proud features. 'I see that the seriousness of the occasion has done nothing to quell your enormous appetite.'

She chuckled softly. 'On the contrary, dear husband, all the excitement has made me ravenously hungry.'

His hand left hers. 'As long as it leaves room for other things, sweetheart, who am I to stop you.' His face creased into a smile which took her breath away, and she wished that the proceedings were over.

She smiled at him with embarrassed pleasure, her skin glowing with eager happiness. She took more food, savouring every mouthful with uncharacteristic bridal behaviour. Silently she prayed that nothing would ever come between them again, that she could hold on to this overflowing happiness that almost seemed too good to be true, that her cup of life would always be this full.

The sun began to slant across the hills when the merry, bantering crowd went out to wave the bridal party and sleepy little Aurora, goodbye. She sat in the wagon, looking crumpled in the new gingham dress, gay with stripes, and promptly fell asleep.

The smiles and laughter seemed so far away as Esther waved to them amidst the jovial cries of farewell. She felt relief as the wagon started with a lurch, dust clouds rising in the air, as the rolling team of oxen surged forward. She and Buck were alone at last.

Night found them camped in a clearing of tall trees near a stream. Rivers of stars were set against the velvet sky, the air crystal clear. The wind had died, and there was the sound of running water. The stream was rendered invisible by the bush and the darkness as it ran, bubbling, along the shallow valley floor. And beyond the camp with its flickering fire, the lonely hills rolled far away into the distance of the frontier.

The night was incredibly dark. Pinpoints of glimmering lights glowed from myriad tiny fireflies flitting in and out of the dense trees festooned with ancient grey monkey-ropes, the gnarled branches hidden with creepers.

Esther took a deep draught of fresh, night air. All around them the undergrowth was alive with the sounds of nocturnal

315

creatures. Buck had thrown more branches onto the fire. He had set up the tent beside the wagon, where Aurora slept, guarded by the watchdog they had brought with them.

Esther stood in silent fascination watching him, glowing with strength, energy and vigour. Her eyes took in the flexing of the iron-hard muscles of his wide shoulders, the broad chest covered with brown curls of damp hair, the lean belly and the length of his sturdy, powerful legs. She could feel the warmth of his body close to hers as he stood looking down at her, and her whole being reached out to him, yearning for him to seize her, hold her and possess her once more. She reached up to brush his lips with a kiss, her hands sliding down his body which gleamed like satined bronze in the warm glow of the rush candle.

Slowly, gently, he slipped her lawn nightgown down over one shoulder, so that first one breast then the other appeared from beneath the concealing shadows of the garment, and, little by little, the rest of her glowing flesh was revealed to him. The candlelight flooded over her, and there was a pungent smell of aromatic shrub and tree outside. Somewhere a nightjar shrieked triumphantly and an owl answered further away. The campfire beyond the tent hissed, crackled, the odour of resin mingling with the fragrance of the earth.

His wonderful eyes caressed every curve of her body, every indentation of her skin, and his obvious delight in her sent the blood singing through her veins. He put his hands up and found hers, and she felt her fingers begin to tremble, her whole being attuned to him, sensing nothing beyond that bond between them which had always drawn them together, and which was as firm and strong as ever.

'This time it's legal, my beautiful one,' he whispered huskily, his hands caressing her face. Her skin tingled where he touched it, sending quivers through the depths of her body. 'You are every bit as lovely as I remember you, and more so. That last image in the dunes has stayed bright in my memory always. You spoilt me for other women, you know that?'

He took her hand and pressed his mouth against her open palm. Her heart beating ever more wildly, her hand went to his cheek, then stroked his thick, brown hair.

'I shall love you until my dying day, Buck Jones. Promise me that nothing shall ever come between us.' She put up a finger to trace the line of his jaw.

'I love you so much,' he said softly, 'We shall have all the time in the world this night, so let us take advantage of it.' As he spoke he unbound her hair, letting the curls cascade to her shoulders. As her hands slid over his chest, she felt the strong grip of his arms and his warm mouth was on hers, drawing her down to the pallet of straw covered with antelope skin. In the darkness outside, the noise of the beetles in the bush was loud, insistent. But she could no longer hear them.

She could only hear Buck's breathing close to her. There was nothing that had any place in the tent, only the two of them who had waited so long for this night, impatient for each other. No more words were said. None was needed with the silent messages flowing between them. He drew her closer, his mouth meeting hers again, at first demanding, then sweet and achingly tender. She could think of nothing but the man, her husband, whose strong body filled her arms, whose hands caressed her with the ease of long practice, whose mouth claimed her for his own.

Closing her eyes in rapture, she felt his lips on her breasts. They swelled at his touch, rising to meet him, eager for his exploration as sensation mounted through the erect nipples.

Reaching out, her fingers slid to the back of his head, and gripped the thick cap of curls with savage and triumphant pleasure. He caressed the shapely contours of her body as if he had all the time in the world. His love-play was agonisingly subtle and delicious, teasing her desire to the limits of endurance, feeling her writhing and panting under his touch as warm, hard breasts, firm thighs, hot belly and moist lips moulded themselves to his body.

Her neck arched backwards, eyes half-closed, her lips partly open; for the second time in her life, Esther was experiencing heaven. Her heart beat in her ears like thunder, her excitement mounted uncontrollably, and she wanted him to take her immediately.

'Love is a slow death, my darling,' he murmured, 'let us enjoy it to its fullest.' His experienced, accomplished hands and lips deterred her as they drew nearer to her trembling thighs. Writhing with intolerable bliss, they parted. Fiercely she held him to her, trying to get as close as she could to him. She watched his face, his changing expressions making him unbelievably beautiful, and sending her emotions soaring even higher.

Giving herself up to total abandoned joy, she revelled in the pleasure she was giving him as his lips kissed the smooth swell of her hips and the copper-shadowed abdomen. When she could bear it no longer, she dug her fingers into his back, holding him in utter, wild impatience. With a long, deep groan, she felt the inexorable and rigid thrust as he entered her, murmuring intimate, sensual endearments. A fainting ecstasy momentarily darkened her consciousness, as his passion rose to meet hers.

She was aware of the incredible joy mounting inside her as she surrendered her proud, defiant self to him, her response spontaneous and all enveloping. For her it was an experience even surpassing that first time, and far more profound. It soared above her memories, the supreme fulfilment, as she responded to him, not as a girl but as a woman.

Later, as they lay in the darkness, with the deep silence all around them, clasped in each other's arms, he said softly, 'There's nothing more beautiful out here than the sound of silence, my darling. I love the bush and the hills more than any other place on earth because of its wildness. There is a great force all around, yet it is so silent.' He turned his head and stroked her hair streaming over his shoulders. 'You have indeed married a strange fellow.'

'I would not have it any other way,' she answered, lying there content with the darkness, and with the warmth and nearness of the man she loved more than any other.

'You know what old Chief Mazwi once told me — that there is no quiet place in the villages of the white man. No place to hear the wind in the trees, or the noise of insects' wings.'

She nestled her head against his neck, wrapping her arms around him. 'What else did the chief tell you?'

He went on, his husky voice low, and pleasant to her, 'He believes we will kill everything — and that what is happening to the wild beasts that have left the colony, especially the shy quagga, will happen to his people. He says we take away all the secrets of the forests and hills.' He was so silent for a while that she thought he must have fallen asleep, but then she felt gentle

318

kisses on her skin and heard him whisper, 'And when everything is gone, dear one, and all the empty places filled with our people, the lives of the Xhosas will become simply a matter of survival.'

'He must be a very wise old man — and perhaps he is right.' She raised herself on her elbow and kissed him, while her finger travelled softly through the hair on his chest, tracing the pattern of muscle. 'And quite unexpected for a black savage.'

'It very much depends upon what you mean by a savage, now doesn't it?' He chuckled softly and she could sense him smiling in the darkness.

She playfully pummelled his chest. 'I am not in the mood to be drawn into your arguments about this or that side of the Fish River, do you hear me?'

She could say no more as, giggling with delight, she was stopped by his lips on her mouth.

The sun had risen just far enough to dapple the tops of the tall yellowwood trees when she awoke the next morning. Esther stretched herself luxuriously, radiant with the self-confidence of a woman who had given herself completely to the man she loved. Feeling with a lazy arm for Buck, she found to her disappointment that the place beside her was empty. And Aurora — she had forgotten all about her small daughter in the full intoxication of her own pleasure.

She swung up her legs and hugged them deliciously for a moment, leaning slightly back on the pallet as she thought of the night before. Shuddering a bit in the raw air, she pulled the antelope skin about her shoulders. Except for the clamouring of early morning birds, she could not hear anything.

Then she heard the snapping of twigs and the sound of an Old English ditty, followed by low, richly-infectious laughter. Quickly she pulled on her pale green peignoir and drew aside the tentflap. A strand of hair spilled down her cheek, dark red and shining in the moving sunlight with streaks of fire.

The morning was still pale and cool, the sun visible but still remote. Overhead, birds wheeled, their wings catching the sporadic golden flash of the sun before they dipped and vanished beyond the treetops. Once more the air fell silent for a brief while and she could hear the clear ring of a shot fired by a solitary hunter, coming from a great distance, which seemed to hang on the air for a long time afterwards, before the cries of the birds became resonant once more.

Cool, soft air fanned her cheeks as she stepped from the shelter of the tent into the morning light, savouring the freshness of the air carrying the aromatic scent of shrub and burning mimosa branches. She had lived on the frontier for seven years, but for the first time the vast space of it was in her, the space of the ever-stretching hills, the great sky viewed from the peaks and reaching into infinity. She could not, on that morning, imagine herself anywhere else.

The camp fire was glowing, the iron kettle swinging on its tripod above it. Buck was down on one knee, blowing gently on the heap of branches. Then he sat back on his heels, smiling at Aurora who crouched beside him. His voice, with a laugh now and then, rose and fell and seemed to shut Esther out. There was something about this close communion of man and child that touched a fibre of jealousy in her. She wanted Buck all to herself, to share him with no one. Sighing inwardly, she was deeply shocked that she could feel in such a way about her own small daughter, her own flesh and blood.

The feeling vanished as Buck raised his head, his eyes lighting up at the sight of her.

'Lud! But you look the way every woman should look first thing in the morning, sweetheart — soft, happy, with just that touch of shameless wickedness about her.' He watched her with that candid, disconcerting expression she was learning to know, his eyes saying things she blushed to think about.

She was ashamed about her former feelings, and wanted to make amends in her own extravagant way. She stepped forward, her bare feet brushing the dew-covered grass, her beautiful hair falling loose about her shoulders. 'And so should I look,' she said, pulling Aurora towards her and hugging her affectionately. 'Aurora and I are very fortunate to have found you, Mr Buck Jones.'

He looked at her without speaking, for the truth of her words was shining in her face. A grin tugged at the corners of his lips, broadening and deepening until it reached his eyes, the dimples cleft in that familiar, smile.

CHAPTER
Thirty-One

On the way back to Eden, Esther regaled Buck with amusing chatter about her early life of ease and fun, and she was very amusing, an excellent mimic, and a shrewd judge of character. She had often been criticized for her indifference to the feelings of others, and her reckless lust for life, but she managed to keep him entertained all those long miles back to the farm.

She took him eagerly into her former life, conjuring it up in vivid detail, and he listened without a twinge of envy. She encouraged him to talk of his past with a voracity to know everything about him, once she had overcome his natural reticence to talk. Gradually he told her the difficulties and obstacles of his childhood, of the loneliness of being an only child of an actress who had a succession of rich and famous lovers, one of whom had been his unnamed father. His mother had refused to divulge his identity, and remained silent on the matter, taking her secret with her to her untimely grave at the age of twenty-seven.

She learned of how, after his mother's death, he had run away from the poorhouse to the army and had lived better than he had ever done in his whole life. She listened without a smile, admiring his lack of bitterness. And as she listened, she watched him, entranced. Moving closer as they rode, she felt his arm come about her and rested her head against his shoulder. He was teasing, smiling, but she had seen the flicker in the blue eyes, a hint of something she could not explain, when he talked of his past. He told her a little of the battles in which he had fought all over Europe, of the dead and dying lying in heaps on the battlefields, especially Waterloo. When he spoke of arriving in

Africa soon afterwards, his expression changed, his tone becoming lighter, more eager.

All the time she was so aware of him, of wanting to always be near him, to share everything with him, of herself, of her life. All about them was the sweep of hills and bush, a sky full of birds rising and wheeling in glittering formations against the puffs of cloud. Deep down, Esther was beginning to learn that there was a Buck that he kept to himself, a Buck of whom she knew nothing. She was realizing painfully that there was a part of him that escaped her, a part she could not reach no matter how hard she tried. And always, a small fear lurked in the back of her mind that this wonderful new happiness she had found was too good to be true.

At last they reached Eden. Esther looked around her and was determined to turn the farmhouse into a home and the farm itself into a showpiece. She voiced her disapproval of the men eating their meals in the kitchen, but on that subject Buck remained adamant that they continue the routine. He explained that as they resented her presence among them, being expelled from the kitchen during meals would only turn them against her completely. He stood to lose good men, except Pike, who had accepted her from the very beginning.

As time went by, Esther came to respect Buck's opinion. It was not long before she had the homestead running smoothly and efficiently. There were no problems in preparing the most tasty meals for the men, and soon there was no idleness among them. They would see her making fresh muslin curtains, polishing the new furniture to a superb gloss and creating a patch for a kitchen garden, where herbs and vegetables were planted. She had no time for idle chat and spared herself nothing in those first few weeks. She was never seen wearing her best apparel, but simple working clothes, her hair covered and hidden under a matron's cap. There was a new trim look to the cottage and the men's huts, the smell of delicious cooking forever filling the air.

In those weeks Eden was transformed into a home. It never occurred to her in all that time that observing her ease in managing a farm where she was the only woman, evoked Buck's admiration for her all the more. Life there was simple and rustic, the work was hard and the sense of danger, as everywhere in

Albany, more or less constant. But the laughter was more hearty and the atmosphere, cheerful and pleasant.

Buck's wagon approached the banks of the Fish River in the late afternoon of a particularly warm day near the end of summer. He had been requested rather suddenly by Major Dundas to parley with some of the Xhosa Chiefs concerning the unrest among them. He had taken his best Hottentot tracker, Oukiep, with him, intending to stop along the way for a spot of hunting.

It was the first time that he and Esther had been separated, and he had left her in a resentful mood, making last minute sauces, jams and preserves before the autumn.

The wagon wound through the dense edge of the forest beside the river coiling and looping through the valley, wide and slow. It began the narrow descent, then climbed up the steep euphorbia-covered hillside and rounded a steep incline which looked out on a wide panorama of the chain of the mighty Amatole Mountains, stretched across the valley.

It was at this moment that Esther, dressed in borrowed men's clothes, chose to appear from the rear of the wagon where she had cleverly concealed herself from the outset of the journey. Her red hair pushed completely under a low-brimmed hat, she stuck her head out of the open canvas flap and stared at her husband, sitting easily on the driver's seat, puffing away contentedly at his pipe.

'I knew you wouldn't miss me, you big liar! Sitting there, enjoying it all without a thought for your poor little wife struggling at home.'

Startled almost out of his wits, Buck swung round, taking the pipe from his mouth. Oukiep screeched with alarm, gesticulating in her direction and bringing the wagon to a halt.

'It's all right, Oukiep,' Buck said sharply, 'this is women all over — shock the heart out of you when you least expect it, by doing the darn'dest things.' He stared at his wife, his face set in hard, angry lines, as Oukiep, thinking better of getting involved in a domestic dispute, turned away and loped ahead beside the oxen, whipping the lead animal to make a start.

'And what do you think you're playing at, Esther, in that ridiculous garb in a territory not safe for women? Where is

Aurora? I would not put it past you to bring her along for the ride.' His face was stiff with indignation. He turned away as the oxen made the slow descent towards the river banks.

Not at all deterred, Esther climbed into the seat beside him. 'I knew if I asked to come, you would refuse without even thinking of it, so I was forced into a harmless deception. I was very cramped back there, having to hide until we reached the river. I knew that, once here, it would be too far from home for me to be returned forthwith — which would have been your intention.' A beguiling smile on her lips, she went on, 'I just couldn't live without you — and I couldn't bear to think of you out there alone, especially during the long, lonely nights.'

Her voice was sweet and whimsical with a deliberate Irish note in it which gave it a peculiar appeal. She smiled again, half-closed her eyes and studied him through her lashes. She was thinking how fine and infinitely attractive he was, and she did not need to tax her memory at all to recall the powerful physique that lay beneath the leather jacket and trousers. And now, there was that ice-blue glance and the angry little curl at the corner of his firm mouth.

'How could you do this, Esther — this childish escapade? What of our child? The men? There will be a devil of a commotion when they tumble to the fact that you have gone — downright irresponsible, that's what you are!' His voice was suddenly defensive. He glanced across at her. Her figure, in the frontier-man's clothing, looked almost as athletic as his own.

'Oh pooh to the men! They know where I am — I told them. True, they were not happy about it, but there was nothing they could do to stop me. Pike promised to look after Aurora, under some duress, I admit. But, when all is said and done, if there's one man I trust, second to you, it's Pike. The men seem to have this inexplicable idea that you will tan their hides, or worse, if they do anything to displease you. Not a very nice reputation to have, is it? Besides I can cook for you much better than Oukiep, and I can provide certain comforts you wouldn't have otherwise.' She tried not to smile as she saw him giving way.

His vivid eyes met hers, and the same sudden gleam of laughter lurked in both. 'Whatever shall I do with you, Mrs Jones? You really are overdue for a good spanking,' he said,

324

surrendering with a sigh, and placing an arm around her shoulders as they reached smoother ground. 'But you will have to behave, and obey my every command.' He paused, considering, 'You do not look too bad in that get-up after all, but from now on you will be my nephew. You will not be comfortably accepted to the Xhosas if they know you are a woman — and you may have to share the quarters of their wives and hundreds of squalling brats.'

'I cannot think of anything worse. It's the nights with you I've been counting on. If I am to be your nephew you had better take your arm from my shoulder. It is not seemly for uncles to be too familiar with their male kinsmen. At night, of course, that will be another matter altogether.' She laughed, enveloping him in the warm light of her teasing eyes.

'Never having had an uncle, I take your word for it — so be it, my dear.' Without another word he took his arm away, but from under his well-defined brows his eyes gave her a silent caress, a wicked intimate knowledge of what was between them.

They halted on the banks of the river at Lower Kaffir Drift. Esther dismounted, walking carefully to the edge of the water, pouring sweat. The oxen slapped away festoons of flies with their tails. The huge footprints of a herd of elephants were everywhere, obliterating every other spoor. In the swampy spots on the bank the evidence of the great beasts lay where they had rolled joyously in the ooze and mud.

Her eyes followed the line of bushes beside the river on the other side, riddled with ancient animal trails and Xhosa tracks. The trees, centuries old and trailing lianas, arched high above the mossy floor, oblique shafts of light penetrating here and there. She wrinkled her nose with sudden excitement. Her mind, now freed of its depression at the thought of being apart from Buck, focussed on the days ahead with him in the world of forbidden experiences and adventures of men.

'We'll camp not far from here tonight,' Buck said, coming up beside her. 'I know a good spot where these great mammoth beasts will not trouble us, and besides they have long moved on their way.'

The trail to the place Buck had chosen for the night was dim, covered with broken patches of light and shadow. Twisted cords

325

of lianas hung in heavy webs in the shadows, whence frightened, chattering birds fled at their approach. Quite suddenly they broke through the trees into another world where the river widened into a secluded pool, quiet and deep with the brilliant sparkle of sun glinting and shifting on its surface, the dull drone of insects breaking the silence all around them.

Oukiep set about making camp, leaving Buck and Esther to themselves. Beyond the pool, the water tumbled away down a moss-bearded cluster of rocks to the valley floor further below. In the clear light, small fish leapt every now and then, from the depths of the water.

'It seems as if it has been untouched since the beginning of time,' Esther breathed, staring around her. 'Oh Buck, this is a magic place where one could almost believe spirits or fairy-people dwell.'

'Irish blarney, dear heart?' Buck said serenely, smiling at her. 'You are getting carried away — talking of spirits and fairy creatures and such. You come from the most wild and fanciful race on God's earth, for sure.' The tenderness in his eyes belied the mockery in his voice.

Hands on her hips, she surveyed him, 'You can take that all back, you unimaginative Englishman! All this beauty, all this timelessness is lost on you, I can see that! But, in my present mood, I will not take back one word — you can say what you like.'

His blue eyes sparkled as he turned to her, smiling. He held up a hand. 'Whoa there, let's call a truce. I would much rather be friends in this magic place where the only spirits that can disturb us are the spirits of Xhosa ancestors.'

Esther's eyes widened in sudden horror. 'That is not true! This spot is too — beautiful, untouched for that.' She looked around with mild terror.

Buck laughed and shook his head. 'You're quite safe — they're quite harmless, I assure you. Anyway, we can frighten them away with a wild, Irish scream.' He pulled a sudden, unexpected face at her.

Seeing his amusing expression, she laughed.

'Come,' he said, 'let's take to the waters my dear, and enjoy its wicked delights.'

326

She hesitated. 'Swim here — without clothes? What about Oukiep?'

He chuckled, pulling her towards him. 'Oukiep will keep to himself. He is well aware of the goings on between men and their wives, for he has known at least three himself. Come — before the last of the light leaves us.'

He led her to the water's edge and stripped, throwing his clothes into an unceremonious bundle on the earth, enjoying the freedom of naked flesh. Strolling to the deepest part of the pool, he dived from the cluster of rocks above it. Surfacing almost immediately, he called to her to join him, droplets of gleaming water clinging to his brown curls, the water swirling about him in broken ripples. 'Come now, Mrs Jones, you've chosen to enter a man's world, so dare to experience it in all its dangers. If you were my nephew, I'd not hesitate to throw you in.'

She shook out her long coat, smiling at him, and kicked off her boots. Unbuttoning the coat and shirt, she allowed them to slip gracefully down the length of her body, to her feet. Excitement leapt into his eyes as he watched her, his eyes falling on the smooth roundness of her breasts, the gleaming shoulders, the provocative curve of her hips.

'You are without doubt the most glorious woman I have ever seen,' he called, as with easy grace she undid the trousers, stepping from them, the creamy flesh exposed now in vibrant splendour.

The low, admiring tone of his voice brought instant radiance to her face, as she said, 'As you keep telling me so often I shall soon get to believe it.'

Walking to the water's edge, she stepped carefully over the damp, mossy ground, the scent of bruised grass and soft, black leaf mould, strong. She lowered herself into the water, its delicious chill shocking her skin, the feel of dark, silky weeds caressing her feet. The tumbled mass of her hair made a rich, red halo within which her face glowed like a pale, exotic flower. Her long lashes threw soft shadows on cheeks flushed with warmth and her moist lips were slightly parted as though she awaited a kiss. When she stopped moving, the water felt colder. A shiver ran through her as Buck waded towards her through the weeds and reached for her.

327

'The hell with the swim,' he said. 'It's you I want, without any more delay.'

She laughed as she looked up into the blazing, blue eyes, allowing him to lift her up and carry her soaking wet from the water on to the damp, moss-covered bank, where young fern unfurled its lace fronds. The greenish light from the trees filtered down on them as he pulled her to him, and she felt the growing tension in his wet body.

'This is indeed one of the unexpected rewards of bringing my wife to Xhosaland.' His voice deepened as she melted completely into his embrace and he played her body like a delicate and beautiful, musical instrument. She writhed and groaned under his touch, revelling in her pleasure and his, until at last he took her, passionately and completely, enfolding her in his flesh, and all but tipping them both back into the pool. They made love again and still were not sated, their bodies seeming to have been created to fit close for ever.

In the deep silence that fell over the bush under the vast blanket of darkening, velvet sky, Esther felt the strength and security of his presence. She moved up and lay against Buck's broad chest, listening to the steady beating of his heart, her damp, red hair streaming over his shoulders. It took a real man to make love, she acknowledged, and Buck had become the fulfilment she would never have known existed if she had not taken the big step of running away from Dwyers' Cross to marry him. Her silent thoughts filtered back over the past. She was sad about the break with her father and uncle but she regretted nothing. By letting go of the preconceived notion of the kind of person she 'should marry', of 'the suitable marriage', she had freed herself to enjoy life to the full. She did not need all the trappings of high society life, all its privileges, to fulfil herself. After all, who really wanted it all without love? All the fulfilment she wanted, lay here, right beside her, and she prayed that it would last forever.

It was then, as she moved to lie on her back, that she saw the face. It was half in shadow in the gloom of a tree suspended above them, the outline lit by an edge of light from the last sun's rays. It was a face she had never seen before, malevolent, wild, hostile.

328

She sat up and screamed. Buck woke up in a frenzy of fright, reaching immediately for his gun lying beside him. 'What is it, Esther? You've frightened the wits of half the Ceded Territory by now.'

A hand to her face, she cowered on the ground, trying to cover her nakedness with her clothes, and pointed to the tree. 'There — there was a face. Someone was staring at us. It was terrible, the most horrible thing I've seen.'

Buck was on his feet in a trice, running up to the tree. For a moment she lost him in the gloom as she hastily pulled on her trousers. He walked back slowly some minutes later, a puzzled expression on his face.

'Esther — are you sure you saw a face?'

Dumbly she nodded, shaking like a leaf. She found her voice at last, 'Yes — it was in that tree, I swear it — just — just staring at us.'

He knelt down beside her, taking her head in his hands. 'Sweetheart, there was no one there. There are no tracks, no trace of anyone. Besides, no one comes here, there is no reason why they should. I know, I have stayed here many times, undisturbed.' He held her against him. 'I think you were mistaken. It was all that talk of spirits that did it.'

She pulled away from him. 'I was not mistaken — I know what I saw — it was there I tell you, there, in that branch.'

He sighed. 'Esther, take hold of yourself. It was the shadows playing tricks on you. There's no way anyone could have got up there. It's too high, infested with monkey-ropes, and snarled up with other trees.'

'Then how could you see there were no tracks, no evidence?' she pressed him, hugging her arms around the top part of her body.

'Because there is clear ground beneath the tree before it becomes jungle growth above with the other trees. Satisfied?'

She shook her head violently, gathering the rest of her clothes as she rose from the ground. 'I will never be satisfied, I know what I saw.' She looked about her. Imperceptibly, with the setting of the sun, the place that had at first appeared so magical, so beautiful to her, was now hostile and frightening, the shadows deeper in the trees, the pool menacingly still and dark. 'I must get away. I'm going to the wagon. You can stay here if you wish,' she called as she turned and started to run through the trees.

'Hey!' His laughing voice followed her as she found the trail. 'Come back here — you mad wench. Do you want all of the Ceded Territory to see you half naked? You've forgotten your shirt.'

Annoyed, she looked down, and sure enough, her coat was flapping open to expose her breasts. Crossly, she pulled the coat tightly about her.

'You bring it, if it's that important to you!' she yelled back, her feet flying even faster to the safety and refuge of the wagon, beside the comforting warmth of the campfire winking as darkness fell.

The hills of Xhosaland were high. They passed through rock-strewn pastures with steep rock faces rising beside them. The valley of the Keiskamma River sloped upwards for some way, and a path ran rough and stony through the bush. Almost at its end, in a clearing, stood the village of old chieftain Mazwi and his people. He was one of the strongest minor chiefs of the Ama-Xhosa, and one of Buck's old friends.

Esther turned quickly in the warm sunshine, looking at Buck sitting opposite the old chief, conversing in the Xhosa tongue which she did not understand. She watched the wiry, wizened old man, his dark inscrutable eyes downcast for the moment, as he dipped his long, gnarled fingers into a basket of boiled beef, urging her and Buck to do the same. Throwing back the magnificent kaross of leopard skin from the thin, hunched shoulders, he gestured to the communal pot of sorghum beer, shaking his woolly cap of white hair in answer to something Buck had said.

His was an interesting and ageless face, the features shrivelled but unusually dignified. Esther had heard all about him, but up until now, she had never met him. It was strange, she thought, that there was so much trouble between his people and hers, and yet, here she was being entertained as Buck's nephew, and Buck was talking to him in a friendly, easy way.

Mazwi's first wife, a quiet, dark shadow of a woman, flitted in and out of his large hut, overseeing the domestic routine. Esther watched her move away, swinging her hips, her buttocks swaying rhythmically from side to side. She had been shocked to learn from Buck that Mazwi had over fifteen wives, his privilege as chief, but causing its problems in the power struggle between the sons of two of them, the notorious Lungelo and his half-brother Nyezi, the younger, but rightful heir.

It amused Buck that the privilege of many wives was a custom the old man would never give up, not even with all the pressure of the white missionaries.

Mazwi's youngest wife, Nomexhagwane, a little older than his twenty-two-year-old son, Nyezi, walked past. She had a clay pot balanced on her head and was holding the hand of her daughter, a child of Aurora's age, her baby strapped straddle-legged across her back. Shapely, bare, dark breasts were adorned with pretty ornaments and beadwork. She saw Mazwi lift his head, a smile of pride lighting his face as his eyes followed her proud, beautiful head, looking neither left nor right. He chuckled and made some remark to Buck, who smiled with amusement.

Esther looked away and studied the fowls pecking the centres from kaffir melons on the ground. Another bare-breasted woman bearing faggots of firewood on her head bent and placed them over the cowdung fires, and in the distance came the lowing of milch cows.

Esther found that she was thoroughly enjoying having Buck to herself without interference from anyone, especially the men. She saw him in a myriad of new lights, ever surprised at his intelligent grasp of situations and the power and force of his personality which never ceased to impress each chieftain they had met.

On this trip she had learned far more about the tribesmen than she had heretofore known. She had learned that the Ama-Xhosa feared the numbers of white men and the way their lands were being used for hunting. Mistrust and suspicion were deeply rooted in them, between brothers, fathers and sons. Until that ended, they would never have real unity among themselves and make peace with the white man, and in Buck's opinion, until that time, they would never be safe from the whites, or the whites from them.

Finally Buck rose, smiling, a new kind of pride in his eyes as they fell on Esther waiting for him in the sunshine. As they walked away together, Buck palmed his sweating hair, replacing the

331

low-brimmed, white hat on his head.

She peered at him. 'And so — was it promising, that long talk between you and the old chieftan?'

He shrugged. 'He's a wise old devil — gives no promises about his people he knows they cannot keep. But then, neither do I. Perhaps there is still a chance that our two races can come to understand each other. I will never give up trying until that day dawns.'

Some evenings later they were entertained in the kraal of Chief Gaika, acknowledged by the whites as the paramount chief of all the Xhosa clans. All his sub-chiefs, including Mazwi, were present and sat with Esther and Buck.

Gaika, a tall, still goodlooking and well-built man, wearing a band of white and black beads around his head and a cloak of leopard skin across his shoulders, imbibed freely of the sorghum beer provided.

As Esther watched, Gaika sprang forward as lithely and sinuously as a leopard, pausing for a single moment before he flung himself into the front row of dancing men, whereupon he led the dance, raising his voice lustily above the rest, becoming more and more uninhibited as the drink took effect. The dance rose to a climax, the air ringing with the elemental and brutal rhythm of the warriors managing to convey deep menace beneath the strong harmony of their voices, their bodies moving to and fro with frenzied thrusts as if in battle. Nearer and nearer they came to the spot where the guests sat, stamping iron-hard calves and hardened feet, thousands of black eyes shining, their powerful, muscled bodies gleaming with sweat.

Buck remained perfectly still, his face impassive, and his eyes fixed on the fierce motions of the dance. Esther caught sight of Nyezi and she watched the handsome, black face smiling as he jested with friends, the fine strong physique outlined in the flickering firelight. Old Mazwi sat behind him, sucking at his long pipe, an enigmatic expression in his dark, sunken eyes.

Esther tried not to draw back, a sudden fear coming to her as the dance grew with savage intensity. She and Buck were two whites alone, surrounded by thousands of battle-scarred warriors. What could they do, she wondered, if they got it in their heads to fall upon them and murder them? She felt numb, the urge to run miles away from this sweat-filled, deafening place, rose up inside her. It took her all her time to control her sudden, obsessive impulse. It struck her with full force that these people had killed Garnet, James Coffee and others. It was they who had caused so much suffering at Dwyers' Cross, and yet, Buck talked with them as with old friends.

She could scarcely believe the reality of the scene before her, the pagan glare of the crackling fire, the black men leaping up and down in motions of a tribal dance, and the bent old figure of Mazwi — all enemies of the men of Dwyers' Cross.

The conflict deepened in her between loyalty to her kinsmen and their opposition to the tribesmen, and her respect and love for her husband who believed in the acceptance of them. It struck her forcibly that the aims of her father and her husband were for the same growth and development of their land, for Buck was now as much a landowner as her father, and they both wanted, above all, peace for Albany, but that was where the similarity ended. They both had totally incompatible ideas as to the achievement of that peace.

Buck wanted closer understanding with the chiefs, a system of treaties to be set up between them and the colony that they could understand. He had explained to her that the black man's concept of the ownership of land and that of the whites differed fundamentally, and this had to be taken into account. Whereas the white man's concept of personal ownership was based on contracts and private monopoly, the black man considered the people on the land more important than the land itself, that everyone living on the chief's 'land' immediately had access to the grazing and water rights by giving the chief a gift. They did not 'own' the land as such. It was there for the use of the whole tribe.

Buck was convinced that, in the long term, no military victory for the whites against the Xhosa was finally possible in this kind of country with its different racial groups. They were only staving off their inevitable inclusion into the colony. Her father, on the other hand, believed that frontier defence had to be strengthened at all costs, to keep the tribesmen out, backed by a system of strict military patrols and reprisal measures.

Who was right, she could not tell. And where in all this conflict, did she now stand? Although she loved and respected

Buck, did she stand with her father and uncle on this point, despite the fact that she was emotionally and bitterly estranged from them. Or did she stand with Buck?

Only time would tell, she sighed to herself, pulling the Phoenix Palm hat lower over her eyes as Gaika motioned the dance to end, urging his guests to eat from the wooden bowls of roasted meat brought before them.

After a long and exhausting first day on the journey back they spent the night with a nomadic Boer and his family beside the banks of the Tyumie River. Overwhelmed by the hospitality of the Boer in the lonely mountain country, where he had encroached into the Ceded Territory, they were taken into his hovel, made from a few poles and reeds and shared by his thirty dogs. After a night on mats of rushes lying on the floor, covered by blankets of tanned, woolly lambskin, they took their leave in the pre-dawn light and advanced southwards and home.

Near the banks of the Fish River at sunset, a wonderful sight met their eyes. Large herds of graceful springbok covered the plain beyond. As the wagon started to approach the river, the animals bounded off on either side, flitting away into the long waist-high grass. It was there that they decided to make camp for the night.

A most productive hunt followed and that night they roasted a small buck. The wagon was laden with meat, and they sat, companionably, beside the fire, letting the darkness and the night move around them. They talked long and low before retiring to sleep in the wagon, huddled together under Buck's greatcoat, redolent of the smells of warm earth and decaying leaf-mould.

A flame burst through the sky as the sun rose next morning. Suddenly a horrendous trumpeting was heard from the banks of the river.

Buck, still shirtless and bare-footed, grabbed his heavy double-barrelled elephant gun. His eyes travelled swiftly from the giant umbrella-shaped mimosa standing in the centre of the camp, festooned with wet buffalo hides, to the surrounding bush bristling with snakes, porcupines, wild cats and leopards, and beyond, where the herds of buck grazed on the plain.

The shrieking started again. 'It's Oukiep!' he said as Esther joined him. 'And it sounds as if he's been cornered by an elephant at the river. Stay here, Esther — I'm going to him.' He turned and ran as silently and stealthily as a Red Indian, down the trail forking and twisting through the bush.

Unable to hold herself back, Esther pulled a musket from the wagon and followed him, the hair streaming about her face under her hastily-pulled-on hat. Her mouth went dry and suddenly the beauty and exhilaration of the land about her became sinister and dark, ominously alive and bristling with danger.

Swiftly she followed Buck making his way towards the bushes skirting the river bank. There was an almost startling contrast between the luminous light over the river and along the edge of the tangled, bushy undergrowth, and the seemingly impenetrable darkness of the jungle growth which screened and, in some parts, completely hid the river banks, here and there forming natural bridges where the trees and bushes were so bent and intertwined.

'Esther — go back!' Buck hissed urgently, suddenly aware of her presence behind him, his eyes never leaving the river bank. 'It's too dangerous for you out here.'

'No,' she whispered, moving up closer behind him. 'I'm here now and I'm not leaving.'

Before Buck could answer, the great, grey elephant cow on the bank raised its trunk in their direction. Buck rammed the charge home, accompanied by its wad of oil rag, as the animal suddenly lowered its head and charged towards Oukiep, not more than two hundred yards away from it.

Esther tried to calm herself as the massive beast crashed through the undergrowth chasing the Hottentot, broken twigs, small stones and flattened leaves flying in all direction. Two elephant calves stood at the water's edge, their heads turned towards the cow.

It was gaining ground fast, when suddenly Oukiep swerved at right angles, obviously hoping to reach the rocks on the other side of the river bank. By this time the two calves had joined the cow, flanking her as they trumpted and bellowed for the kill.

Esther crept in the direction of where Buck had taken a stand near some rocks. She rammed her charge home, feeling safer with a loaded gun though without the faintest idea of what she would do, should the necessity arise.

Buck dared not get any closer as he had not had the time to take the usual precaution of stripping and smearing himself with elephant dung, in order to get closer to the beasts. He could usually get thirty yards from the animal for a clear shot, but today it was a different story. He was forced to take cover behind the rocks and creep up on them unseen. Oukiep rushed for the water and the safety of the rocks, striving to keep the distance between himself and his three, noisy pursuers. The trumpeting grew to such a pitch that he turned around to see the beasts bearing down on him. Esther could see him trying to hold his gun steady and cocking it, aiming at the head of the large cow. To her rising dismay, she thought that his powder was damp, because the gun would not fire. Then she saw him taking it to his shoulder, where it suddenly went off, the shot merely grazing the side of the advancing elephant's head.

The rapid progress of the animal was checked for one hopeful instant, then it rushed forward in maddened fury. Oukiep took a step forward and fell, his legs buckling, thrown to his knees in the path of the elephant.

Esther's mind was numb with shock as, with the single tusk it possessed, the cow made a sharp thrust at Oukiep, missing him narrowly by inches. With the unerring instinct of the soldier, Buck, holding his heavy elephant gun, ran towards another group of large rocks overlooking the water. He crouched behind the largest one, pulling himself slowly up until he had a good view of the banks below.

In cold horror, Esther saw Oukiep's body beneath the massive feet of the great, grey cow. He was lying flat on his back, moving his arms and legs back and forth in a painful effort to twist away from the animal as it trumpeted and bellowed into the air. She ran quickly forward to join Buck as he took aim and fired at the furious beast. Without thinking, Esther aimed at the same time, her throat drier than a desert. The scattered burst of fire hit the animal squarely in the shoulder with such force that it was knocked sideways and away from Oukiep giving him a last cuff with its hind feet as it fell. The other two elephants, obviously very young, trumpeted wildly, lifting their trunks, and seeming bewildered, retreated. They trumpeted once more before turning and disappearing into the bush, much to Esther's relief.

For a moment all was still. As Esther waited with indrawn breath, her eyes never leaving the body on the ground, Buck turned to her, and she heard him saying hoarsely, 'Well, I'll be damned — you actually helped me to shoot an elephant, Mrs Jones!' He gave an involuntary chuckle, his eyes a mixture of scolding and approval. 'You really are the darnedest wench both sides of the border.'

She did not answer at once, staring wide-eyed at Oukiep's body, still lying on the sand. Then she murmured as if to herself. 'Thank the Lord — he's alive. Buck, he's alive, I saw him move.'

With a great wave of relief, they watched him slowly rise to his feet, picking up his gun as he staggered towards them.

'He's about the pluckiest little fellow I've met,' Buck observed, as they watched the two departing elephants, wondering if there would be any more trouble. The largest turned around as it reached the edge of the bushes. Buck waited, his gun already reloaded and in the aiming position. They watched in tense silence as the beast hesitated, then after some moments it disappeared, trumpeting into the trees, accompanied by the other calf and the sharp crackling of branches and undergrowth in its path.

'Come, Esther — we're taking Oukiep back to camp. He's badly bruised and all but done for.'

Slinging the strap of his heavy gun about his shoulders, he carefully lifted the small Hottentot as he would a baby, and slowly carried him back to camp, preceded by Esther pulling back offending branches in their way.

Fortunately Buck had a certain rudimentary medical knowledge, picked up during his years in the bush, and the wounds were treated and bandaged. Once Oukiep was settled and lying fairly comfortably in the wagon, Buck pulled out a flask of brandy and handed it to Esther, saying, 'Oukiep will soon mend, he's a strong little fellow. Try this, sweetheart — it's the best medicine in the world.'

With relief she took a few large gulps, and wiped her mouth with her sleeve. Buck took back the flask, cocking a questioning eye at her. 'And where did you learn to shoot that well? I had no notion that you could aim so straight.'

As she felt the fire of the golden liquid going down her throat, and curling warmly in her belly, Esther giggled shakily, 'And neither did I — no one is more surprised than me. Why, at Dwyers' Cross under Uncle Cady's tuition I never had to hit anything more real that a target made up of empty porter bottles.'

She was oblivious of everything as the brandy warmed her body and her mind, except the special smile that lit his eyes for her alone. He had been slowly drawing nearer to her, now he pulled her to him and, unresisting, she started to laugh and raised her lips to his.

'You see, I love you so much that I could not bear you chancing your life for Oukiep alone.'

The dimples played deeply about his cheeks as he murmured, 'I love you too, and when all is said and done you are one hell of a woman.'

She pressed herself against him, moulding every inch of her body to his. 'Then prove it to me now,' she breathed. 'Soon we will have to leave and it will be a long time before the night hours.'

In that glow of early morning, she felt like the conqueror, and all other thoughts were driven from her head.

CHAPTER
Thirty-Two

Esther returned to Eden a different woman. She had experienced and seen many things denied most of the women of her time, and slowly she began to gain knowledge previously hidden from her.

She became aware as the days slid into weeks, of the bond between the men on the farm as they came together to work and to talk and drink after dinner. She saw that it was an easy friendship which effectively shut out the loneliness and danger that lurked outside, and she no longer tried to keep them out of her life with Buck. Gradually she came to know them and the way in which they lived — the hazards and the problems they faced, wresting a living from the unrelenting earth. Her former critical distaste gave way to a more tolerant understanding.

It took Aurora a much shorter time to ingratiate herself with them, and especially with Buck, with whom she developed a very special father-daughter relationship. The child seemed to expand and develop more in his company, and Esther was pleased to accept the fact that the little girl had won a very special place in her husband's heart, a place she herself could never fill. She tried hard to switch off the odd twinge of jealousy as she watched them together, enjoying each other in a way she never could.

As the days passed, Esther became an increasingly beautiful woman. Her smile grew more warm, the sparkle in her eyes, deeper. She ceased being afraid of the larger centipedes, spiders and snakes, learning how to deal with them, and to make effective Hottentot poultices of special leaves for the very painful bite of the centipede. She learned how to keep the accounts and to help manage the affairs of the farm. Despite the hard work and the climate, she loved the life and the creating of a real home. She enjoyed making order out of the easy-going, masculine chaos, unexpectedly showing a formidable talent for organization.

The towns of Port Elizabeth, Bathurst, Salem, Sidbury and Somerset East grew steadily. A Commissioner-General for the Eastern Districts was appointed and Andries Stockenstrom was placed in charge of the officials in the area.

The Cape Corps was finally abolished to be replaced by the Cape Mounted Rifles, on a more economic basis. There was talk of freeing the Hottentots and other persons of colour, and allowing the Xhosas into the colony, to cut down the labour shortage. This step alarmed many settlers, but not Buck Jones, who employed a handful of tribesmen, among them young Mazinga who was to prove most loyal in the coming years.

At last the freedom of the Press was granted and the right to hold public meetings. The existing system of government was augmented by the Governor, assisted by an Advisory Council.

Buck was among the first of the colonists to buy wool-bearing, merino sheep from Australia from an enterprising settler, helping to start the wool trade in the Eastern Cape. The Boer farmers up until then had shown very little interest, preferring the long-haired, fat-tailed sheep, which was suitable for mutton only.

Buck had known nothing about sheep-rearing and breeding, but he proved quick and keen to learn. A few of the settlers had begun breeding from the Spanish merino for wool and it was from these men that he learned. The start was slow and uncertain, but his determination to succeed won out. He was the first to start burning the grass on the hills of his farm in rotation, to overcome the problems of the sour grass of the area which the sheep disliked. It was the first time in his life that he had ever owned land and stock, and with it came the sense of belonging, somewhere to lay down his roots. He ordered more merinos, four rams and six ewes, costing fifty pounds, and eagerly awaited their arrival as the wool factories in Yorkshire cried out for more wool.

Esther was fascinated by the processes of sheep breeding, which she learned alongside him, gleaning as much as she could at every opportunity. The crude cleaning processes of the sheep however, she left distastefully to the men. Subtly, the men, who were fed and looked after far better than ever in their lives before, began to accept and even like her, but Marsden Pike remained her devoted slave.

Before his marriage, Buck had earned himself one thousand pounds in hides and ivory from his last trading expedition, in the land beyond the colony owned by the black tyrant, Msilikazi, a former captain in Shaka's armies. He had run away to form his Matabele tribe, far to the north, and now there were rumours that he wanted to get to know the white man, Jones. He sent messengers to the missionary, Robert Moffat at Kuruman, in the land between the colony and his territory. Moffat, in turn, relayed the messages through his coloured servants, into the colony, where they finally reached Eden. So far, Buck had not ventured again into the far north, usually leaving in the winter so that he could return before the summer storms. As ivory was fetching incredibly high prices on the Ivory Floor in London and Eden was on its way to becoming one of the finest farms in the area, it was a tempting offer from the capricious black chief, who chose very selectively those he allowed to hunt on his lands.

At Sunfield Park, in the Blaaukranz Valley, Roydon Wilson heard these rumours. An idea took hold of him and a plan began to slowly form in his mind. When Buck Jones left again for the interior, and he was sure that the offer was too tempting to miss, he wanted to be there beside him. He remained silent, biding his time and divulging his plan to no one. But as the days of departure drew nearer, his plans began to take concrete form. He did not know that, silently, Esther was also making her plans to join her husband. She had found that one taste of the wilds beyond had not been enough — it had only whetted her appetite for more.

Esther threw another log into the flames of the kitchen fire and watched the sparks flying up the chimney. She leant back on her heels as the waves of morning sickness swept over her. It was late May and already cold, the short splash of autumn over for another year, to be replaced by the coral blush of the peach protea, the sugar bush and the red candelabra of the bitter aloes. I am carrying Buck's second child, she thought.

She rose, looking up quickly as the kitchen door flew open revealing Aurora, her cheeks rosy and bright from the crisp air outside. She was followed by Buck, spilling over with rugged, early-morning, good humour. After the usual clumsy hugs and kisses for her mother, Aurora was sent to play in the care of the new, gentle Mantatee maid, a beautiful girl of about fourteen, who adored the child with the black woman's outgoing love for children.

As the feeling of nausea subsided, Esther sat down at the table. Buck stood, legs astride, before the fireplace, cradling a large pewter mug of steaming coffee in his hands. His face looked older, tough, somewhat moody and hardened by experience, a perpetual air of cynical amusement emanating from him, which carried him, unscathed, throughmost circumstances. Yet she was learning fast that what sometimes was overlooked was the keen self-mockery beneath the surface.

Esther looked at him for a few seconds, then plunged right into her news.

He set down the mug, and reaching out, touched her cheek. He smiled warmly, the dimples deep and mischievous. 'You have made me very happy, Esther my love — that I am to be the father of my second child at the rather ancient age of thirty-five.' There was a slight pause. And then, 'Do you know, I never thought of ever being a father — or married to a lady of the gentry, for that matter.'

'Perhaps I should banish you from the bedchamber for a while,' she said teasingly, a delighted smile playing about her full, generous lips.

He grinned wickedly at her, patting her stomach. 'No door will be strong enough to keep me out.'

He sat down at the table and gazed at her. 'We will have to look after you, Mrs Jones, for you carry the rightful son and heir of all you see about you right now.'

Trying unsuccessfully to control the sudden acceleration of her heartbeat, Esther looked at him speculatively for a moment. 'May I suppose then, that your expedition up to the north, to that tyrant Msilikazi, is postponed — until after your child is born?'

His face was suddenly non-commital, his intensely blue eyes meeting hers steadily. 'Unfortunately, sweetheart, this expedition is of the utmost importance. It is not everyone who gets a chance to hunt on Msilikazi's lands. It could mean several thousands of pounds for us — for our children.'

342

Esther's eyes turned hard, beginning to glitter with the old fire, accentuating the strength of her jaw, the proud line of her head. He smiled as he saw in her his own indomitable will.

She gave him a withering look. 'It's nothing less than shameless for you to consider leaving me when there is a child on the way. You shall reconsider and not go, do you hear me?'

He raised one thick eyebrow. 'Never fear, I shall be back for the birth of our child. I have never to my knowledge missed an important event yet — though I own to have been a little late for our wedding.' He smiled ironically. 'Besides, you now belong to me as my lawful wedded wife, and it is you, dear one, who'll do as you are told.'

She shot him an angry glance. 'Your first duty, Buck Jones, is to me as your wife — especially now. You may think you own me, and in the eyes of the law it may be so — but that you never will. You shall not go.'

Propping his arm up on one elbow, his face supported on his hand, he looked at her with a crooked grin. 'And how do you intend to stop me? By taking away the wagon or the oxen, or both?' She saw a muscle in his jaw flex and unflex. Even in his teasing mood, she could sense the note of sudden constraint in him. 'Everything is planned and ready. I cannot put it off now, and that, my dear, is the end of the matter.'

His words and expression were as close to a reprimand as they had ever been with her. She was surprised to discover that he was very firmly and coolly keeping her in her place — a fact, which at any other time, she may even have enjoyed. But now she rose, her dark blue eyes flashing. 'You are as stubborn as an Irish mule! I do not want you to go, do you hear me?'

She had changed in an instant from a radiant wife. She was no longer shining and yielding. Now there was all the fierceness, the arrogance, the self-will of the Dwyers.

'Why is it, do you suppose, that when I am with child, my husband must go off to some black tribesman or other. You intend to leave me at this difficult time — but little do you care!'

Buck's face hardened. 'By God, woman, you try me hard. You prattle on without one idea of what you ask of me. My fortune, for what it is, has been built on such expeditions. Msilikazi is the most difficult, capricious man in all of known Africa. He has turned away hunters, missionaries and traders from the richest hunting grounds known to us. And this is the man who begs me to hunt on his lands for some mysterious reason I have yet to discover. He is handing me the fat of his land on a plate, when there are many in this colony starving and bankrupt.'

Esther stood up and looked at him. She realized that his charm, his wits and experience were weapons against which one as young as she had very little chance. His mind was made up. He would not change it for her. Their conversation now was a whole world of hard, angry words.

She heard his voice continue. 'I want you to understand, once and for all time, that this expedition can enrich us beyond everything we have so far achieved — it can give our children all the chances that should be their right.'

A faint smile edged his lips. 'Only the good die young, you know that — so you and I have a very long time together yet, my dear.'

She knew all these things as her temper uncoiled itself to blaze through their first quarrel, but she could not break him down. He was as determined as ever to start for the north in the next few weeks, at the beginning of winter. She closed her eyes, remembering her first months with him, recalling their brightness, the warmth and excitement ...

'You, Buck Jones, are the most unfeeling cur!' she yelled at him.

'You were always good at calling me names, but know your place now, woman!' He was crisp, cold, implacable.

'You are nothing but a baseborn bastard, that's all you are!'

'Don't you ever use that name with me again, do you hear? May I remind you that it was you who crawled to me on your hands and knees, begging me to take you in. And that name will never be used between us, ever!'

'You won't stop me!' she cried, her face flushed with rage. She stood before him, her head thrown back as she looked at him with taunting defiance. Her features were darkened and distorted by her anger as she tried to think of the things that would hurt him the most. She looked like some wild, beautiful animal as she threw her lawn cap on the table, leaving her face framed by the untamed tangle of red curls, her eyes narrowed to two slits.

He rose and took a step towards her, holding her strongly to him as she fought him off. She could feel the flexing of his shoulders, his muscles tautening, as he continued to hold her against the rough leather of his coat, until she became still, overpowered by his strength. Normally she would have melted into his arms, surrendering, but now she was too angry.

'Say that word again, Esther — I dare you to speak those words once more — you know that I fight fire with fire, my dear!'

He kissed her as she opened her mouth and continued until she began to respond urgently to him. She was suddenly aware that he was laughing, his brilliant blue eyes alight with fire. He thrust her from him, a reckless look about him, his rollicking laughter ringing to the rafters.

'That is how you must be treated, my beautiful tigress,' he said, throwing her a mocking glance. 'This way I know you will never leave me, and you will do as I say. Now I must get back to my sheep, who do not have to be broken in as hard as you, sweetheart.'

He strode through to the sitting-room and took down a musket and a priming powder-horn from the wall, then he walked back to the kitchen.

She stared after him. 'How dare you treat me like that!' she hissed, her hands planted firmly on her hips, the cloud of red hair framing her angry face.

'It's because I dare that you love me so much,' he laughed. 'And while I am at work in the sheep pens, I expect to see you hard at it preparing for the expedition that will bring many riches to you and our child.'

He opened the back door, letting in a cold gust of air, and closed it in one swift movement, leaving her to gaze at the closed door with a new storm brewing in her eyes. She checked the angry tears which threatened, her stomach tightening with another wave of nausea. A great empty silence fell about her, an emptiness she had not felt since leaving Dwyers' Cross. She so wanted to go with him, but she also wanted to have his child. And she dreaded being apart from him for months.

It was then that the pain of longing for her father and Uncle Cady, and Sam, began. She wished she could go to them and tell them about the baby, close the ugly chasm that was between them, gaping like some large, black hole. She missed them, and with Buck going away she knew she would miss them all the more, for without his presence there was nothing to shield her from that terrible void inside her.

Thirty-Three

Buck's plans were to be thwarted that winter, but not by intervention on Esther's part. Far more ominous shadows darkened the affairs of the settlement as May passed, then June, and Colonel Henry Somerset returned, reinstated as Commander of the new Cape Mounted Rifles.

During these two months the news spread that two marauding bands of Zulus were advancing on the colony, one taking the northern route and the other steadily progressing down the eastern seaboard. There were gruesome stories of the countryside laid to waste in their paths, of cattle captured and some of the Xhosa tribes ravaged and forced to flee into the bush. Thefts of settler stock by the Xhosas living near the border increased when the Xhosa crops, which usually ripened in March, were already harvested.

Esther was only concerned at that time with the child growing inside her. She was already bigger and heavier than she had ever been with Aurora at the same stage, and as a result, suffered far more fatigue and irritability. She still continued her daily chores, wasting nothing of the animals slaughtered by the men and brought to the kitchen. Fat was melted for cooking and for soap and candles, the good hides were used for clothes and the flesh for roasting.

The cold of the grey, wet winter spread itself like a blanket over the land by the end of June. The subdued murmur of men's voices in the sitting-room reached her as she cut vegetables at the kitchen table, wearing out a path from it to the fireplace, where the heavy iron stood heating and a bundle of clothes lay waiting to be ironed.

She had been immediately alarmed by the arrival of Captain Summers and Mr Josiah Wood, a prominent settler, well-known to her. They had been cloistered with Buck for an hour already. Sighing with exasperation, she wiped the skirt of her pinafore and reached for the large iron kettle. In the warm silence of the room, she drew forth a canister of tea. The atmosphere in the kitchen was aromatic with her herbs, stored in stoneware jars on the wide window-ledge behind her, the glow of the firelight falling on the neat row of shining copper pots ranged on the mantel.

Pursing her lips irritably, she wondered what was being discussed, as she poured the steaming water into a teapot and rattled the crockery on to a wooden tray, with a platter heaped with golden-brown johnny cakes. She felt tired, her back ached more than usual, as she untied her apron and carried the tray into the sitting-room.

The three men in the room — which was now more than a credit to her feminine eye, and in excellent taste — looked most grave. She stood on the threshold, immediately alert, the tray balanced in her hands.

Buck stood with his back to the fireplace, a clay pipe clamped in his mouth. He looked from one man to the other, with the slightest trace of impatience. The firelight flickered and winked in the open fireplace. The huge ivory tusks on the wall above him were thrown into bold relief, a fitting backdrop for his tall, robust stature and confident stance.

She stood very still, listening. Captain Summers waved a restless hand. 'Come now, Jones, as Commandant of a Burgher Command you can use all that valuable experience of the bush and the tribesmen that we need. It is highly necessary, dear fellow, to have a small band of settlers, as we haven't nearly enough regular men to defend the settlement against these Zulu marauders. You yourself stated that very fact.' He coughed, stroking his moustache. 'These young men are ignorant of bush warfare. They have never fought against any tribesmen before. Led by you they will quickly learn the tactics they must use.'

He leaned forward urgently, a deep frown creasing his face, his large moustache gleaming gold in the firelight. 'We have the Xhosas begging our help on one hand, and large tracts of undefended border on the other — tracts of land you know like the back of your hand. You know the Zulu, you understand the way they think. That is our only real hope, you see.'

Josiah Wood nodded. 'Mr Jones, these beardless youths need a strong, experienced leader such as yourself. Besides, old Mazwi's son, Nyezi, has agreed to fight alongside you with his warriors. He wants you to be there, he trusts you, and you speak their language.'

Esther froze. Her heart hammered wildly against her ribs. Her worst fears had become reality. They were asking Buck to lead a settler commando against the Zulu invaders.

She heard him say, 'I am well aware of the panic among the Xhosas. Heaven forbid that, in wild chaos, they get through our ineffective lines into the colony — that would be disastrous.'

His eyes now rested on Esther, who came forward. He stopped speaking and went to help her, taking the tray from her and placing it on the long, low, central table. As she bent to pour the tea, she knew that he was going to agree to lead the commando. Polite, courteous conversation broke out for a few minutes, as the men spoke to her, tactfully avoiding any mention of her kinsmen.

She remained long enough to pour the tea and hand round the cakes, her heavy body well concealed by her voluminous skirts as they fell from beneath her full breasts, a white fichu demurely gracing neck and shoulders. Then she left them, but remained within earshot of their resumed conversation.

She heard Captain Summers' voice. 'Every able-bodied man has been called out to man frontier posts, but we want you and your commando to march with the regular troops.'

Her heart sank as she heard Buck's answer. He did not mince his words. 'The way I see it, gentlemen, the die is cast. There is no turning back. We are forced to fight — myself along with the rest of you — for the safety of our womenfolk and children. However, may I stipulate that each man in my commando be given a pocketful of beads to buy cattle from the tribesmen for food, and that each be served with good, serviceable firearms.'

Esther sank against the wall, the core of fear hardening inside her. Would they never be left alone — to live peaceably together? Would the fear, the danger around them, never end? She had run away from it at Dwyers' Cross, but she could not run away from it here. It pursued her at every turn, twisting and coiling itself about her insiduously, a reptile of hate and destruction. She put up a hand to brush away the hair from her sweating forehead. Oh dear God, let it all stop before it is too late, and my children, our children, are old enough to be sucked inside its violent tentacles for ever.

She leant there, repulsed beyond anything she had yet experienced. It gripped her. Then something made her look down. Her small daughter was looking up at her, plucking her skirts. The blue eyes, so like Buck's, but without his lively expression, were puzzled in the face crowned by glossy brown ringlets. Esther drew a breath, visibly shaken, and knelt down, gathering the small bundle into her arms.

She could not let go, she could never give up the fight so long as there were those who needed her, depended on her. She had to go on, her will to survive strong, no matter what happened. Aurora, her unborn child, they depended on her — on Buck.

Oh, please let Buck be safe, she prayed silently, clinging to her daughter, her lips pressed against the silky, soft hair. Please bring him back safely to us. We need him. I'll do anything to make him safe.

Yet when he came into the kitchen after the men had left, her control broke down once more.

'Whatever will I do if anything happens to you?' she cried, her mind obsessed with Garnet's death. 'I've lost one husband — I just could not bear to lose you too.'

He saw the fear in her face. 'Hush, Esther — there's no need to panic in this way. I don't get killed that easy, sweetheart. Have you forgotten the Bama Pass?' The ghost of a smile lit his face; his expression softened slightly. 'I don't want to fight anymore, you know that. I have striven for peace, but still I must go to war to protect the lifeblood of the settlement, and to help those Xhosas who can one day be our allies.' His voice was soothing as it had been so often in the past, but she hated his words. 'We have to fight — so that our children will still be here to bring our ideas of peace to reality, for it will come, one day.'

She turned away, not daring to look at him, but forced herself to submit to his decision and his authority. He moved towards her. His hands were on her shoulders, turning her around to face him. His lips touched her cheek, his free hand moving about her waist possessively.

350

She wanted to argue with him, but his lips closed over hers as he gathered her up, and there was nothing more to say. She was aware again of the current of incredible vitality in him, of the nearness of his beloved, strong face, and the feel of the familiar hard lines of his body beneath his clothes.

'It's just so hard to say goodbye,' she said, near to tears as she clung to his strength, wishing she could be convinced of his indestructibility, that he had been blessed with some special gift of endurance.

He was looking at her intently and his magnetic eyes, his calm face, stirred her painfully. She knew that though one part of him was reluctant to leave her and the farm, the other part had sprung to life with the call of a challenge. She knew that once again the disciplined soldier in him had taken command, his energies bent towards the campaign in which he would lead thirty-one Dutch burghers and twelve raw, young Englishmen, his brother-in-law, Roydon Wilson, among them.

He laid his fingers over hers. She closed her eyes, her hand still gripping his, not letting him go.

'Just remember, my darling,' he whispered, his lips pressed into her hair. 'Just remember one thing, and brand it into your heart, for it is all you need to know in life — that once you have conquered your fears, you have conquered everything.'

She felt the strength of his muscles as he held her tightly, then released her. 'And now I must reluctantly leave you. I love you, and nothing will ever change that, believe me.'

He walked swiftly to the sitting-room where the guns hung on the wall. She looked after him, her face very pale, the vision of Garnet's departure seared into her brain. With trembling hands she pushed back her dishevelled hair, then let them fall helplessly to her sides. She only understood some of his parting words then, but they were to become more real and meaningful as time passed.

Early the following morning, as the heavy mist lay in tufts and rolls on the earth, Buck and the men cantered away into the damp, cold air, leaving Pike behind to watch over the farm.

Esther turned away. A fine rain was falling and the trees and bushes were dark and vaporous. She returned to the sitting-room, pulling a thick, wool shawl closely about her shoulders. Bending

351

to the fire to light a taper, she experienced another wave of melancholy.

She put the taper carefully to the candles on the mantel-shelf, her brows contracting in deep thought, and watched, with a sense of deep weariness, the wicks spring to life. Life seemed to her then, a long series of partings and reunions, and she had come to hate the partings more than anything else. Blowing softly on the burning taper she slowly turned, and stood staring out of the window towards the long avenue of mimosa trees, hidden in the depths of the misty rain.

For weeks Esther waited for news of Buck and the men. The only information that filtered through was that the army that had invaded the colony was not, after all, comprised of Zulus; but another tribe called the Amangwane or Fetcani. So it was with growing fear that she paced restlessly outside, in between her farm chores, which seemed to grow heavier all the time.

The sky was clear of thunderclouds and spring was in the air once more. It was warm and when the wind blew, the fragrance of mimosa hung in the air, cloying and sweet, mingled with the more pungent odours of aromatic shrub, damp, salt air and the scent of white-starred jasmine, falling in profusion over the low picket fence bordering the kitchen garden. The world was a riot of colour wherever the eye fell — the clouds of white quince sprays in the hedges, splashes of bright red pomegranate flowers, and the foamy pink of peach blossom. Esther, Pike and the servants had worked hard throughout the winter weeks, continuing the work the men had done in the summer, and Eden was surrounded by burgeoning gardens and fields under cultivation.

Esther, heavy with child, watched pensively as Pike studied the rough plans for the new outbuildings some way out in the fields. He could not read, but his understanding of plans was amazingly accurate. She carefully adjusted the outspread skirts of her full dress as she sat on a cushion in the wooden farm-cart.

Aurora played in her clumsy, babyish way, with Beauty, the young Mantatee maid. In the bush the rhythmic churring of the cicadas blotted out the quiet lowing and bleating of the cattle and sheep. High up on a hillside, Esther could see the herd of merinos grazing, and across the rolling fields, the green leaves of the trees made streams of rustling silver in the light, their branches a dazzling network against a cobalt blue sky. Closer at hand, the fields of wheat and Indian corn were set out in pale green lines separated by deep, dark furrows.

A small, irritated frown settled between Esther's finely drawn brows. She always seemed to be waiting for something these days. She looked out towards the fields where far above, an eagle swooped and soared, and a couple of plump quail alighted on a bush of wild honeysuckle nearer by. She loved Eden, with all its moods, its activities, its peace amidst the violence and the danger of her world. To her, this farm was Buck, who every day meant more and more to her. She sighed loudly.

'Won't be long now, ma'am,' Pike announced, coming up to the cart. He smiled at her ill-concealed impatience. 'I am that sorry, I am, to keep you waiting so long, but just think how pleased the Sergeant will be when he finds out how we worked these plans out for him, and now we're ready to go at his orders, ma'am.'

'If he does come back, Mr Pike — we've heard nothing since he left two months ago.' She looked at him for an instant, her blue eyes wide and restless. Then she smiled. 'Very well, Mr Pike, you finish the plans.'

'The Sergeant'll be back, ma'am, I feel it in me bones, I do. 'E'll be back and no mistake. I think we should go back now, ma'am — it's a sight too hot out 'ere in the sun. You should've stayed back there in the house.' He stared at her for a moment, seeing the shifting pain that came and went behind her eyes. His seamed, scarred face mirroring concern, he quickly called Beauty.

'If anything 'appens to you or the babe, ma'am, the Sergeant will 'ave me head for breakfast, on a plate just like John the Baptist, for sure,' he mumbled as he prepared the horse for the drive back.

Esther leaned back, feeling uncomfortably hot and weary as she waited for Aurora and Beauty, letting her eyes roam from hill to hill, taking in the fields bordered by blombos, and the open country further away, rolling out of sight, down to the sea. She remained deep in thought as Pike climbed up on to the driver's seat beside her, a look of anxiety on his face.

Slowly the cart started, Pike taking every care to drive as carefully as possible over the ruts, guiding the horse away from the deep gouges. Esther had refused to let him take over the complete management of the farm, taking added responsibility herself, despite his protests. She had relied on him to teach her all that she did not know, but the reins of mastership she took strongly into her own independent hands. It had given her an added interest, filled her mind and her time more satisfyingly in the long weeks of Buck's absence. And it had kept her from thinking too much about Dwyers' Cross. Eden had become a substitute for her longings and her loneliness. She had become progressively more troubled by the rift between her father, Uncle Cady and herself, and missed them more as time passed. The pain in her heart grew as large as the child she was carrying, because she knew that they would never see it.

She knew that her father's inflexible pride forbade him coming to see her, and that she could, if forced, humble herself and go to him, begging his forgiveness. But she also knew that he would never accept Buck or his child.

She had a quick mind, penetrating to the core of most matters, and a knack for quick decisions which had at first alarmed poor old Pike. She was clear in her intentions, which he felt was not seemly in a woman, but she was keen to learn, and he found that it was not unpleasant to teach her the ropes of farm management and sheep breeding, unladylike though it was.

She went to the market once a month with him, even though he was beside himself with anxiety about her condition. As he bargained, bought and sold, she sat beside the driver's box of the wagon, hiding her condition beneath her full skirts. She remained seated so that it never became obvious to any of the men present. Proud and resolute, she spoke to no one, but all the time she listened alertly to all that went on about her. She kept such dignity and aloofness that no one dared to sneer at her or laugh, even behind her back.

As the weeks passed, the discomfort of her pregnancy increased, reaching the stage when she could only lie on her side through the lonely nights, feeling the movements of the child growing within. And all the time, she watched and waited for the men who had left so many weeks before.

354

The only news of any great importance to break had been that Ordinance 50 had been passed, giving the Hottentots and other coloured persons their freedom. It was resented by most of the colonists, as it took away all the controls from their biggest source of labour, and allowed the coloureds to wander around the colony, squatting where they pleased.

Turning her head to the distant farmhouse, Esther saw clouds of dust, rising from the fields and converging on the walled farmyard. It took her a moment to realize what it was, then she sat up slowly.

'Mr Pike, the men are back, I know it. Look, look how the dust rises out there. It can only be them. Do hurry, go as quickly as you can,' she urged, holding fast to her seat as Pike shook his head dispairingly.

'Don't upset yourself, ma'am, it's not good for you. It could be anyone out there. Now you just calm down, I am not going any faster. I mean to get you to the house in one piece, and better for it.'

Esther was forced to curb her growing impatience as they made their sedate way back, her eyes forever turned in the direction of the dust clouds with mounting anticipation and dread.

Then she saw him coming up fast across the fields towards the cart, hooves throwing sand clods high across the fields. It was Buck. Esther held her breath, thinking she would faint from the relief.

They had reached a very rough patch and Pike slackened his reins. The ground was pitted and deeply rutted, the cart jolted and swayed dangerously. Then he saw Buck. With much creaking, he stopped the cart and Esther watched Aurora climb clumsily out, her small slippered feet stumbling unsteadily across the grass, cotton skirts and dainty, cambric pantoffles bobbing up and down with her slow, irregular progress. Buck stopped for a brief instant to pick her up.

Esther did not move or speak as he dismounted and walked towards the cart, the little girl beside him. He had a bundle strapped to his back. She looked at this man who had held her heart for so long, her eyes suddenly misting over. Despite his unshaven appearance, the dust and grime, he was hers, with that air of distinction in his face and bearing which always set him apart from all other men and which never failed to affect her. Her mind and body filled with the sweetness of her love for him as he stopped and looked at her, his face crinkling.

He reached out for one of her hands, raised it to his mouth and kissed the rough palm. Neither of them spoke as he put his arms about her, drawing her gently to him.

Pike puckered his eyes in his deeply corrugated face and motioned Beauty out of the cart, then they tactfully melted away in the direction of the farmhouse, leaving Mazinga to bring back Buck's horse.

As Buck kissed her and she felt his arms close about her, the days and weeks of loneliness, of fear, of longing and separation were forgotten. They were broken apart by Aurora's unintelligible babbling at being left out. Buck laughed as they drew apart to let her come between them.

'I have another baby for you both,' he said, unstrapping the bundle from his shoulders. He lifted it down and gently knelt on the grass, holding the bundle on his knee.

Esther and Aurora looked down and saw a small, black face with the largest, softest, black eyes they had ever seen. A head of short, woolly, black hair peeped from the cloth tightly bound around it.

Esther frowned. 'And what do we have here?'

Aurora's bland, vacant eyes stared at this new arrival, then she clapped her chubby hands awkwardly together with acceptance. Buck gave a husky chuckle, giving Esther a penetrating glance.

'We've called this little fellow Moses because we found 'im hidden in an ant-bear hole on our return from the Umtata River in Xhosaland. He was crying his tiny lungs out, and we didn't have the stomach to leave 'im to the mercy of the scavengers of the bush. It was obvious he'd been left by his mother who had fled or been killed by our troops.' He grinned affectionately. 'There was some fight about who should take 'im home. I just beat Roydon Wilson by the weight of my authority as Commandant. It caused much disappointment among all of 'em, I can tell you.'

Esther gave him a look of displeasure, showing clearly the deep, translucent lustre of her eyes, brilliant now with suppressed emotion which he chose to ignore.

'And who, may I ask, is going to feed him? He cannot be more than three months old by the look of him.'

She gazed at Buck as his face took on a new look in the sunlight enveloping them both. She saw the crow's feet fanning out from his startling blue eyes, the thick, brown lashes, the strong nose and the brown beard hiding the strong jaw. The sudden quizzical look he sent her threw her into momentary confusion, the slightest hint of impatience in his eyes accentuating the weariness about him.

'Oh, come now, Esther, you cannot turn this defenceless mite out into the bush. Besides young Beauty can help look after him — she loves children. I feel sure there'll be one among the servants to take pity on him.'

He rose to his feet, looking down at her. A smile just shadowed the tanned skin of his face, hiding the strange sadness that flashed into his eyes. 'Is it because this is a child of our so-called enemy, Esther? Is that why you cannot find the heart to take him in?'

His eyes suddenly burned into hers, until she forced herself to look away. Dismay at the full realization of his words robbed her of speech. She drew herself up, making a blind, confused gesture. 'You could have been killed by such a savage, you know that — it's almost like condoning such wrongs to take a child of theirs and raise him.'

She fell silent as she watched him place the baby carefully in the cart, then he leaned towards her and lifted her hand.

'This child is helpless, sweetheart — he has not asked to be abandoned. And I know full well what abandonment means, believe me, though I was already eleven when I lost my only parent, and could fend for myself. He — he has not tools for his survival yet. Is there no pity to be found in your usually generous heart?'

Unable to resist him, she smiled. 'I love you, you big opportunist, and that is why I will still find some room in my heart for your baby Moses, even though he is from the enemy, and I feared for your life at the hands of his people every waking hour of the past days, and most of the nights. Beauty will be asked to give him a home, even though she is not of his tribe.'

The firm mouth before her creased into that wonderful smile. She had been so aware of his disappointment in her that she had almost forgotten the effect of his dazzling smile, reaching his eyes like the sun creeping over sombre hills. It transported her for the moment to a level of joy almost too painful to bear. He gave her a slow and intimate look, causing a sharp thrill to run along her nerves, when suddenly she gave a cry of anguish, clutching her belly, as a vicious pain streaked through her body. For a moment she could not breathe.

'What is it, Esther? Is it the child?' Buck demanded with intense concern, taking command of the situation immediately.

She nodded weakly as the spasm reached its height and then very slowly eased away, leaving her trembling with relief. 'It is the child — it seems too early yet, but I know too well the signs.'

Without another word he climbed up beside her, with Aurora in his arms, and started the cart. Then he urged the horse on with all swiftness, never stopping once until they reached the yard.

CHAPTER
Thirty-Four

Esther lay back on the pillows of her bed, a full three days later, the mother of lusty twin boys, born three weeks before their time. Deep shadows lay under her eyes, but the eyes themselves were brilliant.

It had been a long and exhausting labour in which she had, as with the first time, wanted to die but also to live, to scream and yet to remain courageously silent. Now it was over, and little Adam and Guybon lay sleeping in the one large cot beside the bed until another could be made.

There was a warm light from the drawn-back curtains and the faint, far-off murmur of voices drifted from behind the closed kitchen-door. She looked down at the red-golden-headed babies, and then at Elizabeth Rowlands who stood before her, a tray of steaming tea in her hands. She had arrived the day before and had wasted no time in taking over the responsibility of the house. She was busy, efficient with no fuss, which suited everyone admirably.

'Trust you and Buck to produce two babies at once, Esther — nothing done by halves. Seems as if you've now got your family,' she said, smiling as she put the tray beside the bed. 'Just think of it — two heirs to the Jones fortune, not one. And Buck is so full of pride, he's fit to burst.'

She sat down on the bed, a wisp of pale hair escaping from the blue housescarf tied about her head. 'He was so worried about you, my dear, it took Higgins and that great bear of a Parker to hold him back during the birthing, when he wanted to break into the room, saying he could bring the child into this world quicker than the midwife. There was such a to-do, you never saw. And then, when he heard there was another baby, it's a wonder he never fainted away on the spot. I swear I've never seen that man so pale. And all the time it was you he was going on about, so anxious he was that you were suffering so. I've never seen him like that, ever.'

She smiled and patted Esther's hand. 'I am that happy for you, my dear, and for him. Buck has that security, that anchor he's needed all his life, in you and his children.'

Esther nodded and tried to smile as for a long moment a shadow stole across her mind. She tried to brush away the deep sadness sweeping over her as she thought of her father. He would never see her children, his grandsons, acknowledge them, love them. And they were everything he had ever wanted in his old-age — robust, full-blooded grandsons to carry on the Dwyer tradition, if not the name — and the heritage built up so long ago.

She leant forward as the midwife came sailing in, the ample folds of her long dress and apron flapping as she glided up to the bed.

'They be two of the bonniest young 'uns I ever did help bring into this world, ma'am. This place will never be the same now they're in it, you mark my words.' She chuckled, her fat chins bobbing and the tight mop of close curls under the dingy cap, shaking. She had produced thirteen children herself and knew all the ropes, and was considered to be the best midwife for miles around.

'And I was so worried about you, ma'am, though I never let on to Mr Jones — you being a redhead and all, and knowing how easy redheads bleed. I was half frightened to death, I can tell you, when you was giving birth to *two* babes not one. But you're a healthy young woman, you are, and built for having children easy like.' She rolled her eyes up to heaven, a massive woman as overpowering in manner as she was daunting in figure. 'But I give thanks to the Lord and me own good hands, ma'am.'

Cleanliness not being a part of good nursing or birthing, Mrs Swattle had arrived from Port Frances with her grubby hands and clothes. She did, however, wear a clean apron which hid an old, stained dress. Now, with her apron rustling, she took over, ordering Elizabeth away in her loud voice. Elizabeth, not wanting to cause Esther any undue trouble, grudgingly obeyed.

Esther leant forward and studied the two babies while Mrs Swattle bustled about the room, talking ten to the dozen all the time about babies she had birthed and the women she had saved from bleeding to death. Esther's ears conveniently shut out the insistent chatter and concentrated on the babies. She already loved them so much it hurt, because they were Buck's children. Every little detail meant everything to her — the closed little eyes, the feathery eyebrows, the tiny mouths, the perfectly-formed, little fingers.

As Mrs Swattle left, she lay back on the cushions, watching the sun shining in the warm sunniness of the room, touching the crowns of each red-gold head. Her lips softened. They needed her; they were so helpless and vulnerable, so defenceless without her.

Her face grew sad as she remembered how her mother had plaited her hair as a child, with such gentleness so that there were never any squeals of anguish before bedtime. Esther remembered the long, inky-black plaits of her older sister Anna, who had always waited so patiently during the plaiting, with her pre-Raphaelite face and dark, grey-green eyes, so like their father's. She had never got on with Anna, who had been so different in every way from herself, loving reading and poetry and the things of the mind so passionately that she had never felt the need for outdoor activities.

She herself had been such a romp, such a tomboy. She thought now of some of her childish escapades with her brother Lewis, that shining, mischievous boy with the red-gold hair so like her sons, and the gift of making the most beautiful music, all that time ago in the Ireland of her childhood. Ireland — that misty, bittersweet country of her dreams. Why, oh why, did she have to think about them all now, after so long?

In her mind it was as if they were all here with her, as real as yesterday. As the silence of the room enveloped her, she let the tears stream down her cheeks.

Oh Papa, she cried out, beating her hands together. You are all that's left of my childhood, you and Uncle Cady. What is there left between us? I still do love you so much. Is everything we had together gone for ever?

And there was no answer in the warm silence stealing in upon her.

It was later that she heard, from the men, descriptions of the battle against the Amangwane — of the horror and fear of those who had never fought against tribesmen before. She learned, as all the settlement now knew, how the might of the fierce Amangwane had been smashed, and the Xhosa and the colony saved from the devastation that would surely have swept through it unchecked. All the Amangwane women and children, hiding in the forests, had been collected by the troops before Hintza, the Xhosa Chief, could get to them. They had been sent to Fort Willshire, where they had refused to care for their children, so had then been sent to the colony in the charge of the Burgher Commando led by Buck.

'It was a sight, ma'am, I can tell you,' Moss said, sitting at the kitchen table. 'All them masses of warriors with their spears shining in the sun. There were many more hiding in the surrounding bush, but we couldn't see 'em. Then the hordes of screaming warriors rushed forward time and time again. It was a comforting sight to see Commandant Jones riding like fury down our lines, roaring at us above the din of 'em muskets and cannons and screaming warriors. Never did he let us lose heart, not once in all that time, not even when 'e had to carry Mr Roydon Wilson to the back lines with an assegaai wound in 'is leg.'

'Aye,' grunted Higgins, 'and I just say that young Nyezi fought like the goddamed devil —'e's a good sort — fighting with us like we were all from the same troop.'

The image of the wild, rushing hordes was frozen in Esther's mind, a picture of intransigent horror, as she waited for Buck to tell his story of the battle.

But he was adamant. All he would say of the affair was, 'From now on all Xhosaland knows the power of the white man's firearms and his use of horses. I only hope, by God, that this does not arouse a terrible dragon who still sleeps across the border — for when he stirs, we shall know his worst.'

The summer days were languid, but busy, the meals long and cheerful, and redolent of a surprisingly good spread of produce. The fields shimmered pale yellow with the stalks of wheat and Indian corn rippling in the light coastal breezes.

Esther recovered from her anxiety and fears as the days passed into the fullness of summer, and still Buck stayed with her. There were picnics to the coast, walks where the salt in the air was strong and sheep bleated in the quiet stillness of an afternoon. There were excursions on shooting ponies after rhebok in the mountains, or on foot after guinea-fowl and other birds, when the continual round of farm work permitted. The days fled by in balmy air, sunshine and laughter and all the time the twins grew stronger by the month, and little Moses with them, now in the enthusiastic care of Beauty, the Mantatee maid.

January 1829 brought a hot bergwind, boisterously blowing yellow-brown veils over bushes and trees gay with the bright leaves of the spekboom and melkboom, and into the dark, shaded greens of the thorny acacia. Behind it there was a faint heat haze over the Amatole Mountains, stretching far away across the Fish River.

In England Lord Charles Somerset had resigned from office as Governor of the Cape, and Sir Lowry Cole had arrived to take his place. Vagrancy continued at an alarming rate, the numbers of stock thefts increasing by the week. Reprisals had been forbidden, and due to the fact that the number of Cape Mounted Rifles had been reduced, matters worsened.

The New Year passed with the refusal of the government to pass an anti-vagrancy law, limiting the movement of the Hottentots. The resentment of the colonists, both Briton and Boer, grew, adding to the bitterness of the latter who were forced to use only English in the law courts.

Old Mazwi, Buck's friend, had died the previous year, effectively removing one of the figures immediately beyond the frontier with whom the colonists could deal. Nyezi, his heir, had become Chieftain. His half-brother Lungelo had never paid him the respect due to a Chief, determined as he was to establish himself and his authority over the tribe. His cunning and agile mind plotted against the trusting younger man, who was overthrown and murdered soon afterwards. It was Lungelo who now took command over the tribe, as old Mazwi had feared while he was alive. The red mabele grain had won. Lungelo and his people had suffered more than once at Colonel Somerset's hands, and their resentment against the colonists steadily accumulated.

It was at this time that Laree and Roydon visited Eden for the first time with their four children. Roydon, who now suffered from a slight limp from the assegaai wound in his leg, wanted to join Buck on his next hunting trip. They decided to venture through Xhosaland, where large herds of elephant still roamed, and into the land of the Zulus, where the herds were the largest. Chief Shaka had been murdered the year before by accomplices of his half-brother Dingane, and it was he who now ruled the fierce tribe.

It was decided that they would leave at the beginning of the following winter. On the day Roydon and Laree departed, the two sisters went out, hand in hand, to the wagon packed for the return to Sunfield Park. Sitting up in the front beside Roydon, Laree looked down on Esther's upturned face. With an impulsive movement, she reached down holding out her hand, and when Esther's hand gripped hers, Esther felt an aching sadness. Looking into Laree's face, she saw her eyes large and bright with unshed tears and she knew that her sister was as much against the trip as she was. Only she would never tell her husband. Laree would remain stoically silent, accepting that a man must do what he felt right.

I wish I was more like that, Esther thought, watching the wagon disappear down the track of mimosa trees. It would make everything so much easier if I could accept it. I don't want Buck to go because I cannot go with him now that I have two young sons, too small to be left without me. With my growing family I am tied to the farm.

That evening, Buck entered the bedroom to find Esther propped up against the pillows before retiring for the night. There was a hot darkness of anger before her eyes. Resentment smouldered in every cell of her body. He closed the door and held up his hand.

'I know from that look on your face that there is a mighty storm brewing, sweetheart. Sometimes a herd of enraged elephants is simpler to deal with than you, my dear. I will hear no more about the expedition.' His eyes held hers in an angry glance. 'You knew the kind of life I led before you married me — and the fact that you are living off the proceeds seems to have escaped you completely. The sooner you get used to the idea, the better for you and for me. You cannot come with me — your place is now very firmly with the children.'

Esther bristled at his dismissive tone. Her eyes flashed like a wildcat, the tangle of her hair bright and disorderly in the flickering candlelight.

His expression seemed to change in the moving shadows as the golden light of the candle pushed the dark back up towards the raftered ceiling. The sudden change in his face warned her. She was all too conscious of the quickening in his eyes as he looked down at her, almost naked in her thin, lawn nightgown, her breasts and shoulders all too obviously glistening, washed softly in the light. Intensely aware of her own power, she used it.

Her generous mouth pouted with ill temper. 'You get out of here!' she flared. 'I sleep alone tonight!'

He took a step closer to the bed. Suddenly his hand tightened almost brutally around her wrist. 'Damn you to hell's flames, Esther — mind your words when you speak to me, do you understand that? I have had enough of your tantrums every time a trip inland is planned and you are excluded.'

His glance flickered over her breasts and shoulders and came to rest on her face. 'If I had a mind to I could rip that wispy thing from your body this instant, and have you at my mercy! But don't upset yourself — I am not about to fight for your favours, because that is what you want me to do — that would satisfy your angry little spirit more than anything else, to see me grovel at your feet! You are right, my dear — tonight you sleep alone.'

He released her wrist and strode angrily from the room, banging the door with such a resounding crash as to almost wrench it from its hinges.

Esther remained motionless, stunned. She felt paralysis set in, at the unexpected temper in him. Suddenly she wanted him with his arms closing out all the dangers, his body feeding the rising passion inside her. She felt that his body belonged to her, that she must be close to it and cling to it, so that they might never again be parted. Her need was almost painful, like a mounting hunger. But she was not going to him to apologize and beg him for what he termed favours.

She lay back, her face flushed with angry despair, locked into the agony of her own womanhood. At least he could go away, roam the earth if he chose, free as a bird. With icy clarity she knew that there was still a part of his life that he would never, could never, share with her. And that was the part she hated, and resented so much.

Her thoughts went back to the one and only trip into Xhosaland with him, in the bright first months of their marriage. That now seemed like a distant and wonderful memory, when he had belonged to her alone. She knew he had aroused in her a depth of passion she had never known, that he could satisfy that depth of hunger in her. She admitted to herself that she was jealous of other women admiring him, even still at times, of her own small daughter. And she knew, with rising agitation, that she would either have to get used to the situation, or become swamped by it. And that she would never do ... for being swamped by anything was not in her nature. She was a fighter born, and now that her passion and anger were aroused there was nothing she would not do to remain the most important feature of Buck Jones's life ...

CHAPTER
Thirty-Five

It was a long way back for the ivory hunters from the soft winds, velvet hills and fertile plains of Natal. They returned with their wagons torn and patched, accompanied by a raucously lively and gaily-coloured parakeet, and a Frenchman whom they had met in the bush.

Daniel Lavoisier was a self-styled hunter-trader, a former officer in Napoleon's service, who had lived by his wits and charm, ever since the battle of Waterloo and the end of the war.

Buck and Roydon had managed to obtain a sizeable quantity of high quality ivory, as the game was still plentiful in Natal. They had killed two enormous crocodiles for the much sought-after skins, cutting them open to find the half-digested body of a Zulu male, swallowed whole, in the stomach of one of them.

The news the previous year, of the assassination of Shaka by his half-brother Dingane had shattered southern Africa, especially the ivory traders who had known him and enjoyed his patronage. Particularly annoying was the fact that the Cape government would give the traders no support or protection. Buck and Roydon had found, however, that the safety of Natal was actually strengthened by the new Zulu chief, Dingane, who had assured them of his peaceful intentions, and it seemed as if a prosperous period of trade was underway with him.

The three hunters turned at last down the long track shaded by the mimosa trees. Roydon lay in the back of the wagon, suffering from a wound in the chest. He had been trampled by an enraged elephant cow. How he had survived at all was a miracle. He owed his life to the excellent marksmanship of Buck and the expertise of their wagon-driver, the faithful Hottentot tracker, Oukiep.

367

Esther looked up from the accounts she was tackling in Buck's new office, built on to the sitting-room. She pushed her chair back from the desk with a sigh, stretching her arms above her head, until the tension ebbed from her stiff neck and shoulders. Her neat copperplate figures on the large account book still danced before her weary eyes. With a mental shake, she pushed the financial matters to the back of her mind as she heard the dog bark and the rumble of wagons in the drive. She rose, and pulled back the curtain hiding the morning light, and saw Buck and Oukiep carefully lift Roydon from the first wagon. A stranger stood in the background near the second wagon, a low-brimmed, slouch hat pulled down over his head.

Pulling on her paisley shawl, she sprang past Pike, standing beside the desk, the sickness of fear deep in her stomach. She sped out into the spring freshness of the morning, her face peaked with anxiety.

'Buck! What on earth has happened to Roydon?' she gasped, as she drew up to the men.

Buck gave her a lopsided grin, slowing his pace as he helped carry Roydon on a makeshift stretcher. 'He'd better tell you himself — he makes a grand tale of it. In fact the story's been so added to in the telling by your brother-in-law that it has become better than any adventure I've ever heard.'

Esther stopped and turned to Roydon, her face drained of all colour as she thought of Laree.

Roydon grinned painfully as he looked up at her. 'I got gored by an elephant cow in Natal, Esther — but I'll live, count on it. And that husband of yours — he tells a better story than ever I could.' He grimaced with pain as they entered the house, and Esther shook her head in vexation.

Buck gently lowered Roydon on to the settle in the sitting-room, then turned towards her. She hurled herself at him, disregarding the dust covering his face and clothes. Then she looked up at him, at his cheeks hidden by a full, brown beard; the dust traced lines about his nose, making him look older and tired. But he was home, and that was all that mattered. With a rush of delight she pulled him closer, and he kissed her, his lips moving deliberately to her bare throat so that she would know all of his heated desire from weeks apart. She clung to him, oblivious of the

368

others, running her hands over the curly, matted beard.

His deep blue eyes shone, flawless and penetrating, into hers. He was wearing a tattered blanket, fastened around his neck by strips of hide, and leather trousers, his head partly covered with a crownless hat. For all his disreputable appearance, he was still desirable to her. She pressed herself to him, feeling the powerful masculinity, the hard muscles, the corded belly. He whispered into the fire-coloured hair falling across her cheeks, and smiled at her, a secret, conspiratorial smile. And she was instantly and willingly his slave.

Suddenly she felt the simple pleasure once more of just being alive. She forgot her annoyance at him over his trip as the joy of living spread through her. All that mattered was his presence, the reconciliation and the love she bore him so strongly that it ached somewhere deep in the very core of her being. She wanted to be alone with him — to banish the others, even Roydon who needed her now in his suffering.

Then they broke free, reluctantly, as Roydon's condition intruded into their private world. Esther turned to the Frenchman, suddenly aware again of his presence, as Buck introduced him.

There was a flash of white teeth as he smiled, taking off his hat with a flourish, and bent to kiss her hand with casual French grace. His hair and beard were bleached by the sun to the colour of burnished gold. He was sturdily built, shorter than Buck, and exactly her own height. He was easily Buck's age, ten years older than herself. He lifted his head, his face bronzed and prematurely lined by years in the sun and wind. Her eyes took in the sculptured nose, the sensuous mouth, the sturdy shoulders and broad arms. Above all, she was conscious of his wicked, light-green eyes. His face was intent and much too close. He was, she realized, with a sharp, uncomfortable shock, the most handsome man she had ever met — not unlike the statues of ancient Greek gods seen long ago in her childhood.

Then he was forgotten as she took Buck's arm possessively, and together they walked arm-in-arm to the settle where Roydon lay. Daniel stared after her, a bold but enigmatic expression in his translucent green eyes. He watched her as she bent down towards Roydon, deciding that she was easily the most beautiful woman

369

he had yet met in Africa. All the while Esther attended to Roydon, soaking the rags away from his broken flesh where it had stuck fast and she was forced to pull them free, bringing blood with them, Daniel watched her, fascinated, through the open kitchen door. He saw the grim determination with which she went about her grisly task in the sitting-room, her face whiter than death, while he sat in the kitchen and ate cold chicken and barley bread, and drank steaming coffee, waiting for the washing water to boil.

After a vigorous cold wash, Buck eased himself into a chair, the dog beside him. He reached for the animal's head and fondled and teased its ears until Aurora awkwardly settled herself on his lap. He looked down at the small girl and smiled affectionately. The little, oval face was barely visible beneath her brown hair, tumbling ringlets which spilled about her cheeks. Happy and relaxed, he stroked the thick curls for a while, then he knuckled the side of her face fondly and sent her out to play while he gave his full attention to his guest. Mid-morning sunshine claimed the room, and the kettle hissed over the flames as Buck spoke with the Frenchman, unaware of Daniel's interest in his wife.

Esther rose at last and looked down at Roydon, swathed in bandages and healing poultices, a weary smile on his face. She winced as she saw him blanch suddenly with pain, a low, almost soundless whistle escaping her lips. Moving into the kitchen to fetch the warm broth she had prepared for him, her eyes fell on those of Daniel. She drew a sharp breath, two spots of colour burning her cheeks. Walking past him without another glance, she busied herself at the kitchen fire. Outside there was the sound of children's laughter, and behind her, in the sitting-room, Buck jested with Roydon.

The talk rose and fell about the expedition, and Esther found herself listening avidly, trying to glean those parts of Buck's life she could no longer share. Daniel did most of the talking, and she was interested and alarmed to learn that it was still a precarious life for the traders in Natal, who lived in shacks, prepared to flee into the bush at the first rumour of Zulu aggression.

Daniel described the traders, mostly very young men, living and dressing as they pleased. The older ones who had been there for some years had married black wives and had become the

370

chiefs of the splinter groups forming about them. He enthusiastically recounted how he and Buck and Roydon had explored some of the lakes, sailing across to shoot hippos in a dug-out canoe given to them by one of the tribes. They had lived in the lush, tropical bush, bristling with all kinds of wild animals and on the far-reaching plains where herds of antelope roamed. Daniel paused to enjoy the awed silence of Esther's interest. The inner core of her wrestled with the demon of guilt at her resentment for Daniel when she heard him trying to persuade Buck to accept Msilikazi's offer to hunt in the lands to the far north, where the game was the best and the ivory the richest. He, himself, had been there, but had been chased away by the Chief, never able to return.

Esther's mind withdrew sharply into its former tortured prison, focussing briefly on Buck's face. She knew instinctively that he would be persuaded to go and would leave her once more. In her mind she heard the shrieking of black tribesmen, the wild trumpeting of elephants, saw Roydon's pain all over again. Her flesh crawled at the images superimposed on her brain.

She became aware that the eyes of the Frenchman had never left her, and she knew he was still looking at her back. Why had Buck brought him here?

She moved restlessly before the iron pot over the fire, tapping the floor with one impatient foot. For all Buck's crazy schemes, she was still in love with him, and more than ever. He was home and they were together. That was what mattered, that and nothing else.

And no Frenchman, no matter how handsome or charming he was, was ever going to spoil it.

During the days that followed, Roydon's condition improved and he was able to return to Sunfield Park with Laree, who had come, distraught, to fetch him. They left together with the promise of the handsome proceeds to be made from the sale of the ivory, the skins and small live animals, which had become popular overseas.

Shearing time drew near, followed by the harvesting of good crops that season. Albany was now firmly established by virtue of its cattle and sheep; there were farmhouses everywhere and Boer and Briton were intermarrying. There was news that Samuel

Pettigrew had finally won the hand of Gert Venter's widow, the lovely, blonde Helena, and had taken her back to Dwyers' Cross to live. At last there was another woman to take the place of Esther at the farm, and she was reputed to make the best mosbolletjies in the district.

With his accumulating wealth Buck was able to buy the adjoining farm, extending down to the sea and adding a good few hundred acres to his land. He built a small, stone cottage on one of the hillsides on the periphery of his land, overlooking the Bushman's River and the sea, a place where the family could escape from the farm routine at times, and relax. It was called Aloe Cottage and became a familiar landmark along the coast, clearly seen from the sea. It was rough and white-washed, with a thatched roof, and was cool, washed by the fresh sea breezes on the hottest summer days with the fragrances of salt and shrub. On clear days they could see across the wide river mouth and the broad tracks of fine, pale sand, and out to sea where the blue of the sky and ocean met.

By that time, most of the farm's dairy produce and wool was being sold, of which sales Esther kept the most meticulous accounts.

Daniel Lavoisier visited them on his way back from a hunting trip, with the news that Msilikazi had again sent messengers to the missionary Robert Moffat in Kuruman, in search of the white man Jones, whom he had heard the Zulus called *Hlambamnzi*, the swimmer. Buck had earned this nickname because he had spent much time in Natal fording the flooded, yellow-brown rivers naked, much to the delight of the Zulu matrons who had crowded the banks to watch these feats, shouting loudly in admiration and pleasure.

Msilikazi invited Hlambamnzi and his friend with the wheat hair who had courageously escaped after being trampled by an elephant, to come and hunt on his lands. Buck pondered the reason for the Matabele King's interest in seeing him, and as the days merged into weeks, his curiosity grew.

And all the time, Esther watched him. She could feel the restlessness about him and she knew, with smouldering resentment, that the call of the far north was too strong — that one day near the winter he would obey it and leave her, to travel further than he had ever been before. She also knew that when he went, it would be many months before she would see him again.

She had given up her tantrums that had shaken the farm whenever the idea was mentioned. She was scarred within by such battles. When another threatened, the scars throbbed like old wounds. Instead she angrily resigned herself to it, shutting her mind to the long, lonely months ahead without him.

Buck found his plans accepted without the usual earth-shattering scenes, but with steady, unconcealed resentment. It was all too clear that the expedition was a detested ordeal which Esther would endure for his sake, sustained by her strong pride.

In November, Chief Gaika died. Though he had not been recognized by the tribesmen themselves as their overall leader, to the whites he represented the Xhosa, and his death therefore removed another link in the chain of contacts across the border. His heir, the young Sandile, was not able to exact any respect from his half-brothers, Macomo and Thyali, who were determined to re-establish their authority in the Mancazana and Kat River valleys. They were supported by the Mazwis under Lungelo, who now lived in close proximity in the Ceded Territory.

Gaika had virtually given away the Ceded Territory by a verbal treaty with the British authorities before the arrival of the Settlers, but this treaty had never been acknowledged by the Xhosa clans who had generally acknowledged Hintza, and not Gaika, as Senior Chief. Now, there were growing tensions across the border and especially in the Ceded Territory, which had quickly lost its empty and neutral character. Boer farmers in the north encroached on it and black tribes still infiltrated into other parts. Traders swarmed into Xhosaland as soon as Governor Sir Lowry Cole gave permission, making matters worse and angering some chieftains, whose own movements were confined to the eastern Amatole Mountains.

Colonel Harry Smith arrived in the colony and invited Buck to act as interpreter for his visits to the tribes on the border. Reprisal raids to recover stolen cattle were once more allowed as the restlessness of the tribes continued.

None knew the currents of unrest more than Buck, riding through the troubled centres of the north. He was sensitive to the currents swaying the Xhosa chiefs. The most alarming incident to him was the action of Lungelo who, without warning, helped Macomo to destroy the kraals of the Tambookie tribe, an apparently peaceful people living near him, who seemed to want to trade with the whites.

Lungelo and Macomo stole large numbers of cattle too and when they refused to restore the stolen cattle it was decided that retaliatory action would be taken by the regular troops, with a Burgher Commando. As nothing came of the parleys with Macomo and Lungelo, the order was given to move into their territory and destroy their crops and kraals.

Buck knew that the orders to destroy the kraals and fields and drive the tribes out of the Kat River Valley would lead to endless trouble. He was all too aware that the indignity to which a Chieftain and his people were subjected would unite his colleagues across the Fish River.

Henry Somerset was also aware of the fact, but he was forced to proceed and Lungelo's people, along with Macomo's tribe, were evicted. The final insult came when their fertile territory was occupied by Hottentots in accordance with plans made by the Governor and Stockenström, the new Commissioner General for the Eastern Cape.

Macomo, Lungelo and their people remained close by, disgruntled and resentful, and their captured cattle was returned to the servile Tambookie tribe.

And all the while, there was a continual pressing for a separate government in the east, from that of the west, from one of the most vocal of voices on the subject, that of Joshua Dwyer.

Autumn held winter at bay that year in a haze of bright, warm weather but at the end of the season Buck finally left Eden to meet Roydon on a hunting trip to the north to obtain skins and live animals to fulfil an American Commission. They left with three wagons between them, Oukiep and a small band of Hottentots. Esther's heart was leaden as she stood at the front door in the chilly, early morning, the twins hugging her skirts; Aurora following as far as she could after the departing wagons, billowing clouds of yellow-brown dust.

Esther looked up; there was not a cloud in the cold sky. She walked back inside, intensely lonely and frustrated. Her restless eyes fell over the lovely pieces of new porcelain, ivory and jade scattered around the sitting-room, bringing to it a surprisingly new elegance. She had adored it all only days before. Now the house had lost its life for her. It was a dead, ghostly shell. She missed Buck with increased longing every time he left her, and she knew with dread that this time it was to be their longest separation.

His two sons were growing into sturdy little boys, bright with mischievous eyes and perky, cheeky expressions. They and young Moses threw themselves into life with gusto, getting into everything with such glee and mischief, that no one could be angry with them for very long.

Esther saw in Aurora much of Buck, her lovely, oval face losing its chubby baby appearance as she slowly became a young girl — but she had the mentality of a child at least four years younger than she was. She could only speak in short, jerky phrases, and then not too well. It took Esther all her time being patient with her, trying to teach her the simplest things. Buck was much more compassionate, seeming to take pleasure in helping the weak, defenceless creature.

At night Esther lay in the bed she shared with Buck, longing to be cushioned by the silent communion between them, until she slept exhausted, the lonely feelings sinking into the oblivion of merciful darkness.

CHAPTER
Thirty-Six

She stood watching Higgins set a new stave on her butter firkin in the carpenter's workshop across the yard, all about her the smell of worked wood and shavings. It was stuffy in there, but the air outside was cool as winter progressed. She stood to one side as he worked on the yellowwood wheel with long, deft fingers. At the sight of his long, lean face, its stubble coated with sawdust, and his bent, wiry figure, Esther felt a homely comfort.

It had been some months since she had last had news of Buck and Roydon. As the silence concerning their whereabouts continued, it was as if the wilds of Africa had swallowed them in its mysterious ancient clutches, drawn them into a countryside, still, withdrawn, beautiful and cruel.

She had no idea of when she would see them again, and was weary of the deep void in her life. There was a tiny pout to the curve of her full, generous lips, as she shot a sharp, frustrated glance at Higgins' bent head. Loosening the blue cloak about her shoulders, her attention turned to the land outside.

In the trodden yard, with its smells of straw and leather near the stables, three new horses were being rubbed down by Mazinga and two other Xhosas. They were fine, big horses, powerfully built, not over-ridden. She stirred restlessly, disturbing the dog, which had its nose on her instep. She bent and patted it down.

Eden was coming to mean everything to her, the more she worked at it, the more she gave to it. She was beginning to understand her father and Buck and their urge to put down strong durable roots into the earth. A sense of the vast, untamed wealth of Africa had taken hold of her in the days since Buck's departure, as she pushed herself ever deeper into the farm's progress and its new lands. Eden had become one of the showplaces of the settlement, where important visitors began to stop and pass some time. Henry Somerset was a frequent visitor, as were others. It had even outstripped Dwyers' Cross with its beautiful orchards and vineyards, which Joshua and Cady with the help of Sam had turned from a wilderness into a beautiful place. But their wealth and their comfort was nowhere near the scale of Eden, and their place in the community, though still powerful and respected, has been superseded by Buck Jones, who had become one of the wealthiest and most influential farmers in the Eastern Cape.

Esther quickly shut her father and uncle from her thoughts.

The final tally from all the ivory sent to the Ivory Floor in London two years before, had come through. Esther was surprised to discover that it had fetched all of forty thousand pounds. And from that amount Buck had received his portion of several thousand pounds. She had at first not been able to believe it. Here they were sitting on a treasure chest and she had not realized until then the full extent of it. It had at once excited and disappointed her. For without Buck, there was a void, a chasm in her life. And not all the money in the world could put that right.

She knew he felt satisfied with the money earned because he could do the things he planned for her, for the children and the farm — but the money itself was of no other importance to him. It had not changed him for he was essentially an unextravagant man who enjoyed the simple pleasures he was used to, leaving the accounting and the managing of it to her.

She thought of their first exciting year together, and came to the conclusion that it could never be repeated. He had the wilds of Africa in his blood and nothing would ever cure it. It was as much a part of him as his love of adventure, the love of danger and activity. And that she would have to accept.

It was not the wealth he was chasing — it was something far deeper. It was the challenge, the excitement, the danger of charting the unknown, of battling his wits against Nature in all its forms. These were the things she had loved about him from the beginning, but she had not realized that it would be these very qualities that would come between them — that they would

377

deprive her of him, of his presence, for months on end.

Perhaps she should have married a duller, less exciting man, for then she would at least have had his company through the lonely nights and seen his familiar face during the long days. And she would be able to have more of his children. During the past few weeks of watching the children growing up, she had become broody once more, longing to have another child of Buck's.

Her mind was so busy with her thoughts that she did not hear the approach of another horse in the yard, or the growling of the dog. The rider was standing in the doorway before she was aware of his presence, and the dog was wagging its tail.

'I see even the magic of my personality has not disturbed you, madame,' a voice drawled behind her, an easily-attractive, French voice.

She caught her breath at the sound of it, and whirled round. Higgins' head came up at the same time, a suspicious look filling his eyes.

'I never did trust 'em Frenchies,' he hissed savagely, but so softly that only Esther could hear. 'Never — not since we fought 'em scoundrels in the bleedin' war.'

Esther perversely chose to ignore him. 'Monsieur Lavoisier, and what brings you to Eden?' She looked at Daniel, her face full of questions, a slight flush on her cheeks. He looked like a golden god standing there, a slow, studied smile playing about his full, sensuous lips.

'Madame Jones, my name is Daniel, please use it. After all, I pride myself on being a friend of the family.' He looked towards Higgins, one golden eyebrow raised enquiringly in his direction, as Higgins savagely spun the yellowwood wheel.

'I will take Monsieur Lavoisier into the Commandant's office, Mr Higgins,' she said quickly, the two ringlets about her ears swinging as she inclined her head towards him. She wore no housecap and the heavy locks of her hair were twisted up securely at the back of her head, catching the light like a flame. She led the way across the yard, clapping her hands for tea when she saw Beauty in the kitchen with the children. The twins' high spirits flooded the air with their childish shrieks of joy at some game with Moses. They were bursting with vitality, their startling blue eyes, so like Buck's, full of wicked mischief which kept the young

378

maid busy with their antics.

'You are fortunate to have such handsome children,' Daniel said, settling back in the riempie-backed chair in front of the desk. He sniffed appreciatively at the woody smell of wine casks rising pleasantly about him.

He was content to watch her as she sat down opposite him behind the desk, letting her cloak slip gracefully from her shoulders over the chair-back. She was a most bewitching woman, he thought, with a lustrous exciting quality to her eyes, and charm and power in her smile.

'And when does your wandering husband return?' he asked blandly. 'The last I heard was that he and Mr Wilson had left Reverend Moffat at Kuruman. They were travelling far into Matabele territory with wagons already loaded with precious, valuable cargo.'

The pale, wintry sun shone through the long sash window and fell across the clutter of papers on the desk. Esther smiled, half-bitterly, half-anxiously, as she took the tea tray from Beauty. She felt better entertaining him in the office; it was more businesslike that way, and the presence of Buck was safely and comfortingly all around them.

'I was hoping that you could tell me more than that, Monsieur — I have not heard from them for weeks.'

He did not answer immediately; he was watching her carefully. 'It is not easy to get messages back from there, my dear Esther — may I call you that? The way is hard, dangerous, and communication is all but impossible. From what I have heard and seen of Msilikazi — if he likes your husband and Mr Wilson, he could keep them there for many weeks. I would not put anything past that wily king, he has the power to do anything to anybody in his territory.' He flicked an experienced eye over her grey, wool dress, and flashed her an attractive smile. 'Your husband really shouldn't leave such a beautiful wife alone for so long — the temptations are too great.'

He gave her a searching look from his fascinating, light green eyes, and she bent her head, hoping that he would not notice that her heart had taken a strange backward flip. Then an angry flash lit her eyes and she looked at him. 'Temptations from whom, may I ask? You are not suggesting that I would betray the man I love?'

He nonchalantly waved a hand, a knowing, mischievous smile crossing his lips. 'No — no, my dear Esther, forgive me. It is I who is susceptible to the temptations, for I find you a most bewitching and attractive creature. Your husband is extremely fortunate to have an invitation from the Matabele king. Most of us have tried to hunt on his lands and failed.' His eyes flashed and he spoke quickly, with an edge of pique in his voice. Then his face cleared and he smiled. 'And he has you. But he is foolish. He does not guard carefully enough that which should be most precious to him. He is too confident of himself, oversure of you, so that he has become careless, especially now when there is a restlessness about you — a yearning for his full attention at all times. You do not love with your heart alone, Esther, you love with everything you have, and it is only right that you should have a man who loves you totally and completely too, wouldn't you say?'

She opened her mouth to defend Buck, her eyes sparking when he raised a hand. 'There's no need to defend such a fine man, my dear, and I never quarrel with beautiful women. He neglects you, that is all — it is plain for anyone to see, and you pine day in and day out. You need to love and be loved completely, and all the time, for that is what you crave most — admiration, adoration and appreciation. You were not made to compete with the mistress of the hunt. You are worth far more than that.'

His voice was soft, seductive as he suddenly reached for her hand, the touch of his fingers unnerving her. She left her hand in his, not wanting to take it away and yet knowing that she should. Aware of every gesture that he made, she had no need to look at him to know that he was examining her closely.

'I have seen you pine for him, this Englishman, Esther. The dreams have gone from your eyes, the light, the life. And I can bring them all back.'

He leaned forward, his light green eyes full on her. 'I want you, my dear, you know that. I have done so for weeks, ever since we first met. You are fully aware of the men around you. More goes on behind those extraordinarily expressive eyes than most people think. You were made for men to admire, to court, to worship.'

'Don't go on, Daniel, please!' She flushed to the roots of her hair. Sitting straight in her chair, she looked away, her hand still in his.

'How well I remember you Irish waiting for our Napoleon to come and save you from the English dogs — they really are a coarse and scurvy lot, my dear. They do not appreciate the refinements, the exquisite things of life. They trample them in to the dust like so many delicate and useless flowers,' he said in an almost off-hand manner, as if to disguise the triumphant contempt in his eyes. 'The Irish are different — there is poetry about your people, imagination, a whimsical quality. The English are as dull as ditch-water, and as thick. They have very little skill with their women. Now I could show you Paris — a city at its best in spring. You would dazzle the best circles of Europe, dressed in the latest French fashions from the hands of the most skilful designers in the world. How you would have liked our Napoleon — that little man had more charisma, more dynamite in his one little finger than all your proper Englishmen put together.'

He regarded her calmly, very much aware of the effect he had on her. Her mind was a jumble of confused feelings. She had been so long without Buck.

Daniel excited her, made her feel a beautiful woman again. He filled her need to feel still young, vital, desirable. She thought of Buck with sick bitterness. He had neglected her, Daniel was right, but she belonged to him, no matter what he said. There was no one else for her, no one.

Daniel rose and came round the desk towards her. She tried to move out of the way from him, but he was beside her in a quiet, swift movement. He stood, facing her, arms outstretched against the wall, enclosing her, trapping her as he bent to try and see her face. She leant against the wall, and hung her head.

'You and I were meant for each other. No one, not even your strong Englishman, can change that.' His arm circled her waist.

She tipped back her head and looked at him, acutely aware of the tightening grip around her waist. She looked away from his questioning glance and tried to distance herself from the sturdy breadth of his body. When she moved away, he gripped her firmly. 'Do my feelings mean nothing to you? I can't go on day after day, week after week, worshipping you in silence, declining into some kind of madness without you. That Englishman of yours — he does not deserve to keep you with such inexcusable

381

neglect.'

In the silence that followed she could hear her own heart thudding, her breath quickening. Then his arms were about her. She started and almost cried out. Instantly his hot firm mouth was on hers; the arms encircling her like arms of iron. His breath was in her throat and his tongue pierced between her lips.

Her mind swirled, suddenly terrified of the passion she felt, until she stopped thinking altogether for a very long moment, still held in the cradle of his powerful arms.

'*Mon Dieu*, you are so beautiful,' he groaned, stepping back and holding her away from him. 'And saved from the boredom of perfection by a wide, wicked smile.'

'No, Daniel, this is wrong! I am a married woman, I have children!' she gasped as his hands caught about her waist, outlining the shapeliness of her figure. 'Let me go at once!'

A cough interrupted them. They whirled around to see Higgins standing in the doorway, the firkin in his hands and an angry, defiant look on his face.

Daniel released her, and with an airy wave of his hand he picked up his curled, beaver-rimmed hat from the desk. His grey greatcoat swirled about his shoulders, with elegant panache. 'Adieu, madame,' he said, lightly brushing past Higgins as he passed through the doorway. 'We have unfinished business to attend which we will complete some day soon.'

Esther and Higgins stood facing each other after he had gone. Before she could utter one word, Higgins broke out harshly. 'That Frenchy is no more than a common adventurer, ma'am — I know the type. He's jealous of the Commandant — 'cos of his going to his Msilikazi fellow — and 'tis but a challenge for 'im to try to take you from 'im. He's taking mighty big advantage of you, ma'am — all alone and all that. Take care — the Commandant does not deserve to be cuckolded, though that scoundrel may think he does.'

'How dare you! How dare you speak to me in that tone of voice, Mr Higgins!' Esther looked across at him, her eyes narrowed like splinters of hard blue ice. 'It is not a matter that concerns you.'

He shrugged his shoulders, his face on fire. 'I've been with the Commandant a lot longer than you, ma'am — and I know 'im.

He does not deserve to be deceived, and there'll be hell to pay if he ever finds out, I can tell you. That rascal is no good I tell you, and you'd better see it before it is too late.'

He stood there, his long fingers angrily working on the steel buckle of his leather belt. Esther flinched at the harsh, stabbing words. She saw, watching him, the fierce, almost frightening anger in his eyes, the bitter, stubborn rebellion — and she was causing it.

'Get out of here, Mr Higgins, at once!' she hissed, her eyes burning. He turned and stalked out of the door, sullen and deeply resentful. She stared after him, the flush of defiance still on her face now tinged with guilt. The blaze had gone from her eyes, and the fire in her heart burned with less heat, the anger dissipated, leaving her feeling restless and impatient. Daniel was right in one thing — Buck should never have left her for so long. He did not care enough, or he would have returned by now, or never gone at all. His mistress was Africa and it would always be. Why should she care any longer? Why should she fight it anymore?

The guilt left her. Rather a sense of new power and strange longing filled her. That kiss was to linger in her mind long after she sat down again at the desk, trying to apply herself to the heap of accounts before her. The image of Buck became hazy and indistinct for the first time, as Daniel replaced it with his easy smile and golden head even though her mind kept fighting to throw him out.

CHAPTER
Thirty-Seven

It was almost three months since Buck and Roydon had left the frontier. Their wagons, loaded with valuable goods, had been burned by the fierce Matabele warriors in the far north, and they were on their way back to the Cape.

They had stopped for their midday meal on the banks of a river coursing its way through the dry, winter veld, when one of Msilikazi's messengers found them. He informed them that the King had sent them a gift of four oxen to invite them to trade and hunt in Matabele territory. Msilikazi had been very displeased by the headman who had ordered his warriors to burn the white men's wagons, destroying all the goods they had collected, and he had punished them. The messenger pleaded with them to accompany him to Msilikazi's royal kraal, for if they refused he would be put to death in fitting Matabele fashion.

After some discussion, Buck and Roydon decided it was too good an opportunity to miss, and a way of recouping some of their considerable losses. They also did not want the death of the messenger on their consciences, so they followed him, cutting a trail through the vast, wide expanses of highveld towards the royal kraal near the mountains of the Magaliesberg range.

It was late August and again the sweetness of ripening spring was in the air. Daniel had carried a tiffin to the beach below Aloe Cottage, followed by Esther, Beauty and the children. There was a view of the sparkling ocean lying wide to the horizon. The surface tumbled and tossed its white foam along the edge of the wide, deserted beach, and there were the sounds of the children's laughter further away.

384

It was a beautiful day. The wind, which had blown almost continually for several days, had dropped. The wide lagoon and the sands spread under a vast, uncluttered sky. The sails of a sailing ship broke slowly across the glinting water, until it disappeared out of sight. Among the rocks, near the Bushman's River, the water spouted and sucked, as clouds of spray flew and fell. There the river narrowed and began to snake inland, the hills behind it thickly wooded. On the surface of the river the sunlight glistened and played, shifting golden patterns along its surface. Seagulls flapped and screamed overhead, a group of waterfowl haunting the water's edge where the river entered the sea.

The coastline was already wrapped in a warm, golden haze as Esther and Daniel sat on the large canvas spread on the fine, pale sands. They watched the boys scamper about after crabs sliding along the beach, their fingers running with the sticky juice of oranges. The dog, glad to stretch its great legs, raced along beside them. They heard Aurora cry out as Adam snatched her beloved China doll and threw it on the sand. Then, as she put her hands up to her face in dismay, he ran away, the dog at his heels.

Daniel was leaning against a large rock not far from the lagoon, gazing at Esther. He was fascinated by her varying moods, her bright humour. He liked the smell of her own special perfume, the brightness of her hair, the shapeliness of her body which he longed to possess. Lately he had grown more jealous. He was too clever to deceive himself. He had started out by wanting to defeat the Englishman, her husband, because he had been jealous of the fact that Msilikazi had asked him, and not Daniel, to visit his royal kraal. He had wanted to take away something precious from him, make him suffer for his arrogance. But, as time wore on, he had fallen in love with Esther himself.

He knew she was strongly attracted to him, but she still was in love with her neglectful husband. He saw her eyes soften when they fell on her sons, his sons, both radiant with their father's large bones and robust strength. To him, Buck Jones had the lusty strength of his kind, whereas he regarded himself as having strength with the subtlety of the French. This, he considered, gave him admirable advantage.

He had also great physical energy, but he used it with more finesse, more calculation than the big, powerful Englishman.

Besides, Esther had not heard from Buck for four months. Daniel stared moodily before him, his hands on his knees, his full, golden beard brightening to copper in the sun. He stared at the fine, ivory-coloured sand, flanked by high dunes covered with coarse water-grass and thorn bushes. Beyond, the bright stretch of sea rippled with waves, and further back the sunlight made diamonds on its glinting surface.

He leaned forward suddenly, his fair brows drawn together, as his eyes met hers in direct challenge. 'Come away with me, Esther — your husband has been too long away. Anything could have happened to him, so far to the north in the land of the fierce Matabele. He should have been home by now. I can give you a finer life — with all the refinements, the luxury you deserve. Your husband is a wealthy man, yet you still live a rustic life far from the civilized centres of the world. You are only existing here, you do not really live at all. I am weary of Africa and its barbarity,' he said, curving the most sensuous mouth Esther had ever seen.

His face with its warm, healthy glow, gave a decidedly youthful effect, despite his rather tired eyes. On closer scrutiny, his eyes were those of an experienced man, pleasure-loving and inflexible.

Esther looked up at the sky, the familiar pain and fear she knew during Buck's absence almost more than she could bear. Her eyes met his without flinching. Her first reaction to his words was alarm that anything should have happened to Buck.

Buck, she thought wildly, will you ever see your sons again? Will they know their father's love and strength once more? Will you ever return safely — am I to remain alone without you, without hope?

Then she felt excited by Daniel's words, by the new world they conjured up, yet embarrassed by their implication. She forced a laugh. 'True, it has been a long time without Buck — but he is still my husband, and until I know what has happened to him, I will be faithful to him.'

'You are quite mad,' he said smiling, showing the edges of his white teeth. 'Look at the valuable time you are losing — it is ebbing away while you wait. You are not growing any younger, though you will always remain a beautiful woman, *cherie*. And here I am, a devoted slave at your feet, waiting to show you just how good the world can be out there. This place,' he gestured deprecatingly, 'lacks culture — it has no traditions. There is, as yet, no substance of history. I long to take you back with me to Europe, where you belong. This is a backwater, if you will but see it — savage and monstrous for most of the time, exciting in its way for a while — but even that can pall.'

He looked up into the dark-fringed, blue eyes facing him, as she stole a look at him from under her eyelashes. 'There are gas-lamps in the streets of London, *cherie*, new fashions, steam engines. They are making ice-cream in America. And what have you got here?'

A smile played about Esther's lips, her face and hair all brightness in the light. She watched his fingers playing idly with the fine grains of sand. 'You paint a pretty picture of Europe, Daniel — but if ever I were to take you seriously, which I do not, I could never leave my children or the farm. This place, however rough and barbaric it may appear, is now my home,' she reminded him.

She was sharply aware, as usual, of his physical presence, his handsome physique and features first, and of his thoughts and feelings long afterwards. She gazed at his strong, suntanned neck, and grew hot and tense. She imagined his body on hers, and tried furiously to obliterate the image. She was always aware of the physical Daniel, before the spirit and character of the man. How different it had been with Buck, in whom the spirit and physical fused so automatically . . .

'If only . . .' He stopped, making a light, helpless gesture as he gave the sand at his feet an impatient thrust.

She inclined her face towards him, her eyes clear under the deep brim of her bonnet, its lemon and blue trimmings framing her watching face. He lifted the wicker lid off the food hamper and produced a bottle of choice sweet Constantia and two glasses. Raising a glass, he peered across its rim and topped her.

'To you, my dear. Do you know, I have been observing your children closely and a surprising fact has come to my attention. Your daughter Aurora shows an uncanny resemblance to your husband — yet, I believe, her father was dark, with dark eyes. Interesting, isn't it?' His gaze left her and travelled down to the beach. 'Strange — it's the eyes, it must be the eyes, and she of all three has his colour of hair. The boys of course have yours, but also his eyes — those remarkably blue eyes, unusual eyes. Has no one mentioned it before?'

He looked at her face, bright and lively with an inward zest that was so much a part of her personality. A pale triangle of neck showed where the ends of a pale, lace fichu met, fastened by a deep golden rose. There was sudden colour in her cheeks as she leaned forward to tuck a loose curl into place.

She sat rooted to the spot as if some chilling finger from the past had tapped her on the shoulder. He knew, or thought he did. Or was he guessing, trying to force her, to have some kind of hold on her? Sinister shivers flicked along her spine as the sunshine warmed her bare arms. It was as if a dark cloud had suddenly obscured the sun, taking all its warmth, though it still beat down on her.

She gazed out over the broad stretch of smooth, pale sand. She had the urge to run away, far from it all. Nothing must spoil the reputation she and Buck and the children had built up of solid respectability in the community. They had fought for it, and won. And no one, not even Daniel would ever take that away.

She was brought back to sudden and sharp reality by his voice, deceptively calm, saying, 'Is anything wrong, Esther?'

Her blue gaze focused on him and she shook her head, watching the small breeze from the sea ruffling gently the skirts of her lemon and blue striped muslin.

'Past dalliances are nothing new, *cherie* — they add spice to an otherwise dull existence. We will keep it to ourselves, shall we? I shall remain very quiet, as quiet as a mouse, if you are very nice to me.' He made a gesture with his hands, 'We could be so happy together. If you come away with me, I will lay the whole world at your feet. And I have never been so serious in my whole life.' He smiled at her, and went on, summoning all his skill to touch her feelings. 'You are so full of pure madness, it excites me beyond words, Esther. I have never met anyone quite like you. I set out to seduce you, but ironically, it is I who have been well and truly seduced — by you. Anything, anything at all you desire, shall be yours.'

Esther could not believe it. He was calmly, charmingly, blackmailing her within yards of her children — and Aurora, the unwitting cause of it. What should she do?

388

Normally she would have denied it and defiantly stood up to him, but he had held her up to ransom through her child, and to deny him what he wanted was not only to commit her own social suicide, but that of Buck and the children too. Everything they had worked for, and overcome, would be knocked down in one overriding blow. Her children would be shunned as the offspring of a whore, and Aurora would be mercilessly taunted until her life would not be worth living. Daniel could ruin them, and she knew that he would.

There was an added problem. It was very difficult for her not to respond when this devastatingly handsome man exerted his charm as he was doing at the moment, deliberately making her feel the most wonderful, desirable woman in the world. And she was so lonely.

Perhaps it was the angle of his face, perhaps it was a trick of the light; perhaps it was a sudden, surprising, yearning softness in his voice, as though he was speaking of a cherished dream, some unspoilt pleasure. Whatever the reason, she had the impression that his face changed. Some of the lines seemed to fall away from it, making it younger, less hard and cynical. She had a momentary glimpse of the young man he must have been before the wars and the African jungles had claimed him. But only the sharp rise and fall of the soft curves of her breasts gave any evidence of that emotion he had touched.

They sat for a while in silence. Esther looked down the beach to where Guy was rolling with the dog, splashing in the shallow water where the river ran into the sea, and scuffling on the sand. Adam squatted beside him, digging in the sand with his hands. She watched for a moment or two the white, combing curl of the breakers.

Then she turned to Daniel, who smiled at her with all his sensual and bewitching charm as her control suddenly broke. He was at her side immediately, drawing her against his shoulder, his voice soft in her ear.

'Come back to Europe with me, *cherie* — come back where you belong.' His words cut through to her and in that second she was tempted. He stroked her hair, and she did not dare speak. Seeing the children otherwise occupied, she leaned briefly against his shoulder, and let him touch her breast, permitting his hand to wander. Her own body responded with a fire that frightened her. Her eyelids dropped, the wide generous mouth moistened as her breasts swelled. She had an almost uncontrollable desire to draw him down to the pale, soft sand, but then she heard the laughter of the children.

She pretended to adjust her skirts, feeling that nothing existed but the feelings in her body as she lusted for him with increasing desire. The imminence of Daniel was maddeningly terrifying, and there was suddenly nothing else in the world but her fear of his knowledge, and her desire.

She sighed heavily, beginning to feel the time was soon approaching when she could no longer postpone this subject, which she knew must be faced. If only Buck was here, if only he would come home — soon, before she would be forced, in her desire to protect him, her children and her own longings, to give in to Daniel.

She looked up at his dangerously close mouth and his eyes, which were so light it was like looking into a mirror.

'You will fall in love with me, Esther. You will. I will make you,' he said in a curious voice of soft violence. 'When will you succumb, *cherie*, when?'

Her eyes flickered to his face, and she caught her breath at something she saw there. No man had ever looked at her quite like that before. She cursed herself for being unable to free herself from the trap he had set for her.

'If you do not my beautiful one, there are many subtle ways one's interesting past can become common knowledge — a careless word dropped here and there — and no one can deny such a resemblance.'

She was gripped again by a terrible fear. Daniel held her life and those of her loved ones in the palm of his hand.

'You make it so very hard for me, Daniel,' she said, trying to keep her voice calm. 'You batter at my feelings until very soon you may succeed in breaking me down against my better judgement.' Silently she pleaded with him to let her go, relying strongly on any mercy in him to leave her alone.

Daniel considered her words, a triumphant gleam in his eyes. It was obvious from his expression that he cared very much that he should get what he wanted.

'I see we are beginning to understand each other, *cherie*. I intend to win this battle of wits with your husband. And the prize is what I want most — you.' His voice was soft with menace.

The sun was gone in an instant, and a great sweep of cloud was pulled over the sea, now wrinkled and grey. They had hardly noticed the change. Esther was afraid, but more for her reputation than of him. 'Will you let me go? I think we must get back to the cottage before it rains.'

But his arm tightened as he spoke. 'I will succeed, beautiful creature, I will make you more happy than you have ever dreamed possible.' His voice whispered in her hair, a change in his teasing expression, turning his eyes hard like two pieces of green glass, the set of his jaw grim and taut.

She turned away, but he pulled her round to face him. 'We are two hunters, your husband and I. We know all the rules, and success goes to him who is the swiftest and the cleverest. Your husband is clever, but not clever enough. He delays too long, leaving me the advantage. I will use his past against him, and yours if I have to — and what about your father? Hasn't he suffered enough from your scandalous behaviour? What will he do when it all gets out? I am not used to losing, my sweet Esther, and your erring husband is giving me all the time I need.'

CHAPTER
Thirty-Eight

Summer was in evidence, washing the coast with its warm, balmy light. The wind that had gusted along the coast the previous night had blown itself out, leaving another calm and beautiful day. Esther stood before the door of Aloe Cottage, watching the children playing down on the beach with Beauty. Great ropes of seaweed lay in heaps along the sand and crabs scuttled away from the eager, clutching little hands. Guy and Adam pranced around the beach like wild beasts, and the dog, barking furiously, circled around them.

The hearth behind her of light-coloured, Bathurst freestone shone in the golden sunlight flooding through the door and windows, casting dancing patterns on the floor. Rafters of keurboom carried from the river banks, stretched across the small cosy room, and a set of assegaai-wood chairs were arranged tastefully around the hearth.

She loved the tranquility and ease of the cottage, spending as much time as she could manage away from the busy activities of the farm. It was six months since she had last seen or heard from Buck, and she had finally grown used to an empty bed at night, keeping her thoughts away from him, focusing on her children.

She stood for a while, her eyes travelling over the wide spread of river and sea. Her gaze wandered to where the river narrowed between the thickly wooded hills that fell to the water's edge. Over the hillside a seagull hovered and swooped, a single flash in the sunlight, then it disappeared over the dancing water with its rippling, lacy foam.

She turned and forced herself to smile brightly at Daniel who was now a constant visitor, forever battering at her defences. He had grown more insistent, subtly threatening to throw her secret to the world. Subconsciously she glanced at him from beneath dark, fluttering eyelashes, and he marvelled at the many things she could say with her eyes. She had, he was forced to admit, utterly bewitched him. His overriding jealousy of Buck Jones, that had at first fed his mind with her attractions until he had been able to think of nothing else, had changed. It was now Esther alone that attracted him. Buck Jones did not matter any more. It was her beauty and spirit that aroused him so strongly that he was unable to forget her. She had succeeded in turning his thoughts from all other women, and he was more determined than ever that she should at last succumb to him. He would rather destroy her and her relationship with the Englishman he loathed, if he could not have her himself. He was determined to use the knowledge he had about her child to wean her from her children and take her back to Europe with him. He had found out many unnoticed details about her life, working back into her past and noting dates of her marriage and of her daughter's birth. He had gone into records of the evidence she had given at Buck Jones' trial, and a pattern began to emerge — a most interesting story that he knew would be gobbled up by a community harried with mounting problems. It would give them the kind of sensational escape they needed at this point of time.

Esther was demure and yet bold in a swathe of brilliant, peacock-blue muslin, gathered under her breasts and falling billowing in frills to her slippered feet. About her throat was an exquisite necklace, links of small turquoise stones held in the warm hollow of her throat. He could see the outline of her strong, firm legs and thighs beneath the skirt, and the clear-cut profile of her face as she turned her head towards him. The glorious, luxuriant hair was upswept, the corkscrew ringlets bouncing about her ears as she moved.

Her beauty and mischievousness delighted his rather jaded palate, and he could not help observing the impudence shining from the dark blue eyes. Daniel knew he had won, for she had dressed up in her finery in this cottage at the beach, just for him. At last the memory of Buck Jones had faded from her mind.

Her heart beat faster as he silently came up closer and stood before her. She was about to compromise herself to save her family and herself from social ostracism, and there was no turning back. She thought that she could buy him off with her body and still save herself from total degradation, and Buck would never know. He was so lost to her after all the months he had been gone, and she seemed to have changed so much since meeting Daniel and learning of his condemning knowledge of her past.

He undoubtedly looked very handsome as the sunlight caught his head in a halo of gleaming gold. He took a step back, pulling her away from the door and into the depths of the room. Then he took her in his arms, kissing her face and hair. He found her mouth, stopping all words and holding her prisoner. Her heart throbbed and tears of pain-driven frustration, fear and longing made her respond to him.

His lips moved to her throat, running one hand round to the back of her neck, his passion racing feverishly high. When his hand touched her intimately, she felt as if she was bursting into flame and could not turn away to leave him. She had eluded him, fenced with him until then, but she was yielding to him at last, she knew that then, and allowed herself to be carried away by the dangerous currents running between them.

She was devastated by her own response. It was hard to fight him when his touch ignited fires that flared immediately out of control and raced along her nerves. All guilt, all doubt fled before the fierceness of her feelings as his hand nestled against her breast.

His face swelling and deeply flushed, he plunged his golden head down, his lips on her soft, full breasts. The hot blood raced through her body as he started to kiss her again, holding her with one hard, muscular arm and with the other undoing the bodice of her gown.

Then she stood perfectly still, her gaze suddenly riveted beyond Daniel to the open doorway. Feeling cold shock run through her, she saw who stood there. It was Buck. His tall, broad-shouldered figure blocked out the light and seemed to fill the whole room.

She wrenched herself free. 'No, Daniel — *no!*'

He looked up at her with some amusement and not a little impatience, thinking she was teasing him. Her face was stricken, her eyes wild as she stared at the doorway. Daniel turned slowly, the smile freezing on his face.

Esther shrank from him, her eyes never leaving her husband's brilliant blue eyes, wide and savagely furious as a wild, wounded beast. He was bareheaded and wearing the sheepskin coat she had made, a full brown beard hiding the implacable and angry jaw. Her first reaction was cold, numbing fright at the terrible, utter rage on his face. Such a transformation had come over his features that she recoiled before the change. All that had ever been good-humoured, teasing and attractive, had given way to hot fury and positive revulsion. The blue of his eyes seemed sheathed in ice; anger and horror fixed his mouth into a straight line, and his temples pulsed with the rapid beat of his heart.

She backed away then, deadened with fear at what she had done. Her eyes ever widening in terror, she clapped her shaking hands to her mouth. He had, in those few, brief moments, become a total stranger to her. An impenetrable barrier had been thrown up between them, which she knew she was powerless to tear down.

'So — Higgins was telling the truth! By God's eyes, Lavoisier,' he roared, 'how dare you make a cuckold of me!'

He bunched his strong fist, his eyes threatening to explode. He looked from Daniel to Esther. His wild eyes took in her hair, a mass of disordered red curls pillowing her head, her body clothed in her best muslin. She remained stricken and frightened, seeing the rage running through him as Daniel sprang forward, eyeing the tall, powerful man warily, bitter hatred in his eyes. He spat in disgust on the floor, measuring his man. His stored envy, goaded and taunted, burst out.

'You do not deserve such a woman, you English dog!' he snarled, his French accent more pronounced than ever. 'You are a rough boor! You do not appreciate what you possess until it is too late. You deserve to lose that which you neglect for worthier men to find!'

'Daniel — please!' Esther's voice was shrill and hysterical, but neither man looked at her as they faced each other in murderous silence.

Buck jumped at Daniel and swung his fists so swiftly it took her breath away. He jabbed the Frenchman hard in the stomach before he was ready to defend himself, and violently punched him on the chin before the look of surprise could fade from his face. Daniel's head jerked upwards from the violent punch and he fell backwards with a crash to the floor.

Esther backed away from the sight, her hand covering her mouth to still her cries of fear. She wanted to close her eyes, but couldn't. After dealing with the enemy, Buck's burning eyes now sought the traitor. He glared across at her, her arms still held to her face. 'And well may you look horrified! 'Twas your doing — you and that French rat!' he spat out at her. 'What in the devil's name got into you while I was away?'

She looked at him, feeling as if the bones in her body had melted to water. She was unable to move, fearing that he would hit her too.

His eyes were two slits of hard, unyielding steel. 'Have you finally lost your fierce Irish tongue, woman?'

'You were away so long — you'll never know what it was — is — like without you — so desperately lonely,' she flared at him, suddenly finding her tongue. 'He found out about Aurora — he was blackmailing me — threatened to expose me before the community.'

'I don't want to know what was between you and this — this scurrilous troublemaker, this wrecker of marriages!'

He stalked towards her, his hands fierce on her as she shrank back in fear. For the first time since she had known him, she was afraid of him. 'I ought to thrash you — I ought to cut your heart from your body. You have taken everything we had together and wrenched it apart — mangled it between your cruel little hands. You couldn't wait for me to be gone to get at that vain, self-opinionated rogue, making Aurora the excuse! There are women who go from man to man with little reason, but there are many who, left alone without a man in their bed for longer than you, do not throw themselves at the first unscrupulous scoundrel.'

She had never seen so much anger, or so much pain in anyone's eyes, and she suddenly thought of his mother. For the first time she knew the blinding humiliation he had kept hidden for so long.

'Where is your control, wench? When will you grow up? You are not a child. You have broken all the trust there was between us — ground it into the dust until there is nothing left.'

Their eyes held in a long, blazing moment, neither yielding an inch. Then he threw her from him.

'You only care about what's happened to you!' she cried. 'Your own wounded pride that I could find another man as attractive as you means more to you than what I feel — what terrible fear trapped me to him. You don't care one jot about the loneliness you caused me to suffer by your own selfish demands, for months on end.' Her eyes shone like blue flames.

'You are a Celtic witch and no fit mother for your children!' He strode to the door. 'Pack your bags — you are going with Pike back to Dwyers' Cross where you belong! The children stay with me until I can get 'em proper care. I will take 'em to Elizabeth until you have been taken away from this farm — I want no trace of you or your belongings left when I return!'

'No! You can't do this to me!' she cried out in anguish.

He turned and flung himself through the open door. The crisp air rustled in and caught the soft folds of her gown, causing it to billow, as he furiously slammed it shut. The last sight of him through the window was a blur of brown leather and sheepskin as he strode angrily from the cottage.

She heard him call Beauty and the children as she stood rooted to the spot, bewildered. A great wave of terror filled her heart as she fell into a chair, sobbing in bitter torment. Am I going mad? she thought wildly. Has some mocking demon taken over my mind? This cannot be happening — not to Buck and me. She knew then the real, desperate meaning of isolation, and the icy coldness of its grip. If she had been alone before, it had been nothing like this terrible, terrifying void. She hated it, and she hated herself. It was as if she had put some wild, destructive force into motion and she would never be free of it again.

Daniel moaned, coming to his senses on the floor. She looked at him, her eyes swollen with tears. All the blinding passion of moments before was dead, burnt-out. She saw him in a new light, observing with stark clarity for the first time, the early signs of dissipation about his face, the weakness and the selfish egoism.

She saw him for what he was — a vain, handsome, utterly ruthless and charming opportunist, and she had allowed him to lead her to the break-up of her marriage, the ruin of her home, the loss of her children. Shuddering violently, she remembered that she had so nearly given herself to him. And now, with great agony of mind she knew that she had lost the only man strong enough for her — the only man she really loved with all her heart and mind and body — that her marriage was broken, finished, all trust gone.

Daniel totally repulsed her now. How could she have done it? How could she have given in to her fear and her selfish vanity? She had pushed Buck aside, just like his mother had done, by giving herself to another man. She had diminished herself and Buck, and most important of all, she had cheapened their relationship.

She turned on Daniel, regarding him with intense hatred through her wet and streaming eyes. She cried out in a passion of deepest rage. 'You have ruined my life — now get out of here! I never want to see you again as long as I live! And if you dare open your mouth in this community and accuse me of anything I will see to it that you are hounded from this colony forever!'

She looked away from the figure dazedly trying to raise himself to a sitting position. Just like a nightmare, there was an agonising moment when she could not move — then she propelled herself out of the chair and wrenched open the door.

She flew up the short, rocky ridge to the trail winding through the bushes, the rhythmic sound of cicadas loud in her ears. The cart which had brought them from the house was no longer standing outside, and Buck's horse was nowhere to be seen. She hardly heard the thunder of the surf on the deserted beach below, which had rung with childish laughter only a short while before. All she knew was that she had to reach Buck and the children before he took them away from the farm. She had to stop him, beg him to stay, to forgive her — even if she was forced to go down on her bended knees before him. She had been arrogant, too sure of herself and her attractions, and too afraid of what Daniel had known — or guessed, and she was more sorry than she knew how to express.

The bushes were dense, hindering her as she ran, tripping over broken branches. She fell into the damp undergrowth, tearing the fine muslin gown and cutting the ribbons of her shoes, which she was forced to discard. All was silence around her as she fell again and again, her skirts, petticoats and stockings torn beyond repair. Her face and hair were matted with earth and cut by the gnarled fingers of spiky branches sticking out into her path. The turquoise necklace was wrenched from her throat and lay forgotten in the mud.

She stumbled over the old gnarled roots twisting over her path like a grey, convoluted staircase, grazing her knees and arms as she raced on like a wild woman, her breath catching in her throat.

It was a long way back to the farmhouse, the path winding through the bushes, but all she could think was that she must reach Buck and the children before it was too late.

Long afterwards, her skirt held well above her bleeding knees, her stockings hanging in shreds, she broke from the cover of the trees into the open fields leading to the farmhouse, shocked once more into full, frantic flight.

Splintered branches brushed her arms, seeming to pierce them and her legs swished past large spider webs strung out between the grass-stalks. Once out of the thick palisade of trees and bush, she spurred herself on faster. The earth was heavy underneath her bare feet, the blades of sheep-bitten grass cutting into her flesh as she hurtled across the field.

She drew a harsh, rasping breath, knowing that her marriage and the love of her husband and children still hung precariously in the balance. She could see the mimosas far away, the tops of the tallest trees spiking the sky, the homestead small in the distance as she raced towards it.

She tore out of the grass to a great, echoing silence. It was broken only by the swishing of her ragged skirts and the hoarseness of her breath. Nothing seemed to move except the quiet gliding of a hawk crossing the fields in search of mice. Her heart stopped still, then started again, pounding furiously against her ribs. It was difficult to breathe, her throat was so dry.

She was too late. They had gone. Buck had already taken the children away. There was no sign of him, them or Beauty. The men were out in the fields and from the rest of the servants there was no sound. The wagon was gone.

There was a terrible fear in her heart as she ran, trembling, through the empty rooms, so unusually quiet. The clothes had gone, the home-made toys — and Aurora's favourite china doll. Heavy with despair she called all their names but only the echoing of her own voice came back to fill her ears. In an agony of indecision, she stood with her two hands pressed tightly over her mouth. She closed her eyes and the tears rolled slowly down her cheeks as she realized fully, with a searing sense of loss, that he had really gone and taken the children with him.

She walked back into the sitting-room where her eyes fell for the first time on the disorderly heap of her clothes thrown carelessly down on the floor. Beside them stood her wooden chest with the brass studs — the same one she had used to run away from Dwyers' Cross. Her best pair of embroidered, midnight-blue, satin slippers lay abandoned on the floor, shunned and discarded like some frivolous reminder of happy, giddy times that had turned into the most hideous of nightmares.

She continued to stand rooted to the floor. He wanted her out of his life, she understood that now, and the heap of clothes angrily tossed out had crystallized it in her mind. He had gone from her forever. He did not want to see her again, or be reminded of her.

She had nothing left. It had all been disastrously snatched from her. She had always feared it was too good to last. She would never see him again in this house. He would keep his word. Buck was not unlike her father in that regard. Her vitality ebbed away into the empty, quiet rooms about her. She had been trapped by her own nature, by her own passion and impulsiveness; now all hope was gone.

A footstep disturbed her. She whirled around with a mad, sudden hope that Buck had changed his mind and come back. But her heart sank when she saw it was Pike. He coughed, his seamed, scarred face flushed with embarrassment.

'The Commandant — 'e wants me to take you back to Dwyers' Cross ma'am — I'm sorry. I be ready when you are.'

Esther's eyes clouded with misery. Everything about her mocked her with its new wealth and luxury. Her eyes wandered about the room she had loved, and came to rest on the small Chippendale table below the long sash windows with the delicate ewer sprinkled with tiny, blue and purple daisies, outlined with goldleaf. For an icy moment she recalled a childhood memory that she had forgotten until then. She remembered how as a very small child, she had tried to spoon out the blue daisies ornamenting the soup bowls at Longwood House. They had almost seemed to swim free below the clear broth, but whenever she discovered she could not spoon them out she had experienced a strange acute disappointment — as if something infinitely special was escaping her. She felt that strangeness again, but mixed with a much deeper sorrow.

And now she was returning to Dwyers' Cross, to her father and his wrath, who would tell her how he knew this would happen. But he would be shocked that it had been she and not her husband who had caused the parting. Ever since she had arrived in Africa, her path always seemed to lead back to Dwyers' Cross.

She hated it all for that moment, the whole house filled with its beautiful and practical things standing side by side, wanting to break some valuable object. She wanted to vent the dreadful unhappiness locked up inside her on all the objects she had helped to choose so carefully.

Emptiness flooded over her as she remembered Pike's presence. His eyes were remote, embarrassed, set in shadowed hollows.

'I will tell you when I am ready, Mr Pike — I do not need you at the moment.'

He nodded and disappeared in haste, relieved to be out of her sight. The room swam dizzily around her as she sank down on the settle. She was afraid to think of the future. It was too painful for her now. There was only the present, and in it there was nothing she could cling to. She gasped, trying to breathe as blackness closed in on her. The last thing she remembered was the look on Amanda Lightfoot's face so long ago that day in her house, just before Esther ran out on her — white, drawn into lines of bitter hatred and jealousy. She remembered her screaming words of hatred before she swooned away and the maid rushed in with sal volatile. Ah Amanda, she thought, I understand you now as I have never understood you before.

Somewhere far away she heard the neigh of a horse, and a bird shrill in the trees. She knew she was fainting and realized there was no one to help her. No one at all.

This startled her back to consciousness. There was no one to help her anymore. Groping for the back of the chair, she pulled herself up, desperately trying to conquer the squeamishness inside her. She walked shakily to the yellowwood dresser on which was laid out a crystal decanter of Constantia wine. Lifting one of the goblets beside it with trembling fingers, she poured out a generous portion of the deep, red liquid. She took a sip, then drained the goblet, pouring out another, and a third.

Her suffering belonged to her alone. There was and never would be anyone else to share it. The main thing to do, she told herself as the wine began to take sly hold of her brain, was not to go to pieces, to think what to do. Uppermost in her befuddled thoughts was the feeling that she did not want to return to Dwyers' Cross in disgrace.

Rising with a swish of torn, muslin petticoats, she snuffed the candle Pike had lit, throwing the room into the same gloom which already enveloped the rest of the house. But she found she was crying, the tears falling unheeded on to her bruised and cut fingers, because she knew that much of what Buck had roared at her in Aloe Cottage was true; she could never undo what she had done — and he no longer loved her.

CHAPTER
Thirty-Nine

The day was warm and overcast, the air heavy and still. The door stood open to the late afternoon quiet and in the trees turtledoves cooed as other birds chattered and piped. The frequent thunderstorms that lit the sky had stopped, and the earth waited for the rain.

Esther sat on the rough wooden bench under the largest mimosa tree at the edge of the orchard. The dog lay in the shade beside her, snapping at the flies teasing his muzzle.

The men avoided her like the plague, especially Higgins, and even Pike. She had dismissed him telling him that she would not return to Dwyers' Cross, and that she would take the full consequences of her decision when the Commandant returned. He had kept out of her way, not knowing what to make of her decision but understanding there was nothing he could do to change it.

She had braced herself for a week now between hope and fear that Buck would return. But he never came. She caught glimpses of the servants sliding across the yard, glancing at her with curious, puzzled eyes. Only Mazinga and little Moses accepted her without question.

Turning her head away, she looked out across the fields bordered by the low-lying hills. A cluster of melkbos caught the sunlight in a gleam of sudden silver that hurt her eyes. She saw, out of the corner of her eye, Higgins emerge from the carpenter's workshop. He glanced once in her direction, scowling before he moved on. Esther felt a sob catch in her throat and took a deep, sharp breath to steady herself.

Inhaling the cool, living smell of the earth, she was somewhat comforted. Unconsciously she tossed her mane of dishevelled red curls. Unusually for her, she was totally uninterested in her appearance in the deepness of her pain. Yet the defiance lurking behind her eyes strengthened. She would not cry again. She would not let herself. And she would stop the drinking in which she had indulged self-piteously in the past days. She had started drinking far too much and it only made her feel worse. There was a lot of life left in her yet, she would pull herself together. And never, ever, would she crawl back to Dwyers' Cross. She still had her fierce pride, her lifetime habits were too strong. Deserted she was, but not defeated.

She did not know what had happened to Daniel, and she did not care. All thought of him made her cringe. All she wanted to do was to forget that he had ever existed.

Unseeing, she looked across the lands, breathing the damp, fresh air, and feeling the soft, early evening breeze moist against her cheek as the purple shadows deepened under the trees. An emptiness hung over everything, like some great, dark desolation. She could not eat anything, had not been able to eat for days. As the minutes passed and the dusk descended like a blanket, she rose to enter the silent, dusty house reluctantly.

She picked her way through the yard. No one was there, except Mazinga, who smiled and darted a respectful nod at her. The men's huts were lit up. Inside the men were talking; the sound echoed, making her feel more cut off than ever. Beyond the quince hedge, bordering the kitchen garden, she heard the voices of the servants, talking quietly while frogs croaked in the long grass.

The bitter taste of hopelessness was again in her mouth as she lit the candles to keep out the darkness from her and from her thoughts. She was not tired or hungry. She was not anything as she wandered through the rooms, the corners now thick with shadows, cobwebbed and lustreless. Her feet made very little sound over the skin rugs encrusted with dust on the floor.

She wandered into the boys' room, listening to the trees near the window rattling drily in the rising wind, the candle glowing red through her shielding hand. Once she heard the hooting of an owl somewhere out in the darkness. A roar of bawdy laughter sounded. There was singing across the yard, broken by quarrelsome, drunken shouts. Something crashed; Parker's voice roared out; the noise subsided, and a different more melancholy song began.

Esther walked back into the sitting-room, and it was then, as she placed the candlestick on the mantelshelf, that she lowered her head, weakening her resolve not to cry.

The tears rolled unchecked down her face and she wept in wracking sobs as she had not wept since Garnet's death. But this was far worse. Then, events had been beyond her control, something final she had been forced to accept. This time, it was what she had caused herself.

It was a week later and, outside, the shadowy tracks of countryside spread under a cloudless sky and a full African moon. The tall silhouettes of the mimosas along the driveway were black against the sky.

Esther sat up in bed, tense and still. She put a hand for a moment to her breast, all instincts instantly alert. She groped for the tinderbox beside the bed. Trembling violently, the flint and steel were clumsy in her hands. After a few attempts the spark caught and she shakily lit the candle, watching the flame curling slowly upward.

Something had awakened her and made her feel uneasy. She had been alone in the house for almost two weeks, and no one had come near her. So completely had she been isolated from everyone, from all support and companionship, that she had become jumpy and nervous. She remembered with a start that she had forgotten to bolt the doors, and she had let the dog out hours before. The bedroom door was slightly ajar. The bright moonlight filtering through from the sitting-room, gave an unreal quality to all it touched. She heard, or thought she heard, the distinct, soft sound of footfalls somewhere in the house. The dog had not barked outside, but some instinct deep inside her told her that she was not alone.

She felt suddenly, a strong sense of another presence groping its way towards the sitting-room. Her eyes searched the darkness beyond the room, her senses aroused and sensitive, pushing all drowsiness to the back of her mind. There was no one to be seen.

She could see dark shadows, the shapes of her wooden chest

405

and valise by the door, packed and waiting to leave in the morning. Finally realizing there was nothing she could do to win Buck back, Esther had asked Pike to convey her to Port Elizabeth.

She could see nothing else, but she knew, in every cell of her body, that she was not alone. Sitting petrified, unable to move, her eyes continued to dart along the sliver of light beyond the door.

Something, or someone, knocked against the settle. She shrank back in terror, unarmed and defenceless. Closing her eyes for the briefest of seconds, she heard the loud hammering of her heart, expecting to be set upon any moment. The sound of footsteps reached her from behind the bedroom door. Her terror grew frenzied as the door was pushed open. She did not move or speak, but gazed at the figure leaning against the doorframe as if it was a ghost.

Then quite suddenly her fear passed, evaporated in the darkness. She recognized Buck's powerful frame in the candlelight staring at her, a terrible fatigue about him. Speechless, with numb amazement, she could only gaze at him. She had never dreamt to see him like this; his pale, unkempt appearance appalled her, shocked her out of all fear, all feeling for herself. He was dishevelled, his face haggard and drawn.

Staring at him with incredulity, she sat bolt upright. Her hair a wild tangle, there were great, black circles under her eyes, in a face washed of all colour. It was the pale wanness of her face that unconsciously reached out to him, thrusting past all the pain in that deep silent moment in a way her beauty never could.

He waited, still leaning against the doorframe. She did not speak, and her face was whiter, if possible, than before.

She watched him advance slowly into the room, his tousled brown curls flecked with silver threads. His beard was matted and untidy as if he no longer cared. He sighed, hesitating. Then he drew up a chair beside the bed and sank heavily into it. In the candlelight his lined face, the anguished eyes and the total despair about the beautiful mouth impressed themselves more vividly on Esther's tormented mind than anything else.

She had done this to him — she had caused this terrible transformation. It was just as well she was leaving him, and

406

taking with her all capacity to hurt him. He had not deserved to be treated so badly. There was something in his stillness that seemed to melt the tension in her.

'I heard you were leaving tomorrow,' he said finally, weighing every word carefully before he spoke. 'I am surprised you stayed so long — it is a relief to find you — alone.' He sighed, his tired blue eyes gazing into hers. 'Mazinga — he found me — he did not want you to leave. He wanted me to come back. I've been riding for miles, anywhere away from this house, this room.'

'Oh Buck,' she whispered thickly, her throat constricted with misery, 'why did you come back? How I have hurt you. I am so very sorry. I never thought to see you again. I was so terribly afraid of what Daniel knew — he threatened me. I am leaving for the good of both of us — and the children. They cannot live in my terrible shadow. I must free them — you — myself. I never gave myself to Daniel, believe me. There has only been you. That — that was a stupid, meaningless escapade.'

He stared at her, the blue eyes strangely dead and lifeless. 'Whatever happened, happened — and no one can change that now,' he said hoarsely. 'It's over, dead, gone.' He was silent for a few moments as she waited tensely. 'Where will you go? How will you live — you haven't much to live on. What will you do?'

She looked away, dashing the sudden tears away with the cuff of her nightgown. She did not look at him when she spoke. 'To Cape Town, and then perhaps back to Ireland or England. I can look for a job as a governess to some wealthy family. I have the education for that. I'll go somewhere where no one will know what I've done. I don't want to disgrace anyone ever again.' When she looked back, the sorrow was etched deep about her eyes and in the lines around her mouth.

He rubbed a hand across his eyes, looking oddly and uncharacteristically abstracted. 'I came back to stop you leaving. If you had gone to Dwyers' Cross I would have fetched you because I can never let you go.'

She did not dare to breathe, knowing how much it was costing him to say these words, because he possessed as proud a spirit as she.

He looked at her untidy hair, at the pale face, the downcast eyes ringed by deep shadows. 'I could not bear the thought of

Eden without you, Esther — no matter what you've done. I realize now what made you do it. I need you, and the children need you, and that is the all of it.'

He waited, not making an effort to touch her. She remained silent, as sweet warmth washed through her. Unbearable relief stirred inside her, seeping back over the terrible suffering and mortification. But he still had not said he loved her. He needed her though, in spite of all she had done. He may not love her, but he needed her. There was so much damage to repair, it would take time to wash away the hurt. There was still too much between them, too many days of despair and betrayal. They had to try to recover the closeness they had once shared. She owed him this attempt, and she had no right to ask for his love until she earned it once more.

She wanted to say all this but she was afraid to tell him. She felt unfamiliarly nervous, and ashamed. She continued to stare at the strong-boned face, the face she loved so much. After some time she spoke in the quietness of the room.

'I never loved Daniel — he meant nothing to me. Please say that you forgive me. I could never stay if you don't.' She turned her face away to hide her growing embarrassment and distress. Struggling for words to adequately smooth a situation that had gone far beyond her, she suddenly felt inept. Turning back to him, she spoke with a rush. 'If you can find it in your heart to forgive me, I will stay and start all over again, and try very hard to make you forget what I did.'

He dropped his hands to his knees. She wanted him so much then, wanted to feel his arms about her, feel his thick, strong hair between her fingers — to give him the warmth and love he deserved. But she could only sit and watch him, distanced by what she had done to him.

'I love you, Buck, more than anyone, more than anything. I have never met anyone like you, ever. I want to make it up to you in every way I can. I need you too.' The words were out, the words she had never been able to say to anyone, ever, in the whole of her life. She did need him, and now he knew it too.

Then his rigidity melted and he allowed the faintest of smiles to shadow his beautiful lips. 'Let's leave the past in the past. The only thing that's important is what's between us, you and me —

408

that we still have that something between us to mend — and that Aurora will never know the truth.'

There was the faintest glimmer of tears in his eyes as he looked at her, then they blazed suddenly with their old vivid light. She breathed deeply, then smiled at him, painfully. Feelings rushed to her in a flood. She loved him so much. He was her destiny, her future and she had to make that absolutely clear to him right now.

She reached for him, pulling him to her, locking her arms about him fiercely. 'I love you so much, believe it, for it has always been true.' It was good to have him back, to feel him, hold him.

He knelt down beside the bed and hugged her body as she moved closer to him. 'I could never let you be a governess to some unsuspecting family,' he said huskily, with a touch of the old humour, 'you might very well seduce the father of the house, and then where would you be?'

She smiled sadly, holding his head in her hands. She brought it to her breast, and pressed it there. 'You always have to bail me out of trouble, my dearest, but that is going to stop. I no longer need you to save me from myself. I am a reformed woman. Don't ever leave me again though, promise me?' Her voice was an urgent whisper, a prayer. 'I am not complete without you, not very much of a person.'

A lump constricted her throat so that she could say no more. She took his face between her hands, loving the feel of his skin. Lovingly she traced the lines of his dimples with her finger. Then she pressed him as close to her as she could with a fierce new protectiveness, her eyes large and bright.

He seemed poignantly touched by the warm spontaneity of her actions, for he said, in the gentlest of voices as he lifted his head, 'Life tends to make fools of us all at times, Esther. We fight to survive, to save face, to keep our small selves together, but in the end we lose our balance and cause such misery around us.'

Her eyes were not smiling, they were unusually soft and filled with welling tears. 'I know what I have done — you have every right to say such things about me. I shall never forget what I have done to you — to everyone.' Her indrawn breath was almost a half-strangled sob, as Buck's words began to take hold, to force

409

into shape the mass of feelings between them.

He shook his head. He did not look at her. His face was drawn and sad and looked suddenly exhausted. He spoke with effort. 'No — I am talking of myself. I am as much to blame as you. I had been looking forward to seeing you again after so long — knowing you would be there with all the things I have grown to love.'

He cleared his throat as if it was even harder to put his thoughts into words, and when he spoke his voice was more husky than ever. 'All the high moments of my life — all those things I consider of real importance — have been with you. You see, you have always given a meaning to my life — to everything I do. Always, inside of me, I have had a kind of loneliness — but with you there has always been some private and special sharing. You have become, sweetheart — in a manner of speaking — my best friend.' He sighed and dropped his head. 'I have never shared so much with anyone — I was afraid to try. Yet, even so, I have not given enough.'

Esther had never felt such a softness in her since she had been a very small child. There was a new confidence in her, an elation born of the knowledge that all she felt he was feeling too. Along with the rush of sweetness, the curl of ecstasy, she felt the beginning of a deep-seated security which would hold them through all that still faced them. She brought her hand down slowly, and closed it over his strong fingers. She turned them over, and lifting them she pressed a kiss against the hard, rough palms, the tears now very bright, pricking her eyes.

He spoke again, his voice laboured and slow as if his thoughts were still agonisingly painful. 'I failed to see that someone else could arouse that passion in you I thought was only mine. Lavoisier was right in one thing — I have neglected you far too long. You were damned right — I was jealous at seeing you in the arms of someone else. I demanded too much of you, of your patience, your life, without giving you enough of mine. We have built up too much to throw it all on the scrap-heap of vanity and false pride, Esther.'

He smiled his old teasing smile, then it faded. 'Lud! I nearly did the most senseless thing in my life — sending you away when you were the best thing that ever happened to me. I am too old

410

now, at nearly forty, to go gallivanting into the wilds and the back of beyond. I must make way for the green youths to prove their manly strength and courage. It is time to settle down and finish what we've started, complete the cycle of growth here with you, before it is too late.'

She kissed him then, with all the old, fierce possessiveness he knew so well. She slid her arms around his neck, and sifted her fingers through his thick hair. How she had longed to do that again! Her lips felt his brows, his cheeks, his eyelids. He sank on to the bed, taking her into his arms and she soared with a sense of overwhelming elation.

She found comfort in his closeness. Tonight he had been weak, weaker than he had ever been, but tomorrow she knew he would be strong again. And it was in this very weakness that she had at last found him, that Buck he had hidden deep inside himself, who had always escaped her until now.

CHAPTER
Forty

Esther and Buck slowly resolved their differences, the mistrust and the suffering, and grew closer than ever. But not before there was an almighty row with Higgins and Parker, who still resented Esther's behaviour with Daniel Lavoisier. Buck supported Esther, and in the end both men left the farm, leaving Pike and Egmont Moss, who remained loyal.

Buck kept his word as 1831 began, and spent his time on the farm, setting up a farm school. The more progressive farmers of Graaff-Reinet and Murraysberg were buying his merinos, and a small revolution in sheep farming was activated in the Eastern Cape. Buck took the risk and started a profitable business of importing stock from Britain, the German states and Australia, for sale to local farmers. Together with a handful of enterprising farmers, he pioneered the idea of a Grahamstown Joint Stock Company. He was still not interested in the details of bookkeeping, accounting and saving, and left it all to Esther, who kept a tight rein on all their financial matters. She was twenty-nine, pregnant once more, and it was largely due to her that their wealth grew and multiplied.

She put Buck's lack of interest down to the fact that because he had never had much money until he was in his thirties, he had lived frugally on what the Army provided, and it was too late to change the habits of years. He loved new ideas, the challenge of pioneering enterprises and making them work. The broad aspects and outlines of a plan fascinated him, and he was content to leave the details of the husbanding of the results to her.

A third son, Jonathan, was born on a cold day in late July, and as time passed his first mop of fluffy dark hair fell out, to be replaced by soft tendrils of brown hair, curling about his small round head. His most outstanding feature was his extraordinarily beautiful eyes, so like his mother's, but of a lighter, more translucent blue and very large, striking in the quality of their colour and the childlike directness of their gaze. He was christened at the Settler's Church at Port Frances, in the same exquisite robe of white satin and Brussels lace worn by Aurora and the twins before him. The only relatives present were Laree, Roydon and their four children.

It was a great trial for Laree who had just lost her fifth child in childbirth and was still recovering. Early autumn was on the land, the countryside awash with the bright flames of aloes and orange-mauve of the strelitzias, when Arthur Wilson died, a month after Charity. Beneath a cobalt blue sky, as shreds of cloud drifted across it and the sweet country air pervaded the surroundings, the last clod of earth was thrown onto his wooden coffin at Sunfield Park. There was a deep silence among the mourners, including Joshua and Cady, who remembered the loyal support of their friend in bad times.

Among the crowd who went up to the house later for refreshments, only Esther, Buck and their children were conspicuous by their absence.

Buck had discovered during his visit to Msilikazi with Roydon that it was his firearms that interested the Matabele king. He had heard of them when Buck had traded in the land between the Orange and Vaal Rivers with the Bahrutsi people some years before. He had waited for two years to see this magic for himself, when Buck had demonstrated his skill by killing a cow instantly with a shot of half lead, half pewter. He and Roydon had successfully managed to depart without giving the King any firearms, as they feared the outcome if they did. They did, however, impress him with Buck's rudimentary knowledge of medicine, when he was able to cure one of Msilikazi's blinding headaches.

Daniel Lavoisier had disappeared, never to be heard of again, and Roydon continued to hunt in the north, visiting the King on occasion and making a fortune in the process. He was forced away from Natal as the trade was not good, due to the undercutting of prices by the Portuguese at Lourenco Marques.

In addition, he had inherited Sunfield Park and set about buying more sheep from Buck.

There was growing enthusiasm among the Boers for Natal, a paradise of grass-covered plains, fertile river banks and warm, soft winds. Back in Albany, the effects of Ordinance 50, giving the Hottentots, Bushmen and freecoloured persons full right to own land if they could get it, and freeing them of all restrictive laws, continued to sour relations between the British Government and the settlers. Yet, in spite of the vagrancy, many satisfactory relationships between Hottentots and Mantatees and their masters developed. Despite its obvious deficiencies, the Ordinance did place the employment of these races and their legal treatment on a more rational and moral basis.

The following year, 1832, passed with many of the leading Boers casting their eyes increasingly towards Natal. They wished to get as far away from the resented administration of the British Government as they could, where there was more land for their growing herds.

Twice Macomo and Lungelo were allowed to return to the Ceded Territory from the dry eastern lands, and twice they were expelled due to friction with the settlers. Macomo was to ask: 'When shall I and my people be able to rest?' It was a question troubling the other chiefs.

Drought aggravated the situation as colonists were already driving their herds far into Xhosaland because of it. Friction mounted at the clay pits, where the number of Xhosas now being allowed to enter the colony grew. Cady Dwyer mounted a guard of his remaining men, and it was their task to drive off any trespassers near the pits before they could steal cattle. The constant changes in the reprisal system led to confusion and abuse as the Government struggled to maintain an impossible system.

Throughout all this time Buck Jones remained a familiar, enthusiastic, and, to some degree, a lonely figure at the meetings of men such as the Dwyer brothers and their peers. The Dwyers and Buck stayed proud, unbending antagonists. Joshua only just managed to control the rising tide of hatred he felt towards the man who had married his favourite daughter. He was wise enough to realize that he had to keep his own counsel and dignity before the man who was now one of the leading merino-sheep breeders, and who it was rumoured had earned one thousand and eight hundred pounds from the ivory hunted on Msilikazi's lands. He and Cady came very far behind him in financial terms. Buck had also built up a fairly large following of respect in recent years, as a man of forceful, though often controversial, opinions.

He continued to make money steadily from the excellent quality of his wool and he and Esther were finally accepted by the influential, new commercial class of settler society. He was recognized more and more as a man of substance, means and sharp intelligence, who had fought his way out of his past and succeeded.

Buck stood at the vortex trying to keep the balance between three opposing forces: the colonists, the government forces and the black tribesmen. He understood the bitterness and hatred of the colonists for the system which opposed them and inadequately defended them; he understood the motives of the military and the government agencies; and he knew the resentment and the anger of the tribesman. He was in a dilemma: where did he stand — for the colonists or against them? For the Xhosas or against them?

Through his contacts in Xhosaland, he had come to appreciate the concerns and the problems of the Xhosas more than most. Yet, he remained a colonist, a new landowner with the love of his land deep inside him. His conviction grew stronger with time that black and white, Boer and Briton must learn to live together peacefully on the frontier. He felt instinctively that without the support of the Xhosa clans, especially those living near the colony, there could be no peace. There had to be, in his mind, some kind of understanding brought about between the races in a border settlement satisfactory to both sides. He also felt that the Xhosa had to come to terms with themselves, make peace among their own kind, before they could make peace permanently with the white man.

As the years sped by, the little village of Port Frances retrogressed and almost disappeared entirely. The treacherous sand-bar had not been overcome. The Government Resident and the harbour master were abolished and all the government buildings sold. And all the time the settlement moved inexorably

415

to a climax, unanticipated by the majority of settlers still living on the border of Xhosaland.

A change was clearly coming now that the great Reform Bill had become law in England. Slave emancipation was carried and letters patent were issued, providing for a nominated Legislative Assembly for the Cape. The new Governor, Sir Benjamin D'Urban, arrived in 1834 to put the new constitution into force, but as had so often happened in the past, violence was to destroy the immediate prospects of reform.

The first day of December dawned clear and bright with a slight breeze over Grahamstown and the rest of Albany stretching away to the east. Even though the settlement had again suffered another prolonged drought, it was forgotten on this memorable day in the town as the Anti-Slavery Law became at last a fact, part of a general movement throughout the Empire. This meant that the slaves of the Western Cape, and the very few in the East, were freed, and the liberal-minded settlers rejoiced in true British style.

There was much bustle and activity in the High Street of Grahamstown, which now boasted itself almost as big, and second only, to Cape Town. The roads were bad and the drifts unsafe, but the town continued to expand. The surrounding hills were now criss-crossed with broad ribbons of rutted, inferior roads leading out from the town to other parts of the settlement.

Everyone had turned out to celebrate. The streets were alive with streams of gaily dressed people, all greeting those they passed on the way to St George's Church at the bottom of High Street. Outspanned wagons lined the streets from outlying farms. All over Albany, at different church centres, similar events were taking place. Buck and Esther had been invited by the Rowlands to stay with them and join in the ceremonies there instead of at Bathurst, their nearer destination.

The simple church, rough-hewn of local stone, was bursting at its seams, as every available place was taken. The aisles were packed to capacity with townsfolk, Hottentots and half-breeds, for the thanksgiving service at eleven o'clock.

Later there were shouts of pleasure and laughter as the children formed a procession with brightly-coloured banners

416

fluttering in the breeze. They marched to the sound of sprightly music up to the elevated ground beyond the town, accompanied by the rest of the congregation, singing and rejoicing. The trees shimmered in the bright sunshine, festooned with flags and banners, as the sound of many voices lifted in song, before the important event of the afternoon, the public meeting to commemorate the occasion.

Esther stood beside Buck, in an off-shoulder, frilled gown of ribbon-striped, aurora sarsenet, covered by a pale lace and gauze fichu, caught by a small posy of matching flowers at her throat. It was a softly shimmering dress, changing colour as the light caught it, and seeming to hold the sun in its folds. Her head tilted slightly to the side so that the red ringlets peeped from her bonnet which was plumed with black ostrich feathers. She did not care a jot today that Frances Somerset, newly returned from Europe, was the most elegantly turned-out lady in the latest fashionable gigot sleeves. All that mattered to her was the presence of her husband, of whom she was so proud. And his eyes paid her tribute.

She relaxed and prepared to enjoy herself. Their affinity was more complete and comfortable than it had ever been, and for that she was content. She was aware every now and then, of female heads turning but Buck seemed completely oblivious to the looks cast in his direction. He smiled at her, a delightful, conspiratorial smile, full of the memories they shared.

She glanced at him, savouring every detail of his appearance. He wore a well-cut, long, dark blue coat, grey trousers, a pale scarf knotted at his throat over a spotless white shirt. In his hand he held his grey, beaver-trimed hat, and his curly brown hair was flecked distinguishedly with silver. A short, close-cropped beard of rich brown hair also flecked with silver, framed his strong face.

She caught sight of the twins and little Jonathan not far away. Aurora, with them, stood behind her twin brothers, holding Jonathan's hand. She, at ten, was tall and large-boned, with silky brown ringlets and ivory skin. Her face, under a gay straw bonnet, was already both pretty and delicate, and her placid eyes now lit up at the sight of Buck.

Esther looked at her thoughtfully. She saw the beautiful eyes of her daughter still fixed on Buck. Those about, singing with full, joyous voices, were too busy to see their exchange of smiles. Lately, Aurora had shown that she had most remarkable healing hands — a massage from her hands had caused headaches and other pains to disappear, and she was much in demand on the farm. But she still played with dolls and childish toys like a six-year-old. Esther wondered sadly what would become of their daughter when she and Buck were gone one day. Most people regarded her as simple, and it was obvious that she could never marry. She would have to remain on the farm, shielded and protected from the world, until the day she died. Recently, the hero-worship Aurora had for Buck was causing complications. It had led to resentment and misunderstandings, and not a little jealousy between her brothers.

Esther was interrupted by the sight of her seven-year-old twins giggling softly in front of their sister. Their red-gold hair gleamed in the sunlight. Trouble seemed to follow them everywhere, their pockets full of snares, slings, worms and cameleons. Their days passed trespassing on shrews and pouncing on guinea-fowl. Yet, for all their pranks, they had been forced to grow up quickly in other ways — to become the children of the bush, who could pick out the movement of an adder or grass-snake, to identify accurately the calls of the birds and to ride the smaller horses bare-backed.

She suddenly felt her heart and mind burst with a joy almost too big to contain. These were her family, they were all she had, and they were all together after the past years of fear and longing, loneliness and despair. The world assumed for her a wonderful glow that had nothing to do with the reality about her, where believers and unbelievers mingled for one day.

Everything seemed transformed before her eyes — the sun giving brilliance to all around her, the trees, the hills, the town huddled below.

As the congregation joined voice again and she added her own not-too-musical voice to theirs, Guy, the more restless of the two, brandished a bright green cameleon, his wicked hand hovering near the back of a small girl's bottle-green velvet spencer. Suddenly there was a flash as Buck semi-circled the crowd in a trice and swooped up the unsuspecting little boy, hauling him off as the children broke away from the adults for sticky cakes and home-made lemonade, and the public meeting began in earnest.

As the bright orange ball of sun hung low in the early evening sky, a large and lively tea-party was held in John and Elizabeth Rowlands' new store, by far the largest in town. Already the windows of the houses in the streets were illuminated by candles, orange points of light everywhere.

Esther looked up for a second from the platters of cold meats, contributed by all of the womenfolk — thick slices of roast beef, chunks of turkey, sliced brown hams, lamb, mutton, pork thick with crackling, loaded on the long trestle-tables. She pressed her way through the large throng of guests humming about her, the room blazing in the light of many candles Then she stopped, the trilling cadences of laughter all around her, the flash and shimmer of silks and satins, and felt an instant sense of alarm.

Her eyes took in the figures of her father and Uncle Cady, approaching the edge of the crowd near the open door. She had avoided seeing either of them ever since that fateful day, seven years ago, when she had run away from Dwyers' Cross. She had dreaded this moment, knowing that some day, sometime, it would come. Now it seemed that there was no way out, they were about to come face to face at last. The moment of reckoning she had dreaded had come before all these people.

Why had they come to Grahamstown, she wondered wildly, why? Why had they not gone to Bathurst? It would have been so much easier if they had.

Nerves tightened the muscles of her throat, and she was curiously unable to move as she stared at them. Faces she loved in that far-off nightmare life that no longer belonged to her. Her heart raced chaotically as her father suddenly looked up at her, startled, their eyes meeting for one transient moment. She thought for one ridiculous second that at last he was about to acknowledge her, that the chasm between them would finally be bridged. She hardly dared to breathe as silence fell around her.

Then he tightened, a shadow of wariness passing across his face, and his eyes darkened. His expression sank into her brain, shaping torment out of pain. She could not bear to look into those wounded eyes, and to see the stern, lined face, framed with its snow-white hair, now showing the weariness, the disillusionment

419

and the thickening of age, become a mask. She flushed feverishly as he tried to hide his surprise, but her quick observant eye saw the varied emotions flickering in his eyes.

Then it was over, the moment was gone. He walked on, recovering, as if she did not exist. She knew that the immediate crowd was watching them with intense interest. She was not thinking clearly, but she felt a stirring of fear — a premonition of a calamity she did not understand. Everything in her demanded that she should go after him ... but she remained where she was, trapped by stubborn pride, misery and confusion. With the pride came the guilt that tore her apart.

Cady had not seen her yet. Trying to fight back the tears, she prepared to slip into a crevice in the wall of guests. But not before she caught Cady's bright, hazel eye. For one miniscule fraction of time she wanted to throw herself into his arms, teasing and mocking and laughing as she had done so long ago in her childhood, when he came to visit them from the West Indies.

Uncle Cady, always good-natured, fiery, amusing — always baiting her because he loved her and saw through all her weaknesses, her defences, always attempting to knock them down, one by one. There had always been that between them, that battle of wits, and how she longed to have those times again. But the naked bitterness in his eyes now made her heart stop for an instant. He was looking at her as if she had betrayed him, betrayed her father. She froze — but there was something else there, a great hurt that lurked behind that look in his eyes.

A change came over his face and she thought, hoped, that he would smile in that old, teasing way. But it was not to be. He looked at her strangely, as if she was a blur at the edge of his vision, out of focus. He stiffened, his eyes alone burning in a face suddenly grown old and blank. Then he turned away, his brows drawing together in fierce concentration, the lines of his face falling into inflexibility and deep sadness she could not bear to see.

She stood there, filled with agony, crucifying herself for what she had done to them — for not being able to go to them and ask their forgiveness, mend the chasm between them. If only there could have been another way, but she knew that there was never any going back.

420

Then her pride rose, stifling the hurt and covering it with anger and indignation. Knowing nowhere else to hide herself, she plunged quickly into the line of buzzing, laughing people, with a flash of silk and a straight, proud back. Whisking up a plate, she heaped it with meat and assorted salads she knew she could never eat. She moved as if in a dream, past the dozen and more cold puddings and pies, indifferent to each tantalising size, shape and colour. Over the whole party hung the veiled sense of unease she had felt since the arrival of her kinsmen. The sun disappeared into the fast gathering gloom as she stood in the close-packed throng, glasses ringing with toast after toast. The clatter and clanking of platters ceased as speech followed speech, and she felt utterly alone.

She tried half-heartedly to join the guests, who with gay disregard for all troubles caused by the British Government, were singing 'Rule Britannia', when she caught Buck's speculative glance. He was watching closely, his eyes alive to every expression that passed across her face.

Summoning up a brilliant, false smile, she suddenly wanted to hide her innermost feelings from him. But she knew there was so little she could hide from those eyes, so wise, so penetrating, as if he could see into her very soul.

Outwardly she was excited and gay, a roguish sparkle about her. She laughed and clapped in a bright desperate charade to hide an unbearable sorrow. All the while as she played the role she had chosen for the evening, she felt as if she was at a funeral and not a party. As she smiled and laughed she prayed that she could continue to play it out until the end of a suddenly sombre and depressing evening.

Forty-One

For fourteen years the feud between the blacks and whites had gathered force. It was that December that it finally exploded. It took only a small spark to set the explosion alight, very little friction to flare the flame after months of tension.

Cattle-lifting had been one of the endemic scourges of the frontier, complicated by other complex problems, that could not, even with twice the forces available to Colonel Henry Somerset, be adequately policed. The colony could not boast of impressive fortifications as there were very few forts. Fort Willshire, the strongest, on the banks of the Keiskamma River was resented by the tribesmen as an intolerable invasion of their ancestral lands.

There were many complexities, but the fact remained that when the new governor, Sir Benjamin D'Urban, failed to visit the tribesmen, who expected him to negotiate with them as promised, they listened more readily to the war parties in Xhosaland. The latter were already exploiting the tensions produced by the protracted drought.

The unrest gripped the border and threatened to pull it apart as Colonel Somerset, anxious to recover any stolen cattle before the long-delayed visit of the new governor to the frontier, whipped up his patrols.

The day before Christmas was bright. The sun shone warmly through the matted gold of the summer flowers at Sunfield Park in the Blaaukranz Valley. Esther, who was staying with her family at Sunfield Park for Christmas, looked at the timepiece about the waist of her pinafore. She smiled to herself as she surveyed the spread before her in the kitchen for the following day — mince pies, turkey, beef and ham. The large plum pudding bubbled away over the fire behind her.

She loved this place, built on a flat shelf between a sloping hillside and a rocky gorge. On its open side were the fields and gardens and the cattle and sheep kraals. One or two cows were grazing not too far from the house; the rest were further out in the fields. Goats and some sheep grazed on the hill, the others were still in the kraal where Buck and Mazinga were assembling them with the new lot Roydon had bought from Eden. Everything here reminded her of Arthur and Charity Wilson and the heritage they had left.

She heard Laree humming to her newly-born fifth child, a daughter she was feeding in the next room, while Roydon was in Bathurst fetching urgently needed supplies. She walked over to the fire, conscious of a satisfying contentment. Happiness had given her an appetite, painted a glow about her face, lent sparkle to her eyes.

Aurora and thirteen-year-old Emma, her eldest cousin, came running back from the orchard, with the peach leaves, held in the folds of their wide aprons, to boil with the egg custard to give it a delicious almond flavour. They tossed them on to the large, scrubbed sneezewood table, sticking wicked fingers into the mince pies arrayed on it.

Esther admonished a warning finger and shooed them away. In another moment they had swamped her, Emma plying eager questions as to their Christmas gifts for the next day. Aurora's face was lit by a childish glow as she babbled away in short, jerky sentences. Laughing, Esther answered her niece briefly and gestured them to leave.

Emma whirled on her playfully, cheeks flushed from running. 'You always say that, Aunt Esther — when will you ever change?'

Esther opened her mouth to reply and found she was facing empty air. Her daughter had run outside, at the heels of flaxen-haired Emma, to the fields where her brothers and cousins played in the grass.

She had no more time to think about them as the cooling bowls for the wine goblets in Irish cut-glass were brought in, and she was required to check them where they stood, sparkling on the dresser. Inside the dresser the home-made Christmas gifts were hidden — gay sashes for the girls, with gilt painted acorns on the ends, freshly sewn shirts for the men, boxes of ninepins for the boys. The rocking-horse for Jonathan had been safely tucked away in the barn.

Beyond the gleaming yellowwood staircase in the entrance hall, the sitting-room was bright and sweet-smelling with gay bowls of flowers. Earlier the children had excitedly planned the amusements for that evening — kiss-in-the-ring and forfeits being the favourites. As she stirred the pudding, Esther viewed the coming arrangements with a tinge of pleasure. She was feeling alive and it showed. This was the first time in years that the Joneses and the Wilsons had celebrated Christmas together. The only shadow over her day was the fact that her father and uncle had refused to come, on hearing that she and Buck would be present.

Esther was tired of giving up family gatherings because of her father and uncle and had accepted Laree's invitation, sad at the absence of her kinsmen. But she was determined not to let their absence spoil her pleasure. Perhaps, she thought, by next Christmas they would be reconciled to the idea and they would all be together at last.

Her thoughts were interrupted by Buck's tall figure blocking out the light in the doorway. He leaned an arm on the bottom half of the stable-door, bent his head and looked in.

'That smells good, sweetheart — food for the gods and their friends.' He stroked his full, silver-sprinkled, brown beard, stirred by the sight of the food on the table. His checked shirt-sleeves were unbuttoned and loose at his wrists, and a brown leather waistcoat hung open. He threw her an engaging smile, wiping his eyes with the back of his hands. 'Roydon should be pleased with the sheep we brought him, they're the best stock we had. Mazinga and I — we've just finished putting 'em in the kraal.'

'He should be back from Bathurst by now,' Esther said, a warm glint in her eyes. 'I need those supplies if we're to finish the preparations for tomorrow.'

Buck was about to answer when a horse came galloping into the yard, its hoofs ringing loudly on the stones. The animal reared with a great whinny. It was Roydon, but without the supplies and without the wagon. They were shocked by his drawn look and the anger of his mouth.

424

'The Xhosas are attacking the colony — a war has started! They've killed all the traders in Xhosaland,' he thundered. 'We've been warned to retreat to the church at Bathurst as a point of defence.' He turned to Buck. 'I'm going to warn the Dwyers and the men in the Coombs — that is the first line of defence and vulnerable to the most danger. Please see to the farm, Buck, and take the women and children to safety at Bathurst.' From all of those within hearing distance there was a stunned silence.

'It can't be true! I won't believe it!' Esther cried, her face stricken by his expression.

'We have to move immediately,' Buck said. 'We've known it would come — it has taken us at an unexpected moment, that is all.' He slammed his fist on the top of the door.

Esther looked at him. She knew that his stark expression at that moment would live in her memory for a long time. Her face froze with shock. 'But what of Laree and the baby? What are we to do?' She was churning inside, her mind spilling with murderous thoughts.

'Go, Roydon — there's no time to lose,' Buck urged. 'Warn the men at Dwyers' Cross — get to the others in the valley — tell 'em to flee while the going is good. I'll send Mazinga to Eden to tell Pike and Moss to take the sheep and cattle to Port Elizabeth. Don't fret about your sheep and cattle — we'll round 'em up and take 'em too.'

He towered over Roydon and the servants who had gathered around him, a natural leader assuming his authority with bold assurance.

'Can you trust Mazinga?' Roydon asked, his thoughts reflected in his grey eyes, careful and wary.

Buck shot him a glance. An odd expression passed fleetingly across his face. He was silent for a moment. 'Aye, I do. He'll know how to avoid the warriors. He's been too loyal for too long to turn against us now.' He looked at Roydon with an expression Esther could not fathom.

Roydon's watchful eyes flickered and were steady again. 'I see. Well, I had better get going — there's not a moment to lose.'

As he rode off, Buck charged from the door. 'Esther, go and tell Laree to get ready to move out of here, and collect all the children.'

Esther hurled herself after him, flinging open the door. 'Buck! Come back! Whatever are we going to do with all this food? There are the gifts, everything! We can't just pack up and leave it all.'

He turned and looked at her cheerlessly, his figure vivid against the sky. 'That food is not going to help you once we are attacked, sweetheart. Your life — all the lives here are more important. I'll get Roydon's livestock together with the help of the servants. Then we'll leave, Esther — it is not safe here anymore.'

'And what will happen to you — what will you do after that?' Her eyes searched his, and for a terrible stabbing moment she knew the squeeze of fear so strong it seemed to take the breath from her body. She strove hard to control it.

There was an unusually brooding expression in his eyes. Then he forced a smile. He placed an arm about her, bracing himself. 'The Commandos will be called out and I must go with 'em, to fight against some of my oldest friends. But I am forced to protect my own — you, the children, our other friends. There is no other way around it.'

How can I wait, she thought agonisingly, wondering where he is, if he will come back?

'It has to be faced, Esther,' he said softly, stopping further words with his mouth. He pulled her hard against him, then he drew away, a fighting spark in his eyes. 'It's time to move — for time is all important to us now.'

He had started to move away, walking swiftly across the yard, his musket slung over his shoulder, when the farmstead was aroused by a mighty din. The horses in the stable all seemed to have gone mad and were rearing wildly. There were raised voices from the Hottentots and the few Xhosas. A sudden high-pitched scream rang out from the direction of the sheep kraal, echoing across the land. One of the Hottentots tore into the yard, gesticulating wildly. Esther caught sight of his face, and read terror in it.

'The sheep, baas Jones — the sheep — the Xhosas are here.'

'Goddam it — they haven't given us a chance!' Buck yelled, immediately alert. The servants all ran up and his voice was hurled at them, barking orders. They all heard him in silence, eyes

426

glittering in tense, dark faces.

Esther's face was ashen. 'The children! They are in the fields!' she shrieked.

Buck whirled round. 'Get 'em — take Laree and the baby and run for the bushes — go to the hills, get away from here and hide. Take muskets with you. I'll find you when we've chased the Xhosas away.'

Her eyes wide, Esther felt fear stab at her once more. 'We can't leave you alone — should we not bring the children to the house and bolt the doors? We can fire at them from here.'

'No — they'll attack the farmhouse and you will be trapped Escape now while you have the time. I'll be fine, I've faced 'em before. Now move it — before it's too late.'

Then he was gone, shouting more orders to the servants. They joined him on the path leading away to the kraal.

Esther stood there taking deep breaths. Something terrible was happening, something too terrible to think too deeply about. She had to act, to keep her mind on action. Without another moment's hesitation, she stumbled inside and ran for a gun.

Once outside again, she slowed herself to a purposeful and headlong stride, not wanting to cause needless panic among the children. The group of six children were spread out in the fields as she began a half run towards them. The twins, in their worsted stockings, were exchanging insults, slaps, punches, until a fight started. The next instant they were both locked in combat. They were equally strongly-built, able to hold their own for some minutes. Usually these slanging and wrestling matches did them good, but today it was the last thing Esther wanted. Terrible danger lurked around them and over those smiling acres of ploughed fields, under clouds combed thinly across the vast expanse of blue, untroubled sky.

Neither combatant was able to bring the other to the ground as Esther hurried up to them, her mind beginning to shriek alarm. She stretched an arm out urgently towards the others, motioning them to her. Something in her expression alerted Laree's eleven-year-old-son Joseph, on holiday from the Salem Academy. He was a slim, but surprisingly strong boy who was quick to sense that something was wrong. He tilted his head a little, and creased his brows. He had seen and understood.

427

Suddenly he stepped forward and wrenched his cousins apart, standing between them. His clear, grey eyes met those of Adam and Guy, who changed their defiant expressions as he pointed to their mother, running swiftly towards them. Esther, seeing their bruises and scratched arms and faces, said nothing, but beckoned to them.

Little Jonathan was not breeched yet, but even in his full skirt there was the same toughness about him as his brothers. His large, light blue eyes widened until his whole little face seemed filled with bewildered blueness. Esther ran to him, her heart contracting at the sight of his vulnerable innocence and hugged him, careful of the gun slung across her shoulder, as though she would never let him go.

She looked back. Plumes of smoke curled into the air above the cluster of outbuildings. The fields and orchards stretched out on either side as far as the eye could see to the hillside, seeming so peaceful. Morris, Joseph's younger brother, came pounding across the fields, pulling up short before them, as Emma scooped up her small sister Charity after Esther had quickly explained the situation.

There was a sudden noise of musket fire from the direction of the kraal. They all stopped chattering instantly as the noise died down, only to start again. In the terrifying moments that followed, the air was rent with blood-curdling yells turning them all as pale as ghosts.

Jonathan and small Charity cried in fright. Esther hugged her small son's curly head, sensitive and appealing in his dependence, and took Charity from Emma. She could not breathe and dared not think about Buck or the servants. Even Aurora was quiet and grave. Her blue eyes were sombre and frightened under the wide brim of her hat.

How Esther loved and feared for them all in that moment. She gave her orders that they were to go and find Laree and then run into the bushes and make their way to the hills where Buck would find them. Without another word they raced off in the direction of the house.

Shifting Jonathan astride her hip, and tying up her skirt ends to free her legs to run as fast as her burden would allow, Esther started after them with Charity tightly holding her hand. Under

428

the sun, hanging high over the blue-green hills, the children were away, speeding to the house. The two older boys outflanked the rest and were soon out of sight. Never had the safety of the house seemed so far away as Esther tortuously made her way back across the fields. It was only sometime later that she realized the yells had changed direction. They were now coming from the direction of the homestead itself.

She stood transfixed, turning a horrified face towards the outbuildings as Buck, followed by some of the servants, rushed up, hurtling towards the homestead. There was a line of blood running from his temple down the side of his face, where an assegaai had grazed it. It was the voices around her that roused her from the nightmare. They awakened her into another.

'Get back, Esther — keep out of sight — run for the cover of those bushes — we'll try to chase the Xhosas away from the house,' Buck yelled, heedless of the blood coursing down his face as he thundered by and disappeared.

She stood petrified with the two small children clinging to her for support. Where were the other children — and Laree? She hoped desperately that they had managed to escape from the house before the Xhosa attack.

There was an instant's silence, a fragment of peace, before the yells began again, and smoke rose from the house, billowing to the sky. She saw Mazinga, the Xhosa, running towards her. Mazinga, who had accompanied them from Eden, bringing the new ewes to Roydon, pounded up. As he drew abreast, he pulled Jonathan from her and beckoned her to follow him into a clump of evergreen thickets not far away, where he dived for cover.

She followed him with Charity, running for her life into the shelter of the thickets, trembling all over. It was all happening so fast. Above the trees and bushes, a large column of flame, wrapped in a thick, black pall of smoke, rose straight to the sky. It was a terrible sight.

The farmhouse that Arthur and Charity had built — all the care and love that had gone into its creation and improvement — was burning, and acres of fields would be destroyed.

She came to painful life as she waited there, crouching beside the children and Mazinga. Her breath caught until it was difficult to breathe. She tried to quieten her mind. These two little mites depended on her for everything. Mazinga, too, was suffering. A loyal young man, he was stunned by the destruction; she could see it in his face. He was trapped by his loyalty to those he knew and trusted.

She turned her head as violent screams of agony came from the direction of the house. Her body and soul seemed to stiffen and grow cold. It was Laree, she knew without a doubt that it was her sister. She came out of fear to knowledge and despair; the hell had only just begun.

Then, leaving the two children with Mazinga, she was running fast, her breath coming in laboured, painful rasps, towards the house.

The Xhosas had been chased away when she stopped dead just within the entrance to the barn, where Buck had carried Laree and her baby daughter from the fire. Her heart pounding painfully in her chest, Esther willed her body to be still. Something about the sudden silence chilled her, as her eyes took in the scene in one single, frozen moment. Buck was kneeling over Laree and her child.

For a wild, unbelieving moment she felt as if the world was crashing down around her as she saw her husband attempting to staunch the blood oozing from her sister's side. Somehow she found herself beside Laree, and in a paroxysm of grief, she knelt down and took Laree's hand. Laree was barely conscious and in terrible agony, an assegaai projecting from her right side. Blood oozed from the great tear in her dress where the cruel weapon had sunk into her body, sapping it of life.

Esther could feel her anger rising, soon to become a flame exploding inside her as the terrible realization swept over her that her dear, sweet Laree was dying in pools of her own blood. She could see her sister's face hazily through the fast-gathering tears in her eyes.

Then she felt a painful, awful heat and her screams filled the barn and vibrated across the yard. She had no recollection of the next few minutes when hands came forward and led her away from the dreadful scene.

'Mama, mama '

Moments later, she looked up from the upturned pail on which she was sitting in the yard, into the innocent blue eyes of Aurora,

430

kneeling awkwardly at her side.

She tried to calm herself; Laree's children depended on her now. She looked across at the group of children hovering not far away, devastated and robbed of speech. Her eyes met those of flaxen-haired Emma and she held out her arms to the girl, who was only a little younger than Laree had been when she had arrived in Africa for the first time.

The girl ran to her with a muffled cry of horror and laid her head against Esther's shoulder, sobbing helplessly, her hair falling over her face in a golden shower.

'I will go and fetch my father,' Joseph said, standing before her. Looking at him, his young face grown suddenly so old and fierce, Esther saw only his likeness to his dying mother.

She shook her head with wild impatience. 'No, Joseph — stay here. It's too dangerous out there. Your father will be back soon. Uncle Buck can use your help, boy — please go to him and see what to do.'

He left and came back with his tiny sister Elise, whom he placed in her arms, her tiny ankle stained with her mother's blood. Esther hugged the small, living body to her, the blood staining the whiteness of her pinafore. She had no more tears left, and when, later, Laree was finally laid to rest in the family graveyard, it was Buck who wept, allowing all the tears of years to come out.

CHAPTER
Forty-Two

In an oasis of deep silence in the late afternoon, they all climbed into Buck's wagon with nothing but the clothes on their backs. They took the remaining servants with them. Mazinga and one of the herd boys had been sent to Eden hours before to relay Buck's message to the men to take the horses, sheep and cattle to Port Elizabeth without delay.

Esther sat on the driver's seat, her shawl drawn across her shoulders and knotted over her chest. The ruins of the house and outbuildings hovered in the shifting, dying light. The sun was pincered between the topmost branches of the line of oak trees, grown from the acorns Arthur Wilson had brought from Cape Town fourteen years before, and now the only evidence left of his courage and determination in the face of awesome problems.

The sheep had been saved and were driven to Port Elizabeth by two Hottentot trackers. Three Mantatees and a Hottentot had been killed and were buried near the oak trees. Joseph had buried two wine jars, stuffed with coins and a pair of solid silver candlesticks, in a hole dug in the ground near some bushes, before he and the children had escaped from the house.

Now Esther sat, all energy drained out of her, waiting for Buck to saddle his horse and accompany them to safety. Bitterness twisted its knife in her heart. She wanted to protest at the grotesqueness of it all, as the pain inside seemed too heavy to bear.

Buck slung his gun over his shoulder and came up to her, the wound at his temple congealed and dried. He touched her hair under the fold of the housecap. He was looking at her closely, his

432

fingers tracing the edge of her ashen face, then he drew the cap back over her head.

'It'll be all right now,' he said, 'I'll take you to Grahamstown where you will be safe with the children. Bathurst is too exposed and difficult to defend.' He smiled, that charming, wonderful smile she would carry in her heart always.

She remembered the day of the Anti-Slavery celebrations, when they had all safely gathered together. It was a precious light, a beacon of warm radiance before the gathering darkness of this storm that had engulfed them with deadly swiftness. Suddenly there was a new fragility to their love, to the relationship between them, the possibility that they may be parted forever. There was a lump in her throat and tears in her eyes of which she was unaware until they splashed down on her hand.

Will we ever see Eden again? And if we do, what will remain of it? Will it be reduced to nothing but ashes like Sunfield Park? And what of Dwyers' Cross, and her father and uncle, and Sam? It was chilling to think that life perched on such a knife-edge; one moment happy festivity, the next, tragedy.

The children were restive, their bellies hungry. The burnt-out ruins stared out at them as they drove past, their faces stark, immovable. Esther drove the wagon, the two older Wilson boys walking beside it, while Buck on horseback patrolled the roadside.

They rode in silence through the bleak, darkening landscape westwards towards Grahamstown. They took the trail away from the farm into a winding lane, wandering through acres of old acacia trees, kaffirboom and evergreen shrubs. The wagon jolted and swayed down the rough, rutted path as the silent, bush-covered hills grew darker and the gloom of dusk hid the pale blue mountains in the distance.

The rising sun exploded off the hilltops the following morning as they reached Bathurst. Dawn filled the groves of trees; further in, the woods were still black. Between the dawn and the blackness, something moved. A man came down through the trees. The occupants of the wagon stared back in astonishment and pain; then with a shock of recognition.

It was Sam, a neighbouring farmer's wife plodding beside him. Behind them Roydon appeared riding with the woman's two

433

children. The stamping of the massive oxen's feet and the creak of the wagon broke the unearthly silence as the wagon advanced on the dirty, blood-stained figures.

Roydon looked at Esther and then at Buck. 'Where is Laree?' he asked. 'Surely she came with you?'

Esther felt afraid, almost terrified. Her heart beat fast, and she was sweating. She knew something dreadful had befallen her father and uncle, but first Roydon had to be told that he had lost his wife.

Buck halted his horse, the muscles tightening about his mouth. Sam stopped, breathing hard and looking utterly exhausted.

Esther turned to Buck, coming alive for the first time in hours. 'It's Laree . . .'

Buck studied her face for a brief second, then said, 'I will tell Roydon.' He moved away, motioning Roydon to follow him. It took only a moment to crush Roydon's world, for him to lock the dreadful, shocking grief into his heart.

And afterwards Esther had never admired him more as he rejoined them at the wagon to tell them about Joshua and Cady, his face ashen, his eyes suddenly lifeless, but his voice as calm and slow as ever. Esther knew that they would never know just how much it cost him to control himself then, and tell them what they wanted to hear. In a blinding flash of revelation she understood only too clearly why her sister had married this quiet and courageous man, and it was his courage in the face of loss that made the most impression on her — a courage she would desperately need herself in the hours, the days that lay ahead.

Roydon's quiet voice told them the full horror of what had happened. 'Mr Dwyer and his brother were escaping in their wagon with Sam's wife, Helena, and her two children, when they were attacked not a mile from Dwyers' Cross. It was Lungelo and his warriors. Cady died almost instantly. Sam and I pulled Mr Joshua to safety, but he's barely alive, I'm sorry. We left him under cover in the bush for he was too bad to bring all this way without transport.' He bit his lip. 'How he survived is a miracle. He's been calling for you, Esther, and I think that's what kept him alive. Helena escaped into the bush with the children — no one's seen her since. Sam was trying to get help when I came upon him.'

Emma let out a muffled cry of horror from somewhere behind Esther in the wagon. Aurora reached for her in her awkward, childish way, and held her, trying to comfort her, raw white fear on her own young face. Emma laid her cheek against her cousin's shoulder, sobbing helplessly.

Esther's heart stopped for a ghastly moment as she heard Roydon's voice continue. 'Mrs Harding here — her husband was killed right before her eyes. Her farmhouse has been burnt down and we found her wandering in the bush.' As a dreadful minute of silence descended on the party, the clouds high above shifted lazily across the brightening sky, sending shadows chasing across the rolling hills.

Buck turned in his saddlle and saw the anguish full on the white oval of Esther's face. Her nails bit into the palms of her hands and despite the early warmth, she shivered.

'I told your father I would bring you to him so that he can die in peace, Esther,' Roydon said.

She stared at him, tension and guilt weighing on her spirit.

Buck sat still on his horse beside the wagon, listening to every word Roydon uttered. His lips tightened to a thin line, then grimacing with suppressed anger, he said, 'This carnage cannot go on — there must be a way to end it, there must be.' He rested a hand on the wagon and stared at Esther. 'I will take you to your father.'

Then he turned to Sam whose face was shadowed with deep lines of sorrow. 'Pettigrew — get up in the wagon with Mrs Harding and her children. Roydon, I leave the wagon and its occupants in your hands until we catch up with you. Head for Grahamstown, it's by far the safest direction.' The level blue gaze lingered on Sam for a moment. 'How was Dwyers' Cross when you escaped?'

Sam looked up at him, his face haggard, the keen, black eyes sunken. 'Razed to the ground — not a stick left, not a tree in the orchard, nothing.'

Esther turned to Buck. 'Take me to Papa now,' she said.

Buck stared at her for a few moments, then he nodded. Esther swung up behind him, and they rode off in a wild, hot fury with their children calling after them, down the winding road between the high, wooded bank of hills. With every stride Buck's horse overhauled the miles, moving rapidly in the direction of the Coombs Valley, the dust they raised soon hiding them from sight.

They entered the Coombs Valley in the afternoon, penetrating deeply into the wild, aloe-studded countryside. A flock of brown sparrows took off from some open ground looking like bars of music as they moved in the still air. Vultures watched them from the branches of throny acacias, while others circled higher up. The horse moved in a pall of dust into a vale of the deepest quiet, a remote, secluded spot not half a mile from Dwyers' Cross.

The horse suddenly moved restlessly under them, requiring all Buck's strength to hold it. It threw up its head and neighed, the noise echoing back from the surrounding rocks in the deep tomblike silence that had fallen. Shafts of light caught the muzzle of Buck's musket, slung over his shoulder. The horse flapped its ears and tail to keep the flies away, still nervous in the surroundings.

Esther's fear had tightened the muscles of her throat now that she was back in the valley after so long. Pain and hysteria screamed through every nerve, every cell, as she smelt the sickly stench of death so heavy on the air.

Then they saw it. The body of a farmer lay beside the track where he had fallen when the Xhosas had overtaken him. Slowly they inched forward, harness and spurs jingling as the horse tried to avoid the sharp, jagged stones in the way. Apart from their own noise, nothing but a vast empty silence lay about them still.

They saw the bodies of Michael Byrne and another man not far from the overturned wagons. Of Hannah Byrne and her three children there was no sign. Esther's tortured eyes fell along the dusty track some distance further along. For a moment such terrible pain twisted through her that she almost fainted. It was all she could do to force herself to look on the ghastly scene. She shivered, as if danger still lurked behind the rocks and lightly jangled the nerves of her body. They were very close now, nauseated by the terrible stench.

Buck, with reins in one hand, musket in the other, pulled up the horse and they dismounted in grim silence.

They stopped at the body of Cady beside one of the wagons, lying flat on his face. When Buck slowly turned him over he was

436

still clutching his stomach with one hand where an assegaai had torn a gaping wound. His back was riddled with gashes. On the ground there were pools of thick, dried blood.

They remembered what Sam had told them of the last, furious fight when Cady had hurled the first assegaai from his thigh back at his attacker. Esther could not bear to look down into the once teasing, now sightless, hazel eyes. She began to cry — the tears welling up from some inner, deep place her thoughts could not reach. The earth was trampled and bloodstained, and covered with the soft white, downy feathers from the mattresses that had been ripped open in a frantic search by the Xhosas for ammunition.

Buck rose, wiping away the film of sweat from his forehead, and went to her. He placed an arm around her shoulders seeing the terrible starkness of her expression and hearing her crying.

'Stay here, sweetheart — I will go and look for your father. Roydon said he and Sam had pulled him under some bushes nearby. They can't have dragged him too far in his condition.'

His eyes hardening into slits of concentration, he went off to search, plunging into the deep folds of the bushes and melting into the darkness of their cover.

There was a deathly silence around Esther as she waited restlessly. A strange, flesh-numbing fear seemed to creep through her. She remained motionless, but the fear remained, the thought of the hideous ambush uppermost in her mind. The smell of the place closed in on her as vultures swooped and soared in the high, arching sky. The long, red feathers of a Paradise Flycatcher caught her eyes as it nested in a milkwood tree, then it was gone with a bright flutter of wings.

Buck came back and beckoned to her. He took her hand and led her through the dusty bushes away from the track into a screen of heavy, undisturbed, matted trees. The moment had come she dreaded most. She saw her father's figure in the deep shade, looking for an instant so peaceful and sleeping. She advanced and stood before him, stunned, unable to believe what she was seeing. Shock kept her immobile, she could feel it, sense it, transmitted through the air towards her.

He was still wearing his spurs and was barely alive. There was a large wound in his shoulder which he had stuffed with his coat collar in a desperate attempt to stop the bleeding. His face was thin and sunken; he had lost that look of almost youthful enthusiasm which had always been so striking.

'Papa,' she said in a hoarse, raw gasp. 'Papa — what have they done to you?' She stretched out her hands passionately to him and took his hand, kissing it as she knelt down beside him. 'Papa — it's Esther Mary — I've come to take you with us,' she said brokenly as she desperately tried to stop the tears spilling down her cheeks.

His face became a blur. He had always seemed so indestructible. Nothing had seemed beyond the reach and scope of his energy and intelligence. Now he was dying, leaving her forever, and taking all her childhood memories with him. A part of her was dying with him.

'What have I done to you, Papa?' she whispered. 'I have caused you so much misery, so much pain. I should have swallowed my stubborn pride and come to you long ago. Speak to me, Papa, tell me you understand.'

He had given her life and all she wanted in those fragile moments was to pull him back to life, to what he had once been. No person she had ever known, except for Buck and possibly uncle Cady, had a firmer grip on this thing called life than her father had, and yet, it was now slipping through his fingers. And there was nothing she could do to stop it or change her past behaviour.

Slowly his eyes opened and he spoke, his breath rattling in his throat. 'Esther — is that you? I waited for you, dear child.' He fumbled blindly for her hand.

'It's Esther, Papa,' she said. It was so hard for her to smile as with another plunge of pain she saw the yellow, waxy look, the pinchness about his nose, the precursor of death.

He was in great pain but through indomitable willpower he had somehow managed to keep himself alive to see her for the last time. Her eyes clotted with tears so that she could hardly see him. She could only feel his hand in hers. 'Papa — we've come to take you away.'

'Laree — where is Laree?' Death clouded his eyes as with a sigh that was almost a groan his head fell back and mercifully, in his blood and her tears, he passed out. There was so much she wanted to tell him, so much to put right, but he was beyond her reach.

Her throat constricted with grief as she could sense the force in him fading. Nothing else mattered anymore. His race was over. He had fought hard, and in the end he had lost the fight, and yet she could never see him defeated. The past no longer mattered, it was gone, completed. His spirit was his own, that he could never lose. He lay, cradled in her arms, his face still wet with her tears.

'He has gone with Uncle Cady and Laree — they are free at last,' she said in a strangled voice. All she felt was the abject misery of loss, the sorrow deadening all fear in her of the surroundings. 'How many times can a person witness death without their nerves dying too? Tragedy should deaden pain — but it never does. Each time is as terrible and numbing as the first.'

She was filled with an icy void. The traces of the past were vanishing, step by step. She remembered him in life, and with him the cold voices of the past warmed to recollection — Uncle Cady, her sweet mother, her sister Anna, red-golden haired Lewis, Garnet and dear Laree.

She did not see Buck kneeling beside her until she felt the pressure of his hand on hers, and his eyes, anxious, suffering, looking into hers.

'Come, Esther — I hear what you say and it is true. But there is no more to be done here. It's too dangerous to tarry long. We will take 'em back as soon as I can right one of the wagons to carry 'em for a decent burial.'

She looked away blindly, not wanting to move. She never wanted to move again. 'All hopes are wrenched away one by one, and torn apart until there is nothing left. I see no point in going on.'

Buck set his hands on her shoulders, then pulled her to him, holding her gently. 'Death is swallowed up in the final victory, dearest girl,' he said very gently. 'It is left to us to go on and make the best with what we have left. It is only the courage we need to take the next step on the way. Your father and your uncle had such courage. That is how they would like you to see it.'

He stood up, raising her with him and led her through the bush to one of the wagons. It had been completely unloaded. Buck went to the front and bending at the knees, he placed his hands carefully beneath it. Slowly with almost super-human strength he began to lift it from its dusty bed. Gradually it moved. It lurched a fraction before halting again as he and Esther now heaved together. Finally it was righted.

He stood back, breathing deeply. 'We have gorged ourselves sick on disaster and destruction,' he said suddenly, the anger in his face replaced by unfamiliar bitterness. 'We will take this wagon — it will take longer with only a horse to pull it, but we will manage.'

He wiped his parched lips with the back of his hand, his eyes hidden briefly from her. Then he looked at her and with a wooden, expressionless face, said quietly, 'Your father and uncle died as they lived, sweetheart — they never sat down and let unpleasant things happen to 'em. They fought in their way to overcome. It may not have been my way, but it was a way. They were strong men, determined to win, to survive, to make some kind of life for those around them, and I respect that.'

In a daze of grief Esther walked the short distance to the farmstead, pulled towards it by an invisible thread. And there, where the house at Dwyers' Cross had been, was a heap of blackened rubble, the yellowwood beams reduced to charcoal, its once bright orchards and vineyards totally destroyed. All the hopes and disappointments, the hard work of fourteen years, had gone in a few hours, forever.

Looking at it, Esther saw it all through a misty haze of pain and tears, remembering that besides the pain and toil, there had been laughter, rough humour and smiling faces in this valley, on this farm. Now there was nothing left and the dying sun was shining on a silent, charred wasteland.

Later Esther sat on the driver's box of the wagon as the horse, ridden by Buck, pulled it. She looked at the sunset unseeing, silent and withdrawn into intense grief. She could not rid herself of the remorse that she had not forsaken her pride long ago and been reconciled with her father and uncle, and she suffered the regret of all those wasted years apart.

Forty-Three

A grief-stricken Roydon had ridden back to meet them, with a pair of oxen to make the journey quicker and easier. They met their own wagon waiting for them on the way to Grahamstown. There Sam took over the Dwyers' wagon, and Buck departed for Eden to find out what happened there.

Esther climbed up on the driver's box beside Emma, holding her baby sister, wrapped in her shawl. Someone's dog they had found on the way from Sunfield Park sat between the children in the wagon. Emma looked exhausted and there was a shadow in the large, china-blue eyes.

'Do you think we're being punished, Aunt Esther — for something dreadful we've done and not known it?' Her face remained blank, pale and motionless.

Esther looked away, not wanting to answer. She breathed deeply, not even wanting to think. 'No, Emma — you cannot hold yourself responsible for the place, the problems you were thrust into. The reasons for all this were already here before we came.' She patted her niece's cold hand. 'You have to keep hope — without it we will all die.'

Emma shuddered. 'I want to live, Aunt Esther — I want to live in peace somewhere with Papa and the family, troubling no one and troubled by nothing. Nothing else matters anymore, beyond that one thing now that Mama and Grandpa and Uncle Cady have gone.' Her voice fell away. 'Uncle Buck seems the only one who is not afraid.'

Esther sighed, looking out from the driver's box. 'It's only because he keeps hope, Emma. He applies himself to the matter at hand, and does what has to be done now, not thinking too much of what lies ahead — not allowing its fears to take hold,' she said, as much to convince herself as Emma.

She wondered what Buck was thinking. He would be at Eden. He had been one of those born to test his fears, and was at his best in dangerous situations. He knew how to meet trouble and make danger work for him, for them.

The road swarmed with refugees, horses, wagons and cattle pressing slowly forward to get away from the onslaught. Behind them, across the broad horizon, plumes of smoke lifted into the sky.

They were overtaken by a troop of redcoats on horseback who told Roydon that Colonel Harry Smith was arriving on the frontier to take command, and all the commandos were being called out without further delay.

Esther stared ahead, trying not to think of Buck leaving and going to war. Young Adam, in his eighth year, walked beside the wagon with a surprising earnestness of purpose, as if he had in his childlike way, taken his father's place as guardian of his mother. His heavy, tousled red-gold hair made everything else look dusty. His arms and face were scribbled with scratches, his clothes torn and caked with dirt, yet through his face's young roundness, a gem-clear profile had already begun to show. Esther looked at him as she drove the wagon, privately proud of his doggedness. It was hard for her to believe that there was already in him a growing impatience to reach manhood. It was a new side of him and one she cherished in that moment. It was at times such as these when she realized that even although they had lost so much, she still had a lot to live for.

They passed numerous small, ragged bands of refugees raising trails of dust as they moved on foot — faces white, sad, sorrowful, sick. We are the lucky ones, Esther thought, watching them straggle along with only the clothes on their backs. At least we have a wagon, and our sheep and cattle are safe. And suddenly the tribulations of the past years seemed insignificant by contrast, diminutive.

During the next week the whole of the Eastern Cape rocked with horrified shock as each day revealed more disaster. The roads were filled with refugees fleeing from their farms in the face of the massive invasion. They poured into the towns as word of the terror began to fly through the settlement. Colonel Harry Smith had raced overland with reinforcements, re-appointing Buck as Commandant of one of the commando units that were called up to escort many homeless women and children to centres of safety in Grahamstown, Bathurst, Salem and Port Elizabeth, until Bathurst and Salem were considered too weak. They were then alerted to leave for Grahamstown and Port Elizabeth immediately. Wagons piled with sacks of flour, baskets filled with meat, hens with their feet tied and bags tied with thong, crammed the roads in endless streams.

Esther and the children went to St George's Church, where Esther had married Garnet in what now seemed like a hundred years ago. Around Church Square wagons were outspanned and formed a barricade. Tents went up, poles were fitted to holes dug into the ground. Dogs and black servants, Boer women, Britons and their children filled the church and the square, guarded by those men who had not gone out on commando. Trade had come to a stand-still, stores and offices were closed. At night the church blazed with candles, filled with armed men — some on guard, others taking their turn to rest. The chancel was heaped with muskets and bayonets.

Joshua, Cady, Michael Byrne and the others were buried. Helena Pettigrew arrived with Hannah Byrne and the five children between them and two Hottentot servants. They had spent three full, hazardous days of travelling through the bush and living off a diet of sweet potato, which the Hottentots had dug up along the way. Hannah arrived, looking like a grief-stricken, old woman, her bonnet blood-stained, her clothes torn and filthy, in time for her husband's funeral. She was in a daze, incoherent, and could not tell them much of what had happened, except that the Hottentots and one of the Xhosa servants had helped them to escape. They heard that Mazinga had been allowed to return to the Bushman's River, where he had left his wife and children, after transporting the sheep and cattle of Eden safely to Port Elizabeth, for the duration of the war. Beauty and young Moses had been brought to Esther in Grahamstown.

As the days passed, Esther sensed a change in Emma. She saw now the weariness in that pretty heart-shaped face, but the greatest change of all was in her eyes. They were as lovely as

443

ever, but the old innocence and trust had gone out of them. Great blue circles of grief ringed them, mirroring the tragedy she kept in her own heart, seeing her own anguish in her niece's eyes.

She glanced at Emma standing at the church door, watching the refugees in the streets moving like clockwork figures, bodies tilted stiffly forward against the rising wind within the barricade of wagons round Church Square. Jonathan lay in the dust, screaming with laughter as the dog pushed its dirty nose in his ear. Emma wore the same soft, grey dress with cream facings she had worn the day before Christmas. It was all she had. Moving nearer, Esther put an arm around her shoulders.

'Oh, Aunt Esther,' Emma said, her eyes glittering with unshed tears. 'I never dreamt it would be as bad as this. I do not know if I can go on without Mama. There is nothing more to live for — everything we built up, gave our dreams to, has gone.'

She looked at Esther, her eyes clouded. Esther's eyes seemed still as direct, as fearless as ever, but the old arrogance, the defiance, were missing.

'At least you know that your Papa is alive, Emma — that he is out there on commando protecting innocent women and children. We must be content just to have life inside us — for our sakes, and those of the children and the menfolk. We cannot afford to give up. And when I think of how we used to turn up our noses at the very things we now value most, in the folly of our former days.' She fell silent.

Emma sighed. 'Perhaps you are right — there seems nothing else to do.'

Esther, looking at her, wondered at the change, the sense of tragedy in her. These responsibilities we hope to escape so often, to evade and run away from, she thought, are what keep us alive in the end.

She stood back, gazing at the men piling more arms and ammunition at the back of the church. Her eyes were clear enough but her thoughts were grim. We will never be young again, not after this.

The heat was intense but there was no complaining. The sky hung threateningly overhead. Piles of storm clouds banked along the surrounding cup of hills, stretching far up into the sky. There

444

was an eerie, luminous light, the forewarning of a summer storm.

Esther stood with Buck outside the barricade of wagons. He was leaving to take his commando as far as the Keiskamma River and the borders of Xhosaland, to assist in the evacuating of Fort Willshire. All ammunition, stores and provisions were to be cleared in an effort to abandon the more isolated forts in the area.

Martial law had been proclaimed and boys as young as fifteen had been called up for active service. The homestead at Eden had been razed to the ground, the garden in ruins, but the sheep and cattle were safe.

They stood in companionable silence for some time, gazing out to where solitary mimosas shaded the street here and there. She had not seem him for some weeks, and now he had come to bid her farewell before the journey to the Keiskamma.

Esther was cold as fear overwhelmed her for a vivid, stark moment and left her trembling. She was seeing him off with the hard-won woman's courage to love and keep silent — to let him go with a smile, though she was bleeding inside.

They walked away, side by side, into the misty, yellow-brown veils of dust whipped along by the hot wind, to where Buck's horse was tethered and the young men of his commando gathered in knots to talk as guns were handed out to all who applied for them at the Free-Mason's Tavern.

'Come now, Mrs Jones, I want a smile to take with me all those miles into the bush.' He gave her a sidelong glance, his whole presence emanating a sense of controlled power straining beneath the cool surface.

She inclined her head, playing with the gold wedding band on her left hand, refusing to look at him. She was trying so hard to be the calm, composed and perfect wife, but it was not working out that way. She tried to shake off her gloom and failed. 'I hate this war — taking you away from me like this,' she said, suddenly unable to stop herself. Her lips vanished into a tight scowl.

He stopped and turned to her, a flicker of laughter in his eyes. He gave her a penetrating look beneath the low-brimmed hat. 'Now that is what I want to hear — that familiar defiance, that bite of temper I have not heard for weeks. I should take you with me — that would be enough to send the Xhosas fleeing for miles around.'

She knew this was his way, always to ease the situation with humour, in his unfailing cheerfulness to make it easier for her, for himself. She always felt better when he was around. He had no fear of death, but he had a love of life, and she knew he wanted to return, to see his children grow.

He took her hand in his firm ones, deeply tanned and rough from reins. Forcing ease into his voice, he said, 'This war is the price we have to pay to live here, sweetheart.' His face was suddenly full of vital compassion. She had never seen his eyes look so beautiful or so sad.

'I would have contempt for myself if I did not do my duty towards you and those who come after me,' he said, through a twisted smile, knowing the defiance in her was only superficial now.

Her eyes suddenly moist, she lowered her head, not wanting to dull the edge of his courage with her womanly fear. Donning a mask of lightness, she put aside her morbid feelings. At least she owed him that. She looked up at him, a faint smile flitting across her lips for the first time.

'Glory be, Buck Jones — I understand your duty well. And you know how bored to tears I would be without this war. It's a change from the endless scandals and intrigues, especially since you and I are no longer causing most of them. It gives us something else to talk about besides the price of wool.'

A smile lit the corners of his mouth and he took her in his arms. He pulled back the small muslin cap and she could feel him laughing quietly, his cheeks deep in her hair. 'I could almost believe you meant that,' he whispered softly. 'I will have to return soon, to think up some new scandals to liven up this place.'

She drew away slightly, her eyes smarting with hot tears which she fought away, blinking. She adjusted her cap with trembling fingers, 'Do not be concerned about us here — we are safe enough,' she said at last, her voice brightly hiding the pain filling her mind.

He smiled again and touched the red curls at her neck, the feeling of his hand reassuring her. He bent his head and kissed her gently on the lips. Against her resolve, she clung to him, her arms like living ropes around his neck.

I will die if anything happens to him, she thought. My body

will go on but my spirit will surely die for it belongs with his.

She knew there would be more pain, more loss, suffering and despair in the long weeks ahead, that they would all remember the shock of death and sorrow, that the grass of the African veld would run red with the blood of men, both black and white, before it was over. But it had come, and in the end there would be no victors, for there would be suffering and bitterness on both sides. She struggled for control. Buck had enough to concern himself about without adding her burdens to his.

But Buck has been right. Courage was what mattered in life, she thought determinedly, proudly suppressing the fear she dared not show. The courage to meet life gallantly, with all its many obstacles.

'Farewell, my darling,' she said. 'Go out there and give 'em all you've got, and when it's done, come back to me. I will be waiting here for you.'

Though there was dust in his hair and on his clothes, he radiated the same warmth and light as he always had. He would come back. She knew he would.

With musket and powderbag on his shoulder, he mounted his horse, his young men falling in line behind him. She looked up at him as he raised his arm in farewell, and then she turned away.

Her heart beat rapidly as she heard the horses gallop off, then she quickened her stride, her head flung back and held high. Though her clothes were cold and dusty, she could feel the warmth of her body inside them. The fire inside her would continue to flicker, to smoulder until it could burn brightly and fiercely once more. She saw Aurora and the boys running towards her as she approached the barricade of wagons. There was nowhere else to go but forward. She did not look back. She would never look back again.